Ravished by Desire

Brand reached out one hand and took hold of the filmy top of her nightgown. With one motion, he ripped it from her. Unhurriedly, his eyes made their inspection. Her hair, usually tied up with a ribbon, hung unbound, falling over her shoulders like small tongues of flame. She felt his gaze, like warm hands moving down, slowly. . . .

Lavished with Love

She bowed her head. He cupped his hand beneath her chin and made her face him, the touch of his fingers setting her to trembling violently.

"Sable," he murmured, his voice filled with incredible longing and need. He picked her up easily and carried her to the bed where he gently laid her down.

She watched him as he undressed, every gesture, every move. She knew a *good* woman would have looked away, but she didn't care. Then he was beside her, his big hands pulling her to him. . . .

SABLE FLANAGAN

BETTY LAYMAN RECEVEUR

AVON
PUBLISHERS OF BARD, CAMELOT AND DISCUS BOOKS

AVON BOOKS
A division of
The Hearst Corporation
959 Eighth Avenue
New York, New York 10019

Copyright © 1979 by Betty Layman Receveur
Published by arrangement with the author.
Library of Congress Catalog Card Number: 79-51324
ISBN: 0-380-41046-X

First Avon Printing, May, 1979

AVON TRADEMARK REG. U.S. PAT. OFF. AND IN
OTHER COUNTRIES, MARCA REGISTRADA, HECHO EN
U.S.A.

Printed in the U.S.A.

To Jack and Bernie Rogers . . . who encouraged me in the beginning, and all along the way.

Prologue
New York, 1832

Keith Flanagan looked down at the tiny, red-faced, squirming mite of humanity in his arms, the pride and sorrow a conflict in him, memory a stabbing, bittersweet thing.

He could still see Maureen's face when she told him that there was to be a baby. Her eyes had seemed lighted from within, and their corners had crinkled the way they did when she was very pleased. He had not seen them look quite like that for how long?—four years. Since that day he had come upon her picking wildflowers near the old, abandoned mill and she had laughed at him and he had kissed her sweet mouth . . .

Neither of them had meant for it to happen, and afterward, those same eyes filled with tears of shame that she had surrendered herself to him. But he had brushed away the tears and held her close.

"Don't you be worryin' now, darlin'," he had comforted. "We'll have the words said over us and every man in Ireland will know you're my wife . . . as you are already in my heart."

And the words were said, but only over the bitterest

1

opposition. His family was Protestant, hers Catholic, and there was a line between the two that staunch Irishmen did not cross. Her father banished her from his sight, declared her dead to him. His own widowed mother grieved in shocked silence and died of a stroke two weeks later.

There was nothing in Ireland to hold them. An only son, he had inherited substantial landholdings from his father and once everything was sold, they had left the island of their birth and come to America, as so many had before them.

Never a word of complaint had he heard from Maureen. She had given him all the love a man could ask, and yet the shadow had been there in her eyes, behind her smile . . . until she knew about the baby. That had made all the difference.

He'd come in and find her humming soft little lullabies as she stitched away on the tiny clothes. And, manlike, never once did he think that anything might go wrong . . . until the midwife walked out of the bedroom, her kind face gone sick with pity, the awful, bright red stain soaking the front of her white apron . . .

Now he sat, rocking back and forth, back and forth, holding the baby close to him . . . his baby . . . all he had left.

The infant stirred, started to cry with the jerking, squalling sound of the newborn, and Keith Flanagan stopped his helpless rocking and looked closely at his daughter for the first time.

"Hush, hush now," he crooned, and miraculously, or so it seemed to him, the baby quieted. "You're wantin' y'r mother, you poor little one . . . and"— he let out his breath in a long, helpless sound—"I'm wantin' her, too." For a moment he thought he would choke. The hurt was so great.

"But—" He swallowed, and the words came out roughly to keep back the tears. "But you and me, we'll have to be takin' care of each other now."

He rubbed one of his thick fingers over the downy

2

fuzz of the baby's head. It was as soft and almost as black as the bit of fur that had trimmed one of his mother's collars. He'd run his fingers over it as a boy. His father always said it was sable fur and had come all the way from over the water. Sable . . . Sable Flanagan . . . a fine and fittin' name for the little one. Maureen would've liked that, she would.

And Keith Flanagan smiled, never dreaming that his wife would have been horrified at the heathenish name . . . she had planned to call their daughter Brigid, for the saint.

Chapter 1
New York, Christmas, 1849

Sable yawned, stretched luxuriously, her eyes still heavy, half-closed with sleep. Very carefully she poked one shapely foot and ankle out from under the blue coverlet, shivered, hastily pulled the foot back under the covers, and snuggled deeper into the plump featherbed.

Dora's heels tapped sharply along the hallway and the doorknob clicked open.

"Mornin', Miss Sable . . . Merry Christmas," she said. And Sable rolled over, smiled sleepily at the short, stout figure of the housekeeper.

"Merry Christmas, Dora." Starched was the word for Dora, thought Sable fondly, suppressing a giggle as she regarded the shiny surface of the dark blue, cotton dress, the wide white collar so stiff it barely touched its wearer's shoulders, the flat white band with its row of lace atop the graying head.

"Is Papa up yet?" she asked, while the housekeeper stirred up the fire, threw another log into the fireplace.

"Yes'm, these two hours past. Already had a bite o' breakfast. Got tired o' waitin' for Miss Sleepyhead."

There was the creak of wheels in the hall and a sharp rap at the door. "Here's the hot water, Miss Dora," a masculine voice called out.

"Thank you, Wilfred." Footsteps echoed away from the door while the housekeeper swept back the floor-length curtain to reveal a small alcove holding a porcelain-covered bathtub, curving high at one end, low at the other, its four feet fashioned like claws.

"Think it's still too chilly in here?" Dora asked.

"No. Go ahead and pour the water." Sable was anxious to get downstairs now that she was fully awake. Papa had promised that her Christmas present would be very special—and Keith Flanagan's word was gospel to his daughter.

Dora pulled the low, wheeled platform with its cans of steaming water into the room. Wilfred, the hired man, had made it himself; each can was cradled in its own stand so that Dora could just tip the cans forward and empty them without lifting.

The water splashed into the bathtub and Sable threw off the covers, stood up to unfasten the buttons of her nightgown, and let it fall in a soft heap about her feet. She caught a glimpse of herself in the full-length mirror set into the wardrobe door and stopped, a peculiar feeling of looking at a stranger coming upon her. The angular, flat body of childhood had been gone for a while now . . . and in its place had come this slim-waisted figure with high, firm breasts, with hips and thighs round and smooth. Sable shivered in the cool air, saw the full pink nipples pucker, and quickly pulled the soft cashmere wrapper about her, suddenly aware that Dora, bending over the tub, had been talking all this time and now seemed to expect a reply.

"What—what did you say?"

Dora tipped the last can. "I said why you want to cover yourself with water like a fish is beyond me . . . can't be good for a body's health. Maybe all right in the summertime, but here in the dead o' winter! Wonder to me you don't catch your death. You could get just as clean washin' up from that basin right there." Dora turned, her face slightly red from the steaming water, one wisp of hair escaping from the starched cap and stringing over her forehead.

Sable grinned at her. "Dora, do stop fussing and help me pin up my hair." The soft black baby fuzz for which Keith had named her had soon been replaced by coppery curls that now hung past her shoulders. Once the bright tresses were fastened firmly atop her head, Sable went behind the partially drawn curtain, dropped her wrapper, stepped into the tub, and sank gratefully down into the warm water.

She could hear Dora busying herself about the room, closing a drawer, plumping the goose-feather pillows, and smacking the featherbed to take the hollow out of it.

She began to wash herself, pleasurably sniffing the new perfumed soap Papa had let her buy.

"Looks like snow," Dora was saying as she walked from one side of the bed to the other, fitting the coverlet in place. "Sky's as gray as death."

"Oh, I hope it does. Maybe I can get Papa to go riding. It's so pretty when the ground's all covered with white."

"Hmmp," Dora grunted. "Just makes a mess . . . gets tracked in on the floors." She was quiet for a moment, then: "You goin' to be in there for a while?"

"No. It's too cold."

"Knew it was," Dora sniffed. "You want me to start your breakfast now?"

"Yes. Give me time to see Papa first, though."

"All right." She heard Dora pull the cart out, grumbling as she went. "It's a Lord's wonder it don't give her the pneumonia . . ."

Sable laughed, splashed herself clean, and got out of the tub, her teeth chattering with the sudden chill, gooseflesh roughening her skin. She grabbed the towel and rubbed herself vigorously dry, then put on the warm wrapper.

Her hair tumbled loosely around her shoulders as she pulled the pins out and gave it a few quick strokes with the brush, then opened the third drawer of the bureau for fresh underclothes. She dressed quickly, pulling on the ankle-length drawers with their rows of eyelet at the bottom of each leg, the chemise with its matching rows of lace, then petticoats—four of them starched stiffly to make her skirt stand out. No corset, though . . . Sable hated corsets, even though Mrs. Cramer, her dressmaker, assured her that no self-respecting young woman went without one. Mrs. Cramer had laced her into one once and Sable had been sure that she'd die from lack of breath before she got out of it.

That was the first time and it would be the last, she told herself firmly. Besides, she told herself smugly, her waist was small enough without a corset.

She swept back the sliding door of the closet to reveal neat rows of shoes, assorted hatboxes along the upper shelf, and the line of dresses like multicolored flowers in a garden row.

Sable selected a soft, green wool and quickly finished dressing. Then she stood back to survey herself in the mirror, which had been a special gift from her father.

The dress was very becoming. The small round collar was edged with white lace, and the tightly fitted bodice had a line of pearl buttons from throat to waist; the skirt fell in graceful folds that barely revealed the green silk toes of her slippers.

She caught up her mass of coppery curls with a wide white ribbon, then turned from side to side. Satisfied at last with her appearance, she took a neatly tied package from the top bureau drawer and proceeded to the top of the stairs.

The dark wood of the bannister gleamed with polish. For an instant Sable grinned, remembering Dora's shrieks when she used to slide down—but that would never do for a sedate young lady of seventeen. Sable gathered her skirt about her and made her way down the stairs with mock dignity.

8

Good smells drifted from the kitchen and mingled with the pungent aroma of the pine and cedar branches that Dora had placed about the house. The warmth of the library was welcome after the chill of upstairs, and the bright color of the fire seemed to reflect itself in the ornate red scrolls of the wallpaper, in the red velvet draperies with their matching silk cords and tassels.

Keith Flanagan stood before the fireplace, his back to the door, thick shoulders drooping tiredly above the stocky length of his body.

"Papa," she said very softly, something about the way he stood causing an aching fear inside her. "Papa . . . Merry Christmas." Her voice was louder this time and he turned quickly, the deep lines smoothing across the wide ruddiness of his face.

"Merry Christmas, darlin'!" He held his arms wide and the momentary unease was gone as she ran to him and gave him a light kiss on the cheek.

"Now, let me be takin' a good look at you, miss." He held her by the shoulders, his head a bare two inches above her own, and looked her up and down for a long moment. Then: "Ooooh," he said, in that way he had of drawing out the sound, "y'r lookin' more like y'r mother every day. She'd be that proud of you, she would . . . And what's this you've got here?" he asked, taking the package from Sable's hand. " 'Twouldn't be my Christmas present, now would it?" He turned his head to one side and closed one blue eye in an exaggerated wink.

"It would." Sable grinned back at him.

"Well now, let's just see what it is." Keith tore away the ribbon and paper, his face beaming as he drew out the red knitted scarf and looped it around his neck. "Just what I been needin'! But tell me now, how many stitches did you drop?"

"Papa! You know I don't drop stitches anymore," Sable protested.

He took off the scarf and examined the even rows of knitted wool. "I guess you don't at that, darlin'. It's fine work . . . good as y'r mother ever did."

"Miss Sable," Dora said from the doorway, "your breakfast is ready."

"Just hold it for a minute or two more, Dora, if you please," Keith said.

"Yes, sir."

The housekeeper gone, Keith Flanagan opened the top drawer of the rosewood secretary and drew out a small black velvet case.

"For you, darlin'," he said as he handed it to Sable.

"Oh, Papa, what is it?" But there was no need for him to answer. The lid was open, and there against the white satin lay the heavy gold locket with its scalloped, lacy edge and plain, round center.

"It belonged to y'r mother," Keith said, and there was that quiet sadness in his voice that sometimes came when he spoke of her. "I know that she'd be wantin' you to have it now that you're such a young lady."

"Papa, oh, Papa," her voice came in a delighted rush, "it's beautiful! It'll be elegant with my new dress!"

Keith's ruddy features flushed with pleasure. "See the little catch right there to the side? Press it and the top opens to show y'r mother's picture."

Sable did as he said, and suddenly a young woman looked up at her, a girl with coppery red curls and blue eyes and an oval face delicate as a cameo—it could have been herself a few years older. Her first rush of delight was tempered; the locket in the palm of her hand became an object of awe, infinitely more precious than it had been.

"I bought this for her . . . had the portrait painted before we came to America. She wanted me to have mine done for it. Can you imagine that, now? A fine thing to be puttin' an ugly face like mine in there when she could be havin' her own lovely one."

Sable threw her arms around his neck and pressed her cheek against his. "You couldn't have given me a better present, Papa. Thank you." But her father's arms had tightened about her in an almost fierce embrace, and suddenly she was frightened again.

"Papa, something's the matter," she said. "Please tell me, Papa, what's the matter?"

His arms loosened. "Matter?" he said, laughing with a false heartiness. "Nothin' a-tall. What would be the matter?"

"Please . . . ," she said.

"Nothin's wrong, darlin'," he insisted. "There's nothin' f'r you to be worryin' y'r pretty head over."

They looked at each other for a long moment and his face sobered. "I hope I've done right by you, darlin'. Dora says I haven't. Says I've kept you too much to myself . . . says you needed friends of y'r own . . . and maybe she's right, selfish old man that I am."

"That's not true, Papa," she said quickly, refusing to admit to herself that she had been lonely at times. Times she had ridden through the city streets and seen girls her own age strolling, their arms linked, whispering together. She had Papa . . . and she had Wilfred and Dora . . . that was enough.

"Well anyway," Keith went on, "I'm thinkin' maybe we do need to have company more often—so I invited Charles Gregg to have Christmas dinner with us." He smiled at her as if he expected her to be delighted, while an unpleasant little feeling stirred in her stomach.

"That's . . . that's fine, Papa," she stammered.

Sable stood at her back bedroom window and looked out toward the carriage house, its weathered brick walls partly covered by clinging tendrils of ivy. The hired man, Wilfred, occupied the two upper rooms; a thin spiral of smoke curled away from the chimney then curved back upon itself in the erratic winter wind. The huge old sycamore nearby looked cold and defenseless, its trunk blotched where great strips of bark had peeled away and exposed the white wood beneath, its branches hanging full of prickly round balls, brown and dried against the bleakness of the sky.

How foolish of her, she thought, to let Papa's announcement that he had invited Charles Gregg to dinner spoil her day. She hoped he hadn't noticed.

It had been something more than a year since the first time Charles Gregg had come to the house, yet she could remember it so well. Her father had said, "Mr. Gregg, this is my daughter, Sable. Darlin', Mr. Gregg is my new lawyer—my adviser, you might say." The tall, thin man in the perfectly tailored clothes said, "Miss Flanagan," took her hand very lightly in his and bowed over it as if he were going to kiss it, though his lips never quite touched her skin. She could still remember the fluttery feeling inside her, the first, intense awareness of herself as a young woman in the presence of a man.

And yet, with his next visit there had begun a certain inward shrinking which she could not explain to herself. He was handsome in an austere way, with long, thin features too finely honed beneath pale hair, not quite blond and yet not brown, that receded ever so slightly at each temple. His manners were perfect, but her uneasy feeling had persisted, grown stronger with each of the dozen or so times he had been a guest in her home.

It was never anything he said—indeed she had the impression that he chose his words with great care—yet there was at times a subtle note, an inflection, as if he knew a great joke that she didn't.

There was nothing solid or tangible, nothing that she could tell Papa . . . and besides, it wasn't the time to bother him, despite his protests she knew something was worrying him.

Sable turned away from the window and settled herself upon the afghan-covered chaise, for a moment feeling again that sudden dread, the indefinable fear that had filled her that morning in the library. But she put it deliberately from her. Whatever was wrong, Papa could fix it. Papa always knew how to make things right.

Sable let her fingertips trace the filigreed edges of the locket hanging from its heavy gold chain about her neck. What would life have been like if her mother hadn't died? She turned it around and pressed the catch, studying for a long moment the unsmiling young woman who looked up at her.

Mama didn't look happy . . . but maybe people never looked happy in portraits. The mouth, so like Sable's own, was set in stiff unnatural lines, the delicate brows curved above blue eyes that seemed determined not to let the artist know what she was thinking.

Sable noticed that the barest edge of the high-collared dress was showing in the miniature—it was pink. Suddenly a bond had been revealed between them. Her mother was no longer an unsmiling flat image, but a young girl who had once cared about dresses and what shoes to wear and how to fix her hair . . .

Sable's new dress was pink. Mrs. Cramer had stated flatly that she couldn't wear pink with her red hair, but Sable had persisted and finally found just the material . . . satin, with a bold, glowing, almost metallic look to it, like pink bronze. She had had Mrs. Cramer make it into one of the elegant gowns pictured in the newest *Lady's Book,* but now that it had been delivered, she had dared do no more than try it on and admire her reflection briefly. It had only the tiniest cap sleeve and the bodice cut so low . . . what would Papa say?

For a moment she was tempted to wear it down to dinner. That might jar the ever so self-assured Mr. Gregg . . . But then she remembered an expression she had seen in his eyes once when he thought no one was looking. She shivered, and changed her mind.

The snowflakes, with a trick of the wind, seemed to pause momentarily in the flickering halo of the streetlamp, turning the yellow glow into blue-white purity, then in the next instant fly helter-skelter into the night.

Charles Gregg took a firm grip on his tall silk hat and once again looked over the carriages that moved slowly along the street. A horse slipped, almost went down on the slick pavement; the driver shouted a curse, jerked at

13

the reins and the struggling animal righted itself, moved on.

He had meant to walk the eight blocks from the Regis, where he lived, to the Flanagan's house, but the snow had started soon after he left. Already there was a thin covering on the ground and more coming down all the time.

At last he saw a cab rounding the corner. He waved the slim black walking stick with its heavy brass knob high in the air, shouting, "Here! Here, cabby!" And the old man up top hunched himself deeper into the shapeless coat and pulled over to the curb.

Gregg quickly gave directions, to which the driver responded with a nod and a surly grunt. Gregg felt a cold anger, started to wave the man on, but just then the wind shifted, driving the stinging flakes into his face. He shrugged, opened the door and climbed in.

He could hear the old man's clucking command to the horse and the cab lurched once, then went smoothly on. He carefully brushed the bits of snow and ice from his greatcoat, removed his hat, hitting it several times against the edge of his hand, frowning at the spots on the black silk, then replaced it. His nostrils flared unpleasantly at the dank, musty odor of the interior.

"Mold." He said the word aloud and looked with distaste at the faded green of the plush-covered seat. He pulled back the length of drapery that covered the window, the fabric damp and flimsy beneath his fingers.

The old houses with their brownstone fronts and gaily lighted windows passed before his eyes. Occasionally a well-muffled pedestrian picked his way carefully along, and somewhere in the distance he could hear carolers, singing their defiance of the weather.

For an instant, the cab window framed a boy standing near the curb, twelve perhaps, maybe thirteen, his thin face foxlike, his eyes sharp, questioning beneath the shabby woolen cap. Gregg had the strangest feeling of recognition, then the face was gone. He leaned back, puzzled, gave a short laugh. Of course—that was it. The boy had reminded him of himself. He must have looked like that fifteen years ago. Fifteen years ago . . . there was a dry, bitter taste in his mouth.

There had been holes in his cap, too. And in his gloves, so that his hands had nearly frozen blue working along-side his brothers, dragging in wood for the huge fireplace in the main serving room while his father sat with his lumpy potato face, splotched purple with broken veins, and his soft, fat belly, swigging down beer and trying to play the gracious innkeeper.

Father . . . father, he laughed softly with malicious sat-isfaction. That swine had never sired him—the others, yes, with the same shapeless faces and slow wits, but never him. He had known that since he was ten years old. He ran his long, slim fingers over the high, narrow bridge of his nose. He had known it and told his mother so.

She had been standing above the big copper stewpot, stirring the bubbling mixture. Her flushed cheeks had gone gray, her eyes had darted about the room to see if anyone had overheard. "Don't you never say that again! You hear me, boy? Never!" she had said.

When Gregg thought of her now, that was the only way he could remember her, standing inside over the cookstove or outside stirring the washboiler. And yet he knew there must have been a time when she was pretty, before hard work and childbearing had blurred the round lines of her body, taken all the grace and youth from her. He could imagine how she must have looked with hair as light as cornsilk and eyes big and round and blue.

And some fine gentleman had stopped at the inn one night, probably when her husband was in one of his drunken stupors, spewed out a son between her white legs, and the next morning went his way none the wiser . . . and very likely uncaring.

Strange that Gregg felt no curiosity about any of his family. They could all be dead these many years, but it didn't touch him. Hadn't since the sharp-faced fifteen-year-old had carefully removed the loose brick at the side of the chimney and reached inside for the tin box where the old man kept his money.

They must have found the hole in the masonry, the box and brick cast aside, but the two hundred and thirty dollars had been safely in his pocket and he far away by that next morning.

It had been so easy after that. It amused Gregg to think how simple it was to use people to accomplish what he wanted. They became puppets if you knew how to pull the right string . . . like the wealthy widow in Cortland or Judge Bradshaw over in Cooperstown—the good Judge who had helped him become an attorney.

This fool Flanagan had been almost too easy—took all the savor away. But the girl . . . he smiled. He had seen that chin go up, that red mouth set itself in tight, ungiving lines . . . seen those eyes go to blue ice. Young as she was, she promised to be a challenge worthy of him.

He was so engrossed he didn't realize that the carriage had come to a stop until the small trap door above his head opened and the driver peered down at him, muttering something unintelligible.

Gregg climbed out, deliberately tossed a coin high into the air just out of reach of the man, who in an instant was down from the high seat, sprawled on his hands and knees, scratching through the snow for the bright metal, mouthing curses beneath his breath. Gregg laughed, mounted the steps, lifted the heavy brass knocker, and let it fall once, twice.

The housekeeper let him in and took his things as Sable walked into the foyer from the library.

"Miss Flanagan," he said, bowing in a slightly exaggerated manner, "good evening."

The crystal chandelier glittered above the dinner table set with the best china and silver. Waxy green leaves and bright red berries of holly spilled out of a ruby glass bowl centered on the white linen tablecover.

"Allow me, Miss Flanagan." Charles Gregg pulled out

16

her chair, smiled down at her. She inclined her head slightly in acknowledgment and seated herself.

Gregg took the place set for him, opposite her, while Keith at the head of the table had already started to carve through the crisp, brown skin of the turkey.

Sable toyed with the silver in front of her, moved the water goblet, rearranged the napkin, anything to keep from looking at Gregg . . . and yet in spite of herself her eyes kept lifting to his.

"Pity the weather had to turn so foul," he said.

Sable lifted her chin, gave him a level look. "I like the snow," she said coldly, with perverse pleasure.

He made no reply, just smiled at her. In his eyes there was an amused satisfaction that made her furious.

"There now," Keith said, unmindful of the small by-play. He passed each plate, with thin slices of turkey and a generous mound of chestnut stuffing, along to Dora, who stood at the buffet and ladled gravy, offered frenched green beans, buttered limas, shimmering red cranberries in their sweet, thick sauce, baked yellow squash, and pickled beets and cucumbers.

"I don't know when I've been privileged to sit down to a finer meal," Gregg said, after sampling his plateful. "This woman is an artist, Keith." He smiled at Dora, who narrowly missed tipping the china teapot into the basket of hot bread.

Positively simpering, Sable thought disgustedly. She'd hear nothing for days to come but "what an elegant gentleman Mr. Gregg is . . ." She softened, realizing almost at once that she was more annoyed with herself than with Dora.

Gregg had been talking all the while. "I insist," he was saying, "that you both come out soon to dinner as my guests . . . of course even at Delmonico's I don't think they can match Dora's cooking. You are, I'm afraid, spoiling a poor bachelor."

"What of your family, Mr. Gregg?" Sable asked. "You've never mentioned them."

Gregg's thin face sobered. "Gone . . . all gone. My

only brother was killed in an accident three years ago. It was a terrible loss to me . . . we were inseparable. Two years before that, Father passed away. And I lost my mother when I was a lad barely old enough to walk. That," he said, "is a bond we share in common, Miss Flanagan."

"Rest their souls . . ." Keith shook his head sadly while Sable looked down at her plate, confused, a little ashamed of her earlier antagonism, not seeing the brief triumphant glittering of Gregg's eyes as he regarded her lowered head.

"But," he said quickly, "we mustn't allow the past to cast its shadow upon this festive occasion."

"You're right, Charles, you're right," Keith said. "Darlin', did you show Charles y'r locket? 'Twas her Christmas present."

"No, Papa," she said and felt an intense discomfort as Gregg looked for what seemed a very long time at the locket nestled against her soft wool dress, just at the point where the hollow between her breasts began its gentle curve. Her hands fluttered upward, covered the locket.

Gregg lowered his head slightly, peered at her from beneath thin, well-molded brows. "It's lovely," he said, "as lovely as its wearer."

Dora passed back and forth offering more food, refilling their cups with hot black tea. She disappeared, to return a short time later carrying a round silver tray proudly before her. On it was a large steamed pudding, its fluted surface glowing with fine blue flame.

Gregg made much of the display, and Dora blushed like a young girl as she topped each serving with her own special butter sauce.

"Well now, darlin'," Keith said, when at last the meal was finished, "if you'll excuse us, we menfolk'll be havin' our brandy and cigars in the library. You—" He seemed suddenly preoccupied. "You come join us a bit later."

"Yes, Papa," she said.

A little more than an hour later, Sable drew near the

library door, which was standing partially ajar. Suddenly her father's voice sounded in a loud, harsh way that she had never heard before.

"But they have to give me an extension," he was saying.

Gregg's cold, clipped tones came back. "Out of the question."

"Charles, you told me—"

"Come now, Keith," Gregg cut him off. "Must we go through that again?"

Sable gave the door a little push and now she could see both men. She wanted to say, "I'm here, Papa! I'm here," but curiosity mixed with apprehension dried her words.

The two men stood outlined against the white marble mantle piece: Gregg with one hand in his pocket, the other holding a slim black cigar; Keith, whose stocky body seemed suddenly smaller within the black wool suit, with his head tilted forward until the loose skin hung beneath his chin.

Papa . . . Papa . . . it was a part of the silent trembling within her. Papa looks old . . . No, no, she pushed it from her, not Papa, never Papa!

At last he spoke, his voice dried, unnatural. "Tomorrow I'm going to speak to Crawford myself . . . Benton, too."

Gregg shrugged. "As you like." As he turned away, he saw Sable standing there in the doorway. "Ah, Miss Flanagan, do come in." He came toward her. "Your father and I have just been passing time until you joined us."

Keith made a visible effort to collect himself. "Yes, darlin'," he said, "come in . . . come in."

Chapter 2

Sable pushed the muffin away. "I don't want any more, Dora. I guess I'm not very hungry this morning."

"My lands!" Dora's round face tilted sideways, the wide-set eyes filled with concern. "What's the matter with ever'body? Mr. Keith barely swallowed half cup o' tea 'fore he left." She cleared away the last of the dishes from the round kitchen table and slid them into the big dishpan to soak in the steaming water, while Sable sat, her chin in her hands, elbows propped against the hard oak surface.

The squat black cookstove gave off a pleasurable warmth, making faint popping sounds as the oven started to cool down.

"Never seen so much good food goin' to waste," Dora scolded as she put the clean silver away. "Night 'fore last you didn't want turkey again, and last night . . ." She drew a long breath. "That beautiful beef roast just a dryin' itself to a fair cinder while we waited for Mr. Keith to come home."

"Papa's hardly been home at all these last two days. Do you know the reason, Dora?"

21

The housekeeper pursed her mouth in its tight, little smile. "Who knows about menfolk? My late husband was the self-same way—always a-rushin' out on some pressin' business. I declare, I never understood the first thing about it. Put these away for me, would you please?"

Sable rose from her place at the table and put the blue graniteware pots in their accustomed places along the shelf, hung the big iron ladle on the hook beneath.

"Oh, Sable!" Dora's voice was half teasing, half serious. "Can't be pretty with a face that long."

Sable tried to smile. "I know," she said.

"Tell you what. You go upstairs and get yourself ready. I'll have Wilfred bring the carriage 'round front. There's still plenty of snow left. You said you wanted to go driving."

"Oh . . . I don't know . . ."

"Nonsense! Be the very thing for you. Get right along now . . . and mind you, dress warm! It's still cold."

She was glad she'd heeded Dora's words when she stepped out of the front door. The wind, as if in defiance of the bright sunlight, stung her face and with her indrawn breath caused a dry ache at the back of her throat.

The waiting Wilfred, his tall, almost skeletal frame nearly hidden by the greatcoat, touched a finger to his brown woolen cap and hastened to her.

"Best take my arm, Miss Sable," he said, and she knew the homely grin was on his face, though she couldn't see it. The wool muffler covered everything except his eyes and his big, hooked nose, which right now was very red and had the tiniest bead of moisture trembling at its end. He made a huge snuffing sound and the bead disappeared as he helped her down the two steps, past the black iron posts that flanked the gateway, and across the icy sidewalk to the waiting carriage.

One of the matched pair of bays struck out at the pavement while the other tossed his head impatiently, his breath forming white fingers of steam that quickly disappeared in the cold air.

"Tuck this in around you good now," Wilfred said, pulling up the lap robe. "I wouldn't be a bit surprised if this ain't the coldest we've had this year. Where to, Miss Sable?"

"Let's drive through the outskirts of the city a while, Wilfred, and then stop by Mrs. Cramer's on the way home. I want to see if she has any new material in the shop."

Sable pulled the soft fur lap robe closer about her and inched nearer to the window so she could see better. The signs of Christmas were still much in evidence. Along one block someone had tied great red bows fashioned of oil-cloth around each lampost, and farther on a small green tree, its branches festooned with popcorn strings, was displayed in a front window. It should be such a happy time, she thought, and yet . . .

She had tried to question Keith about the overheard conversation between him and Gregg, but he had just patted her hand in that preoccupied way he had adopted lately and told her that women didn't understand business. She was sure she'd understand if he'd just tell her.

But she returned to the same thought again and again —Papa could fix it, whatever it was . . . Papa could always fix things. Yet no matter how often she said it, the old comfort, the feeling of absolute certainty, was not quite complete.

The carriageways were cleared north of the city, but the grass was still well covered with drifts in spots that looked as deep as a foot and a half. Bare-limbed trees reached upward, stark and naked beside their evergreen sisters.

Sable heard a shout, loud sounds of laughter, then she saw them—boys sledding on the hill. They shrieked their excitement as one, smaller than the rest, skimmed down the icy incline, his blue muffler streaming out behind him, his body clamped belly-down to the shiny new sled. He pulled sharply to one side to avoid a tree, the sled tipped over, and he rolled, tumbling end over end into a drift. It was like a small explosion in the powdery snow, then he was up waving gaily to his companions, grinning.

The carriage rounded the bend and she could no longer see the boys, though the sounds of the laughter could be heard for some little distance. It was deserted here—too cold, she thought—but no, there was someone up ahead, a woman walking by the side of the road.

The wind pulled at the folds of the dark cape she wore; her head bent forward so that only the back of her bonnet showed. Then she turned and for a moment, Sable saw her clearly. It was a strong face, yet womanly —not too much older than herself, she thought. In her twenties, perhaps . . .

Then suddenly she disappeared from view. Sable heard Wilfred's warning shout, the carriage lurched heavily, stopped, one of the horses whinnied shrilly.

Sable threw off the lap robe and struggled out onto the packed snow of the roadside. The woman was a dark heap on the icy pavement and Wilfred was crouching over her, moaning, "My God, my God, we've run her down!"

Sable sucked in the cold air, her legs trembling so violently each step was a jerk. She saw the dark lashes flutter against colorless cheeks and dropped to her knees.

"Help me, help me, Wilfred," she said, and together they lifted the woman's shoulders and rested her head in Sable's lap. She quickly undid the bonnet strings.

The lashes moved again, swept open. Brown eyes looked first at Sable then Wilfred, then the well-shaped, strong lips formed themselves into an O and she struggled to sit up.

"Oh, I'm so sorry," she said, her voice shaking.

"Wait! Don't try to stand up," Wilfred said, "you might be hurt." But the woman was already on her feet.

"Are you sure you're all right?" Sable asked, feeling the rigidity of the arm she held, the trembling.

"I . . . I think so."

"Praise God!" Wilfred moaned under his breath, then louder, "I thought sure one of them hooves had hit you. It gave them such a fright when you stepped out so suddenlike in front of 'em. They're most o' the time gentle as a team o' lambs . . ."

"Yes . . . yes, I'm sure they are . . ." She passed a hand across her forehead. "I'm afraid my mind was . . . on something else. It was completely my fault . . ." She shivered.

"Here, Wilfred, let's get her inside the carriage," Sable said.

"No, please—that isn't necessary! I'll be quite all right in a minute. I'm sure I wasn't even hit. I was just startled when I turned and saw the horses so near . . . I think I slipped on the ice."

But all the time she had been talking, they were propelling her toward the carriage, and now Wilfred helped her in.

"If you'll just tell us where you live, ma'am," Wilfred said, "we'll take you home."

Sable sat beside her. "Yes, we insist upon it," she said.

The young woman looked from one to the other of them. "All right . . . maybe that is best." She was quiet.

"What's the address, ma'am?" Wilfred prodded.

She started to speak, stopped, looked away for a moment. Then all at once that strong mouth set itself in a straight, firm line. She reached to the inside pocket of her cape and drew out a neatly folded bit of newspaper.

"Would you be good enough to take me to this address instead?" She opened the paper and pointed to the bottom line.

Wilfred peered at it. His muffler had fallen away from his lean face, and Sable noted that the bead was back at the tip of his nose.

"Why, that's down near the waterfront, ma'am. You sure you're wantin' to go there?"

"Yes, please."

Wilfred gave his nose a mighty swipe with the back of his gloved hand and shut the carriage door.

"I don't know what you must think of me." The woman turned to Sable as the carriage tilted forward then settled into its gentle, rocking motion. "I owe you an explanation." The brown eyes were serious, troubled.

"No, of course you don't," Sable said. "I'm just so glad you weren't hurt."

"You and . . . your driver are very kind, Miss . . . ?"

"Flanagan . . . Sable Flanagan."

She nodded her head and smiled. "I'm Amanda Peters." She seemed to notice the loose bonnet strings for the first time and hurriedly pulled the gray felt bonnet from her head. "Mercy me! I must look a sight." Her hands made quick, strong movements over her brown hair, smoothing, tucking a stray wisp into the soft bun at the nape of her neck. She replaced the bonnet, straightening the slightly bedraggled blue feather, tying the strings in a tight, neat bow beneath her chin.

She shivered again as she had back on the road, and Sable realized that her own teeth were chattering.

"Here, let's pull this around us." Sable tugged at the fur lap robe. "No reason for us to freeze to death while we have this," she said. Amanda Peters made a small, grateful, humming sound and tucked her half of the robe firmly around her.

The young woman was silent for a moment. Then, "I was trying to decide something—something important. And I didn't have anybody I could talk to about it. That's why I was walking there in the snow by myself."

I should tell her, Sable thought, tell her that she needn't explain. But there was a spreading warmth inside her . . . like a hunger she hadn't even known was there, now suddenly satisfied.

In her life there had been one housekeeper that she could remember before Dora—Mrs. Edmiston, that dry little woman, colorless, like a wisp of dust. And there had been Mrs. Cooley, stern and demanding, the teacher Keith had hired to come in three times a week to hear Sable's lessons. There was Mrs. Cramer, the dressmaker, good-natured, always smiling, but well past middle age. But there had never been anyone of her own sex who was even near her age. And now suddenly this young woman was sitting next to her in the carriage, looking at her with quiet confidence as if she wanted to talk to her.

"I guess I've already made up my mind," Amanda Peters said. "This is where I told him to go." She reached again for the clipping and Sable noticed the neatly mended spot near the collar of the dark wool cape.

"Read it," she said, her voice low but steady.

The small printed words, framed by a neat black rectangle, stared up at Sable.

Wanted . . . Women of good health and character willing to go to San Francisco, in California territory, to become the wives of honest men . . . the man being responsible for the payment of her passage. Character references from a reliable source must be produced. Those interested, contact Captain Judd Grayson, #19. . . .

She stopped, the rest of the address unread. "California," she said. "I remember Papa talking about that. Isn't that where they discovered a lot of gold?"

Amanda nodded. Sable looked down once more at the clipping.

"But . . . you'd . . . have to marry a man you didn't even know," she said, as the full meaning of the words came to her.

"Yes . . . that's what it says." Amanda's voice was curiously flat, then rose suddenly. "But you can't have things just the way you want them all the time. You have to make compromises—sometimes big ones."

"But why?" Sable questioned, then remembered herself. "Miss Peters," she said, "I do beg your pardon . . . it's none of my business, of course."

The firm lips softened, and Amanda put a hand on Sable's arm. "I want to talk about it," she said. "I want to hear it out loud so I'm sure once and for all that it's what I want to do."

Sable looked at her for a long moment, nodded.

Amanda took a clean white hankerchief from her pocket, passed it from one hand to the other nervously.

"I don't have anyone to leave behind me," she said. "Both my parents are gone . . . died within two days of each other during the cholera outbreak . . . must be more than five years now.

"They left me some money—not much, but I've managed . . . taken in some sewing and such as that. But when I saw that piece in the paper . . ." She stopped and smiled, the color coming back to her cheeks. "I think I knew it right then, that I was going . . . I just didn't want to admit it."

"But Amanda," said Sable, the first name coming so easily neither of them even noticed it, "I still don't understand why . . . If it's help you need, maybe I could talk to Papa—"

"No . . . no, it isn't that, though I do thank you. I'm going because it's like beginning all over again . . . It's like having a new life handed to you on a plate—and that's what I want."

They rode in silence for a while, a slight creaking in one of the wheels forming a perfect accompaniment to the pleasant rhythm of hooves against pavement. Then Amanda leaned far over to the window and pointed.

"Look!" she said.

They could see a part of the harbor, ships lying at rest, and yet even at this distance there was something about them—alive, mobile, Sable thought, as if they could never be completely still. The sun glinted on tall masts; for a moment she thought she could see the figure of a man, scrambling with incredible agility along one of the yard-arms. Then Wilfred pulled the carriage around a corner and tall buildings blocked their view.

"Maybe I'll be sailing on one of those," Amanda said.

Sable looked at her with undisguised admiration. "Aren't you frightened?"

"Well . . . a little," Amanda admitted.

The carriage came to a stop and Wilfred opened the door. "This is it, ma'am . . . right there." He pointed across the sidewalk to the glass-fronted door, a green shade pulled three-quarters down, the number 19 showing clearly at the top.

Amanda drew a long breath. She looked at Sable. "I guess this is goodbye, then."

"Oh, no—we'll wait for you, drive you home when you've seen . . . whoever it is."

Amanda shook her head, smiling. "I couldn't let you," she said firmly. "You've been kind enough already."

"But . . . but I want to," Sable stammered. "Besides . . . I'd like to hear about it—while we're taking you home, I mean."

"Are you really interested?"

"Yes."

"Then come in with me." Amanda's eyes were suddenly wistful, not at all as certain as her voice had been.

At their knock, an edge of the green shade lifted slightly, then the door swung open.

"Good afternoon, ladies, won't you step inside?" The tall man smiled pleasantly at them and lifted his visored cap briefly from thick, black hair touched lightly at each temple with gray.

Sable and Amanda exchanged quick looks and entered. The room contained only a desk and some chairs, and from one of the chairs sprang the oddest looking man Sable had ever seen.

He was skinny, and not even five feet tall, but his arms were quite long and his chest wide for his size. As if, Sable thought, the various parts of him really should have belonged to several different people.

The gentleman who had opened the door for them motioned them to the two chairs in front of the desk.

"I'm Judd Grayson, captain of the *Betty Kay,* and this," he said, motioning to the other man, "is my first mate, Nimrod Jones."

Nimrod, his hat in hand, made a funny little dip with his neck that was supposed to be a bow, looked solemnly at Amanda, then at Sable, from a face whose features seemed almost as mismatched as the rest of him.

The captain sat down behind the desk, opened the top drawer and drew out several papers. "I presume," he said, "that you ladies have come about the advertisement in the paper?"

"That's correct, sir," Amanda said primly. "But"—her voice faltered—"well, I would like to find out a bit more . . . before I commit myself to anything."

"Oh, it's all fittin' and proper, ma'am," Nimrod said, and his brief smile suddenly made the odd features all of a part. Sable decided that she liked him then and there.

"I'll be happy to explain the situation fully, ladies." Captain Grayson shoved the dark blue cap back on his head. "Some seven months ago, I was in San Francisco. I'm sure you must know that there's been a big gold strike there in California, and men have come from everywhere. Now there are lots of shortages, but I guess the biggest one is . . . women." He smiled at them again, his tough, windburned face breaking into leathery creases.

"Some of the men have been there long enough that they've decided they want to make it their home . . . settle down, raise their families.

"When I was there last, I was approached by a committee. They had a petition signed by three hundred. They agreed to pay for the passage of the ladies. There'll be a preacher waiting when the ship docks and all you ladies will have to do is make your choice among the men waiting for you.

"Now," he said matter-of-factly, "are you still interested?"

Amanda just sat there for a moment, not saying anything. Then she took a deep breath and nodded her head.

"Good . . . good. And what about you, miss?" He turned to Sable.

After the first stab of surprise, Sable suppressed the desire to giggle. "Oh, no," she said quite firmly, "I'm just here with Miss Peters."

"In that case, let's get down to business. I'll have to ask you a few questions, Miss Peters. What is your age?"

"I'm twenty-six."

"And you are in good health." His eyes flickered over her and it was more a statement than a question. Amanda nodded her head.

"Have you ever been married? I mean are you a widow?"

Amanda hesitated for the briefest moment than answered quietly, "No."

His pen had scratched across the page after each answer; then he scrawled a few last words at the bottom.

"Now then," he said. "have you brought your reference with you, Miss Peters?"

Amanda reached inside her cloak and brought out a small, white envelope. "It's from the minister of my church."

The captain tore it open and scanned its contents quickly. "Yes . . . yes, this seems to be quite satisfactory. Now if you'll just sign this contract. Read it over if you like. It just states that in return for passage to San Francisco on my ship, the *Betty Kay,* you will, on arrival, choose a husband from the men who come down wanting a wife. And," he added with a dry chuckle, "I think you'll have plenty to choose from. There must've been five hundred down to see the ship off, and there'll likely be more than that waiting for us to come in."

"That's the Lord's own truth, ma'am," Nimrod spoke up. "I recollect one man sayin' he'd give a thousand dollars in gold dust if he could just see a real lady . . . like yourself, ma'am."

Sable saw the slight trembling in Amanda's hand as she signed her name, saw the tip of her tongue run quickly over dry lips, then it was done.

"One more thing, Miss Peters," said Captain Grayson. "As we are limited for space aboard ship, each woman may bring only one large trunk and perhaps a small case. That will have to be all. We sail with the tide on Sunday morning."

"I understand, Captain," said Amanda.

As they rose, Nimrod scrambled to the door to open it for them, and again made that funny, little dip that was supposed to be a bow. And there they were, back out on the sidewalk again, the sun shining brightly.

The soup simmered in the heavy iron pot, sending out its hearty aroma to every corner of the warm kitchen. Wilfred tipped his bowl so that he could get the last spoonful, scooped out the last bit of shredded meat with a piece of cold muffin.

"Mmmmmm," he said, his long, thin face showing his satisfaction. He finished the hot black tea with one swallow, drew the back of his hand across his mouth.

"Wilfred!" Dora protested.

He grinned, the prominent Adam's apple moving noticeably in the over-long neck. "Sorry. I'll use the napkin next time." He took his greatcoat from the peg by the door and left for his rooms over the carriage house.

Dora held the sieve in one hand, struck it lightly and rapidly against the other so that the flour showered down into the large, wooden bowl.

"And you, miss," she said to Sable, "I thought you'd come back cheery as a bird in springtime, and here you are a-pinin' around as bad as before. I wonder if you oughtn't be dosed with a good tonic."

Sable made a face. "Ooooh . . . not that awful stuff! Besides, I'm fine."

"Well . . ." Dora measured out the butter with a practiced eye. "When I get this cookie dough made and rolled, maybe you could do the cuttin' and sprinkle the sugar for me."

"All right."

Dora glanced up at the ornately carved wooden clock that hung on the wall above the table. "My lands, I hope Mr. Keith ain't late again tonight."

"I hope not, too," Sable said dutifully, though in truth her mind wasn't on Keith at all but upon the tall, brown-haired young woman with features so strong and regular you'd think she was plain unless you took a closer look.

It had been hard to say goodbye to Amanda. She had known her little more than two hours . . . yet it had been hard.

They had driven her back to her rooming house; it was like her—genteel and proud, but poor.

The doorknob had been polished to a soft luster, the wooden panels scrubbed spotless, even though the white paint had peeled away in several places. One shutter was missing—taken down, Sable guessed, rather than allowed to sag on a broken hinge. It was easy to imagine the boxwood hedges as they must look in summer, trimmed to a neat perfection; yet she could imagine just as surely that the roof leaked.

If only she could have met Amanda long before this . . . but on Sunday the ship would sail, and that was that.

The front door knocker sounded loudly, repeatedly, and Sable waved Dora back to the cookie dough. "I'll get it," she said.

As she came into the foyer she could see a man's figure outlined through the colored glass inset. The door open, the distinguished-looking man removed his tall beaver hat, ran a hand over his gray hair in what almost seemed a gesture of distress.

"Miss Flanagan?" he said, his voice uncertain.

"Yes."

"Miss Flanagan, I am Jason Crawford. May I step inside, please?"

"Certainly, sir." Sable stepped back, waited, puzzled.

The man turned the hat round and round in his hands, looked down at it. "Miss Flanagan, I have had business dealings with your father . . . in fact, we were having a meeting this afternoon, just a short time ago . . ."

He glanced up at her, shifted his eyes quickly back to the hat. "I shouldn't be the one to do this. We . . . tried to find Gregg. I know he's a friend . . . but . . ." He looked directly at her now. "I'm afraid I've brought very sad news to you . . ."

Sable was suddenly aware of her own heartbeat; her

skin felt clammy, cold. "Papa. . . . ? Papa's ill," she said.

The man looked at her for a long moment, his face working oddly. "No . . . no, Miss Flanagan. He's dead."

She heard the words, heard him go on talking, and yet her brain had ceased to understand.

"I'm so sorry," he was saying. "We were having this meeting . . . several of us . . . and he just held his chest and fell."

An awful nausea gripped her stomach, rose upward to her throat.

". . . They're bringing him home . . . should be here soon . . ."

Dora was crying . . . tears on Dora's face . . . flour on Dora's skirt . . . Dora's dark blue starched skirt . . . No, that wasn't right . . . Dora never spilled flour on her skirt . . .

"Catch her—catch her!" Dora's voice sounded loud and unnatural. "She's going to fall!"

Chapter 3

There weren't very many
people there. Not very many for Papa, Sable thought, as
she stood in the cemetery beside the awful, dark hole
they dug in the ground.

The wind, out of a gray sky, tugged like fingers at her
hair, pulled at the skirts of the ill-fitting black dress and
coat that had been borrowed so hastily.

There was Mr. Crawford . . . he was the one who had
brought the news. Those others—five, no, six of them
—business acquaintances, they said, when they stum-
blingly offered her their sympathy.

There were Dora and Wilfred . . . what would she have
done without them? They had taken care of everything.

And there was Charles Gregg. Charles Gregg, who
even now was standing beside her holding her arm as if
he had the right. At first she had tried to pull away from
him, but he had tightened his grip until it hurt and she
had looked up sharply at the cold, handsome, expressionless face, the thin lips pressed tightly together.

"The Lord hath given; the Lord hath taken away."
The minister's voice was a deep, rich baritone. He bowed

his head, hiding for a moment the turned-about white collar.

Her eyes felt hot, burning with dryness. What could tears mean now? The ache had become a part of her very tissue and fiber, so that she couldn't have told where it started or ended . . . it was her.

Four brawny men in stout work clothes stepped forward, grasped the heavy ropes. The walnut casket with its heavy brass handles was lowered slowly. For one terrible moment, Sable felt as if she might shatter into a thousand small pieces, as glass shatters when struck sharply.

"Dust to dust."

Papa wasn't dust . . . Papa was warm, Papa laughed, Papa— No, not that cold, waxlike figure closed away in the casket! It was a scream inside her.

Gregg's fingers tightened on her arm, and she realized that the minister had said something to her, was holding out something toward her.

She took the handful of dirt, looked down at it for a long moment. It was wet, would leave a brown stain against the black kid glove . . . She stepped forward, Gregg along with her, his hand still firmly on her arm, and with head erect, eyes straight ahead, she dropped it into the open grave.

Her whole body jerked as the dull thump echoed in her ears . . . Then it was over and they were walking back to the carriages. There had been a sudden thaw; the clean snow was gone, and underfoot the ground had become wet and spongy.

Gregg handed her into the carriage, climbed in beside her, and told the driver to start.

"Where's Dora?" Sable asked quickly.

"I put her into my carriage. My driver will bring her along home," Gregg replied.

They rode in silence, Sable dry-eyed, her body rigid with grief. Yet even then something, some unnamed thing caused an instinctive shrinking within her. Gregg sat with eyes straight ahead, his face impassive, his profile etched in the gray light like a mask.

Back at the house he alighted from the carriage first and held his arms out to her. She tried to pretend that she didn't notice, but his hands were already around her waist and he swung her to the pavement. She tried to sweep past him, but he caught her arm and turned her around to face him.

"I realize, Sable," he said smoothly, "that this has been a trying day for you, so I won't come in with you now. But I shall call on you tomorrow at two." His eyes rested for a moment on her lips, which she knew were trembling.

"That really won't be necessary, Mr. Gregg," she said coldly, clamping her mouth firmly.

"I'm afraid it will be." His voice suddenly was harsh. "As your father's attorney, there are certain facts of which I must inform you. I'll see you at two."

With that he turned away from her and signaled his driver, who had just pulled up to the curbing with Dora.

Atop the white marble mantelpiece, the slim black hands of the clock pointed to the two and the twelve. Sable paced back and forth. She had dressed in a simple blue muslin, the only sign of mourning the narrow black band pinned to her sleeve. It would be several days before Mrs. Cramer could deliver her mourning clothes.

She heard the heavy brass knocker fall; she waited, afraid of this meeting and yet strangely anxious to get it over with. She would simply instruct the man that she would no longer require his services . . . that she would arrange for someone else to take over her affairs. That would end it. Then he stood in the doorway.

"Sable," he said, inclining his head in that overdone bow. "You may be excused, Dora; I prefer to speak to your mistress alone." He all but closed the sliding doors in the housekeeper's face.

He turned and surveyed Sable from across the room,

offering no added word of greeting, just looking at her with insolent eyes, examining her with thoroughness.

She felt the hot flush of confusion, felt the false front of confidence cracking. "I hope you'll be as brief as possible, Mr. Gregg," she said quickly. "You understand, of course, that if it weren't business I wouldn't receive you at all at this time."

"I understand you perfectly, Sable. Now perhaps it's time you understand me. Sit down, please," he said, pointing to the old, leather sofa.

"I prefer to stand."

"Very well, if that's what you want," he said, crossing the room to stand beside her. "I had hoped that there would be a way to soften this for you, but perhaps it's better to stop beating about the bush. Sable . . . you are penniless."

She stared up at him, unable to believe she had heard him correctly. "What are you saying? That's impossible," she finally stammered.

"I'm afraid it's true. A few months ago, your father got word of a good deal involving Jamaican rum. His assets were overextended already. I advised him strongly against it but he insisted on borrowing the money on a short-term basis, sure that he could recoup before it was due. He risked everything he had . . . and lost."

"I don't believe you! Papa trusted you—he would have listened to whatever you told him!"

He shrugged. "I suppose it's useless to try to convince you. I even put up some of my own money to help him out."

She stood there, stunned. "Everything's gone? Everything?"

He nodded. "You own nothing but the clothes on your back." He paused, his eyes moving avidly over her. "And some of those haven't been paid for."

He took out one of his slim black cigars, lit it, threw the burned-out match into the fireplace.

"The house . . ." Sable looked about the room with its mellow polished wood and soft old leather, the two fine paintings in their gilded frames above the sofa, the milk-glass bowl on the table. She let one finger touch the smooth marble surface of the mantle beside her. "Who owns this house now?" she asked.

He blew the cigar smoke slowly from his mouth, looked at her coolly.

"I do," he said.

"You . . ."

"I bought it from Crawford and Benton. Signed the papers last night."

She bit her underlip, completely confused, distraught. "But why?"

"For you . . ." There was that silken tone she'd heard before. "For us."

She looked at him for a moment, then drew her chin up proudly. "Mr. Gregg," she said, trying to control her trembling voice, "you forget yourself!"

"Hear me out, Sable." He threw the unfinished cigar into the fire. "I need apologize to no one for my means or position. What's more, I'm an ambitious man, Sable. I've decided to go into politics. Someday I'm going to be governor of this state—I know, because it's what I want and I always get what I want. I want you, too, Sable."

"Please—don't, Mr. Gregg! Perhaps we'd better continue our business at another time." She tried to pass him but his arms were suddenly around her. "Please!" she pleaded, her voice no more than a frightened whisper.

"I'll take care of you. You won't have to worry about anything. The governor's lady. That's what you'll be . . . beautiful and elegant . . ."

He pulled her closer to him, his arms tight about her, and bent to kiss her. She frantically turned her head to one side. He laughed. Holding her with one arm, he entangled his fingers in her long red curls, pulled her head forward until her face was very close to his.

"You'll marry me, Sable." The silk of his voice was suddenly roughened with harsh edges of anger. "After all, what else can you do? You have no money, no place to go. Even if you wanted to work, what would you do? I'll bet you don't even know how to do housework!"

His thin lips drew back in a smile. "Of course," he said, "your obvious charms could bring high prices . . . but somehow, I think you'd rather share my bed than sell yourself to many men. Be thankful that I'm willing to marry you!"

With the last, Sable's fear gave way to blind anger. She jerked away, felt the sudden pain as her hair pulled through his fingers, heard the harsh sound of material tearing as he caught at the neckline of her bodice.

She saw the momentary surprise in his eyes as he stared down at her, then that other thing . . . the avid look she'd seen before.

She looked down at herself, saw the parted buttons, the eyelet-trimmed camisole ripped open, showing one white, rose-tipped breast. Gregg's long, thin, almost womanish fingers reached out and cupped it, caressed the nipple.

The power of movement returned to her and she jumped away as if his fingers had burned her. Clutching the open bodice together, she turned on him.

"Never!" she spat, her loathing full in her voice. "I'll never marry you!" Then she turned and ran from the room, up the stairs, and into her own bedroom.

She heard his "Come back here, Sable!", heard his running footsteps behind her. She barely slid the bolt in place before he turned the knob. The door shuddered beneath the pounding of his fists, then there was sudden silence.

"All right, Sable," he said, his voice coming clearly to her, "I'll give you a little time to get used to the idea . . . but make no mistake about it, you'll meet my terms. There's nothing else you can do. I'll be back here at six tomorrow evening—and make sure that your welcome is all it should be!"

Sable stood, her back pressed against the door, her hands to her face, her whole body trembling uncontrollably.

She heard him walk away, heard the front door slam.

Now the hot flood of tears threatened to break, thrusting her into hysteria, but she held them sternly back. There could be no weakness now. She had to think . . . think . . .

You'll meet my terms. There's nothing else you can do. His words hammered at her.

"No! no!" she said aloud, "I won't marry him . . . I can't." The shame of memory scorched her. She looked down at her open dress, pulled the torn camisole together as best she could, then fastened the buttons.

Charles Gregg had killed Papa—killed him just as surely as if he'd stabbed him with a knife or taken a gun and shot him. He had lied to Papa, manipulated him. Why? The house? The money?

. . . I always get what I want. I want you, too, Sable.

Papa . . . oh, Papa . . . it was a numbness inside her. If only he were here to make things right. But he wasn't —and it would never be the same again. It was like dying and having to begin to live all over again. A new life. Amanda had said that.

There was a hesitant knocking. "Miss Sable . . . ?"

It was Dora's voice. Sable turned and drew back the bolt. The housekeeper's eyes looked suspiciously red, but her white cap was stiff as always and firmly in place.

"What day is this?" Sable asked before Dora could say anything.

"Why . . . why it's Saturday."

What was it Captain Grayson had said? *We sail with the tide on Sunday morning.*

"I want you to help me pack, Dora. I'm going to leave New York," said Sable.

One hand fluttered to Dora's mouth. "Oh no, Miss Sable!"

"Dora, I have to. You must have heard what Gregg said when he was shouting outside my door."

Tears welled in the wide-set eyes. "Miss Sable, I always thought he was such a fine gentleman. To think he'd use such language to you—"

"Listen to me!" Sable cut her off. "He said he'd come

back at six tomorrow evening, but he might change his mind and come sooner. We have to hurry."

She pulled a small carpetbag out of the closet. "I'm going to California, where he'll never find me."

"California! But Miss Sable, you can't—you can't go all that way by yourself!"

"I'm not going by myself. I have a friend who's going, too." Sable opened the top bureau drawer, put handkerchiefs and hose into the bag. "There's no more time for talk. Have Wilfred get the big trunk out of the attic and bring it here. Then you come back and help me."

"Yes, miss," Dora said. There was a new note of respect in her voice, but Sable was too busy to notice it.

It was hard to know what to pack. She didn't even know what the weather was like in San Francisco. She decided to be prepared for anything.

The only time she hesitated was when she came to the pink satin dress, the one she'd never worn. It would take up precious room in the trunk, and she might never have a chance to wear it . . .

Her velvet jewelry case was open atop the bureau, the gold locket in plain view. Her mother had worn a pink dress for the portrait inside. She'd take her own pink satin, she decided. It would be worth the space it took.

It was growing dark outside before Sable was ready. She took a last, quick look around the room to be sure she hadn't forgotten anything.

Her room . . . for as long as she could remember. For a moment panic rose up to suffocate her and she hurried out the door, knowing that if she stayed for one instant longer she might not have the strength to go.

Wilfred had taken the trunk and the small carpetbag out to the waiting carriage and now he stood in the entrance hall, his cap in hand, his Adam's apple working. Dora, beside him, was weeping openly.

Sable handed them each folded pieces of paper. "These are references for you. I'm sure you won't have any trouble finding other positions," she said. "And remember what I told you both . . . Don't tell anyone where I've gone—not anyone. He mustn't find me."

She put her arms around Dora and kissed her on the cheek, then, not trusting herself to speak, she motioned Wilfred out to the carriage.

As they pulled away, she watched the big stone house for as long as she could see it in the dim light. Then she turned her face resolutely forward.

Chapter 4

Amanda Peters's capable fingers drew the needle through the fabric one last time, firmly catching the edge of the hem, put the thread up to her mouth and snapped it between strong teeth.

A knock sounded at the door; she put the petticoat aside, stuck the needle into the plush pincushion.

Who could that be? Surely not her landlady again. Amanda had told her a dozen times that she'd leave the room clean in the morning.

She swung the door open, looked into the blue eyes, desolate, lost, saw the young face with features far too pretty to be so white and strained.

"Sable . . ." she said, almost unable to believe that it was the same happy-looking young woman she'd met just three days ago.

Sable smiled weakly. "I've been standing here," she said, "afraid that you might have forgotten me."

"Nonsense! Come right in here!" Amanda drew the

girl into the room. "Take off your coat," she said. Sable did as she was told, as a child might follow directions.

Amanda glanced at the one chair, remembered the broken spring in the cushion. "Let's sit here," she said, and drew Sable down beside her on the edge of the narrow bed. "What's happened?"

The girl looked away for a long moment. "Papa's dead," she said.

She went on talking, tonelessly, impassively, but it didn't fool Amanda. She studied Sable intently as she listened to her story and she sensed that Sable was holding herself in check by sheer strength of will, afraid to let the tears come for fear of giving way completely to her fear and shock.

Only once did Sable's voice start to tremble. "He—he tore my dress," she said, her hand lifting as if to cover her full young breasts. She was quiet for just a moment, then told how she had run up to her room.

Finally: "I had to get away," she said, her hands twisting together. "You were the only one I could come to. Do you think Captain Grayson would let me go along to California?"

Amanda patted her hand. "Of course he will. We'll go together right now and talk to him."

"I was hoping you'd say that," said Sable, "that's why I had Wilfred wait for me downstairs."

"Good!" said Amanda, busily tying her bonnet strings. "It might be dangerous for us to walk to the docks after dark."

The staccato beat of the horses' hooves sounded loud and hollow in the dark streets. Sable wondered why they had never seemed so noisy to her before. She was so frightened that someone would see and recognize the carriage . . . that in some way Gregg would find out her plans.

"Now just stop it," Amanda said sensibly. "There must

be hundreds of carriages that look exactly like this one. There's no need to worry."

Sable drew a long breath. "What if Captain Grayson's not there?"

"Then we'll go down to the *Betty Kay* and ask for him," Amanda answered calmly.

But when they pulled up they could see the light shining with a pale green glow through the drawn shade of the office door. There was a chill wind blowing. They shivered and drew closer together as they stood waiting for an answer to their knock.

Captain Grayson opened the door and stood there a moment adjusting his eyes to the darkness outside.

"Why, ladies . . . this is a surprise! Do come in," he said, and as they entered, "Just a few more minutes and I . . . we would have been gone."

There was a look on his face that seemed half embarrassed, half amused. "Ladies," he said, "I'd like you to meet Miss Flossie Tucker." He motioned toward the short, blond girl standing near the desk. "This is Miss Peters and—I believe, Miss Flanagan?" He looked to Sable for confirmation.

She nodded, so preoccupied with the business she had come on that she paid little attention to the young woman's throaty "Glad to meet you."

Amanda took the initiative. "Miss Flanagan has decided to sign up and come along with us. We thought it would be better to see you tonight rather than wait until sailing time in the morning."

"Oh?" Judd Grayson fastened Sable with a quick, inquiring look. "We'll be happy to have you with us, Miss Flanagan. You make fifty-three. Not as many as I had hoped for, but . . ."

He rummaged in the top drawer of the desk and drew out a paper such as Amanda had signed.

Sable answered the same questions, and with a feeling of relief, made her signature at the bottom.

"Now," Captain Grayson said amiably, "I'll just take your reference . . ."

"Oh," Sable said, dismayed. "I forgot that!"

"But she only decided to go tonight," protested Amanda. "Besides, I'll vouch for her."

"I'm afraid that's not quite the same, Miss Peters. I'm really not supposed to accept anyone unless they have the proper character reference. The committee made that quite clear."

"Please, Captain Grayson, I must go with you!" Sable could hear the desperation in her own voice.

Flossie Tucker, who until now had stood quietly by, put one arm possessively through the captain's. "Aw, Judd, let the kid come with us. You can see just by lookin' at her that she's proper as afternoon tea."

Judd Grayson looked from one to the other of them, let out a long breath. "All right."

"Oh, thank you, Captain Grayson . . . thank you very much. And thank you, too, Miss Tucker." For the first time since entering the room, Sable looked closely at the blond girl.

She was rather pretty in a flamboyant way; her figure generously proportioned, the bust and hips voluptuous. Her dress, though of good material, was a bit too frilly and loudly colored to be becoming. Her face reminded Sable of a china doll—the skin a little too white, the lips and cheeks a little too red to be real.

"There ain't nothin' to thank me for, honey, and just call me Flossie. Ain't nobody called me Miss Tucker since old Preacher Harris come callin' to try and reform me. I always will wonder why he left in such a hurry. All I did was ask him to fasten my dress for me. It was way back here, and I couldn't hardly reach the hooks . . ." She made her green eyes very wide, then turned and walked over to the chair in a swinging way that Sable had never seen a woman use before.

"Sable, it's getting late." She felt Amanda's hand tighten on her arm. "I think we'd best be going!" Amanda steered her firmly toward the door, nodding coolly to Flossie Tucker and the captain.

"Better be here early," Captain Grayson called after them, that same look of half-amused embarrassment on his face. "No later than six."

The air of the waterfront was heavy with smells of salt and tar, hemp and fish, and a hundred other unidentifiable odors. Ships were loading cargo; wagons full of supplies blocked the road. The noise, the shouting beat at Sable's ears.

She had spent a sleepless night lying beside Amanda on the narrow, sagging mattress. And then while it was still dark and quiet, they had crept down to the kitchen and eaten a quick breakfast, gulping two cups each of strong black tea to guard them against the chill morning air.

Wilfred had been waiting patiently for them . . . dear Wilfred with his long, sad face and the persistent drop of moisture at the end of his nose. He had carried them and their luggage down to the dock where the *Betty Kay* was tied.

Maybe that had been the hardest of all—his leaving, severing the last tie with the stone house and her happy life with her father.

Amanda nudged her arm and from their vantage point on deck near the rail they watched the smiling Flossie Tucker starting up the gangplank, moving in that sensuous, swinging way Sable had noticed the night before.

Half a dozen seamen in their tight blue pants and heavy wool jackets sprang to help her, but suddenly Captain Grayson was standing at the top, and the men eyed one another and moved away to various tasks. Flossie slipped her arm through the captain's and they walked aft.

Amanda lifted her eyebrows, sniffed.

Nimrod Jones paused in front of them, stuck the open ledger under one arm, snatched the cap from his head. "Mornin', ladies," he said, with his peculiar quick nod. Though he included both of them, his smile was obviously for Sable. He was away then, the stub of pencil making quick, sure strokes on the opened page.

Amanda gave Sable a teasing smile. "I think you've made a conquest."

Sable looked after the ill-formed figure. "I like him," she answered seriously.

They watched a fragile-looking girl struggle aboard carrying a large wicker basket on her arm, refusing to relinquish it to the outstretched hands, her eyes big and frightened in the thin face.

"Surely, she'll be the last," said Amanda tiredly. "I didn't know there were so many different sizes and shapes of women."

"Mmmm." Sable nodded her agreement. But there was one more.

A black-cloaked figure came with sure, steady steps up the gangplank, stepped on deck and paused to look about her. The black eyes looked almost feverishly at Sable, then passed on, the drooping mouth pulling down even tighter.

Suddenly, the black-cloaked woman dropped to her knees. She threw her head back, lifted her black-sleeved arms high—like some great, black bird, Sable thought.

"Oh Lord!" her deep voice rang out. "Guard us through the treacherous months ahead. Protect us from the sea and rocks and winds that would destroy us . . . and from worse, the evil and vain and lustful among us. Cast them from you. Protect your righteous servants. Deliver us safely to our new land. Amen."

There was a sudden quiet on deck. Then the woman stood up laboriously, and normal activity was resumed.

Sable and Amanda looked at each other, then back at the woman, who sat down on a low trunk and stared out toward the sea. It seemed to Sable that her sober features had assumed a look of grim satisfaction—as if, having done her duty, she would now await the evils she was sure were coming.

There was a quick shout and Sable turned to see the gangplank swinging away. There was an odd tightening through her middle, and for a moment she wanted to cry, "Wait, wait, let me go home!"

But Charles Gregg was there . . . and if she stayed, he'd win. She knew that somehow, had always known.

She felt Amanda's hand slip into hers, felt the firm, warm, comforting pressure. Sable looked up, was able to smile.

Chapter 5

Sable heard the low wail of distress, heard the gagging, gushing sound from the bunk to her left, and turned to see the vile white vomit spewed out upon the floor between them. The woman gave her an apologetic look and sank weakly back against the coarse, unbleached muslin pillowcover, her face the color of unbaked dough.

Sable turned away and covered her face with her hands, her own stomach heaving spasmodically.

The roll of the ship had increased hourly. She heard the woman's small portmanteau sliding across the floor again. Her own carpetbag and Amanda's leather satchel were fastened securely to the legs of their bunks. Nimrod Jones had tied them there.

The affable first mate, himself, had helped them down the companionway to the 'tween-deck area, explaining that it had been used for cargo until Captain Grayson had the *Betty Kay* refitted to carry passengers. The remodeling had consisted of installing draft vents on both sides of the bow and enlarging the fore and aft hatches for ventilation. Rows of bunks lined either side of the long room, leaving

53

a narrow aisle in the middle and a small space at each end.

"You'd best take these bunks here," he had said. "It'll be cooler when we go through the tropics." He had pointed out the draft vents close by. "It gets hotter'n . . . I mean . . . it sure enough gets hot down here then!"

It had not occurred to either of them to wonder why the first mate had taken such duties upon himself. Much later they discovered that Captain Grayson had given Nimrod the unusual task of caring for the female charges and keeping the rest of the crew as far removed from them as was possible in the close area of a sailing ship.

It had been enough for the moment just to have a place to lie down, since they were rapidly finding out that they were far from being "natural sailors." And before long the 'tween-deck area had been filled with the groaning and weeping of their fellow travelers.

The first day at sea dragged on. The call for lunch and then dinner came with everyone refusing.

Once, from somewhere close by, Sable heard a voice that she recognized immediately as that of the praying woman, mumbling between groans something about punishing the innocent with the wicked. And she and Amanda exchanged weak grins.

Finally Captain Grayson called down the companionway, asking permission to come down. The sight that met his eyes, the odors that assailed his nostrils, must have been dreadful. But he tactfully gave no hint of it. In fact his face assumed an expression of complete sympathy as he walked up and down the aisle looking at the sufferers.

"Ladies," he said, "I'm very sorry to hear you're not feeling so well, but let me assure you, this will pass."

"But, Captain," came a querulous voice, "is this a storm, or will the goin' be this rough all the way?"

"No, this isn't a storm," he replied patiently, "these heavy seas are quite normal for this position at this time of the year. You'll see a big difference as we push farther south . . ."

Suddenly a peculiar yipping noise interrupted Captain

Grayson. He turned his head to one side as if to hear better, his forehead knotted into leathery ridges. Then he strode down the aisle toward the sound.

He stopped in front of Sable's bunk, staring at her suspiciously, but turned away as the yipping came again from the bunk directly opposite her where the thin girl Sable noticed boarding the ship sat. Now the big, dark eyes looked more frightened than ever, as the captain bore down on the wicker basket she had beside her on the bunk.

He fumbled with the top a moment and then reached in and pulled out for all to see a small, white dog, extremely wooly and, at the moment, wriggling violently.

"Christ!" The one word exploded from Captain Grayson's mouth. The struggling bundle of fur barked nervously and, twisting out of the captain's grasp, jumped into the waiting arms of its mistress.

Judd Grayson stood looking down at the two of them. "I hope, Miss Moore," he said, his voice brusque, but perfectly controlled, "that you have a satisfactory explanation for this. I believe I told you emphatically that I do not allow animals aboard this ship!"

The girl clutched the small dog closer to her. "Yes, sir, you told me . . . and I'm real sorry, but I just couldn't leave her behind. I ain't got nobody but Bitsy. I'll see she don't cause you no trouble . . ."

The captain shook his head in exasperation. "Miss Moore, can you imagine what my ship would be like if I had allowed everyone to bring a pet?"

The clearly defined chinbone set itself in a stubborn line. "I couldn't leave her behind!" she said again, staring up at the captain with more defiance than Sable would have thought her capable of.

Captain Grayson yanked off his cap, ran a hand over the thick black hair. "Might have known," he muttered. "With women aboard, anything can happen . . ."

He clapped the hat back on, shrugged. "Well, there's one thing certain," he said resignedly. "We can't take her back, so it looks as if she's going along whether I like it or not. See that you keep her out of trouble!"

"I will, sir, I will," the girl said happily. The captain turned away and strode back toward the companionway, muttering something about fifty-three sick women and a dog.

He paused. "Oh, yes, I came down to tell you, Mr. Jones and the cook are bringing some hot soup from the galley. It'll make you feel better."

At the chorus of protest, he said sternly, "See that you eat some, or I'll have to send the ship's doctor down!"

Once he was gone, Sable reached across the short space between bunks and poked Amanda. "Look who's in the bunk next to the Moore girl," she whispered.

"Well!" Amanda's voice expressed a certain satisfaction. "It's Flossie!" The young woman they had met just the night before lay there, her eyes closed, her face pasty-looking. Amanda grinned wickedly. "Looks like she really needs that paint on her face today."

The soup arrived. Nimrod passed among them with bowls, while Herman, the cook, a big rawboned man twice his size, ladled from the big black pot.

The homely face of the first mate was suddenly transformed by a shy grin as he handed Sable her bowl. And after he had moved on, Amanda leaned over and whispered: "I told you you've made a conquest. Look, he gave you a bowl with more soup in it."

Sable looked down at the soup. A chunk of beef and a piece of tomato showed above the surface of the thin broth; a layer of orange-colored grease shimmered over the top.

"Oh," she groaned. "I don't know if it was such a favor!"

The oil lamps, hanging on hooks at intervals around the wall, cast a soft, flickering light, and the women seemed strangely subdued. There was even less groaning, as though they were becoming, if not indifferent, at least inured to the monotonous regularity of the ship's rolling.

Some lay in the same clothing they had worn when they had boarded that morning. But Sable and Amanda, knowing they would be much more comfortable, had changed into nightgowns.

The young Moore girl across the aisle had followed their example and was now sitting up in her bunk with the pillow at her back. The dog, Bitsy, was curled up asleep at the foot.

"Do you think we should speak to her?" Sable asked, seeing Amanda looking at the thin girl.

"I don't know why not." Amanda's voice was matter-of-fact. "After all, we're going to be living together for the next few months. We should make it as pleasant as possible."

They watched their chance and the first time the girl looked up they both called out a soft hello across the aisle.

She returned their greeting with a quick, eager smile.

"I'm Amanda Peters and this is Sable Flanagan," said Amanda.

"And I'm Willa . . . Willa Moore," said the girl shyly.

"Willa . . ." Amanda repeated it. "That's a beautiful name."

"Thank you."

Sable started to ask why Willa wanted to go to San Francisco, but caught herself in time. Remembering her own reasons, she knew that was one question they wouldn't be asking each other for a long time—maybe never. Instead, she pointed to the sleeping dog.

"He's awfully cute," she said.

Willa smiled. "He's a she."

"Oh, I forgot. I never had a dog," said Sable, almost wistfully.

"I had one once," said Amanda, "when I was a little girl. But it died."

"Land! I guess I'd mighty near die, too, if Bitsy did," Willa replied.

"I guess you don't have to worry. She looks healthy enough," said Amanda.

"She is now," Willa assured them, "but she sure was a

puny one when she was little. She was out of a litter of six. Seems like she was just wasting away . . . wouldn't even try to nurse. Tom and Lucy—that's my brother and his wife—was set on doing away with her, but I begged them to let me have her. They claimed it was just foolishness to fool with her, but I wrapped her in a piece of warm flannel and fed her milk with a spoon. Pretty soon, she started growing and . . . she's been mine ever since."

Sable looked at Willa with a new respect. "How in the world did you know what to do for her?" she asked.

"I've lived on a farm all my life," Willa answered simply. "Ma and me been living with Tom and Lucy since I was eight. I always had a fondness for newborn things. Tom used to say I had a way with 'em."

She wasn't really looking at them now, but past them . . . to a happier time. And for the first time since Sable had seen her, the fear was gone from the big eyes.

But quickly, with an all but visible effort, Willa brought herself back to reality . . . and the fear was back again. "They've got so many younguns of their own now . . . and another coming every year . . ."

Sable's unasked question had been answered.

The warmth of the dining saloon felt good as Sable and Amanda closed the door on the chilling, damp wind. The cramped room was nearly empty—most of the passengers still could not leave their bunks—but a small group had gathered for breakfast at the far end of one of the three long, narrow tables.

Sable caught sight of Willa Moore, with the bright-eyed Bitsy on her lap, and she pulled Amanda toward them.

They were welcomed with friendly smiles, except for the praying woman, who gave them one blank look and then sat with eyes downcast. A plump, motherly-looking woman, with thick braids, more gray than blond, encircling her head, waved them into two of the straight wooden chairs and suggested that everyone introduce herself.

"That seems like the best way to get acquainted to me,"

she said, the laugh wrinkles around her eyes deepening. "I'll start off. I'm Martha Abernathy. Most everybody calls me Ma."

Sable tried not to stare at the girl sitting next to Ma Abernathy. She was covered with freckles—her face, her neck, hands, wrists. Her hair, caught up in a topknot, was so blond it was nearly white. When she opened her mouth to speak, Sable saw that her teeth protruded slightly.

"I'm Carrie Thorne," she said, her light skin flushing a brilliant red between the freckles.

Next it was Willa's turn, then Sable's, and then Amanda's.

The praying woman looked for a moment as if she wanted to ignore them. Finally she said, "I'm Widow Parker." She gave a quick nod and the narrow nose pinched in even tighter.

A tall, lank woman with a New England accent introduced herself as Marian Foley, and then the last one, a plump little robin of a woman, said, "My name is Katy Johnson."

"Not much like home, is it?" Ma Abernathy said with humor, as they all looked about them at the dining room, bare except for chairs and the long tables, which were covered with new white oilcloth, the slick surface pulled tight and tacked along each side. "Captain's table," she said, nodding toward a smaller table over to one side.

"Well, at least it's clean," Amanda said, and Martha Abernathy nodded agreement.

The door to the galley swung open, and the big, rawboned cook came in balancing trays on either hand, lined with bowls of oatmeal, a platter of fried meat, and one of biscuits. Another trip brought butter and apple jelly and steaming hot coffee which he served in tin cups.

Sable looked at the greasy meat, passed it on without taking any. The oatmeal was not entirely free of lumps, but it was warm and made her stomach feel better than anything had since the previous morning. The biscuits were surprisingly good, but the metal cup burned her mouth and the unfamiliar coffee was bitter.

A few more women drifted in, started to eat. Suddenly a knife dropped to the floor with a loud clatter. Sable looked up, followed Amanda's eyes to the door where Flossie Tucker stood.

There wasn't a sound. Everyone had been too ill to notice Flossie the day before, but her casual entry into the dining room now, her lips and cheeks unmistakably rouged, made quite an impression.

She started toward them, a pair of cheap metal bracelets on her wrist clicking together, then suddenly she stopped. And Sable saw that the women at her table had turned their faces away in an unmistakable rebuff.

Flossie looked at them for a moment, smiled her knowing smile, shrugged. She walked over to the captain's table and sat alone.

Sable lifted a spoonful of the oatmeal to her mouth, but let it fall back to the bowl uneaten when she heard chair legs scrape harshly against wood planking. The Widow Parker stood slowly erect, her eyes fastened on Flossie and burning with a strange, almost personal resentment.

"A painted face—the mark of a harlot," she said, her normally sallow features a dull red. She threw her head back and closed her eyes. "Oh, Lord, we beseech Thee to smite down in Thy wrath the painted women who do the devil's work!"

She turned and stalked from the room, but her words stayed behind . . . to echo and reecho in the painful silence.

Ma Abernathy planted her fists on well-padded hips and looked around her at the mess.

"There's no doubt about it," she said, "we've got to have mops and brooms and a scrub brush—with plenty of hot water and lye soap."

"I'll go on deck and ask," volunteered Amanda.

"I'll go with you," said Sable. And while the others started to fasten down their luggage, Sable and Amanda made their way onto the deck.

The swollen clouds of the morning were now a flat gray

ceiling above them, and rain fell in a chilling mist. The lead-colored sea ran in small, choppy peaks.

Amanda undid her woolen headscarf and held one end out to Sable.

"Here, we can hold this over our heads," she said. And they huddled close together, walking carefully on the slippery deck.

But suddenly the planking beneath their feet slanted. The scarf jerked from Sable's grasp as Amanda lost her footing. Her arms flailing, she made several wild steps toward the rail.

Before Sable could do anything, a tall, broad figure strode along the deck as easily as if it had been dry land and caught Amanda firmly to him.

"There now," he boomed. "Steady as you go, miss!" Her benefactor was a dark, husky man, his face windburned to the color of mahogany—that is, what could be seen of his face, for most of it was covered with a black, curling beard.

Still supporting Amanda with one arm, he swept off his cap with the other, to expose a head that was absolutely devoid of hair—not even a fringe. The pale, protected skin of his pate looked all the more incongruous when paired with the luxuriant beard.

He laughed, a great, gusty sound. "Give you a week and you'll think you'd been born to it," he said, his arms still firmly around Amanda, whose thanks were being all but drowned out by his big voice.

Suddenly Sable saw her friend start, saw her eyes go big and round with accusation. Amanda pushed the man away from her.

"And what are two sweet lasses like yourselves doing up here all alone?" he asked, the pleasant expression of his face changed not one whit.

"We came to ask for some cleaning supplies," Amanda said primly. "We'd like a broom and mop, some scrub brushes and pails—and plenty of hot water and good strong soap."

"I'll see to it myself," he said, "just as soon as I escort you safely back to the women's quarters."

"That won't be necessary. We'll be quite all right." Amanda's voice was frosty.

There was a flash of white teeth through the black curl of his beard. "As you wish, lass, as you wish," he called after them.

Sable had to walk fast to keep up with Amanda, who was walking along the unsteady deck at a furious pace.

"Amanda," she said, tugging at the woolen cape, "whatever is the matter with you?"

Amanda slowed her steps, two bright spots of color on her cheekbones. She took a quick look around. "He pinched me!" she all but whispered.

Sable stared . . . realized that her mouth was open. "He what?"

"Pinched me!" Amanda said again.

Sable looked at the heavy wool cape. "But how . . . ?"

Amanda shrugged. "I don't know . . . he slipped his hand—" She shook her head. "I don't know how he did it, I just know we'll have to watch out for him from now on."

Sable nodded, suitably impressed.

But they soon found that the man was as good as his word, for they were hardly back below when the supplies they had asked for were delivered. The women who were well enough now set to work to make the 'tween-deck area livable again. Sable had never before had a broom in her hand, but when Amanda shoved one at her she took it and put it to good use—awkward at first, but thankful not to be helping Martha Abernathy and some of the others down on their knees scraping away at the foul, dried messes.

Within two hours, the wide planking of the floor had been scrubbed nearly white and the bunks were all neatly spread up, but for the ones that still held passengers. And those poor sufferers were clean and comfortable.

There was a feeling of accomplishment, of pride even,

for Sable, as she sat on her bunk and looked around her, her nose sniffing at the fresh smell.

"Lye soap." Amanda laughed at her, sat down beside her.

"Smells good."

"Not good, just clean." Amanda seemed to know what she was feeling. "Many hands make light work," she said. "That was my father's favorite expression."

Sable felt the sudden twisting inside her . . . tried not to think of her own father. "It must have been terrible for you to lose both your parents so close together," she said quietly to Amanda.

"Yes, it was . . . Father was a doctor. Don't think I ever saw him when he didn't have his pockets stuffed with pills and his vest stained with cough syrup or reeking of quinine or some such. But he always found time for me.

"He used to teach me, read to me. He always said a woman should be educated same as a man. Mother always asked why. She said you didn't need an education to get married and have babies, and that that should be a woman's biggest job in life . . ."

Amanda's voice trailed off. A shadow dulled her eyes. "I have some mending to tend to," she said.

That evening when the ladies who were well enough—about half of the group—assembled for dinner, they found the captain and his officers already seated at the smaller table.

Captain Grayson stood up at their arrival, and the other three men hastily followed his example.

Sable felt the quick nudge of Amanda's hand at the same moment that she saw the fifth diner still seated at the small table: Flossie Tucker.

A small, whispering rustle went through the group of women and Flossie's blond head lifted high. She was obviously aware of the sensation she was causing, seated at the captain's right, and obviously enjoying it immensely.

Captain Grayson remained standing until they were all

seated, then raised his hand to get their attention—a gesture which was completely unnecessary.

"First, let me say that I am delighted to see so many of you are feeling better." He smiled with good humor. "I thought this would be a good time to introduce you to these gentlemen. I believe most of you already know my first mate, Mr. Jones."

Nimrod gave his quick nod and looked down at his plate.

"And this," Captain Grayson continued, "is my second mate, Mr. Finchly."

Sable and Amanda exchanged quick looks. There was no mistaking the curling black beard, the bald head.

"My third officer, Mr. Creighton," the captain went on, "is busy seeing to the ship; you'll meet him later. But we do have Dr. Blair with us," he gestured to the final gentleman at the table.

The ship's doctor drew his long, stringy body to its full height and inclined his iron-gray, slightly shaggy head.

"And now that the introductions are concluded—ladies, enjoy your dinner." Captain Grayson reseated himself and started his meal.

The slick oilcloth surfaces had been covered with crisp white tablecovers, and it was obvious that Herman, the cook, had gone to extra trouble with the food, but there was little eaten that night. The good ladies were too busy watching the low exchanges of conversation, the sudden bursts of laughter at the captain's table.

Once, Flossie leaned toward the captain to whisper something in his ear, and her low-cut bodice gaped to show so much of her ample breasts that several gasps were heard.

Amanda tugged at Sable's arm. "It's a good thing Widow Parker felt too sick to come to table," she whispered.

Flossie was getting her revenge.

Chapter 6

One by one the travelers recovered from their attacks of seasickness. As the days passed and became weeks, everyone settled into the routine boredom of life aboard ship.

As the weather stayed cold and rainy, they were necessarily confined a good deal of the time to the cramped quarters of the 'tween deck. There was little to do except sew or read or just sit and talk.

One topic of conversation that never grew old was Flossie Tucker. It was rumored that one of the crew members had overheard the Widow Parker remonstrating with the captain for allowing such a woman to join their group and demanding that she be set ashore at the first port of call. The captain's retort had been that Flossie was not a regular member of the group but a paying passenger, and that he had no control over the character of a paying passenger. The Widow Parker was said to have flounced furiously out of the captain's cabin.

"She wasn't in her bunk again last night," Carrie Thorne whispered, as her eyes moved slightly to indicate the sleeping form of Flossie, two bunks down.

The four of them—Carrie, Sable, Amanda, and Willa Moore—sat on the coarse duck cover of Amanda's bunk, catching up on their mending. With a sigh, Sable laid the sewing in her lap. She wasn't used to doing her own mending yet, and her fingers were covered with a dozen needlepricks.

"I know that none of you agree with me," she said, "but I can't help liking Flossie—a little bit."

"Sable!" Carrie's nearly white topknot trembled with indignation.

"Well, it's true. She never complains. She always goes out of her way to be friendly . . . and that Widow Parker is so hateful to her all the time I don't see how Flossie can keep from talking back to her. Some of the things she says."

"Well . . ." Carrie's tone was grudging. "I don't have no love for that old psalm-singer either. But you *know* where Flossie is when that bunk's empty at night!"

"Maybe that's the way she's paying for her passage," Amanda said dryly. Willa looked shocked. Amanda laughed, "Men will be men, you know."

They were quiet for a moment. Amanda finished her sewing, put it aside, reached out for Sable's. But Sable shook her head, doggedly began again.

"No—I guess I *don't* know," Carrie said suddenly.

The other three looked at her questioningly.

"About men . . . less'n you want to count my pa. Wasn't a man in forty miles'd look at me back home."

"Now, Carrie, don't say that," Amanda protested.

"It's gospel truth. Why, even old Finchly don't bother me—and you know that's saying some. I bet there ain't another woman aboard this here ship ain't been pinched" —she instinctively lowered her voice—" 'cept maybe the old psalm-singer . . ."

The Widow Parker had just passed down the aisle and stretched herself upon her bunk—ironically enough, just across from Flossie.

"Anyway," said Carrie frankly, "that's why I'm here

now. I figured it was the only way I'd ever get myself a husband."

"But, Carrie," said Willa shyly, "don't you ever worry . . . ?"

"About what?"

"Oh, what they'll be like, and all."

"At least we'll get to take our pick," said Amanda.

"I know." Willa's eyes looked even bigger. "But it ain't like being courted and having a man know you the way you are, and want you that way. I mean there we'll be— two strangers. And maybe he won't like me. I mean—" Her cheeks grew redder. "I mean—"

Flossie's throaty laugh stopped her. "Don't you worry, honey," she said, sitting up on her bunk. "You just lay down and he'll like you."

Before any of them could recover enough to answer, the Widow Parker jerked her slat-thin body erect.

"You slut!" she fairly screamed, "boasting of your sins of the flesh! Luring good men to the devil with your painted mouth and your sinful body! God will strike you down—in His wrath, He'll strike you down!" Her black eyes glittered.

Throughout the length of the 'tween deck, every head was turned.

Flossie smiled her most pleasant smile, stood up and patted her disarrayed hair into place, then slowly crossed the aisle to stand beside the Widow Parker's bunk.

She looked down at her for a long moment, the smile suddenly gone. "Maybe I have sent men to the devil," she said, not in a loud voice, but very distinctly, so that everyone present heard quite clearly. "But people like you have sent just as many to hell. No wonder your husband died. He probably couldn't stand living with a self-righteous, evil-minded, old bitch like you any longer."

The Widow Parker caught her breath sharply. Her eyes went dead, like burned-out pieces of coal.

"I pity the man that gets you." Flossie's calm voice was merciless. "That is, if you can get any of 'em to take you. A man knows what he wants in his bed, and I ain't never seen one yet that wanted a hatchet-faced, skinny, no-tit woman like you." She waited, as if daring the woman to say more, but the Widow Parker turned her head away, for once quiet.

Flossie walked down the aisle toward the companion-way, silk petticoats rustling, the pleasant smile once more on her face.

Sable didn't know what had awakened her—but at least she could be grateful that it wasn't the dream that had tortured her again and again at the beginning of the voyage. The dream where Charles Gregg was every-where, no matter how she turned, waiting for her with that cold, assured look on his face. No . . . it had been weeks since she'd had that dream.

She turned in her bunk, no longer minding the rough muslin of the sheets and pillow cover. It was so quiet in these few hours before dawn, she thought, as she looked down the double row of sleeping figures toward the one lantern that burned near the companionway.

So quiet that if she closed her eyes, she could almost imagine that she was the only person left anywhere, safe in the surrounding darkness, rocked gently, cradled in the palm of the sea.

But she wasn't the only person. Way back over all those miles there was Charles Gregg. And somewhere far ahead was . . . who? The unknown man she had chosen over Gregg . . .

"Sable . . ."

The soft voice startled her. It took her a moment to re-alize that it was coming from the bunk next to her. "Amanda," she whispered, "I didn't realize you were awake."

"I haven't been very long. I was dreaming . . . it woke me . . ." There was a certain catching in her voice and Sable suddenly knew that Amanda was crying. Strong, competent Amanda was crying.

Sable got up quickly, sat down on the side of Amanda's bunk. "Move over," she said, and scooted underneath the scratchy, wool blankets. She waited while Amanda wiped away the tears, made a soft, snuffling sound in her nose.

"I was dreaming about Jim."

"Who's Jim?" Sable waited for a long moment. "Do you want to tell me?"

"He was my husband."

"Was . . . ?" Sable said, carefully keeping the surprise out of her voice.

"He's dead now. I married Jim Peters when I was twenty. We'd been married three years when he was killed."

"I'm sorry, Amanda."

"No need. I can hardly remember what he looked like. With him three years . . . and three years gone . . . and I can't really see his face anymore. Even in the dream, I couldn't. Just the words. I could hear the words . . ." The pain in Amanda's voice seemed a thing apart, alive, throbbing. "That last year . . . that's when it was really bad," she said. "The quarrels . . . the awful things we said."

"What was the matter?" Sable asked.

Amanda was quiet again, her breathing deep and rhythmic, almost as if she had dropped off to sleep. Then: "I didn't give him a child . . . and he blamed me bitterly for it.

"Once, I was so desperate I went to an old woman on the other side of town. People claimed she was a witch. Seems like I drank gallons of some vile, black stuff she brewed up for me . . . God knows what was in it." Sable felt her shudder. "But she said if I drank it on certain days . . ."

Amanda's voice trailed away and Sable tried so hard to think of something comforting to say, finally just pressed her hand. Somewhere above them bells rang with a thin, tinny sound.

"They're changing the watch," Amanda said.

"Yes." They listened until the bells stopped. "What happened to him?" Sable asked.

"He started to drink a lot toward the last. One night he

came out of the tavern, tried to get on his horse . . . it threw him . . . His head hit the curbstone."

They lay silent for awhile. Then Amanda spoke. "You must be wondering why I lied to Captain Grayson that day in his office."

"No, I never thought of it," Sable said honestly. "What I've been thinking is . . . you helped me so much when I needed it, and now I feel so useless."

Amanda's strong fingers pressed firmly, quickly against her own. "You listened . . . that's what I needed."

Far down toward the end of the row a woman stirred, rose from her bunk, and disappeared behind the length of canvas that the group had hung up for privacy. A few moments later, she came out, climbed back into her bunk; all was quiet again except for a soft snoring that came from Ma Abernathy's bunk. Ma always snored when she rolled on her back.

"Why didn't you tell Captain Grayson?" Sable asked. "There are lots of widows aboard. It wouldn't have made any difference."

"I'm not really sure myself. I had the feeling that if I told about Jim it'd be like deliberately breaking a mirror and inviting bad luck. I know it sounds silly . . . but I wanted to start all new. I didn't want to take any of my past with me."

Later, in her own bunk, Sable again looked down the double row of sleeping figures. They all had someone or something those miles back, she thought . . . and maybe dreams that came in the night . . . and all had chosen the unknown up ahead.

It should have made her less lonely . . . but it didn't.

The classical Greek figure that adorned the *Betty Kay*'s bow held her proud head high, her draped bosom thrusting forward, her sightless eyes gazing out over the watery miles as the vessel plowed through them with stubborn persistence.

The long-awaited warm, Southern sun was finally with them. The travelers reveled in it, spent hours on deck.

Color, the expanse of sea and sky, took on a new depth,

a brilliance that Sable had never experienced before. Nimrod told her that it was always so in these waters, though he didn't have an explanation for it.

He seemed always to be there if she had a question or needed some small task done, popping up beside her with that shy smile that made his homely face almost comely. And more than one aboard noticed the growing friendship between the striking young girl and the nearly grotesque first mate.

Sable was standing at the rail one day, leaning slightly forward to watch several fish swimming near the surface of the blue water. Their quick, darting movements caused the sunlight to glint against the bold yellow and black stripes along their wide, flat bodies.

"Pretty ain't they?" Flossie's rich voice sounded at her elbow. Sable looked up, nodded.

Nimrod walked past, two crewmen following him. He saw Sable, gave that quick bob of his head, went on.

Flossie laughed, watched him. "If he ain't stuck on you . . ." she said knowingly.

Sable, who had already had some teasing, felt a vague annoyance. "He's a nice man. He's been kind and helpful to me," she said shortly.

"Nice! That little monster! I'll tell you how nice he is. He threatened to slit the Crab's belly if he touched you."

Sable stared at her uncomprehendingly.

Flossie suddenly burst out laughing. "You know, the Crab. That's what the crewmen call Finchly." She made a pinching movement with her thumb and forefinger. "Course he's being more careful than usual, 'cause Judd —that is, Captain Grayson—made it pretty plain what'd happen to anybody'd bother one of you. The captain says he aims to get you there in the same condition as you came on board."

Sable couldn't get what Flossie had said out of her mind. And the next day for the first time she noticed the knife that hung from Nimrod's belt, its long, narrow blade hidden in the leather sheath. It was hard to realize that the kind and thoughtful, even shy, first mate she had come to know these last weeks was not always the same man that others saw. Yet, she was deeply touched that he wanted to protect her.

"I can't drink it," Sable said, waving away the tin cup that Amanda offered her.

"They put some vinegar and molasses in it. It helps a little." Amanda passed the cup of brackish, rust-colored water on to Willa and ran a sodden handkerchief over the small beads of perspiration that stood out on her face.

They and most of the other passengers had brought their thin bunk pads up and spread them out beneath the night sky, trying to escape the brick-oven heat of the 'tween deck.

The *Betty Kay* had lain becalmed for eight days now, the tropic sun beaming mercilessly, the sea around them like bright, green glass. Captain Grayson had assured them that it couldn't last forever and that with the first wind, they'd be on their way to Rio, where they'd put in for fresh water and provisions. But his assurances were small comfort for now.

There had been a noticeable breaking down of discipline. The crewmen had stripped to a bare minimum of clothing—sometimes no more than the tight, blue pants cut to the thigh in ragged peaks. And even now they lay on a portion of deck barely out of sight of the women, who themselves had discarded corsets and petticoats . . . but no one seemed to care. Even Widow Parker just made one feeble remark about it "not being very seemly."

Sable tried not to think of how hot she was. She closed her eyes and lay very still, pretending that she was back home and sliding into a tub of cool water, right up to her chin, the clean, clear liquid splashing up against her face . . .

She awakened some time later, the night air covering her like a hot, wet blanket. The saltmeat and beans she had eaten at dinner lay undigested, an alien mass in her stomach. She was afraid she was going to be sick.

No one stirred except Bitsy, who popped her head up

and looked over Willa at Sable, the small fuzzy head turned quizzically to one side.

Quietly, Sable rose and stepped carefully around the sleeping figures. Perspiration beaded her forehead, trickled between her breasts, down the small of her back.

She walked past the shadowy bulk of canvas-covered lifeboats and came to stand at the rail. The moon looked swollen, ripe to bursting, and its light made a long, bright aisleway across the ink-colored water.

She lifted the heavy, damp mass of her hair away from her neck. It did seem cooler here, perhaps because she was away from the hot press of bodies.

The light suddenly dulled, and she looked up to see a cloud edging across the moon's face. How long since she'd seen a cloud?—two weeks?—more? If only it meant rain and fresh water to drink. And wind . . . wind to take them on to Rio, where there'd be vegetables and fruit. The cloud moved on, the swollen moon face seemed to mock her.

Impulsively, she lay down on the hard planking of the deck, pressed her cheek against the smooth coolness of the wood. She dozed, woke up . . .

At first she thought she was dreaming, then the low voices came to her quite clearly.

"Oh, Harry, I shouldn't have agreed to meet you." The feminine voice sounded vaguely familiar.

"Katy . . . my Katy . . ." The words were muffled as if the man's mouth were partly covered.

Sable turned her head, realized that the voices were coming from the shadows behind the nearest lifeboat.

"I've been so frightened, Harry"—it was scarcely louder than a whisper—"since you told me Captain Grayson said he'd hang the man got caught with one of us."

"Don't think of it, love . . ."

"Oh, Harry . . . oh, Harry, we shouldn't . . ." The woman made a strange, little whimpering sound, and Sable lay there for a moment, trying not to hear, inexplicably shaken, her skin rising in gooseflesh despite the hot night air. Then she rose silently and crept away, back along the shadowy deck.

Bitsy had been the only one to see her leave and now she watched her come back and slip onto her pad between Willa and Amanda.

Katy . . . Katy Johnson . . . demure, round-faced, Katy . . .

The next time she awakened it was daylight. Two big, flat drops hit her face and Amanda was shaking her.

"Sable . . . Sable," she was saying. "Wake up! It's raining!" And Sable opened her eyes, saw the fat white sails ballooning in the wind.

Chapter 7

The woman smiled and her fat cheeks lifted, nearly hid her warm, black eyes, as she fished into the bubbling kettle of fat with the slotted spoon and brought out another golden brown meat pie. With a deftness born of long practice, she flipped it onto the long tray to cool with the others, then wiped her fat hands on her full skirt, brilliant with wide horizontal stripes of red and blue.

The women waiting alongside the open stall murmured appreciatively while Mr. Finchly looked vaguely amused and pulled at his beard.

"Don't say I didn't warn you," he boomed, "you'll have the summer complaints for sure!" But the women were already handing over their money and reaching for the hot pastries.

Sable bit into the turnover crust to the chopped meat at the middle. "Mmmm, delicious," she said, turning to Amanda, who was nodding her head vigorously, her mouth too full to answer. And the fat Brazilian woman, her shiny black hair pulled into a huge coil at the back of her head, made contented clucking sounds as she watched.

The harbor at Rio had been a welcome sight and the

women had plagued the captain to let them go ashore. Finally, after three days in port, he had detailed Finchly and three of the crewmen as escorts and said that half might go, with the others to go the following day. There was immediate argument as to who would go on this, the first day, but Captain Grayson settled it by saying that those who had bunks to starboard side would go first and those to port side would go the next day. But the women were not content, and there was much bargaining back and forth.

Willa and Carrie were on the starboard side, so were assured of going ashore with the first party, but Sable had to trade a pair of amber beads for the privilege, while Amanda promised to do a woman's mending for a month. Ma Abernathy dug deep into her trunk and gave up a jar of apricot preserves she had saved even through the awful days when they'd had only saltmeat and beans.

The water had swirled and eddied quietly against the pilings, leaving a froth of bright green slime. The air had hummed with the rhythm and sound of the docks; men moved gracefully, their dark-skinned faces shaded by sunbleached straw hats, women like exotic birds in their color-drenched skirts and low cotton blouses.

Sable had stepped onto the weathered planking and for a moment it had seemed as if it might come right up and hit her—as if it were moving and the ship had been still. But that sensation soon passed and the group of women, with Finchly in the lead and the other three crewmen scattered among them, had walked along the length of dock, the people smiling, calling out to them, waving, their words pouring over them like liquid music.

But it was only when she felt the grass beneath her feet that the full impact of being on land had come to her. It was as if right through the leather sole she could feel each blade, the soil beneath it. She could smell it—not the salt air, or the rotting fish, or the gull droppings, but the earth itself, the rich, full, fecundity of it.

A small boy had tugged at her skirts, held up his basket of strange fruits, and she had smilingly shaken her head. He had grinned back at her, his face puckish, friendly, the taut-skinned, rounded expanse of his belly curving above ragged blue pants, his dirty bare toes curling into the grass as if he shared her feeling for it.

Mr. Finchly had herded them to the hired carriages lined all in a row with their fringed canopies of striped canvas, and they had spent a pleasant two hours riding through tree-lined streets.

Leaving the carriages, they had walked among the open stalls of the marketplace, where the swarthy, smiling people displayed sturdy pieces of pottery and bright scarves among the bins of vegetables and fruits, strings of fresh fish with blue-green flies buzzing about them, and displays of cheap metal trinkets glittering in the sunlight.

They had stopped for a time to watch a big bird held captive by a thin chain attached to the band around his leg, the other end fastened to the large oval ring in which it perched.

"That there's a macaw," Finchly had said. "Can talk as plain as you or me, if he's a mind to."

But the big bird had just smoothed its beautiful blue and yellow plumage with its massive hooked bill, while the owner smiled and bowed, clutching his straw hat to his chest and saying words which they had come to know meant, "You want to buy? You want to buy?"

Now, their appetites quieted despite the amused warnings of the second mate, the group moved on and at Mr. Finchly's direction entered the open central area of the market. A crowd was gathered, and Sable heard one of the crewmen mutter something under his breath, saw the quick looks exchanged between the men and the silencing frown of the black-bearded second mate.

"Now, ladies," Finchly boomed, "before you, you see the famous slave market of Rio. Auction should be starting most any minute now."

There was an uncertain silence, then: "I don't hold with slaving," Martha Abernathy said in a firm voice.

"Me neither!" another joined in.

"Why, ladies, some o' these blacks have just been unloaded off the schooners that brung 'em from Africa. You don't want to miss seeing that."

The women looked at each other, wide-eyed, hesitant. Sable remembered an Abolitionist poster she'd seen once. It had been tacked up to a storefront and had a picture of a Negro man, his shoulders slumping, his head bowed down, his clothes hanging in tatters, while the snaking end of a whip curled just above his back.

Carrie leaned closer to Sable to whisper in her ear. "I heard my pa say they bring out the women, stand 'em up on that block, and pull their dresses right off 'em. Then they let the men come up and touch 'em if they want to."

Sable's breath sucked in, her mouth a round circle of shock as she looked at Carrie.

"I ain't standing here watching no darkies being sold," one woman said loudly.

"Mr. Finchly," Amanda said, "we'd like you to take us back to the ship."

"Now, just be patient, ladies, be patient," the second mate said, and started to talk to one of the men who seemed to be in charge. Another man, standing up on the scuffed wooden platform, raised his arm and signaled toward the shack to the rear.

Sable saw the stir through the crowd, and all of a sudden one of her fellow passengers shrieked out: "Good Lord o' mercy, that black heathen ain't got his clothes on!"

Sable swallowed hard, caught a glimpse of sleek, brown flanks and a stretch of hard-muscled legs. The man straightened tall, facing full front. Sable gasped, closed her eyes tightly.

"Come on, we're leaving here!" Ma Abernathy said, dragging Sable a step or two.

"Mr. Finchly!" Amanda was calling. "We'll go back to the ship alone if you don't come at once!"

Willa still had one hand over her mouth, and Carrie clutched at Sable's other arm, her face red as a strawberry, each freckle looking as if it had been pasted on.

"All right, all right, my lasses . . ." Finchly came back to them, smiling his most engaging smile. "We'll be off if that's what you're set on. They ain't gonna put up no women afore tomorrow, anyway," he said cheerfully.

"Katy Johnson didn't come back with the others! . . . maybe lost . . . or even kidnapped . . . I've heard what can happen to a defenseless woman in a foreign place . . . maybe . . . poor Katy . . ."

Despite Judd Grayson's efforts to keep it quiet, the news spread among the passengers. The women gathered in small groups for frightened speculation.

For four days, the captain made frequent trips ashore to meet with the authorities and sent out searching parties of crewmen, but demure little Katy was nowhere to be found.

When on the fifth day, Nimrod told Sable that one of the crew had jumped ship their first night in port and had not yet returned, she was almost sure she knew the answer to Katy's disappearance.

"What's his name?" she asked.

"Harry Cranshaw."

She knew she was right. All through the day, she wondered if she should go to the captain and tell him what she had overheard that hot night. But he didn't come aboard until late in the afternoon and immediately called them together in the dining room.

"We still haven't been able to locate Miss Johnson," he said. "But I have made arrangements with the local authorities to put her on the next ship bound for San Francisco if she should turn up. Under the circumstances—" He paused, and there was a sudden look in his eyes that made Sable sure he had guessed the truth. "—that's all we can do."

So once more they set sail and in those next weeks, the crew was never idle. There was much to be done, rigging strengthened, canvas sails repaired, preparations made for the inevitable rough weather ahead.

The days grew shorter and the women, who had only a

few weeks ago sweltered in the torrid heat of the tropics, dug deep into their trunks for sweaters and shawls to protect them from the chill wind that was but a preview of the frigid storms of the Horn.

Despite the extra woolen blankets that had been handed out, Sable woke one cold night, chilly and uncomfortable. The wind was a soft whooshing and the ship was rolling more heavily then it had since those first days at sea.

She rubbed one foot against the other, wishing she'd taken the pair of knitted bedsocks Amanda had offered. Across the aisle, in the bunk next to Willa, there was a sudden thrashing of blankets and a low moaning sound.

So Flossie was in tonight. Must be cold, too, the way she kept moving about. There was an incoherent mumbling followed by a sound that was nearly a cry. She's dreaming, Sable thought, she'll wake everyone.

Sable threw off her blankets and, shivering with the chill, went across to Flossie, her bare feet shrinking from the cold oak planking.

She'd just touch Flossie's shoulder. That should be enough to stop the dream. She reached out her hand, and with the touch, the heat was apparent even through the silk sleeve of the nightgown. Flossie threw her arm upward in a wild, unknowing way and cried out in a voice harsh and frightening.

"What is it? What's wrong?" Amanda was pulling on her wrapper, and there was a general stir through the 'tween deck.

"It's Flossie," Sable said. "She's got fever . . . I thought she was dreaming, but when I touched her . . ." Her voice trailed off. Someone lit the nearest lamp.

"Here—put this on before you freeze," Amanda said, shoving a robe at Sable. She laid the back of her hand lightly against Flossie's flushed face, gently lifted one of the closed eyelids for a brief look.

She pulled the blankets up and tucked them firmly around the unconscious girl, then turned to the rest of the women gathered around in various stages of undress.

"We'd better get the doctor down here," she said.

A short time later, the ship's doctor came down the aisleway between the bunks, his gray hair, never neat, now standing in odd, tufted peaks.

"So the doxie's sick, is she?" He set the bag on the floor by Flossie's bunk. "Likely picked up something in Rio. God help us if she's brought plague aboard!" He started his examination while the women looked at each other with fearful eyes. Flossie had left the ship as soon as it docked and hadn't come back until sailing time.

"How long's she been complaining?" he asked.

There was a long silence, then: "She didn't complain," Sable said. "I heard her moaning a little . . . that was the first we knew."

"Ummm," Dr. Blair grunted, leaned his head forward until his ear rested against the full breasts. He listened for a moment, raised up. "She's good and sick. Pneumonia. Going to need good nursing. Who'll take the first turn tending her?"

Again there was a long silence. The doctor stood up, looked from one to another of them sharply.

Sable looked down at Flossie, her hand outstretched on the blanket as if in mute appeal, and suddenly remembered her saying, back in New York, *Aw, Judd, let the kid come with us . . .*

She drew a deep breath. "I'll take the first turn," she said. There was a rustling through the women as they looked at her.

"And I'll take the second," Amanda said firmly.

The doctor gave a businesslike nod. "Good. Now this is what I want you to do. I'll have Herman fix up some turpentine and lard and coal oil. It'll be hot. Mind you don't burn her. Rub her chest and back with it, and put on a square of flannel . . . do you have any flannel?"

Sable looked to Amanda, who nodded.

"Keep her warm," he went on, "even if you have to tie her down. I'll leave these powders. Give her this much every four hours."

He put the medicine in Sable's hand, looked around at

the others, who now whispered together and cast them sidelong glances. He fingered his chin.

"Seems to me," he said dryly, "you've bitten yourselves quite a chew!" He snapped the black bag shut. "I'll be back in the morning. If she gets worse meanwhile, you can send for me. Not much I can do, though."

Then he was gone and the women eyed each other. The Widow Parker shoved to the center of the group. "It's an outrage," she said in a low, intense voice. "Decent women being asked to tend that slut!" She looked around and there were several nods of agreement. "This is the Lord's way o' punishing her for her sins. If you help her, you're going against the Lord." She spoke directly to Sable and Amanda.

"I don't know as I believe that." Willa's voice trembled, but she walked forward to stand with Sable and Amanda.

"I guess I don't neither," Carrie Thorne snapped.

Widow Parker sucked in her breath. "Then you ain't got the grace o' the Lord in you. This is Devil's work . . . she's one o' his!" She looked down on Flossie, the lines deepening in her sallow face. "I know her kind, all right," she said, her voice hoarse with hatred. "She works on the weakness of men—uses their sinful desires to make them fall to the Devil, her master. I should know," her voice rose hysterically. "I should know. It was a woman just like her that damned my own man.

"I tried to warn him, tried to tell him to put down his sinful wants. He died calling her name—just pushed me away from him he did—called for that harlot with his last breath."

Her face suddenly crumpled like a piece of tissue and she covered it with the long, thin fingers.

There was no sound for a moment except Flossie's labored breathing. Sable felt a sudden pity for the woman before them, but then Widow Parker straightened, put her hands firmly at her sides. Her face was as stern as before.

"You must let the Lord have his vengeance," she challenged.

Sable felt her stubborn Irish pride rise up, but Amanda said quietly, "We plan to do the best we can for her."

"By their company ye shall know them, saith the Lord!" the Widow Parker thundered.

"Now just hold on there." Martha Abernathy confronted her. "I know my scriptures same as the next. There ain't no such words in it!" Her usually placid expression was gone, her eyes flashed. "I been a God-fearing woman all my life. I ain't never had no truck with loose women . . . but I do remember something about casting the first stone. I don't make any excuses for the way this woman has acted, but she is a human being and she needs nursing and I guess the Lord would take it right unkindly if I didn't do all I can to help her."

They were quiet for a moment and then Marian Foley stepped up to stand before Sable and Amanda. "I'm going to bed now," she said in her sparse Vermont accent. "I'll take my turn tending her whenever you want."

One by one, the women nodded and returned to their bunks until finally the Widow Parker stood alone.

How much younger she looks, Sable thought, as she smoothed Flossie's blond hair away from her feverish forehead. It was the first time she had seen Flossie without makeup.

The single flickering lamp nearby cast an unsteady glow, the shadows shifting somberly as the ship rose and fell in a sea growing hourly rougher, but in the dark rows of bunks the women slept, oblivious to the mounting waves, the howling wind.

Sable had sat nearly two hours with the sick woman . . . two hours of tossing and incoherent babbling interspersed with the dry, hard coughing spells. It was something of a shock to look down now and find the green eyes, rational and lucid, staring up at her.

Flossie slowly raised a hand to her lips, already dried into deep ridges that would soon crack. Sable reached for the small jug of water that sat among the other things she and Amanda had gathered, poured a cupful, and lifted Flossie's head.

She drank eagerly, then sank back to the pillow, her eyes closed. Sable thought at first that she had slipped back into unconsciousness, but presently she opened her eyes again and spoke in a low voice.

"I heard what the Widow Parker said . . . I want you to know I'm beholden to you for helping me." Her breathing was shallow, rasping.

"It's all right," Sable assured her. "Now you close your eyes . . . try to rest."

"I'm awful sick, ain't I." It was a statement. "That Widow Parker reminds me of my pa. My pa was sure a religious man. Am I going to die?" She looked directly at Sable and waited for an answer.

"No, no, of course not! But you must rest now."

"Pa said he wouldn't have no Jezebel living under his roof . . . said being young didn't make no difference. Me and Jason was gonna get married—we was. But then Pa told Jason's folks about us . . ."

"Hush . . . hush now," Sable protested, alarmed at the labored breathing. "Don't try to talk. You'll tire yourself."

"Pa told me to get off the farm and never come back . . . Ma cried." Flossie looked for a moment as if she might cry, too. Then much to Sable's relief the thick lashes swept down to hide the green eyes and Flossie lay quietly, her breathing easier.

Outside, the wind howled and the waves rose higher until the timbers creaked and groaned like living creatures.

Fifteen minutes had passed when Flossie opened her eyes and began to talk again, just as though there had been no interruption.

"I aimed to get work in town . . . scrubbing floors or . . . There was a man . . . He thought I was pretty . . . there's been lots of men since him. Am I going to die?" She clutched Sable's hand wildly.

"Of course not." Sable tried to make her voice calm

and soothing, wondering all the while if she should send for the doctor.

"I could change," Flossie went on, her voice half-questioning, half-pleading. "If I get well, I could change. I could be like the rest of you and choose a husband when we get to Frisco. I'll be faithful to him, too . . . no other men . . ."

Her voice trailed off peacefully but a moment later her face twisted fearfully. "Maybe they won't have me! Will they have me?" She struggled to raise her head from the pillow.

"Yes, Flossie, yes . . . I'm sure they will." The reassurance must have calmed her, for she closed her eyes and slipped back into the state of half-sleep, half-unconsciousness.

Sable sat and watched the shifting light play across Flossie's strangely young-old face, the frightened words still ringing in her ears.

Chapter 8

Sable heard the commotion at the top of the companionway. Food, she thought wearily. She looked up, saw that it was Nimrod handing the containers down. She pushed her way past the women on the steps.

He braced himself against the wooden frame of the hatchway and grinned when he saw her, his face half-hidden under a days-old stubble of beard, crusty with ice.

Sable took one of the pots from his hand, passed it to the woman below her. "Nimrod . . . ?" She almost stuttered; the wind was so cold coming through the open hatch. ". . . Nimrod, how bad is it?"

One bushy eyebrow shot up, the other down. "It's sure enough bad, I ain't gonna tell you no different. But"—he grinned again—"we still got a good chance. The *Betty Kay*'s a fine old lady, gives with the waves, she does. If she didn't, we'd have foundered long since."

The women had been warned that rounding the Horn would be rough, but none had dreamed of anything like this. For twelve days, the *Betty Kay* had pitched and screamed with the pounding waves, rain and sleet coming down in stinging torrents until none of them dared venture on deck. Three times a day food was passed down, and Dr. Blair visited frequently; otherwise the women were isolated in the 'tween deck.

Nimrod passed another kettle to Sable. "How is she?" He looked toward Flossie, lying tied in her bunk.

Sable shook her head. "The same. Do you think you could get something hot for her to eat?"

"Too dangerous to have a fire, ship pitching like this . . ." He must have seen the disappointment on her face. "I'll talk to Herman," he said. "We'll try."

Back down below, Sable braced her feet against Amanda's bunk and tried to eat some of the cold stew, picking out the pieces of congealed grease and shoving them aside. The stew was three days old now. That was the last time Herman had risked a fire.

If only she could get some good, hot broth for Flossie. She put the tin plate down and, fighting the slanting floor for every step, went to where Amanda sat by the sick girl.

Flossie had not uttered a rational word since that first night. She just lay there, the fever eating away at her, sometimes quiet, sometimes tossing as wildly as the storm outside, her skin dry as parchment, her full figure shrunken beneath the wool blankets.

Throughout the 'tween deck, the women formed small clusters and huddled together. A few stayed in their bunks where they were warmer. Occasionally, soft weeping could be heard, but for the most part they had displayed remarkable control.

The dog Bitsy howled dismally, and Willa tried to comfort her; the Widow Parker chanted her monotone of prayer, as she had constantly since the storm began, pausing only long enough to warn them that it was God's punishment upon them for trying to save Flossie.

"Let the Devil have his own," she'd said over and over, "or we'll perish with her."

But that day passed and the *Betty Kay* was still afloat.

Dr. Blair came down, a knitted watch cap pulled low over his unruly hair, a triumphant gleam in his eye.

"Give her this," he said, holding the tin cup filled with oatmeal as if it were a rare jewel.

Sable patiently spooned the watery but hot cereal between Flossie's sore lips.

"Nimrod did it," she said.

The ship's doctor nodded shortly. "Nimrod and Herman . . . damned near set the galley afire."

Three days later they awoke to find themselves in the calm, blue brilliance of the Pacific, the sea lapping gently against the ship's hull, the sun a promise of warmth in the clear sky. And as if it were an omen of things to come, Flossie weakly opened her eyes and smiled at Sable, who touched the cool forehead and smiled back.

"How about some breakfast?" Flossie said, in that throaty way that sounded almost like her old self.

Sable and Amanda opened the door and stepped out into the clean morning air of the deck, almost into Flossie.

"Ummm." The sleepy-eyed girl winked at them, her blond hair tousled, her lip rouge smeared slightly. She pushed past them and went on down the companionway to the 'tween deck.

Amanda looked after her, one corner of her mouth drawing down sharply. "She might have looked puny after she was sick, but she sure doesn't now. Looks like she might pop right out of that dress!"

Sable grinned. Flossie's recovery had been amazingly rapid once her fever had broken—just as all things aboard ship had seemed to go well once Cape Horn was behind them. It was as if Nature were determined to make up for the mischief she had made.

The winds had been favorable and the blunt-bowed *Betty Kay* had made good time, sailing north up the coast of South America.

The one disappointment had been when the ship put in for provisions in Valparaiso. Remembering all too well what had happened in Rio, Captain Grayson had firmly refused to allow the women ashore.

Sable and the other passengers had stood on deck for hours, looking longingly toward the shops and houses visible from the dock, but their grumbling and pleas alike fell on deaf ears.

Now they had dropped anchor again, but this time there were no shops, houses, or people to tempt them. They had put in to one of the Galapagos Islands—one, the Captain told them, of a chain of small islands that sprawled across the equator.

"Look! They've already started." Amanda pointed toward the rail, where a group of the women were gathered to watch.

The crewmen worked the winch, their shirts already dark with sweat beneath their armpits, across their backs, even though the sun was barely up in the blue-glass sky. With heavy ropes, they hoisted huge turtles over the side one by one. Their patterned shells were dark and crusty looking.

"I never dreamed they'd be so big," said Sable.

"And ugly!" Amanda shivered. "I don't think I can eat that, even if we don't have any fresh meat."

Nimrod stood by them. "Just you wait, ma'am," he said, "wait till you taste one o' them steaks. Best you ever ate, sure enough."

Amanda wrinkled her nose and looked doubtful. "How will you keep all that meat from spoiling in this heat?"

"Oh, that's the easiest part. We'll just put 'em in the hold and kill 'em as we need 'em."

But in spite of Nimrod's assurances, that evening at dinner Sable looked down at the piece of meat on her plate with something less than enthusiasm, until she heard pleased sounds as some of the more daring tried their first forkful. With that to encourage her, she cut a small piece of the fried meat and cautiously tried it.

"It is delicious," she said, turning to Amanda beside

her, who was nodding her head between bites. "I never would've believed it!"

"Maybe it's so good 'cause I'm so sick of salt pork." Carrie Thorne waved her fork in the air for emphasis.

"I think it tastes like beef," someone said.

"No," came the disagreement, "not beef, chicken. That's what it tastes like—chicken."

But though they argued over the exact flavor, they all agreed that it was good. Herman had done himself proud with the meal—fried potatoes and fresh-baked bread, along with some kind of edible greens, vaguely like chard, which the crewmen had picked on the island.

And the big cook beamed at the cries of appreciation as he brought out the dessert—pans of fruit grunt: dried apples cooked in a rich dough, flavored with molasses and cinnamon.

The meal would be talked about for many weeks to come.

The good fortune of the *Betty Kay* continued, and one day, nearly six months after their departure from New York, Captain Grayson called them all together in the dining room.

"Ladies," he said, tucking his visored hat under one arm, "I know you'll be happy to hear that your travels are nearly ended. That is"—he laughed—"so far as the *Betty Kay* is concerned. I expect to make San Francisco within the week."

There was a sudden silence, then a few scattered exclamations, strained laughter.

Amanda pulled nervously at a stray tendril of hair that had somehow escaped its hairpin. "Isn't that fine . . . isn't that fine," she said almost helplessly as she anchored the strand of hair firmly into the bun at the nape of her neck.

Sable stood there, suddenly fighting tears, remembering how she had stood at the rail that afternoon, pointing out a lone gull to Willa. And as she had leaned forward, the heavy, gold locket that held her mother's portrait caught on a loose bolt, the chain snapped, and it fell to the water below. Sable had watched, stricken, as the warm, glowing metal held almost motionless in the blue-green water . . . and then slowly, slowly sank from view . . .

That night, for the first time in months, the old nightmare returned . . . and Charles Gregg's handsome face was before her, smiling, assured, mocking.

Chapter 9

Lansing Wakefield moved his dark head restlessly on the pillow as the piercing sunlight fell across his face.

"Damn it, Jace!" he cried, opening his gray eyes and then closing them instantly with a groan, "draw those drapes!"

"Yes, sir, Mist' Lanse," the huge, grinning black man said, and reclosed the heavy maroon drapes. He knew full well how his master's head must be pounding after last night. "Mist' Rob is waiting downstairs. He's powerful excited this morning."

"Tell him to come up." Lanse ran his hand over the scratchy stubble of beard on his chin. "And fetch me some hot water," he shouted at the broad back disappearing through the doorway.

He threw the thin sheet off his nude body, eased his long sinewy legs over the side of the bed, and cautiously stood up, closing his eyes tight until his muscular frame reached its full six feet three inches. He groaned again and ran his fingers through the tousled hair as a throbbing pain shot through his head. The pain subsiding, he picked up the trousers that Jace had laid out for him and, with an effort, pulled them on.

The rap of knuckles sounded at the door, and a blond-haired man of average height and weight came in, his fair skin sunburned except for small, white lines around his eyes from squinting into the sunlight.

"Hurry up, Lanse, I want you to come with me!" he began excitedly and then stopped short. "Oh—I see you're feeling last night." He grinned, much in the same way Jace had.

"Goddamn," Lanse swore softly. "If I ever take more than three drinks of whiskey again, Rob Cooper, I want you to kick my backside up against my teeth!"

Rob swung into the chair nearest the bed. "I never saw you drink like that before."

"I know better than to drink like that," Lanse admitted ruefully, his voice betraying the unmistakable slurring tones of the South. "I can't take much of the damned stuff. And I wouldn't have last night if we hadn't made such a pretty profit on that piece of ground across the Bay. I couldn't very well refuse when Tom Atkins wanted to celebrate our deal."

Jace entered the room silently, placed the steaming water and a fresh cake of soap on the marble-topped washstand, then opened the door below, drew out a clean towel and a straight razor, and placed them beside the pan of water.

"Tell Melissa I won't be eating this morning," ordered Lanse, splashing the water vigorously and working up a rich lather with the soap. "And get that idiotic grin off your face!" he spluttered.

"Yes, sir, Mist' Lanse!" Jace left the room, the grin still very much in evidence.

Lanse scraped away at the dark stubble on his chin. "What happened last night? I can't remember a damned thing after we left the Eureka."

Rob draped one leg over the arm of his chair and leaned back comfortably. "That's the hell of it," he said, scratching his close-cropped blond hair thoughtfully. "I never saw a man act so sober. The more you drank, the soberer you got, until . . ."

"Until what?" asked Lanse, reluctantly.

"Until you ran amok at Lil Carstairs's whorehouse."

"Oh, no! What did I do?"

"Well, I couldn't rightly keep up with you, but those girls were running around squealing like piglets. That little Chinese gal ran by spouting that sing-song lingo a mile a minute."

Lanse wiped away the last vestiges of soap, grinning wryly. "Lil will kill me. I guess I'd better go over today and fix it up with her."

"Never mind . . ." Rob handed him the ruffled white shirt. "She was yelling about you driving all her other customers away, so I paid her off last night."

"Thanks. Now, if we have my transgressions taken care of, what's this you're so excited about?"

"Christ!" Rob exclaimed. "I'd forgotten all about it. She's here! The *Betty Kay* is here! Joe Phillips stopped by the house and told me. The signal's up on the Summit. Hurry up. She's probably docked by now."

"Rob Cooper, do you mean you're still set on marrying one of those women?" Lanse sounded incredulous as he pulled on the glove-soft leather boots.

"Of course I am," Rob retorted in his usual calm manner. "I been planning to for over a year, ain't I?"

"Yes, but I thought you'd come to your senses before now." Lanse straightened up and put on the brocaded yellow vest, and then the light gray coat.

"I'm thirty years old and it's time I settled down and raised a family," countered Rob firmly. "And where else could I find a respectable woman? I sure as hell ain't going to marry any of the bawds that work in the houses here."

Lanse just stood and looked at his friend and partner, exasperation in his eyes. Then his white teeth flashed in a grin.

"All right, if you're determined, let's go. Jace," he

shouted as they came to the top of the wide staircase over-looking the huge main hall, "saddle Satan."

Minutes later they galloped down the shady drive, stir-rup to stirrup, Lanse on the big black stallion and Rob on his roan. Lanse reined in for just a moment when they reached the main road and looked back with pride on his newly built home. It had taken months of wheedling and cajoling, begging and bribing, to get enough men to work on it. The only workers available in this gold-crazy town were men who needed a grubstake, and the moment they scraped enough together, they were off to the foot-hills of the Sierras, confident that their fortune lay in the first shovelful of dirt.

But in spite of the difficulties, his home was now a reality, with slim white columns rising gracefully in front of the wide verandah. It was very like his family home in Virginia, except for the extra verandah at the side. That had been his own idea.

Satan, the black stallion, danced sideways, anxious to stretch his legs. The tall Virginian gave him his head and the two horses dashed madly down the well-worn road.

In the center of town, they picked their way across a dusty, crowded street, dodging a stylish, rubber-tired buggy, pulling the horses to a standstill to let a creaking wagonload of building stones pass, the bearded driver swearing stoutly at the six-mule team, the blacksnake whip snapping noisily just above their gleaming backs.

"Now, Lanse, why don't you come along with me?" Rob's expression was one of comical chagrin.

Lanse laughed. "Because," he said, "somebody's got to take care of business while you're off courting. I'll come over there later—after I get that lot of picks and shovels we bought yesterday moved over to one of the ware-houses. Now you go ahead, pick out one you like the looks of, and start talking!"

The tips of Rob's ears turned a bright red, but he grinned and nodded, set the roan into a brisk trot, and gave Lanse a jaunty wave of his hand.

Nearly three hours later, Lanse arrived at the dock where the *Betty Kay* was anchored. It was, as he had suspected it might be, one of the biggest crowds he'd ever seen gathered in San Francisco.

He pushed and shoved and elbowed his way through the grinning men until finally he was able to see the women who were causing so much commotion.

Some stood shyly, obviously embarrassed at the many eyes upon them, while others seemed to be enjoying themselves thoroughly. Lanse felt a sudden rush of nostalgia at the sight of pale, natural pink cheeks and lips, a wisp of white lace, a small cameo brooch . . .

My God, he thought, how long has it been since I saw a respectable woman? Almost two years . . . Why would they want to come out here?

He thought of San Francisco as it must look to them— a lusty, brawling, roaring town. Buildings made of anything on hand that was quick and easy, lots of them just canvas stretched over wooden frames. The harbor was dotted with ships that had been left to rot away, even their crews and captains falling victims to the lure of the goldfields.

And as for the population—what a polyglot meltingpot! There were red-shirted miners with unkempt beards, knives and pistols bristling in their belts, flashy gamblers swinging huge nuggets of gold on fancy chains, shuffling Chinese with long pigtails swinging behind them, Spanish grandees with tight-fitting velvet jackets and silver spurs, Mexicans, kinky-haired natives from the Fiji Islands, Russians. No sight seemed strange in San Francisco. Why, New York must seem like a sedate matron in comparison . . .

Shrill barking caught his attention and he turned to see a thin, big-eyed young woman catch the small white dog up in her arms and whisper something into its ear.

He caught sight of Rob, leaning forward slightly and talking earnestly to a tall, well-built woman, her dark hair pulled back into a bun at the nape of her neck. And the girl . . . the red-haired girl who stood near them and yet discreetly aside.

Lanse stared. Her dress was a shade of blue the exact color of her eyes. The low-cut bodice and short sleeves revealed a creamy white expanse of throat and arms. The sunlight caught and glistened in her hair, turning it to fiery copper.

My God, she's beautiful, he thought, unable to take his eyes from her. And it was apparent that he wasn't the only one to notice, for several men were cleverly maneuvering her away from Rob and the dark-haired woman. Two of the most disreputable looking eased out the others and cornered her for themselves.

Lanse watched the taller of the two men talk to the girl for a moment and walked closer so that he could hear what was being said.

"Honey, you'll never get a better offer than mine." The big fellow grabbed her arm, his grin displaying wide-set, tobacco-stained teeth, the reek of his whiskey breath carrying even to Lanse.

She drew back from his touch, her blue eyes wide and frightened, only to step unwittingly back into the waiting arms of the other. She whirled away in revulsion as the dirty, matted beard brushed her face.

"She don't want you, Clem, she wants a real man, like me. Ain't that right, sweetie?" the bearded one chortled.

Lanse could see her slim body trembling. She looked like a frightened child, though the swelling breasts beneath the blue bodice belied this.

On a sudden, overpowering impulse, he strode to the middle of the group and stood protectively by her. "That's enough . . . move on," he drawled quietly, the hard edge not quite disguised by the velvet softness.

"We got a right," complained the one called Clem, "they're here to marry us, ain't they?"

"The lady is going to marry me," retorted Lanse, his dark brows rising slightly in astonishment at his own words.

"Is that right, miss?" asked the bearded one, a little more respectfully.

Lanse, towering over her, drew in his breath in admiration as she turned her face up to him, searchingly regarding him with cornflower-blue eyes. The once creamy oval had darkened slightly with the long months' exposure to sun and wind; the bridge of her small, straight nose showed just a trace of tiny freckles, like a scant sprinkling of gold dust. She lowered the thick, curling lashes and was silent for a moment.

"Yes . . . that's right," she said at last.

The two men slouched away, muttering curses under their breath. Lanse gazed at the girl, his usually glib tongue silent now that they were alone.

"Lanse!" Rob's voice came from behind them; Lanse turned to see his partner with the dark-haired woman in tow. "I've been looking all over for you."

Rob threw the young red-haired woman a puzzled glance and then drew himself up proudly. "Lanse, this is Amanda Peters . . . right now, that is, but before the day is over she'll be Mrs. Robert Cooper." He drew Amanda forward, tucking her arm through his while her face flushed girlishly. "Amanda, this is Lansing Wakefield. He's going to be our best man."

Lanse bowed gravely to Amanda. "You have my very best wishes, ma'am," he said smoothly and in the same even tone, said, "Rob, I guess I'll have to ask you to do me the same honor—be my best man, that is. You see, this lady . . ." He turned questioningly to her.

"My name is Sable Flanagan," she said in a low voice.

". . . Miss Flanagan and I are going to be married."

Rob's jaw dropped. "Well, I'll be damned."

Lanse saw Amanda's sharp eyes look him over and then glisten their approval to the girl. He felt a quiet amusement at himself that he should be so pleased to pass inspection.

"I spoke to the preacher over there," Rob said, his voice still hollow from the shock of Lanse's announcement. "I told him we'd be ready for him as soon as you came. He should be over any time now."

He fished deep into his vest pocket and came up with a small gold band. "Might as well do this up right," he said, turning to Amanda. "It belonged to my mother. I've been saving it a long time."

Lanse felt a quick consternation, drew Rob aside. "I've got to find a ring for her. I'll be back as soon as I can."

Rob caught at his coat. "But the preacher . . . ?"

"Make him wait," Lanse flung over his shoulder and was swallowed up by the crowd.

A little less than half an hour later, Lanse elbowed his way back through the milling mass of people, smiling his satisfaction. Another gold wedding ring lay in the palm he extended to Sable.

"Thank you," she said simply, but the expression on her face showed him how much it meant to her, and he was glad he'd taken the trouble.

The preacher came puffing up, sweating profusely in a black woolen coat under the July sun. He removed the tall black hat and mopped his face and balding head.

"We've got to hurry right along now," he cautioned, rapidly turning the pages of his well-worn book, "I got lots more waiting for me."

"We're making it a double wedding," Lanse informed him.

"So this gentleman tells me." He nodded at Rob and then peered over his spectacles at the four of them. "You can be each other's witnesses."

He intoned the words hurriedly—so hurriedly, in fact, that they couldn't understand part of them, but he made sure they said "I do" in the right place. He had scarcely said, "I now pronounce you husband and wife," when he shoved a paper at them to sign, opened his purse to receive the gold pieces that Lanse and Rob held out to him, and then hurried off to more waiting couples.

The four of them regarded each other, not knowing quite what to say, strangely let down after the incongruous ceremony.

Lanse broke the awkward silence. "We'd better go get the horses, Rob. The ladies must be tired and hungry by now. I'll send Jace back in for their trunks."

Leaving Sable and Amanda comfortably ensconced on a bale of hay, Lanse and Rob made their way through the noisy crowd across the dusty street to the hitch rails.

"Rob Cooper, don't you say one damned word," Lanse growled.

"Not me, Lanse, I wouldn't say anything," Rob retorted, his eyes twinkling with merriment.

But while Lanse was able to silence Rob, he couldn't silence the small voice within himself. For it had just begun to dawn on him what he had done. He could recall his own words as though it were yesterday, when Rob had first advanced the idea. "You just don't marry a total stranger!" he had argued.

Satan was far down the line. Lanse unhitched him, led him slowly back to Rob and the roan, the stallion snorting and tossing his head at the noise and flying dust. And Lanse experienced a feeling of growing discomfort. He pictured his father in his mind's eye, tall and strong despite his sixty years, his shock of gray hair brushed neatly back, and beside him, his diminutive mother, her body still slim after bearing four lusty sons. He recalled them as they had admonished his brother, George, who had been courting a girl who had caused talk by straying into the woods with a man at a neighborhood barbecue.

"George," his father's deep voice had rung out, "you are a product of the alliance of two of the oldest and finest families in Virginia. That is a privilege that carries with it a responsibility. Choose the woman to whom you will give our name with the greatest care. You're a Wakefield, sir! Don't ever forget it!"

The hollow thump of the horse's hooves against the wooden dock jarred him back to the present. As the crowd opened up to let them pass, he saw the young girl again, sitting quietly beside Amanda on the bale of hay, her face still a little frightened, and his misgivings seemed somehow unimportant.

The two women stood at their approach. Lanse turned apologetically to Sable.

"Sorry I didn't bring the rig in this morning, but—" He stopped in midsentence. He had almost said he didn't know he was getting married. "Satan can carry both of us," he finished lamely.

The glossy black animal whinnied softly and pawed the dock, impatient after his enforced idleness at the hitching post. Lanse quieted him with a word.

A small figure pushed toward them. "Miss Sable . . . Miss Amanda . . ."

"It's Nimrod," Amanda said, and then to Lanse and Rob, "first mate . . ."

Nimrod held out his hand, looked embarrassed. "Your gentlemen will have to fill out these papers before you leave," he said.

"Here, let me." Rob scanned the pages quickly. "It just states how much we owe Captain Grayson and that it has to be paid within the week." He scrawled his signature at the bottom of one of the sheets and then passed the other to Lanse.

Sable turned away so that her face was hidden from him, but Lanse thought she must feel as if she were being bought. He signed the paper hurriedly and thrust it back at the odd-looking little sailor.

"Miss Sable . . . ma'am," he stammered. "I . . . I wanted to tell you goodbye." And there under the quizzical eyes of Lanse and Rob, the small man gravely shook Sable's hand. "We'll be weighing anchor 'fore long, but if I ever get back here again, I'd sure enough like to see that things are all right for you."

Sable looked questioningly up at Lanse.

"Just ask for Wakefield Manor," he directed the seaman. "Most anybody can tell you how to get there."

Nimrod nodded his thanks. " 'Bye, Miss Sable."

"Goodbye, Nimrod," she answered, her voice suddenly unsteady. And he bobbed his head and backed away.

"Well, now," Rob said heartily, "we'd better get started." He grinned at Amanda. "I'm getting hungry."

Lanse mounted Satan, reached down one arm, and with a swish of petticoats, lifted Sable easily to the saddle in front of him.

He put both his long arms firmly around her to keep her from falling. His pulse quickened as he felt the unexpected softness of her uncorseted body, and he could see the color mount to her cheeks.

They waited until Rob had Amanda securely seated in front of him and then set off at a comfortable pace.

Lanse wished the ride twice as long as he enjoyed the intimate nearness of this young woman who was a stranger . . . and who was his wife. Now and again a red curl blew caressingly across his cheek and the faint, sweet fragrance of her came to his nostrils. But almost before he realized it, they reached the wide drive that led up the gently sloping hill and gave an unobstructed view of the house. They reined in the horses.

"There it is," Lanse announced, unable to repress the note of pride, "Wakefield Manor." He watched Sable closely for her reaction. Her eyes widened at the sight of the gracious white house, framed at back and sides by tall oaks.

"It's beautiful," breathed Amanda, "like a painting."

"You save that for later." Rob's eyes sparkled. "We've got our own house to see."

Sable twisted around in the saddle, concern in her eyes. "Will I be able to see Amanda again?" she asked Lanse gravely.

"Every day if you want to," he assured her. "They're our neighbors—only live a quarter of a mile away. Besides, Rob and I are business partners."

She smiled happily at that, her eyes crinkling at the corners. It was the first time he had seen her smile.

"Sure you won't stay to dinner with us?" Lanse asked Rob. But that young man had already turned his horse.

"No, thanks." His impish grin and a wink of his eye betrayed his eagerness to be alone with Amanda. "We'll see you tomorrow," he called over his shoulder as they rode away.

Once at the house, Lanse dismounted, then lifted Sable from the saddle and set her gently on the ground. "Jace! Melissa!" he shouted as he drew her across the cool expanse of verandah through the big door and into the spacious front hall.

Jace came first, almost running in response to his master's voice, surprisingly light on his feet in spite of his huge size, his teeth gleaming like ivory against skin the color of rich chocolate. But his smile faded when he saw Sable. He stood regarding her soberly.

Close at his heels came a tall Negress, dressed in a bright yellow dress. On her head a snowy white kerchief was tied like a turban, a startling contrast to her skin, which was not chocolate like Jace's but ebony black. Her face bore the lines and wrinkles of age but her black eyes were bright and searching, her figure slim as a girl's.

"Jace, Melissa . . . this is your new mistress." Lanse gestured to Sable. "We were married an hour ago."

Jace's eyes rolled in astonishment, but Melissa set her mouth in an unperturbed line and only the bright gleam of her eyes betrayed her surprise.

"Hitch up the team, Jace. I want you to go into town after Mrs. Wakefield's and Mrs. Cooper's trunks. When you're ready, come in. I'll give you directions." As the black man went toward the stables, Lanse turned to Melissa.

"Mrs. Wakefield is hungry. Bring a tray to my room . . . something cool."

"Yes, sir, Mist' Lanse." The Negress started toward the back of the house but paused to take one more look at Sable. "Should I fix something for you, too, Mist' Lanse?"

"No. No, nothing." He waved her away.

Sable had not spoken a single word since they entered the house, but Lanse had seen her eyes darting here and there, taking everything in.

"You must be dead tired," he said, taking her elbow and gently propelling her up the broad staircase.

"I have been up since dawn." Her smile was somewhat

wan—and small wonder, he thought. This must all seem terribly strange to her.

He opened the massive oak door at the end of the upstairs hall. "You'll feel much better after you've had something to eat and rested awhile," he assured her, motioning her inside.

She stopped abruptly at sight of the bed and took a nervous step away from him. As if I were going to push her into it right now, he thought, hard put to hide his amusement.

"I'd better get down and give Jace his instructions," he said reassuringly. He paused at the door. "Melissa will be up directly with your tray. Is there anything you want? Anything at all?"

"The dust was so bad . . ." She ran the tips of her fingers over her throat. "Could I—if it wouldn't be too much trouble, I'd like some warm water for a bath."

"Of course, how stupid of me! I'll have Jace bring in my own tub before he leaves."

"Thank you, Mr. Wakefield."

"Lanse," he corrected.

"Lanse," she repeated hesitantly.

Her eyes flickered toward the huge bed once more and her face flushed scarlet. He just grinned at her and shut the door.

Billy had been the only one to see her leave and now she watched her come back and slip onto her pad between Willa and Amanda.

Katy . . . . Katy Johnson . . . . demure, round-faced, Katy . . . .

The next time she awakened it was daylight. Two big

Chapter 10

Sable stared at the door, the realization that she was alone coming slowly. It was a strange sensation . . . to be alone in a room, after the long months of close contact aboard ship, the total lack of privacy.

She turned to take a closer look at the room, and womanlike, the first thing she rested her eye on was the mirror hanging above the marble-topped washstand.

Have I changed? she wondered, walking slowly across the room. For six long months she had only glanced at herself in borrowed hand mirrors. In her hasty packing, her own mirror had been left behind.

She examined her reflection carefully, frowning slightly at the sprinkling of freckles Lanse had found so enchanting. She had been almost afraid to look, afraid that her face would be as changed as her life had been; but aside from the freckles and the slight tan, the face that looked back at her from the glass was much the same.

Satisfied, she turned to survey the rest of the room. The massive furniture was of mahogany, singular in that it was perfectly plain, having no ornate carving or trim, its beauty lying in the polished, gleaming grain of the wood. There were several chairs, almost like small sofas, a high-boy, the washstand, a table, a low chest at the foot of the bed, and finally the bed itself, with tall, square posts at the four corners.

She suddenly felt small and helpless in this room. It's so big and overpowering, she thought, so . . . so *male* . . . like him . . .

A light knock sounded at the door. "Come in," she called reluctantly, scarcely knowing what to expect.

The stately, white-turbaned Negress entered carrying a napkin-covered tray. "Miz Wakefield, ma'am, I brought your food."

"Oh, yes, thank you . . . uh . . ."

"Melissa, ma'am."

"Thank you, Melissa."

The woman busied herself with the tray, all the while keeping one speculative eye on Sable. "Jace, he have your tub ready soon."

Sable made no reply, feeling ill at ease with the woman. She had the uncomfortable sensation that the snapping black eyes could see right into her mind.

The two Negroes had come as a distinct shock. The idea of slavery had been completely repugnant to her since the marketplace in Rio. Still . . . there was very little comparison between the defeated, humiliated man on the Abolitionist posters and that huge, black giant down below. Big—like everything else here, she thought, suddenly irritable.

"Now, you just set yourself right down here and eat," said Melissa, motioning to the chair pulled close to the table.

"It looks very tempting, Melissa," said Sable, surprised to find that it was true. The woman beamed.

There were cold slices of chicken breast, muffins, a kind of melon that Sable was unfamiliar with, but which she found to be sweet and delicious, and a tall glass of cold milk. She drank the milk eagerly, her throat feeling parched and gritty from inhaling so much dust.

"I fetched it from the springhouse other side o' the hill. That water stays icy all year long," Melissa said in answer to Sable's questioning gaze.

They both turned at the sound from the still-open doorway. Jace stood just outside, regarding Sable intently, his face set and unsmiling. He bent slightly as he entered, his head clearing the doorjamb by scant inches, then stooped to place the heavy raffia mat he carried on the thick maroon carpet.

Fascinated by his size, Sable watched him as he stood up, watched his hands, the size of small hams, swinging at his sides as he went through the doorway.

"No need to be afraid o' Jace," said Melissa, seeming to know in her uncanny way what Sable was thinking.

"I'm not," Sable lied.

Next, Jace brought the tub. It was made of porcelain covered cast iron and must have been terribly heavy, but he carried it easily into the room, turning it sideways to get it through the door, and then set it down on the mat.

"You, Jace," scolded Melissa, "hurry up. Can't you see this poor little missus wore out?"

Jace caught his lower lip between his teeth and dutifully hurried out.

"Some folks is scared o' Jace at first 'cause he's so powerful big, but he's a fine boy . . . He's my boy."

"He's so—so grim," Sable said nervously.

Melissa's laugh rang out. "That's just 'cause he's bashful 'round white ladies he don't know."

Only partly reassured, Sable watched him make the three trips necessary to bring the water for the tub. And each time he regarded her as soberly as he had before.

After Melissa had tested and retested the water to see that the temperature was just to her satisfaction, she shooed Jace out the door. "Now you get along out o' here and fetch them trunks home like Mist' Lanse told you."

The door safely closed, she advanced upon Sable and started to unbutton her dress. Sable drew back.

"I always took care o' my lady back home in Virginia. Mist' Lanse, he say, 'Melissa, you tend to Miz Wakefield.' " She continued calmly to undress Sable as though if Mister Lanse had said something, that was all there was to it.

After the first surprised moment, Sable relaxed and found herself welcoming the assistance; it brought back a luxurious pampered feeling that had been missing for long months.

Melissa nodded her approval at the lack of a corset. "I always say the good Lord never meant for ladies to lace theyselves in till they can't breathe," she said as she dropped the petticoats one by one to the rug.

Sable felt her nakedness keenly as Melissa stood back and studied her appraisingly, as though it were the most natural thing in the world to do. She nodded her approval the second time. "Yes, ma'am," she cackled, "you going to make Mist' Lanse a fine wife. Those hips made to bear lots o' fine, big boys." She laughed again as Sable blushed right to the roots of her hair.

Sable stepped quickly into the tub, anxious to put an end to the conversation. Melissa competently pinned the red curls high to keep them from the water, then reached matter-of-factly for the soap and washcloth.

"No, please," protested Sable firmly.

This time Melissa relented. She chuckled softly as she gathered up the discarded clothing lying in a heap on the rug. "I done heard that Northern ladies did these things for theyselves, but I ain't never believed it till now," she muttered. "I be back directly," she called over her shoulder as she took the rumpled clothing away.

Sable gave a small sigh of relief and sank deeper into the water. She stretched out her legs as far as she could reach, but her toes were still nowhere near the end of the tub. The bath she had thought would be so satisfying was for some reason strangely disturbing.

She pondered the why of it. The tub felt alien to her. She was lost in its bigness; suddenly, unbidden, the image of Lanse, leaning back in the warm water, his long legs reaching to the end where her shorter ones would not, flashed through her mind.

She closed her eyes quickly, as though that would erase the picture from her thoughts, feeling an urgent anxiety to get out of this tub that had come into such intimate contact with him.

She finished hastily and was out of the water, standing on the mat, wrapped in the big towel she had found lying nearby, when Melissa reentered the room.

"All clean and ready for your nap," the smiling Negress said—much in the same manner that she would address a child, Sable thought.

"Yes, only I don't have anything to put on." Sable looked helplessly around.

"You just leave that to Melissa." She drew open a drawer in the washstand and brought out another fluffy, soft towel. She removed the damp one from around Sable, patting a few remaining drops of water dry on the smooth back, and then brought the dry towel under Sable's armpits and knotted it securely to one side, leaving her arms and shoulders bare. It reached almost to her ankles.

"Now, then," said Melissa, surveying her improvised garment with satisfaction. "Jace'll have your trunk back, time you wakes up." She started to turn down the bed.

"No!" protested Sable with a vehemence that surprised even herself. "I'd prefer to lie on top of the coverlet . . . it—it's hot." She dropped her eyes under Melissa's penetrating gaze.

"Yes, ma'am," said Melissa. She turned at the door to see Sable safely settled on the bed, her head on the soft bolster, and then closed the door behind her.

Sable was left with the uncomfortable feeling that Melissa knew it wasn't the heat that had made her protest against the turning down of the bed. And yet, she hadn't been consciously aware of her reason herself until she felt the woman's shrewd eyes upon her. Then, she had realized that she didn't want to feel again the intimate awareness of him, lying between sheets where he had lain, that she had experienced so keenly in the tub.

Once more her eyes searched the room, coming to rest first on the handsome set of matching brushes, the bold "W" inlaid in silver on the backs, then on the table and his pipe rack, all the pipes neatly in place except the one lying carelessly by the humidor of tobacco, as if it were waiting for him to come along and pick it up again.

Strange, how everything that belonged to him, everything he touched, seemed to come alive, vibrating with the force of his personality.

Her lids grew heavy in the cool dimness of the room. She slept.

Awakening came slowly to the distant clanging of pots and pans somewhere on the lower floor. The aroma of fresh-baked bread drifted to Sable's nostrils. For a sweet, fleeting moment she was home . . . safe in her own bed at home. But then came the reality of full wakefulness.

From somewhere in the house she heard a clock chiming, and counted the six chimes with some surprise. I must have slept for hours, she thought.

She stood up, tugging at the towel around her; the knot had loosened while she slept. Across from the bed, the maroon drapes, which she had supposed to be another window, were now drawn back to reveal a large closet, and the various articles of male apparel had been pushed to one side to make room for her own things. For one awful moment panic gripped her. Had he—had Lanse been in this room while she slept? She had a vivid picture of herself lying there without a cover, the knotted towel slipped loose and parted.

"Of course not," she said aloud, comforted by the sound of her own voice. "It was Melissa."

She found a clean pair of drawers and her best camisole lying neatly on the chair, and put them on quickly, glad to be rid of the towel. Spying her hairbrush lying beside his monogramed pair, she put it to good use, brushing the tousled curls until they gleamed.

She surveyed her scanty wardrobe with dismay. She hadn't been able to bring many things in just the one trunk and after six months, all her dresses were sun-faded and worn-looking—except for the pink satin . . .

Satin was awfully dressy . . . still . . . It was her first evening here and she really didn't have anything else that was nice. She pulled it from the hanger and was holding it across her arm when Melissa quietly entered the room.

"Oh," said Melissa. "I was just coming to wake you, ma'am. It's almost time for supper."

"I'll be down as soon as I finish dressing," said Sable, laying the dress aside and pulling petticoats and a pair of white slippers from the closet.

"Let me help you, Miz Wakefield." Melissa dropped the petticoats one by one over Sable's head until four billowed out from her slim waist. Satisfied that that was enough, she helped Sable into the pink satin dress, fastening the hooks securely in the back, and stood back admiringly.

"Mmmm . . . Mist' Lanse is going to be mighty taken with you in that dress," she predicted, and a grin split her face.

A short time later, as Sable slowly descended the stairway, she could see the truth of Melissa's words in Lanse's eyes as he watched her appraisingly from the bottom of the stairs.

She flushed slightly, wishing that she had worn the faded blue, painfully aware of the bareness of the low-cut bodice, relieved only by the merest wisp of tiny cap sleeves. Her breasts were displayed to perfection, pushed high into two white mounds, the deep cleft showing plainly between them. She stood before him and he gazed at her for one long moment of silence.

"You look very beautiful this evening," he said.

"Thank you," she said, embarrassed.

"You rested well?"

"Very well," she replied. "I was surprised to find that I'd slept so long."

He offered his arm. She put her hand on it shyly.

"I had Melissa set a small table in this sitting room," he said, guiding her through a door to their left. "We'd be lost in the big dining room."

Across the room, double doors opened to the outside, and a pleasant breeze wafted through. It was an intimate setting; the table barely big enough for the two of them. The snowy white table cover was of the finest linen; in the center, a single white rose had been placed in a silver bud vase.

Lanse opened the door of the glass-fronted liquor cabinet, selected a decanter, and poured himself a brandy.

"Would you like some sherry?" He turned to her.

"I've nev—" She stopped. "Yes, I would like some." Sable was sure she could detect a faint gleam of amusement in his eyes as he handed her the fragile stemmed glass of amber liquid.

With dark eyebrows raised, he watched her as she swallowed quickly, the deceptive, bittersweet flavor suddenly stinging the back of her throat, scalding its way down. She choked, then coughed, much to her embarrassment.

"Sip it slowly," he instructed, the corners of his mouth twitching.

To Sable's relief, Melissa entered the room at that moment, pushing a small tea cart before her.

"Ah, yes . . . here we are," Lanse said, and he held the chair for Sable and then seated himself. "We'll serve ourselves, Melissa. I'll call if we need anything." And then as Melissa stood hesitantly, "That will be all, Melissa. Thank you."

"Yes sir, Mist' Lanse." And she left the room.

"Melissa's dying of curiosity." Lance chuckled.

"Has she been with you—I mean have you owned her long?"

He looked at her curiously. "She's been with my family since before I was born. I brought her with me from Virginia."

114

While they talked Lanse served them from the cart—thin slices of ham with a faint fragrance of cloves, sweet potatoes covered with sugar glaze, green peas, chilled bowls of small, round melon balls, and hot, fresh bread with butter and honey. For dessert, there were delicious-looking pastries covered with sliced peaches and smothered with cream.

They ate in silence for a time, and then Lanse poured a thin, dark stream of coffee from the silver pot into her cup and then his own, watching her thoughtfully. "I do believe I've married a little Abolitionist," he drawled.

"No . . ." she stammered, "it's just that . . . well, I saw the beginning of a slave auction while the ship was docked at Rio. I never saw anything like that before . . . it wasn't very pleasant . . ."

He frowned. "No, I suppose not. But if it'll make you feel any better, I gave Melissa and Jace their freedom when I brought them out here."

"Then why do they stay?" Sable asked, thoroughly puzzled.

"For reasons you Northerners can't seem to understand. They could leave here any time they chose, but they won't—because I'm their 'family.' "

"But if you knew they would stay with you anyway, why did you bother to give them their freedom?"

Lanse took his time, breaking off a piece of bread and buttering it thoroughly. "I wanted to be sure that they came with me of their own free wills," he said at last. "You see, my family thought I'd lost my mind when I told them I was coming out here. Mother said I was just like Uncle Macon. That's her brother," he explained. "Never content to stay in one place, always on the move. But that's not true. I just wanted something that belonged completely to me. With three older brothers at home, Father didn't need any help with the plantation."

He picked up the platter of ham. "More?" he said.

"No, thank you, I have plenty here." Though the food was delicious, Sable found that she was not very hungry, and a quick glance at his plate showed her that the greater part of his food had been left untouched, also.

"Even if I hadn't given them their papers three years ago, I'd do it now. California is coming into the Union as a free state—that is, if those damned, lazy blockheads in Washington will stir their stumps and admit us," he said bitterly. "Last October, the governor called a convention with representatives from each community in California Territory. They drew up a state constitution and formally asked for admission into the Union as a free state, as the representatives had voted.

"There were some Southerners who were disappointed in the decision—not me!" He grinned, forestalling her question. "But some of them still hope that eventually California will be two states, North and South, with the southern half, slave. That will never happen."

Sable toyed with the food on her plate, feeling somewhat awed at his talk of statehood and conventions and state constitutions, but at the same time impressed with his intensity.

As if suddenly aware of her feelings, he stopped abruptly. "Enough of such serious talk." He stood and touched the back of her chair lightly as she got to her feet. "There's a full moon tonight, and it's cooler out in the garden," he said, guiding her through the double door.

The moon was full and butter yellow, and the stars glittered against the inky velvet sky. The warm air was filled with the fragrance of roses. Turning away from the stone path, she saw the bushes, with pink roses and white, like the one that decorated the table, and behind them taller bushes of hibiscus, their deep red blossoms purple in the half-darkness.

She sat on the wooden bench; he stood looking down at her.

"Are you very rich?" she asked.

His expression was at first startled and then amused. "You're damned direct!" He grinned. "Yes, I suppose I am—at least I intend to be," he amended. "Why do you ask?"

"I heard the women talking on the ship. They said gold is just lying on top of the ground out here—that a man can pick up a fortune in one day . . ."

He threw back his head and laughed loud and long.

"Well, after all . . . this house and the furnishings, the linen and silver—and that wine glass was real crystal . . ." She felt a rising irritation at his laughter.

"Forgive me," he said, recovering himself. "I couldn't help being amused at the ideas people have back East. There are fortunes made in the goldfields, but a man doesn't just pick up nuggets. It's labor—hard, backbreaking labor, and for every one that strikes it rich, there are a hundred more that barely eke out enough to live on, sometimes not even that. But the Gold Goddess beckons and they run. The ones who do get a little dust in their poke break their necks getting to town so they can throw it all away on liquor and gambling and . . ." He stopped and Sable dropped her eyes to her folded hands; she knew full well what he had left unsaid.

"No," he continued, "I didn't pick my money off the ground. I made mine from the only sure gold out here—trade. Consider all the things a man's got to have before he can even start to pan or dig—food, clothing, equipment, gunpowder—that's just to name a few. I make it my business to get the supplies to them first and at the best price."

"But, it must have cost a fortune just to build this house," reasoned Sable. "Why, there must be a dozen bedrooms upstairs."

"Fifteen."

"All that money from just selling supplies to the miners?"

"That and a few deals in real estate. It's hard for you people back East to realize," he went on earnestly, "what it's like in this gold-crazy town. Things that we take for granted back home are either scarce as hen's teeth or non-existent out here. The things we do bring in sell for twenty times their normal price."

"I have a great deal to learn," she said, but he went on as if he hadn't heard her.

"Right now, it's rough and violent and raw. It's like a kid growing up too fast—all arms and legs and elbows, clumsy and sometimes even ugly; but someday it'll be different. The gold fever will run its course, but the people will stay—the worthwhile ones anyway—stay and build San Francisco into the city she can be—a good place to live and raise your sons . . ."

He sat down on the bench beside her and took one of her small hands into his big, tanned one. His voice was low with conviction. "I want to be part of all that. That's why I built this house. I knew some day I'd find a woman to share it with me. Today on the dock when I first saw you, I knew you were the one I wanted."

The moonlight gleamed palely on the pink satin of her dress; his eyes seemed almost to devour her. And though his hand held hers lightly, she suddenly felt trapped.

"Why would a girl, young, beautiful as you are, come out here?"

"My father died . . . I was all alone; I had no money."

"What about your mother?"

"She died when I was born." Something within her cried out to tell him about Charles Gregg. Lanse knew there was more than she was telling, she could see it in his eyes, but somehow she couldn't bring herself to speak.

"I'm sorry about your father," he said quietly. He waited, giving her a chance, but she was silent.

He put his hand out, wonderingly, and touched her hair. "Beautiful," he said, "beautiful." There was a faint, rough edge of huskiness in his voice. He bent his head. His mouth came closer to hers and swift panic rose and pulsed in her throat. She turned her face so that his lips brushed her cheek. Then he put his hand under her chin and forced her to look up at him, his gray eyes steady and sure.

"I'm going to kiss you," he said firmly.

She could feel her heart pounding madly as this time his mouth found its mark. His lips were very gentle on hers. He released her, but his face was still only inches away.

"It's late," he said. "You go up. I'll give you a few minutes."

Chapter 11

Sable found that Melissa had turned down the bed and laid out her prettiest nightdress and wrapper. She undressed with feverish haste, her fingers fumbling and clumsy, terrified that she would hear his footsteps outside the door before she could complete the change.

She stood in front of the mirror, tying the velvet ribbon at the throat of her demure, white wrapper. It fell in soft, flowing folds from the wide yoke, daintily embroidered with pink rosebuds.

Thank God you can't see through it, she thought, then laughed at her reflection in the mirror. As if that would make any difference.

Unable to stay still, she paced back and forth, her footsteps making no sound on the thick carpet. She remembered Charles Gregg's long arms around her, his hand cupping her breast. Oh, please, she prayed, please don't let it be like that. But, no, it won't be . . . this is different, she tried to convince herself. She stared down at the wide band of gold encircling her finger; its weight felt strange. He is my husband, she thought. And he has a perfect right to . . . do whatever he wants with me . . .

She pictured him: saw again the tall, muscular body, slim-hipped and broad-shouldered, the wide-set gray eyes overshadowed by dark brows, his mouth sensitive and yet firmly masculine. She remembered the feel of that mouth on hers. His kiss had been incredibly tender. Perhaps . . . if only he weren't such a stranger to her . . .

She stopped short, drew a deep breath as she heard footsteps in the hall. She turned resolutely to face the door. The knob turned slowly, the door swung wide.

He stood looking at her a long, slow minute, then closed the door firmly behind him. Two strides brought him to the table where the single lamp burned.

"The light of the moon is enough," he said. He leaned over, his eyes never leaving hers, and slowly, deliberately, blew out the flame. He was right. The moonlight flowed into the room like silver liquid, gathering in shimmering pools.

She fought down an almost uncontrollable urge to back away as he came closer. He towered over her, his broad shoulders shutting out the room.

"Very pretty," he drawled, "but I think we can dispense with that." He grinned, untied the bow at her throat, pushed the wrapper off her shoulders. It slid down her arms to the floor.

Her face flamed as his bold, gray eyes appraised her in the all but transparent gown. The nipples showed clearly through the gauzy stuff as her breasts rose and fell in agitation.

"Damned pretty," he drawled again, his voice husky with desire.

He put his arms around her waist and drew her lightly to him. His hands burned her through the thin material.

"Please!" she cried, trembling at his touch.

He bent his head; his mouth closed over hers. His kiss was soft and gently reassuring, as it had been before. But then his breathing quickened.

He caught her roughly closer, pressing her body hard against him. His fingers reached under the thin stuff of the gown. His mouth moved on hers brutally, hurting,

122

bruising, forcing her lips apart, the tip of his tongue a burning, darting flame.

Her recoil was unplanned, sheer reflex. She struck out blindly, unthinking. It was completely by accident that her open palm caught him squarely across the face.

The slap echoed in the terrible silence. Sable put her hands to her trembling mouth, her eyes enormous.

He stood staring at her, the dark brows drawn into a single black line, his eyes like granite. A dull flush spread over his face; the pulse at his temple throbbed violently.

His eyes held her hypnotized. She opened her mouth to speak . . . to tell him she was sorry, to tell him anything to take that terrible look off his face. But her throat was closed, her lips unable to form the words.

He stood there for what seemed like hours, his eyes burning into her, but in reality it was only a few seconds. Then he turned without uttering a word and strode from the room, slamming the door behind him.

For a moment she was rooted to the spot, staring at the closed door, and then a low, moaning wail tore from her bruised lips and she threw herself full-length across the big bed.

The hard knot of unshed tears dissolved at last, painfully. She cried. For the first time in all those months, she cried . . . hard, terrible, wracking sobs, crying out her grief for her father, her fear of Charles Gregg, her loneliness, her anxiety at marrying a complete stranger. And she cried, too, for the look that had been on his face, that, try as she might, she could not put out of her mind.

Lansing Wakefield had been wounded in his most vulnerable spot—his pride. His violent anger had completely wiped out the desire that had engulfed him a moment before.

He was almost to the head of the stairs when he heard her first anguished sobs. He stopped, his hand outstretched to the railing, listening in spite of himself.

"Let her cry," he growled softly, feeling still the stinging slap. But he also remembered the stricken look in her eyes, her unsuccessful effort to speak. His anger began to subside as the terrible, painful sobbing continued.

His foot was on the first step. He willed himself to descend the stairs, but couldn't. Her tormented crying held him there as if he'd been bound.

He remembered her as she had stood on the dock that morning, fearful and strangely childlike in spite of the ripening body. Barely eighteen, he guessed. His anger had been quick and now his contrition was equally quick. His conscience smote him painfully.

She never laid eyes on me before this day, he rebuked himself, and yet I went in there like a goddamned fool and treated her like one of Lil Carstairs's whores.

He remembered the one word she had spoken. "Please," she had cried. Her voice, her eyes, her whole body had implored him to be easy with her, to be patient. And what had he done? He swore softly in disgust.

He walked back to the bedroom and quietly entered, easing the door shut behind him. She was still lying across the bed, her face buried in the pillow, her body silhouetted in the moonlight. Her sobbing had subsided a little, as though from sheer exhaustion. He drew nearer the bed.

"Sable," he said gently.

She stiffened. The soft sobbing stopped abruptly.

"No . . . don't be afraid," he tried to reassure her, "I'm not going to touch you . . . I promise."

A new paroxysm of sobbing shook her shoulders.

"Please, please don't cry." He wanted to reach out, gather her in his arms and comfort her, but dared not. He had given his promise and she might think that was violating it.

"No . . . don't cry . . ." He sat down on the bed beside her. "Look at me . . . that's right."

She rolled slowly over, freeing her face from the pillow, turning the tear-stained cheeks to him.

"There, isn't that better?"

She nodded, sniffling a little, like a child. "I—I didn't mean to hit you."

"I know you didn't," he assured her quickly. He grinned

at her. "Married one day and you've already discovered my damnable temper."

She smiled a little.

"Look," he went on seriously, "I should have given you more time. If you can forget what happened tonight, I'd like to start all over again . . . take time to get to know each other. How would that be?"

Her mouth trembled a little. "Oh, I do need time!" She lowered her eyes, her face colored. "I want to please you," she said, her voice very low. "I truly do. If you'll just be patient with me for a little while . . ." Her eyes implored him.

"I give you my word as a gentleman that I won't so much as kiss you until you ask me to," he promised. The sober look on his face was broken now by a wry grin. "But for God's sake," he said dryly, tossing the sheet over her body, so temptingly outlined in the moonlight, "and mine, let's not make it any harder than it has to be."

The usually stoic Melissa started with surprise the next day, when Lanse ordered her to prepare the bedroom next to his for her mistress.

"Miz Wakefield ain't going to share your room, Mist' Lanse?"

"No. Mrs. Wakefield isn't feeling too well . . . her long sea voyage has been very tiring. I think it will be best if she has a room of her own," he said lamely, "for the time being."

Melissa searched his face shrewdly at this unexpected development, but she asked no more questions.

"You know," he told her, "fix it the way a lady would like it. What will you need for it?"

Melissa narrowed her eyes in thought. Presently, she nodded her head. "I expect we got everything we need, except a mirror." She nodded her head again, pleased with herself. "A pretty lady like Miz Wakefield needs a mirror."

"Take the one out of my room," suggested Lanse.

"No, sir, we need a big mirror"—Melissa gestured with

her hands to show the size she meant—"so she can see herself all the way down."

"Well, I don't know." He scratched his head thoughtfully. "But if there's one in San Francisco, I'll get it for her. Anything else?"

"No, sir, that's all, but I'll be needing Jace to help me move some of the furniture from the other rooms. I'll have to do some sewing, but I think I can finish before tonight."

"Good." Lanse crossed to the window, hearing horses coming up the drive. "I'll tell Jace to let everything else go, and help you."

"Don't forget that mirror!"

"No, I won't," he promised as he headed for the stairs.

Sable had been cutting flowers in the garden, but she, too, had seen Amanda and Rob coming up the drive. Now, as Lanse came down the stairs, she was already rushing toward the great door to greet them, her face attractively flushed from the sunshine.

She threw open the door before they had a chance to lift the heavy brass knocker. "Amanda!" she cried delightedly, taking both of Amanda's hands and drawing her inside.

"I hope we're not too early." Amanda's face was radiant.

"Goodness, no, I've been watching for you for hours."

Rob poked Lanse in the ribs with his elbow, grinning. "You'd think they hadn't seen each other for a year."

"I know it," Lanse agreed. "Sable's been watching that drive all morning. But I am glad you've come. I'd like you to help me transact a little business in town."

"What kind of business?"

Lanse motioned to the still chattering women and shook his head. "I'll tell you after we get started. I want it to be a surprise."

"Mandy, honey," Rob broke into their conversation. "I'm going to take a little ride into town with Lanse."

"All right, Rob." The warmth in their exchanged glance was evident.

"We won't be long," Lanse told Sable, and the men left.

Sable led Amanda into the sitting room and motioned her to one of the big chairs while she finished arranging the freshly cut flowers in the vase on the table. The brilliant red of the hibiscus was startling against the white china. She had cut some four o'clocks, but those delicate blossoms had closed completely and she decided not to use them. She looked closely to find a place for the last hibiscus, then spying an opening, worked it carefully in.

"There, how does that look?" She stood back and surveyed it.

"They're beautiful."

Sable gave the flowers one last touch, then sat in the chair facing Amanda. She studied her face, a long, searching, wondering look. "I just can't get over it."

"Can't get over what?" Amanda's eyes fairly sparkled.

"You . . . you look so . . ." She searched for the right word and then turned her hands up in defeat. "So different," she finished, for want of a better word.

Amanda laughed. "Does it really show that much?"

"Yes, it does. I've never seen you look so happy before."

"Oh, Sable, he's wonderful . . . he's kind, he's good, he's—" she stopped, laughing a little at her own exuberance. "He's everything I hoped for."

Amanda leaned forward earnestly. "Oh, I know what you must be thinking—that I couldn't possibly know all these things about him in such a short time, but . . . just the same, I do. We talked for hours last night. We like the same foods, like to do the same things . . . we want the same things out of life."

"Did you tell him, Amanda, about being married before?"

"No . . . I didn't." A little of the happiness went out of Amanda's eyes and Sable wished that she hadn't asked. "I just couldn't tell him about Jim. It's not that I thought he'd mind, because I really don't think he would . . . it's just that I want nothing of the past hanging over us."

Amanda blushed, suddenly looked down at her folded hands. "I was afraid I'd have to tell him last night when ... I was afraid he'd know ... but if he did, he didn't say anything. Oh, Lord," it was almost a prayer, "if I fail him the way I failed Jim, I think I'll die."

"Now stop that, right now," Sable said sharply, "you mustn't even think that. You haven't said a word about your house." She deliberately changed the subject. "Tell me about it."

Amanda's face lost the forlorn look and grew softly radiant again. "It's a fine house," she said. "Not big and fancy like this one, but built real well. There are eight rooms, four up, four down, and a great big front porch—it's got a swing at one end of it. Rob decided to build the house when he knew I was coming." She laughed. "I mean when he decided he was going to marry one of us.

"Anyway," she went on, "the house is real pretty. Nice furniture and all ... It was messy yesterday. You know how it is when a man's all alone. Rob's had a Mexican woman come in once a week to clean but, mercy me, a house has to have more attention than that." She looked around her at the spotlessly clean room, the tabletop next to them gleaming with polish.

Sable explained quickly about Melissa and Jace in answer to the question in Amanda's eyes. "Melissa is really quite nice," she said, "though she does make me feel just the least bit uncomfortable at times. It's like she knows what you're thinking all the time. But the one I'm really uneasy about is her son, Jace. He's an absolute giant."

"Giant?" There was a teasing disbelief in Amanda's voice.

"Well, almost. Why, he's half a head taller than Lanse, and his hands are—" She measured off the distance with her own hands. "His hands are this big. He stares at me with such big, solemn eyes ... never smiles, at least not at me. But you'll see for yourself."

Amanda nodded and idly fingered one of the velvet-covered buttons on the tufted seat of her chair. She looked at Sable pointedly.

"So far, you haven't said a word about Lanse . . . Maybe it's just that I've talked about my Rob so much you haven't had a chance."

Sable blushed under Amanda's close scrutiny. "He's very nice . . . He's been very kind to me," she said truthfully. She kept her eyes lowered, fearing that Amanda would guess the truth. She didn't want anyone, not even Amanda, to know she had acted like such a baby last night.

"The house," she went on hurriedly, "is more than I ever dreamed of, but—it's too big. I feel lost in it. Even the furniture's too big. Look at this chair I'm sitting in —there's room for both of us and to spare."

She leaned forward, aware that her voice was betraying some of the anxiety she felt, but unable to hide it. "Please, Amanda, you and Rob stay to supper tonight."

Amanda hesitated a long, slow moment. "All right, I'll ask Rob."

The big clock in the hall was just striking six when the men returned from town, and Lanse had scarcely gotten the door ajar before Sable met him.

"Lanse," she said, the smallest edge of uncertainty in her voice, "I asked Amanda if she and Rob would stay to supper with us."

"Good . . . good!" he said at once. The door swung wider to reveal a large flat object, oblong in shape, wrapped in burlap, on the verandah. Lanse threw Rob a dismayed look, while Rob just stood there and grinned.

"Rob and I—we have to get this upstairs," he said. They hefted it between them and started up the stairs. "Sorry to be so late—my business took longer than I thought it would."

A few minutes later they were back and, as if nothing unusual had taken place, Lanse put a hand on Rob's shoulder. "Well, that's settled then . . . you're staying to supper. Though I'm afraid we'll have to fix it for ourselves. Melissa has some work that she can't leave right now. But she always has plenty of food in the kitchen."

"You just lead us to it," Amanda said, "and then leave it to Sable and me."

"Let's eat in here," Sable suggested. The kitchen was warm and homey, and she felt more comfortable than she had since entering the house.

The round oak table was similar to the one in the kitchen at home in New York. A dough bowl and rolling pin sat on the oilcloth-covered counter, and beside it was a white crock, filled with sugar . . . and when Sable lifted the lid she caught the faintest fragrance of vanilla. Dora had always put a vanilla bean in the sugar crock, too.

One whole wall was taken up by a stone fireplace, with gleaming copper pots hung overhead. The stonemason who had built the wall had left several recesses to form small shelves, and now they held jars filled with sweet potato vines, lushly green against the pink stone.

As Lanse had predicted, they found food in abundance . . . ham, cheese, muffins, potatoes, which Amanda popped into the oven of the big black cookstove to roast, and fresh peaches, sliced and sprinkled with sugar.

The men were in high good humor at supper, and Rob regaled them with stories of his and Lanse's first experiences in California, when they had landed in '48.

"Do you remember, Lanse," he asked, laughing so hard he could hardly gasp out the words, "the look on that hotel clerk's face when you told him you'd be damned if you'd pay twenty dollars to sleep in a room with six other men? And then, you stubborn mule, we had to sleep in the stable. Next morning we smelled so of horse manure that people crossed to the other side of the street to get away from us."

"Yes, only if my memory serves me correctly, you weren't laughing then. In fact," Lanse chuckled, "I seem to remember some pretty fancy cussing."

They kept up the friendly raillery all through supper, recalling their hardships with the added humor that time gives, until Sable found herself gasping with laughter at Lanse's account of Rob's adamant refusal to join the volunteer fire company, even though everyone who was anyone in San Francisco belonged, until they agreed to let him lead the next parade through the city.

"There he was," Lanse laughed, "high-stepping it around the Plaza in that fancy new uniform they gave him, so busy watching the crowd admiring him that he didn't watch where he was going. He led the whole damned bunch of us, uniforms and all, right through a knee-deep mud puddle!"

Rob whooped as loud as the rest of them, and forthwith started to tell one on Lanse.

Sable was surprised to find how many times her eyes met Lanse's, freely and easily, laughing, relaxed, without any of the tension that she had felt before.

After a while, Sable and Amanda cleared the table, and though Lanse insisted that Melissa would clean up the next morning, they washed and dried the dishes, while the two men lingered at the table over one last cup of coffee.

"I'm so glad you stayed," Sable said in a low tone, taking a dripping plate from Amanda.

"I am, too." Amanda glanced over her shoulder at the two men, off on yet another tale. "They do talk kind of rough, don't they?" she whispered. "Poor dears, they've been out here so long they've forgotten how to speak in front of ladies. Really, when Rob told that story about them sleeping in the stables and smelling like—manure." She didn't even whisper the last word, merely mouthed it and her face turned bright pink.

It struck Sable as terribly funny and she started to giggle, then Amanda joined in and they went into peals of laughter. And though the men begged to be let in on the joke, they only shook their heads and laughed all the harder.

Rob and Amanda soon took their leave, Amanda still wiping the tears of merriment from her eyes as they said goodnight.

Lanse dropped the big latch into place, locking the front door, and turned to Sable. "Now, young lady," he said, feeling a pleasant anticipation, "I have a surprise for you."

Thoroughly mystified, Sable followed him up the stairs. Melissa was waiting for them on the top step.

"Is everything ready?" Lanse asked her.

"Yes, sir, Mist' Lanse, I just finished a few minutes ago," Melissa said proudly.

Lanse opened the door next to his and stood back with a flourish for Sable to enter first. "Madam, your room!"

Sable drew her breath in delight. "Oh! It's lovely!" she exclaimed. It was all pink and white, as dainty and feminine as Lanse's room was masculine. The furniture was of light cherrywood, the bedspread, canopy, and vanity skirt of white organdy with deep, pink flounces. White lace curtains as delicate as frosted fern hung at the windows, with heavy pink silk overdrapes for privacy.

"Melissa—you did all this today?" Sable asked incredulously.

"Oh, I just brought some things from the other bedrooms . . . did a little sewing . . ." Melissa smiled.

Sable spied the full-length mirror. "So that's what you brought upstairs!" she said to Lanse. Then she ran over to it, turning gaily around, her full skirts whirling about her ankles.

Lanse smiled at her pleasure. Thank God she doesn't know where it came from, he thought uneasily, afraid Rob would let it slip to Amanda despite his oath of secrecy. Women could be mighty touchy about little things like that.

The mirror had hung, until this afternoon, lengthwise over the bar at the Eureka, and was the pride and joy of Mac, the owner. It had taken considerable wheedling and cajoling on Lanse's part to induce him to part with it. Finally Lanse promised to commission an incredibly bad artist by the name of Porter, who frequented the place, to paint a picture of a reclining nude to replace the mirror, and Mac capitulated.

Sable, blissfully unaware of the origin, smiled at Lanse's reflection as he came to stand just behind her.

She spoke softly, so that Melissa, standing just outside the door, wouldn't hear her words. "You really meant what you promised last night."

"I gave you my word. A gentleman doesn't break his word," he said seriously. Even if it kills him, he thought wryly.

Chapter 12

The following Sunday afternoon, Sable heard Lanse say he must make a short trip into town for some papers that he had left at his office, and she begged earnestly to be taken along.

"All right, get your bonnet. I'll have Jace get the rig out." He smiled his pleasure that she had asked to accompany him. "And hurry up!" The last was completely unnecessary, as she was already speeding up the stairs.

I must change into a fresh dress, she thought, as she scanned her wardrobe, depleted no longer since Lanse had lavishly replenished it. She chose a green-and-white checked taffeta from among the row of silks, satins, laces, and fine, soft cottons. Because there were few expert seamstresses in San Francisco, Lanse had let her choose the clothing from shipments ready-made from the East, but Melissa had had to take in the waists of the dresses to make them fit correctly.

Sable had known instinctively that Melissa was responsible when Lanse first suggested the new wardrobe. And later, Melissa had owned up to it. "I said to myself, Melissa, that little Missus ain't going to tell Mist' Lanse that

135

she needs some new clothes, so you better tend to that yourself," she had chuckled.

Sable shook her head, smiling at the recollection. She found herself relying more and more upon the old Negress.

She gave her hair a final pat and tied the perky bonnet strings beneath her chin, carefully pulling forward a curl on each side, then hurried down the stairs, fearful lest Lanse grow impatient waiting for her.

The light carriage was ready, and she found Lanse beside it talking to a man she decided must be a Mexican. His well-lined face was quite dark, his hair and the small mustache very black but with a sprinkling of gray. Though of average height, he appeared short next to Lanse, as he stood turning around in his hands the huge brown *sombrero,* its crown marked with sweat stains, old and new.

As Sable approached them uncertainly, Lanse turned to her with a delighted smile and proudly drew her arm through his. "My dear," he said, "this is Manuel—Manuel Garcia. He is the one responsible for the flowers you've enjoyed so much. I think he must have a touch of magic; before I found him the garden would grow nothing but weeds."

Manuel's white teeth gleamed, his swarthy features flushing with pleasure.

"How do you do, Manuel," said Sable.

"So this is the lovely *señora* with the hair of flame. I have heard much already of the beauty of the *señora,*" said Manuel gallantly, "but truly the reports have not done justice enough." His voice had a smooth melodic quality like water flowing over the pebbles of a brook. And this time it was Sable's turn to color with pleasure.

"May I take this opportunity," he went on, "to congratulate the *señor* and the *señora* on their marriage?" He bowed with old-world charm. "May your years together be filled with happiness and your union be blessed with many little ones."

"Gracias," said Lanse, and he looked at Sable in a way that caused her to grow quite flustered.

"Do you have many children, Manuel?" she asked quickly.

"Alas, no, *señora,"* he shook his head sadly, "my Rosita and I have been wed for many years, but . . ." He shrugged, and Sable suddenly thought of Amanda.

"Manuel hasn't been able to get around for the past couple of weeks," Lanse told Sable. "That's why you haven't met him before."

"I hope it was nothing serious."

"No, no, *señora,* just a—how do you say it?—a sprain of the ankle. See, it is all better now." He flexed his ankle to prove his words. "And it is just in time; my garden needs attention." He shook his head, smiling, "A garden is like a woman—give her lots of love, lots of attention, and she blossoms for you; leave her unloved, neglected, and she soon fades."

Lanse laughed, clapped Manuel on the shoulder. "I forgot to tell you, my dear," he said to Sable, "that besides being a gardener of considerable talent, Manuel has the soul of a poet." Then to Manuel, "Stop by the kitchen, *amigo,* and have Melissa fix you something to eat before you set to work."

Lanse swung Sable up into the open carriage and then jumped lightly in beside her, taking the reins.

"Gracias, Señor Lanse." Manuel waved the big sombrero. *"Adiós,"* he called as the carriage pulled smartly away.

They found the streets of San Francisco busy with vehicles of various descriptions, carts, wagons, a few carriages like their own, not to mention the milling pedestrians. Progress through the streets was slow, but Lanse took the opportunity to point out the sights of interest to Sable.

The town, lacking the time to grow gracefully, was a strange mixture of old and new, of crudeness and elegance, of rawness and polish. The plush new hotel, but recently finished, was scarcely a block away from a rough lumber saloon; the respectable newspaper office, the likes of which one might find in any good-sized town, was right next door to a structure of wood and canvas.

Lanse avoided any reference to the saloons, though they were too plentiful to go unnoticed, and even on a Sunday afternoon, music and harsh male voices blared from every doorway. And he was careful not to get too near the long line of brothels where the "soiled doves" plied their ancient trade. They ran the gamut, from the elegant, plush bawdyhouses like Lil Carstairs's place, right down the line to the rough lumber shacks, the tents, the hole-in-the-wall places where things went on that made Lil Carstairs's place look like Sunday prayer meeting by comparison—where a man, for a price, might satisfy any desire, no matter how bizarre.

Presently they came to the Plaza, and Lanse pulled the horse to a standstill. There was always a gathering here, and this afternoon proved no exception.

"This is it," he said. "Portsmouth Square—but we mostly call it the Plaza."

"We have a Plaza back home," she said, suddenly wistful. "It's all around the City Hall."

Lanse looked about him. The fanciest saloons and gambling houses in town faced Portsmouth Square— hardly places to impress a girl like Sable. And the Plaza itself was a plain dirt square marked off with a rough rail fence. It had rained during the morning—nothing more than a summer shower, but enough to turn the thick layer of dust to mud, and careless boots had turned that into a sticky mire.

If there was one thing a man learned to ignore in San Francisco, it was mud. There were times in the winter when the streets became almost impassable, and it wasn't uncommon for a drunk to stumble off the rough sidewalks and drown in the oozing stuff before anyone found him.

"I know it's not much right now," Lanse said gently, "but give us time. We're young yet."

She was quiet for a moment, and then an amused look

wiped the sadness from her face. "Is this where Rob marched the fire company through the puddle?"

He nodded. "Right over there. In fact, I think I see another puddle in the very same spot."

She giggled outright at that. "What is he saying?" She pointed to a tall, stoop-shouldered man standing atop a good-sized wooden box and waving his arms vigorously as he spoke to a gathered crowd.

"Lord knows. Anytime a man has anything to say, from politics to who's got the best horse in town, he's apt to shout it out at the Plaza. I'll pull over closer and we'll listen for a minute."

". . . and I don't have to tell you," the man was saying, "that you'll get a fair deal at Moffat and Company. You know that without me saying so. This coin right here will pass in trade anyplace." He waved a small object high above his head and then hunched his shoulders and fished through his inside coat pocket until he found a paper.

"Right here's a copy of the government contract locked in the safe at the office. And soon's I read you some of it, I'll pass it around so's you can see for yourselves."

He held the paper far out in front of him and shaded his eyes with one hand. ". . . says right here—Moffat and Company . . . to assay and fix the value of gold in grains and . . ." He read on in a slow, exaggerated voice.

"What is he talking about?" asked Sable.

"He works for Moffat," said Lanse. "They assay and smelt. Turn out damned good coins, too . . . standard mint value."

"You mean they make money?" Sable's eyes mirrored her disbelief.

Lanse laughed at her expression. "Yes, and on a semi-official basis since they got the government contract. Of course, there are plenty of other private mints that operate without the government's blessing. It's been a necessary thing out here. We're so far away from the other centers of trade that it's impossible to get a normal flow of coin— regular mint issue, that is. People were using dust and get-

139

ting six to eight dollars an ounce when it was worth eighteen. That couldn't go on. These private mints are a temporary answer."

He reached into his pocket and drew out a handful of coins. Scanning them quickly, he selected a ten-dollar gold piece and handed it to her.

"Here's one of Moffat's pieces."

She turned it over so that it lay face up in her small gloved hand. "But it looks just like the ones back home!"

"Not quite. See what's stamped on Miss Liberty's coronet—Moffat and Company. And on the back it says, California Gold."

Sable peered more closely at the coin, turning it back and forth. "So it does. I don't think I would have noticed the difference if you hadn't told me."

"That's probably the reason they got the contract. They know their business. We had all hoped for an office of the regular mint to be set up here, but—" He shrugged. "When you've been here longer you'll learn it's very easy for Washington to just ignore us."

While they talked, the speaker climbed down from his wooden box and passed through the crowd showing the copy of the contract to anyone who cared to see it.

Most of his audience had begun to look for a new amusement, and Lanse could see the quick interest that sprang to their eyes as they caught sight of Sable sitting demurely beside him, quite unaware that she was rapidly becoming the center of attention.

"If you're ready, we'll go on now," he said quietly, and without waiting for her answer, he touched the horse lightly with the reins. As their carriage moved off, Lanse caught the looks of awe, of longing, of envy; saw the nudgings, the whispered phrases. A sudden flare of anger that they should so openly stare at Sable wrestled with the pride he felt that she belonged to him.

Once away from the Plaza, they drove through block after block that had been devastated by the two disastrous fires they had suffered earlier that year—one on May 4, and the last one barely a month ago, on June 14.

"But it's almost all rebuilt," Sable said in amazement.

"They started building as soon as the ashes were cool enough to clear away," Lanse said, proud of the indomitable spirit of his city.

"We'd better leave the rig here. It's only another block," Lanse said. "Do you mind walking?"

"Of course not."

Lanse tied the horse to the hitchrail and held out his arms for Sable. She smiled down into his face as she placed her hands lightly on his big shoulders and allowed him to lift her over the muddy stretch of street and onto the rough plank sidewalk, as always keenly aware of his bigness, his masculinity. She saw the guilty look in his eyes as his hands lingered at her waist for one second longer than was necessary, then he released her and offered his arm.

"Sable? Yes, it *is* you!" They turned at the feminine voice behind them. "I was sure it was—who else in Frisco's got hair like that?"

Sable faced Flossie Tucker, dressed spectacularly in dark red satin, a fluffy pink feather boa tossed carelessly around her shoulders, the rouged cheeks and lips to which Sable had become accustomed aboard ship now looking garish and hard in the bright afternoon light.

She was on the arm of a middle-aged man, tall, prosperous-looking, but a bit paunchy. He tipped his hat to Sable, nodded, reservedly, to Lanse.

"Hello, Wakefield."

"Winston," Lanse acknowledged, with an equally reserved nod.

Sable recovered quickly from her surprise. "Hello, Flossie," she said hesitantly.

"I've been wondering what happened to you," Flossie chattered, her arm tucked possessively through Winston's. "How are things going, honey?"

"Just . . . fine, thank you," Sable stammered, stealing a glance up at the scowling Lanse. "How . . . how about you, Flossie?"

"Oh, couldn't be better. We're on our way to the fights —the bear and bullfights." Flossie shivered. "I don't know if I'll like them, but Winnie says everyone goes." She gave his arm an exaggerated squeeze. "Is that where you're headed?"

"No, it isn't," Lanse said curtly. "As a matter of fact, we're late for an appointment." He took Sable's arm and firmly steered her away with a barely perceptible nod of goodbye to Flossie and her gentleman friend.

"See you again sometime," Flossie's throaty tones floated after them.

Lanse snorted angrily. He strode briskly along, his long legs making it difficult for Sable to keep up; his jaw set, his eyebrows a scowling, black line.

"Please," she gasped, finding herself almost running, "I can't keep up with you."

He slackened his pace somewhat. "Madam," he said, his voice low enough not to be heard by passersby, "I cannot imagine how you came to know that woman, but you may as well learn right now that the wife of Lansing Wakefield does not stop to speak with tarts on the street . . . or anywhere else, for that matter!"

Sable felt her temper rising at his tone of voice. Perversely enough, she refused to admit to herself that she had been embarrassed to have Flossie speak to her in Lanse's presence. They had been friends, almost, on the *Betty Kay*. She struggled to keep her self-control.

"But, Lanse, you surely wouldn't have me be rude to anyone?"

He ignored that completely. "Since you seem to be on such friendly terms with her, you must be aware that she is being kept by Winston, the man she was with. And if you think there's any question of marriage, you're badly mistaken. The . . . gentleman has a wife back East. Your friend lives in his home, eats his food. He supplies her with clothing like that gaudy thing she had on, and in return for all this . . ." He stopped walking and turned to

142

face her squarely. "I don't think you're so innocent that you don't know what she gives him in return."

Sable felt her face grow hot.

"I will not have my wife consorting with such people," he said curtly.

"I am not consorting with anyone!" Sable's Irish temper soared out of bounds. "I merely spoke to her . . . and I'm quite sure, Lansing Wakefield, that you've done a lot more than speak to her—or if not her, others just like her!" She stopped, thoroughly shocked at herself.

He drew in his breath; his eyes flashed, but his voice was completely controlled. "I think you have said quite enough, madam," he said, with such authority that Sable dared not say another word. She stamped her foot in frustrated anger.

Burning with indignation, she accompanied him up the stairs to the good-sized room in which he and Rob conducted their business affairs. Waiting at the door, she coldly turned her back on him, disdaining even to examine the room, while he gathered the papers he had come for.

The walk back to the rig was completed in icy silence. He lifted her to the seat impersonally, each of them carefully avoiding the other's eyes. Climbing in beside her, he slapped the reins smartly; the horse bolted ahead with a jolt.

As they wound their way back through the crowded streets, Lanse betrayed his impatience more than once with whispered curses that were too low for Sable to quite make out, but at last they reached the outskirts of town and the clear road.

They had covered approximately half of the distance to Wakefield Manor in absolute silence, when Sable stole a look at Lanse. The scowl on his face had been replaced by a look of feigned indifference—a look that scarcely acknowledged her presence beside him. Suddenly, she saw the ridiculousness of the situation and started to laugh . . . softly at first, then louder.

He didn't move, made no sign to show that he had even

heard her. But Sable was determined. She leaned closer to him, turning her head to one side, and looked into his eyes. He would have had to turn completely away to avoid looking at her. She grinned at him impishly and knew she was winning when she saw a smile play about the corners of his mouth.

"Married little over a week and already I've discovered your temper twice!" she said, leaving out the word he had used, *damnable*.

That brought complete capitulation; he laughed outright. "I'd say you've a pretty good temper yourself," he teased.

"Oh, I admit to that freely. My father used to say, 'There niver was an Irishman without a good, honest temper, and Keith Flanagan with the best of them all.'" She mimicked Keith's tone of voice perfectly. "The old fraud," she said. "I never saw him angry in my life."

"Well," Lanse grinned, "I'm not Irish, but now that you've caught me in a weak moment, I have to admit that the Wakefield men are about the most stubborn, hotheaded lot you're ever likely to run up against. Fact of the matter is . . . ." He slowed the horse to a comfortable walk. "I sometimes wonder how the Wakefield women have been able to put up with us long enough to propagate the line."

He looked pointedly at her; she blushed.

"I do want to explain to you about Flossie," she said, changing the subject. "It was so crowded aboard ship, there just wasn't any way to avoid her. With all of us in the 'tween deck . . . and then when she got pneumonia—"

"My God!" Lanse exploded. "You don't mean she was aboard the *Betty Kay?*"

"Of course."

"Good Lord! What kind of women did they bring out here?" he asked incredulously. Sable set her mouth hard.

"No, no," he said, turning to look at her, "don't get all riled up again, I didn't mean it like that . . . I just can't help wondering how they'd accept a woman like her."

"She wasn't one of our group," explained Sable stiffly.

"Her passage was arranged privately . . . with Captain Grayson."

"I can well imagine," said Lanse dryly.

Jace ran out to meet them as they pulled up in front of the big white house. "That sure was a quick trip, sir," he said, grinning as he always did when addressing Lanse. Then, realizing that Sable was looking directly at him, Jace sobered instantly.

He took the horse's head as Lanse came around to help Sable down. "Mist' Atkins here while you was gone."

"Did he leave the mare?" Lanse asked.

"Yes, sir, Mist' Lanse."

"Fine!" Lanse said, pleased. "Bring her out."

Jace went to obey while Lanse turned, grinning, to Sable. "Well, I hadn't exactly planned it this way, but she's going to make a dandy peace offering."

"You mean it's something for me?"

"Not 'it'—'she'." He laughed. "The prettiest little mare you ever laid your eyes on. Part Arab, I think, from the looks of her. Wait till you see her."

They walked slowly toward the stable, and through the open door Sable could see Jace leading the animal out of her stall. He brought her outside, the sunlight gleaming on her smooth sorrel coat, breeding showing in every line of her, even to one knowing nothing of horses, like Sable.

"You can put up the rig and attend to the other horse now," Lanse told Jace. "Better give him a good rubdown." Then, when they were alone, "Well, what do you think of her?"

From the look in his eyes, Sable knew that her expression had already answered his question. "She's beautiful!" she said, patting the glossy, arched neck. The sorrel mare whinnied softly.

Lanse dug into his coat pocket. "Here. Give her this." He handed her some small bits of sugar. "I always carry some with me for Satan."

Sable held out her hand, shyly at first; the mare, equally shy, tossed her head and whinnied again. Then, curiosity overcoming shyness, she nuzzled Sable's hand with a velvet nose, eager for the sugar once she discovered the sweetness.

"What's her name?"

Lanse rubbed his chin thoughtfully. "I don't really think she has one. Tom just called her 'the sorrel'. Too bad. Guess you'll have to think up one yourself."

She looked up at him with a smile that answered his teasing grin. All of a sudden she thought how very pleasant it was to be Mrs. Lansing Wakefield, and she felt a sudden stab of guilt.

"Lanse," she said, her fingers still entwined in the thick mane, "I like her very much . . . and I'm grateful for her, but . . . please don't get me anything else."

"Why not?"

"You've given me so much already."

"You're my wife. It's only right that I should give you things."

"But," she protested, her voice very low, her eyes avoiding his, "it seems I'm taking all these things from you and . . ." she stammered, "and I'm not . . ."

Lanse smiled at her discomfiture, but his eyes were very gentle. "Don't worry about that, my dear. I expect to collect, with interest. We have a whole lifetime ahead of us . . ." He took her hand and his fingers were strong around hers.

"Let's go in. It's getting late," he said, glancing at the sun dipping close to the horizon, filling the sky with gold and red. "You can put her up now, Jace," he called back over his shoulder to the big man in the stable.

They walked up the path toward the house, with Sable acutely conscious of his fingers still closed over hers.

"Let's get up early in the morning," he suggested, "and take a ride before breakfast."

Sable stopped short. "Oh, my goodness," she said weakly. "I'm not sure if I can ride her. Papa used to let me ride one of the bays—but only when he was there to lead him. I was just a child."

Lanse at first looked incredulous and then as if he might laugh. She felt utterly miserable.

"I suppose to a Virginian it's unthinkable that anyone wouldn't know how to ride a horse," she said defensively, but gave it up, feeling completely woebegone. "I'm sorry," she said.

"Never mind," he consoled her. "I'll teach you."

Chapter 13

And teach her he did. Each morning for the next five weeks, Lanse instructed her with remarkable patience, for to him, who had been in a saddle almost before he could walk, riding was as unconscious as breathing. To have to learn how seemed completely unnatural.

At first, Sable had perched tensely upon the sidesaddle, hanging on grimly, reluctant to let go of his hand, but then gradually she began to relax, to keep her back erect instead of clutching for the horse's neck, to sit easier in the saddle.

"Trust her . . . trust your mare," he'd urge. "She knows better than you do."

At last, after five long weeks, Lanse decided that she had made enough progress to try a real ride along with him and Satan. The big black stallion danced sideways, arching his neck, showing off for Princess, as Sable had decided to call the mare. And Lanse felt a moment of alarm as the mare tossed her head and snorted in response, but then he relaxed, smiling his satisfaction as he saw Sable set her mouth firmly and, without too much difficulty, quiet the excited Princess. After that ride, it was harder to say which one was prouder, himself or Sable.

The six weeks they had been married had been one constant social whirl, for Lanse had a wide circle of friends and acquaintances, all curious to meet the new Mrs. Wakefield. Also, women who had come out aboard the *Betty Kay* attracted much attention in San Francisco.

Sam Brannan, the fiery little editor of the *California Star,* had invited the Wakefields to the new opera house as his guests. They had dined with Tom Atkins, a real estate broker and the former owner of Sable's mare; with young Will Coleman, a Kentuckian who owned the contracting company at the corner of Sansome and Jackson. They had attended a party given by Chris Russell, retired from business but still very active in civic affairs. The list seemed endless. And those who hadn't extended an invitation came to call at Wakefield Manor, their intention clearly to see the new mistress.

Most of the men in San Francisco were bachelors or had left their wives back East, and they showed their admiration of Sable openly and unabashedly. Lanse could see in their eyes the good-natured envy they felt. God, how they'd laugh if they knew the truth.

Countless times during that six weeks, he had had to remind himself of his promise to Sable, and then in the next instant called himself six kinds of a jackass for ever making it. Every time he lifted her to the saddle, the fetching green riding habit emphasizing the gentle swelling of breasts, the softness of her body tempted him almost beyond endurance. She'd look down at him, her blue eyes crinkling at the corners, her mouth curving bewitchingly, completely unaware of what she was doing to him.

And if the days were bad, the nights were worse. He'd lie awake, hot with desire, torturing himself with mental pictures of how she must look lying in the bed only a few feet away in the next room; the sight of her in the thin nightdress etched clearly in his memory—until, finally, utter exhaustion would release him to sleep.

His first instinct was to pay a visit to Lil Carstairs's

place to ease himself temporarily—But, no, he rejected the idea immediately. One visit there and half the men in town would know about it and guess the truth.

And I'll be damned, he thought savagely, if I'll have anybody saying that Lanse Wakefield can't ride his own filly.

Rob and Lanse puffed contentedly on their pipes, the picture of male satisfaction after Amanda's excellent supper. The two couples were together a good deal, with scarcely a day going by that they weren't at one house or the other.

Lanse sniffed the aromatic smoke appreciatively. "Nothing like good Virginia tobacco from home," he said.

Rob nodded his agreement, stretching out his legs in front of him and resting his booted feet on the low walnut table. "I'd better not let Mandy catch me," he chuckled, stealing a quick look at the kitchen door. Reassured by the clatter of pots and pans, the soft voices of Sable and Amanda, he relaxed.

He spoke again, his voice purposely low. "Since when did you start carrying a gun, Lanse?"

The big Virginian touched the telltale bulge under his coat. "Since yesterday," he replied. "For God's sake, don't say anything in front of the women."

"No use getting them upset," Rob agreed.

"Then you've heard talk, too?"

"Nothing you can really put your finger on, but there have been rumors . . ."

"Exactly the same with me—just little hints here and there. But I tell you, Rob, there's trouble stirring . . . It's bound to come."

Lanse rose and crossed to the fireplace. He methodically cleaned the ashes from his pipe, stuck it into his jacket pocket, and then went back to his chair. He listened for a moment to the sounds from the kitchen, and then, assured that the women were still busy, he leaned forward and spoke earnestly to Rob.

"I thought it was the end when we ran the Hounds—or

the 'Regulators' as they called themselves—out of San Francisco last year."

Rob snorted. "They were the Regulators all right—wanted to regulate the whole town for themselves."

Lanse grinned. "That's the truth. But when you come right down to it, they were just a handful of young toughs who thought they could cash in on a wide-open town. It didn't take much to rout them out. But this . . ." He shook his head. "Another shipload from Australia yesterday."

"More for Sydney Town, huh? That's what they're callin' it over by Clark's Point now," Rob said.

Lanse nodded. "I saw some of them when I went down to the docks to get those bills of lading. Rough-looking bunch. God knows what they were sent to prison for. Australia keeps them six months and ships them out of the country . . . cheaper than keeping them, I guess. And what better place than California? Nobody seems to care a damn . . ."

Amanda's voice came from the kitchen. "We'll be with you men in a jiffy, now. Almost finished."

"All right, hon," Rob called back. His face grew even more sober; the sound of his wife's voice had reminded him of his added responsibility. "If only we had some real law out here," he said irritably.

"It'll come . . . but it's going to take time. If we could just get statehood! but even after we're admitted, it'll still take time to set all the necessary wheels in motion. Meanwhile . . ." Lanse patted the gun bulge significantly. "It's just as well to be prepared for anything."

Rob nodded. "I guess I'd better get mine out and oil it up, though Lord knows if Mandy sees it she'll get all stirred up."

"Then make sure she doesn't see it." Lanse leaned over and grasped Rob's arm. "And Rob, whenever you have to go out of town, why don't you bring Amanda over to the house—Jace will always be there, even if I'm gone." The eyes of the two men met, held.

They straightened up quickly, Rob snatching his feet

off the table, and assumed a casual air as the women came in from the kitchen.

"How about some more coffee?" Amanda asked cheerfully, as she set a tray down on the table in front of Rob.

Lanse felt a quick surge of pleasure as Sable, with a smile, chose the chair nearest to him, her full skirts brushing against his leg.

"I don't know why you won't let me get that Mexican woman in here to do the work," Rob scolded Amanda fondly as she handed him his coffee. He turned to Lanse and Sable. "You'd think we were poor as churchmice."

Amanda calmly finished passing the coffee around and offered cream and sugar before she answered him. "It's not a question of money. I know we could afford it, but I enjoy taking care of the house myself." Her eyes reflected a quiet contentment as she glanced about the room, from the antimacassars on the chair backs to the row of framed pictures along the wall, from the cream-colored curtains edged with ball fringe to the soft orange-and-yellow braided rugs. She ran one finger lovingly along the edge of the table in front of them, suddenly suspicious as she found the few specks of dust near the rim.

Lanse had trouble suppressing a grin as Rob took up a spoon and began to stir his coffee vigorously, though he always took it black, and then shook his head in feigned exasperation.

"Well," he said, "I'll give in to you for now, but one of these days I might have to put my foot down." The pretended sternness faded from his face, was replaced by a grin. "It may be all very well for you to do the housework now, but when we get a couple of young ones running about underfoot, you'll . . ."

He got no further. Amanda's cup had dropped with a clatter. It lay broken on the tray, the dark stain spreading rapidly across the white linen napkin. With some surprise, Lanse observed her pale face, her trembling hands.

"Why, Mandy, honey," Rob said teasingly, "you surely aren't embarrassed that I mentioned babies in front of Lanse and Sable . . ."

"No . . . of course not." Amanda shoved her hands into her apron pockets. "I'm afraid I'm just clumsy."

"Not a bit of it." Rob went to her and, despite their guests, gave her a comforting hug.

"Here, let me help," Sable said, taking her napkin and mopping the few drops that had splashed onto the polished oak floor. "There."

"I'll take the tray into the kitchen," Rob offered.

"No. Amanda and I can manage." Sable looked pointedly at her friend and Amanda seized upon the suggestion with obvious gratitude.

"Yes, we'd better take care of this right now," she said. "I'll put that cloth to soaking in cold water, else the stain won't ever come out."

When they were alone, Rob's eyes met Lanse's briefly and then flickered away. "And what was that all about?" he said uneasily.

Lanse shrugged. "Women . . ." he said dryly. "Who understands what goes on in their minds?"

Rob gave a short, forced laugh. "I guess you're right."

The sound of water splashing into a basin echoed from the kitchen. Rob twisted restlessly in his chair and then pulled his big gold watch from his pocket and compared it to the clock on the mantle.

"Damned clock," he muttered, "Always fast. Knew I shouldn't have bought it." He was on his feet at once; opening the glass cover over the face, he moved the heavy black minute hand until it corresponded to his watch.

"There now. Everything's cleaned up," Amanda said from the doorway, and but for the two bright spots of color that marked her cheeks, she seemed her normal self again.

"Then," said Lanse, "I expect now is as good a time as any to tell the big news."

"What big news?" Sable was instantly all childlike curiosity.

"What do you think, Rob? Should we tell them?"

Even Amanda was beginning to look attentive and Rob

played it up. "Well," he said, grinning, "maybe they wouldn't be interested."

"Rob Cooper," Amanda said, "don't tease. Tell us."

"I guess we'd better." Rob's blue eyes twinkled. "Mr. Wakefield." He made an elaborate bow to Lanse. "You do the honors."

"How would you ladies like to go to a ball?"

There was a moment's silence, and then: "A ball!" they said in the same breath.

"Who's giving it?" Sable asked, her eyes shining.

"We are," said Lanse. "That is, the volunteer firemen are. We're going to hold a Firemen's Ball, and if it turns out to be a success, we're going to make it an annual affair."

"When is it going to be?" Amanda asked.

"Two weeks from tonight," answered Lanse.

"Good. Gives me time enough to get a new dress."

Rob moaned in mock despair. "I knew we shouldn't have told them—knew it was gonna cost us money."

Their announcement having gotten the results they had anticipated, Lanse and Rob settled back and shook their heads over the women, who in typical female fashion spent the remainder of the evening in raptures over the coming ball, planning how they would arrange their hair, what they would wear, speculating as to who would attend . . . Whatever their small upset had been, Lanse thought, it was forgotten now.

Amanda caught them at the door just as they were leaving. "Oh, Sable, I forgot the most important thing. Rob found out about Willa Moore. She married a nice young fellow, he says."

"That's right," said Rob. "You know him, Lanse. That Mason boy—remember? The one that just opened the small hotel on the other side of town."

"Oh, yes, I know Mason . . . smart young man."

"Rob's going to drive me over to see her on Friday. Want to come along?" Amanda asked Sable.

"Yes, please come by for me. I'd love to see Willa again."

Willa made no effort to hide her delight. She proudly poured cups of tea and then took the brown stoneware jar from the wall shelf and filled a plate with sugar cookies.

"We can go in the parlor," she said.

"This is fine." Sable looked around the small kitchen, modestly furnished but scrupulously clean, the crisp red-and-white striped curtains bright against the pale walls.

"Yes, let's stay right here." Amanda pulled a chair up to the round table and placed her steaming cup of tea before her on the white enameled top.

They had arrived just in time to meet Willa's husband coming out of the door of the neat whitewashed cottage. Tall and thin, he looked more boyish than his twenty-one years, but he gravely acknowledged Willa's introduction. Then, making his apologies, he continued on his way.

"Jed has to be away so much of the time," Willa explained, as they sat sipping the tea. "I get awful lonesome without him . . . 'specially at night."

"Does he have to be away all night?" asked Amanda.

"Not the whole night, but sometimes it's close to midnight 'fore he can get home. There's lots of work to running a hotel."

"Lanse—my husband says you seem to be doing a good business." Sable helped herself to another cookie.

"Right well." Willa's big eyes reflected her gladness. "Jed's worked so hard to make a go of it. Near to a year and a half of panning up in the hills 'fore he had enough to start it."

"I must say, Bitsy seems to be thriving," said Amanda, looking at the small white dog curled contentedly in a wooden box from which the front had been cut away; a faded comforter served as a cushion. Her tail gave several small thumps at the sound of her name.

"Too much," said Willa, her mouth drawing into a half grin. "We hadn't been here two weeks 'fore she had herself in trouble." She pointed out the telltale roundness. "No tellin' what the pups will look like. I never did know who the pa was." The small dog looked at the three of them with an almost guilty look on her face that sent them into peals of laughter.

"Tell me," said Willa finally, smoothing back the straight brown hair from her forehead, "how did you know where to find me?"

"I had Rob ask around," Amanda answered her. "There was so much confusion that last day on the dock . . . We were just cut off from everybody after we left."

Willa nodded. "It was the same with me. I did hear that Ma Abernathy married a man from Sacramento and they left for there that same day. Carrie and her man moved there, too, but not more than two weeks ago. I went to visit her before they left. Hated to see her go. Jed told me her man was all right 'less he got likkered up, and then he could be right mean. Nice enough when I saw him, but you just never know . . ."

"Poor Carrie," said Sable. "I hope things turn out all right for her."

"I do, too," Amanda agreed. "But Carrie might have stayed right at home and been courted for a year or more and still had a chance of being miserable after she married. Sometimes, no matter how much you want it to be right, it just isn't."

Sable watched Amanda nervously rolling a cookie crumb back and forth between her thumb and forefinger, knowing that she was thinking of that first marriage, which by her own admission had been so unhappy—knowing, too, the reason for that unhappiness, a reason that had become once more a constant, gnawing anxiety. *You couldn't expect anything the very first month*, Amanda had said only a few weeks ago, but her eyes had given her away.

"Oh, yes," Willa was saying, her face lighting up. "This news will do you the most good. Widow Parker is married to a Bible-toting man. She must have thought she'd sure enough found the right one to marry. But the joke's on her, 'cause I hear he makes her step about good and proper. Everytime she don't toe the line, he reads that part about a woman being subject to her man, and she has to knuckle under."

"So the tables are turned at last." Amanda chortled shamelessly.

"Good enough for her," Sable agreed. Then, since they were discussing their old shipmates, she told them about her meeting with Flossie, omitting of course, her subsequent quarrel with Lanse.

This started a flood of reminiscences. The afternoon was gone almost before they knew it, and Rob was back for them. They left, promising to get together again very soon.

Sable's heart constricted as she heard Lanse's light tap on her bedroom door. She had taken such pains to look especially nice. Though they had attended many parties, there had been nothing that could equal this. The Firemen's Ball was being looked upon as the most important social event of the year, and she did so want Lanse to be proud of her.

She turned slowly in front of the full-length mirror, trying to see herself as she would appear to him. She was dressed in a magnificent white gown of Chantilly lace, lined with gleaming satin; her hair, piled high atop her head, formed a cascade of curls that reached well below the nape of her neck. She wore no jewelry, not even a necklace, preferring to show off the low-cut, rounded neckline of the dress in all its beautiful simplicity.

She suffered a moment of panic. What if he thinks it's too plain—perhaps a brooch . . . ? There was a second knock at the door, accompanied by Lanse's deep voice speaking her name.

"Come in," she called, carefully keeping her voice level, and then held her breath.

He stepped inside, looking tall and very handsome in black, unrelieved except for the fancily brocaded white vest. He saw her and stood quite still for a moment, his

158

mouth curving slowly into the grin she had come to know so well.

"You're breathtaking," he said, his eyes leaving not the slightest doubt that he meant it. He walked slowly to her and took both her hands in his.

"Like snow and fire . . ." As his eyes moved from the dress to her hair he leaned toward her, a barely perceptible movement, but it sent an unknown, disturbing tremor through her, half-frightening her. She pulled her hands away from his and turned toward her dressing table to hide the confusion.

"I know Melissa put my gloves out." She made a great show of searching, though they were there in plain sight. "Oh, yes, here they are." She pulled on the long white gloves, buttoning the tiny pearl buttons at the wrists.

Lanse opened the cover of his gold pocket watch and glanced at its face. "It's time we were going," he said. "But just let me warn you, madam," he teased, "I intend to keep a sharp eye on you tonight. I just hope I don't have to call anyone out. There won't be a man there can keep his eyes off you."

Lanse had spoken jokingly, but the words turned out to have a certain element of truth in them. The men at the ball, of course, far outnumbered the women. There was no danger of any woman being a wallflower that night, but even so, Sable unmistakably turned every male head.

Only the cream of San Francisco society attended; the Volunteer Firemen's organization was the equivalent of a highly exclusive club. The large hall they had hired for the evening was decorated lavishly with flowers. Pink and white paper streamers, fastened to the center beam along the length of the ceiling, stirred softly in the air currents. One whole end of the building was taken up by a long table loaded down with delicacies of every description: platters of beef, pork and chicken; small bowls of sauce ringed with fat pink shrimp; assorted cheeses and fruits;

pastries and small iced cakes. There were cups of fruit punch for the ladies and stronger drinks for the men.

At the opposite end of the hall, the musicians sat in a small alcove hidden by a curtain of the pink and white streamers, so that the music seemed to float into the room from nowhere.

Lanse danced the first dance with Sable, his arm light about her waist, as though he didn't trust himself to hold her any closer, but even so she felt unnaturally shy with him . . . more so than she had for weeks.

When the music stopped, they were surrounded immediately by a group of eager males. After the introductions were completed, Lanse good-naturedly stepped aside and allowed them a chance to dance with her.

She found the music heady and exhilarating, the admiration in her partners' eyes equally so—partners who changed often, not giving her a chance to catch her breath, whirling her endlessly around with a swish of petticoats, her white satin slippers hardly seeming to touch the floor.

There was one bad moment, while she was dancing with Chris Russell, the very nice older gentleman, a friend of Lanse's, at whose home they had dined only recently. They were close to the sidelines and the words of two men standing there carried a bit farther than they were meant to.

"That's Lanse Wakefield's wife," said one. "Look at him. Never takes his eyes off her."

The other let out a low, suggestive whistle. "Can you blame him? Good God, wouldn't I like to have that tonight!"

Chris Russell danced her quickly out of earshot. "No need to be embarrassed." He gave her hand a small squeeze and there was something of a twinkle in the strong blue eyes. "Those gentlemen were making some very thoughtless remarks, but I'm sure they were meant to be compliments for a very lovely lady."

The old gentleman's graciousness eased her through the uncomfortable moment, but from that time on she was deeply conscious of Lanse's eyes upon her. She saw him dance by with Amanda, who was fetchingly dressed in pale yellow silk, and then again at the punchbowl, another time chatting with Rob, but always his glance came back to rest upon her.

At intermission, he rescued her from her ring of admirers, but they were alone scarcely a moment before Rob and Amanda joined them. The two men left briefly and returned carrying small cakes and cups of punch for them.

"Come on, Lanse." Rob gestured toward the corner where the men were pouring out liquor.

Lanse shook his head. "I've had enough."

"You've had enough, too, Rob Cooper," Amanda said between bites of cake.

"Now, Mandy, honey, I've only had one drink . . . well, maybe two," he said, as she gave him a disbelieving look.

Sam Brannan, the newspaperman, stopped to chat for a moment, his sentences like small explosions, Sable thought.

"Lovely, ladies . . . lovely. You must each save me a dance. No need to protest, gentlemen—I insist." He winked broadly at Sable and Amanda. "Be back later." The peppery editor of the *California Star* pulled at one of his bushy side-whiskers and continued on his way, chewing at the black cigar that jutted at an angle from his lips.

One man, who had obviously made too many trips to the liquor, stumbled and muttered loudly. Lanse stepped in front of Sable, shielding her, while two men took the unsteady fellow by the elbows and eased him toward the door.

Lanse bent down, placing a hand on the back of her chair. "Are you having a good time?"

"Yes." It was a casual question and answer, but his eyes held hers and suddenly she felt quite breathless, as if there weren't enough air in the room. "It's so warm in here," she said, fanning her throat vigorously with her small lace handkerchief.

"Oh? Perhaps we could walk outside."

"No, no. This is fine," she answered quickly—too quickly, she thought, as she saw the sudden look of amusement in his eyes.

The music started and she wished fervently that he would dance with her again, and then in the next instant she was afraid that he would. Her dilemma was solved when Rob asked her. Lanse threw her an amused look, one dark brow quizzically aslant as he led Amanda out onto the smooth wooden floor.

The evening was almost over now, and Lanse had made no further attempt to dance with her. Relieved at first and then piqued, she made a great show of enjoying herself, dancing every number, laughing gaily, even flirting just a little and then glancing in Lanse's direction to see if he noticed.

"Miz Wakefield, I ain't seen the likes of you for many a day." The tall, rawboned youth bowed so low she could see the back of his neck, red and bulging out of the too-tight collar. "I sure enough do thank you, ma'am, for the dance."

"You're most welcome, Mr. Dean." She gave him what she hoped was a dazzling smile, and the young man stumbled over his own feet as he backed away, still looking at her.

The soft strains of music sounded again and instantly there were three others around her, each one insisting that she had promised this dance to him, when she heard Lanse's deep voice at her side.

"Sorry, gentlemen," he drawled. "I'm claiming my wife this time." Was she only imagining the hidden meaning in his words?

She turned to him. He held out his arms and stood waiting, smiling a little as he looked down at her. The hand she held out to him trembled. He swept her onto the dance floor, holding her close to him this time. Sable had a wild feeling that they were dancing not to the beat of the music but to the pounding of her own heart.

The disturbing sensation she had felt earlier in her bedroom, was back—a sweet, wild pulsing that was both frightening and fascinating. She knew from the expression in his eyes that he was aware of it. She couldn't bring herself to look up at him again, but ducked her head low, feeling the rough texture of his wool coat hard against her cheek.

They left immediately afterward and began the ride home, alone and yet not alone, since Rob and Amanda were but a few yards ahead in their carriage. Rob, in excellent spirits, was singing a lively tune at the top of his lungs, pausing only long enough to call back periodic invitations to them to join in.

Then at last, their goodnights over and Rob's voice fading into the distance, they started up the long drive toward the house, the trees casting blue-black shadows before them, the sound of the horse's hooves muffled in the soft gravel of the road.

She had been strangely anxious to say goodnight to Rob and Amanda; yet now, alone with Lanse, she felt uncomfortable, unsure of herself. She sat to one side of the seat, as far away from him as possible, casting about in her mind for something to say—anything to break the silence, anything to deny the existence of this thing that was between them, this feeling that permeated the very air, that drew her to him irresistibly. The best she could do was to remark hesitantly about the brightness of the stars, and even as she said the words she was aware how foolish and contrived they sounded.

He made no answer, but turned and looked at her and the gray eyes said more than any spoken word could have. She looked away in quick confusion.

They were met in front of the house by a sleepy-eyed, yawning Jace, who, impatient to get back to sleep, jumped to the seat as soon as they were down and drove off toward the stables.

The house was unlit save for a single lamp in the downstairs hall. Sable hurried toward the stairs, expecting Lanse to bring the lamp along with him, but he passed it by and she could hear his footsteps following closely behind her in the shadowy darkness. She walked carefully, feeling her way up the stairs and down the hall to her door.

She stood for a moment, motionless, and then turned to face him. Her eyes grown accustomed to the shadows now, she saw clearly the intensity of his gaze, the lean, hard length of his jaw.

"It's . . . it's been a wonderful evening . . . the ball was . . ." She faltered.

He clenched his fists and then opened them again. Suddenly he put his opened palms against the closed door on either side of her. She drew in her breath sharply as he leaned toward her until only inches separated them. His eyes were questioning.

He stood that way for a long, slow minute, waiting for her to speak. When she didn't, he stood straight again and smiled at her . . . a funny one-sided smile.

"Good night," he said, his voice husky and deep. He walked down the hall to his room and entered without looking back.

She went inside her bedroom and stood with her back pressed against the closed door, tears stinging her eyelids. Oh, why . . . why didn't he . . . She had wanted him to, but . . .

She knew what had stopped him. He was waiting for her to speak; he had given his promise that he wouldn't touch her until she asked. She could hear his words clearly even now: *I won't so much as kiss you until you ask me to*, he had said.

At first, that promise had given her a feeling of security, of safety, when she had realized that he would keep his word no matter what. She had thought of the time when she would finally have to be a real wife to him as a distasteful duty that must be faced when she couldn't put him off any longer. But she had reckoned without his charm, his generosity, his gentleness . . . and yes, his patience. Never once during the two months they had been married had he rebuked her for making him wait.

It had taken her a long time to admit to herself how much she missed him when he was gone from the house, how she listened for the sound of Satan's hooves pounding up the drive, listened for Lanse's footsteps in the hall, the sound of his voice. And only now, she admitted that her heart beat a little faster every time he smiled at her, whenever his hand touched hers.

Yes, she gave a soft, bitter laugh, his promise to her had been her security at first . . . but now . . .

My God! It was hard to ask a man a thing like that. What could she say? "I want you to . . ." She stopped, her mind rebelling at the words, her face growing hot in the darkness.

Chapter 14

Sable sat on the ground, her back resting against a smooth, round boulder. Lanse, nearby, lay stretched full-length on the sweet-smelling grass, watching a cloud, a puff of white with pink edges against the hard, bright blueness of the sky. The warmth of the September sun caressed them through the half-shade of nearby trees.

Sable had been the first down to breakfast that morning and had felt somewhat reluctant to see Lanse after their tense parting of last evening. But if she had expected to see a reproach in his eyes she was pleasantly surprised. When he appeared, he was smiling and by all visible signs relaxed.

He had been his most charming self at breakfast. Lingering over coffee, he announced that he felt like taking the day off and suggested a picnic. She agreed eagerly, and he sent Melissa hurrying off to the kitchen to pack a lunch for them.

The site Lanse had chosen was ideal. They were sheltered on three sides by natural outcroppings of rock; a small brook dropped down one stone face, forming a miniature waterfall, and then wound away through the trees.

Sable eyed Lanse furtively, wondering if he were really as placid as he appeared. One fact stood out clearly. He had scrupulously avoided touching her, even to the extent of pretending to adjust Satan's bridle while she dismounted without his assistance.

"What are you thinking about?" she asked him, tracing a line through the grass with her forefinger.

He rolled over on his stomach, his mouth curving into a slow, lazy smile. "I was thinking that a married man shouldn't be taking the day off in the middle of the week to go on a picnic. After all, I've got responsibilities now."

"I'm glad we came."

"I am, too. But seriously, I have been neglecting my business terribly. I'm going to have to make a trip through the mining camps soon; I've put it off too long now."

"Why do you have to go?" she asked.

He shrugged. "Good business. You see, Rob and I have been sending supplies straight to the camps. That saves the miners a long trip to the nearest settlement. It also saves their trade for us. We've been going up every so often to check and see that all the supplies are getting through, what goods are in the greatest demand—things like that. Rob made the last trip four months ago. It wouldn't be fair to ask him to go again."

"No, I suppose not," she agreed, reluctantly. Then her spirits lifted with a new thought. "Can I go with you?"

"Good Lord, no!" he said firmly.

"But, why not?" Sable made her lips into a pout.

"My dear Sable, it's out of the question. The trip is much too rough for a woman."

"I don't see why. I can ride well now—you said so yourself." She forestalled the words of refusal she knew were coming. "And I could stay where you stay—"

"You don't understand, Sable. These men . . . well, they live under pretty difficult conditions. They're not there because they want to be, but because they're obsessed with the idea that tomorrow they'll strike the big money. Some of them have been there for a long time, and they—they miss seeing women." He scratched vigorously behind one ear. "Damn it, you'll just have to take my word for it. It's no place for you."

Sable had seen Lanse set his mouth like that before, and she knew there was no use arguing, but she felt disquieted at the thought of his leaving. "Can't you put it off a little longer . . . please?" she said. Her voice sounded small in her own ears, but she saw the quick response in his eyes.

The hard line of his mouth softened. "Well . . . all right, as long as I can."

Satisfied now, Sable watched him chew thoughtfully on a blade of grass. Satan and Princess grazed peacefully a short distance away, and every now and then Satan would sidle up to the little sorrel mare and nuzzle her gently, then they'd whinny softly to each other.

Lanse flicked the bit of grass away, rolled over and sat up, hugging his knees to his chest. "There is something I want to talk to you about."

Sable braced herself. It's about last night, she thought, carefully keeping her composure, trying to think of the things she'd say . . . the words she'd use . . .

"Are you afraid of Jace?" His question was so abrupt, so different from what she had expected, that she found herself stammering out the truth.

"Yes . . . that is I . . . how did you know?"

"It shows." His voice was quiet. "Now tell me, why does he frighten you?"

"I don't really know." She nervously smoothed her full skirts with her hand. "Maybe because he's the biggest man I ever saw . . . and then, he doesn't act toward me the way he does you and Melissa . . ."

Lanse fought back a grin. "Believe me, Sable, there's nothing for you to be afraid of," he said. "When I do have to make that trip through the camps, I don't want to leave you feeling this way. Why, I don't know anybody I'd trust more than I would Jace. We were raised together —played together as boys. One spring we sneaked off down to the river and went swimming. It was too early in the year. God, that water was cold." He hunched his shoulders, as if he could still feel it. "I got a cramp and would have drowned if Jace hadn't pulled me out. He risked his life to save mine."

Sable looked at him closely. "And you, Lanse—you'd do the same for him, wouldn't you?"

He nodded. "Yes . . . I suppose I would." He plucked at the grass, his face pensive, and slowly stripped one of the tender green blades, peeling the center out to leave the heart white and exposed.

Sable watched him quietly, remembering the things she'd heard her father and his friends say about slavery when they thought she wasn't listening—whispered words about cruel masters and humans treated worse than animals.

"Back home," she said, "I used to hear terrible stories about the South . . . and slaves. Then when the ship stopped in Rio, I saw the start of that auction. It's not always the way it was between you and Jace, is it?"

He was silent for a time, his gray eyes dark as slate. "No," he said slowly, "it's not always that way." Then suddenly defensive: "But the things the Abolitionists make such a big fuss about are more often the exception than the rule. Why, I don't ever remember my father having a slave whipped. He's always been kind to them and seen to it that they were well cared for—better than lots of poor-whites that could call themselves free. Some of our people are the third generation to belong to the Wakefield family. Besides, the whole structure of the South is built on slavery. Take it away and a whole way of life would crumble and fall."

She shook her head, puzzled. "I don't understand," she said. "You told me there would be no slaves in California, and yet, in spite of what you just said, you still plan to make your home here and you've given Melissa and Jace their freedom."

"Sometimes it's hard for me to understand, myself," he conceded. "I'm a Virginian, a Southerner, and that kind of heritage can't be put aside easily, but . . . slavery just doesn't seem to belong here. We're beginning something brand new. There's something about this California." He flung his arms wide to include everything around them. "It puts its own kind of stamp on a man. It takes all the elements that make him and then remolds them . . . and he finds that, whatever he was before, he's now a Californian.

"There's land here, so rich it'll grow anything . . . and trees bigger than any you've ever seen before—so tall that if a man could climb up to the top he could reach right out and grab a piece of the sky." His eyes were seeing faraway things, then he looked at her with awareness once more.

"I'm sorry," he said abruptly. "I guess women aren't interested in such as that." He cocked one eyebrow at her. "Besides," he drawled, "seems to me we've gotten pretty far afield of what we started to talk about."

"You mean Jace," she said reluctantly.

"Yes. You haven't given me any real reason for being afraid of him."

She fidgeted under his steady scrutiny, pulling nervously at the lace edging on her pocket, then looked up in surprise as she heard his soft chuckle.

"It's really pretty funny," he said. "Jace is as nervous around you as you are around him. He almost dies of bashfulness every time you look at him."

She smiled a little. "Melissa told me almost that same thing the first day I came here."

His eyes twinkled. "It's a little unnerving, isn't it—that way she has of reading you like a page in a book."

They laughed together, Sable nodding her head in agreement. "But what ever would I do without her?" she said. "It's funny, Melissa's skin almost blue, it's so dark, but Jace's skin is brown. You'd think a mother and son's coloring would be more alike. He must be like his father—"

"Melissa isn't his mother," Lanse interrupted her.

"But I thought . . . Melissa said that he was her boy. Naturally, I took that to mean that he was her son."

"That is the way she thinks of him. She's taken the place of his mother for so many years now, that I think she's almost forgotten that he wasn't born to her."

"What happened to his real mother?"

"She . . . died."

"How did she die?" she pressed him.

He frowned and shook his head, his eyes gone to slate again. "Let's not go into all that. It's not a very pretty story, and besides, it all happened a long time ago." He stood up.

"It's much too nice a day to spend on such serious subjects. Besides," the grin made his face suddenly boyish, "I'm starving."

Lanse watched while Sable unpacked the lunch from the wicker basket, watched her spread the cloth and set the places, watched how her body moved beneath the pale green fabric of her dress until he had to look away to keep the bright embers of his desire from bursting into new flame.

Then she called him and they laughed together at the sight of the rapidly wilting wildflowers that she had picked from the edge of the stream and stuck into a cup for the center of their "table."

They ate like two healthy young animals, the fresh air whetting their appetites, and Lanse finally leaned back against the tree trunk, ruefully eyeing the partially eaten slice of apple pie on his plate.

"I don't think I can quite make it," he said, rubbing his full middle in contentment.

"You shouldn't have eaten so much chicken," she teased him, kneeling and packing the remains of their meal back into the basket.

"I'll take care of these," he said. He took the two plates to the creek's edge and rinsed them in the shallow, cold water.

When he came back, Sable had the tablecloth spread wide and gave it two quick, strong snaps in the air to rid it of crumbs. He put the plates into the basket.

"Anything else I can do?"

She wrinkled her small, straight nose at him and shook her head. He felt the easiness between them, was glad for it. But behind that easiness, he wondered, how did she feel about last night . . . ?

She folded the cloth neatly and covered the leftover food. "Melissa sent enough to feed an army," she laughed, tucking the heavy cord-bound handles up over the basket. "Let's walk a bit," she suggested, standing again.

"Good idea. I could do with some exercise myself."

After a glance at the peacefully grazing horses, they set off along the path that followed the creek. The branches of the trees interlocked above them to form a thick, green ceiling, making the path deliciously cool. The water sparkled with patches of sunlight and then swirled into blue-green shade with a faint melodic whisper.

"Look," Lanse said softly, pointing to a low branch where a small, drab bird, obviously the female, scolded and chattered at her more colorful mate.

Before them a large fallen tree lay across the path, and dammed the little stream, forming a small pool. Lanse jumped easily across the weather-worn trunk, then turned and held out his hand to Sable. With that one gesture the ease between them vanished. He saw the quick flush of color that touched her cheeks and her hand fluttered to her throat. Then she took his hand and quickly, self-consciously stepped to the top of the log—but slipped in her hurry.

Lanse heard her small gasp of dismay as she fell against him with a flutter of petticoats. He caught her and clutched her almost fiercely to him. They laughed in mutual nervous relief at the near-fall. Then suddenly, abruptly, the smiles faded from their faces as he cradled her.

The color drained slowly from her cheeks and the big muscles of Lanse's thighs tightened and then grew strangely weak; a weakness that spread up the flat, hard length of his belly to his chest and throat, where it became a raw, hot ache.

"Put me down, Lanse," she said and her voice was all queer and trembly.

He held her for a moment more, trying to fathom what was behind the clear, blue depths of her eyes. Then, reluctantly, he set her gently on her feet.

"We've got to talk," he said, his voice almost gruff. He pulled her to the edge of the path and down beside him onto the thick carpet of grass. He turned his face away.

"I promised you I'd wait," he said. ". . . until you were ready . . . and I will, no matter how hard it is . . . but—"

"Lanse . . . I want to tell you—" she interrupted in a small, uncertain voice.

"No, wait! Just let me say what I have to, and then—" He gave a wry grin. "—I'll behave."

He took a deep breath. "When I came down to the docks the day the *Betty Kay* came in, I had no intention of marrying any of the women aboard. I just came along with Rob."

He paused for a moment, trying to find the right words. "Naturally I intended to marry someday, but, as I told you that first night, when I saw you standing there, the sunlight on your hair, I knew you were the one I had to have. You were the most beautiful thing I ever saw . . . and I had to have you the way I had to build Wakefield Manor . . . the way I had to have Satan the first time I saw him." He heard the little catch in her breathing, but went ahead, determined to tell the truth. "I always wanted the best, the most expensive, the most beautiful . . .

"That's why I wanted you at first . . . but now, I want you because . . . because I love you." His voice was low and husky. "I've never said those words to a woman before—I swear it."

She touched his arm. His flesh quivered and he turned quickly to face her.

"Lanse," she said, her red mouth trembling, "I tried to tell you before . . . I'm ready to—" She suddenly leaned against him and buried her face in the hollow of his neck, "—to be a . . . dutiful wife to you."

For a moment he sat quite still, unable to believe that he had heard the muffled words correctly; that the sweet, fragrant softness of her was pressing against his chest. Then his long arms slipped easily around her as they had been aching to do for so long.

"Sweetheart!" His voice made the very word a caress. He put his hand under her chin and brought her face up. His eyes searched hers for a moment, then he brought his mouth down over hers as gently as he could, trying mightily to hold himself in check, remembering only too well what had happened the last time he had kissed her.

For a moment she was passive under his lips, then he felt her arms slide up around his neck. Her mouth came alive under his, moving hotly, passionately, the twin points of her breasts thrusting hard against his chest.

He pulled her back in the sweet-smelling grass and they kissed again, hungrily, endlessly. His fingers fumbled at her bodice and then inside, found her warm, rounded breasts. He heard and felt the small, moaning gasp.

"No . . . please, Lanse . . . not here," her voice trembled. It was such an effort to say the words.

He reluctantly pulled away from her. "Let's go home," he said hoarsely.

"Yes, oh, yes," she breathed, "let's go home."

They rode home silently, communicating with mute, yearning glances. Once Lanse held out his hand across the short distance that separated the two horses; their fingers met for an instant and Sable felt a sudden, sharp tingling that pulsated through her whole body.

They approached the house from the side, and over the low stone wall that surrounded the garden, they could see Manuel weeding the rose beds. Sable caught the flash of white teeth as he straightened to watch them.

No sooner had they rounded the corner of the house, past the clumps of privet, than they saw the two figures on horseback headed up the long drive.

Lanse shaded his eyes. "Looks like Tom Atkins and Chris Russell." He swung off Satan and helped Sable down from her sidesaddle, pulling her against him for one teasing moment.

"Damn," he swore. "What do you suppose they want?" He tucked her arm possessively through his as the two smiling men rode up and dismounted—Tom Atkins with the springy bounce of youth; the older man, Chris Russell, a little more slowly.

"Gentlemen, I believe you've both met my wife," Lanse said.

"Yes, indeed." The older gentleman brushed the shock of gray hair back from his forehead. "I had the honor and the pleasure of a dance at the ball last night." He smiled at Sable.

"Mr. Russell, of course," said Sable, remembering his gallantry with gratitude.

"Tom," Lanse said, turning to the slight, sandy-haired man, "we missed you at the ball. Where were you?"

"In Sacramento," he replied. "Been there since Wednesday. Just got back this morning."

"Gentlemen," Sable interrupted, "I don't know where my manners are. Please come into the house. I'll have Melissa fix something cool to drink." It was the first time that she had assumed the role of mistress of Wakefield Manor. She stole a quick look at Lanse, who was regarding her with warm pleasure.

"Sorry, ma'am," Tom Atkins declined. "We'll take you up on that another time. Right now we want to steal Lanse away from you for a little while."

"Where to, Tom?" Lanse asked.

"Jim Carter's place," Tom answered. "Some of us are holding a meeting there. We'd like you to come. Stopped by Rob's place, but nobody was at home."

"They were planning to go into town to do some shopping," Sable volunteered. "Is . . . is anything wrong?" She asked it hesitantly, not wanting to pry into Lanse's affairs, yet she couldn't help noticing the small, restless motions of Tom Atkins's hands.

"Certainly not!" Russell said. "Just a civic meeting, Mrs. Wakefield. Your husband is one of the leading citizens of the community, and we need his views and advice."

"I'll be with you directly," Lanse said.

"Good day, gentlemen," said Sable. The two men bowed.

Inside the house, Lanse took the hand still tucked through his arm and pulled Sable around to face him.

"I'm sorry, sweetheart," he said. "I'll get back as soon as I can." He leaned down and kissed the tip of her nose. "Did I ever tell you," he murmured, "how fascinating that sprinkle of freckles is?"

"And to think I've been trying to bleach them with buttermilk . . ." she whispered, just before his mouth found hers. Her feet left the floor as his arms tightened about her, but the maddening sweetness was over too soon. He let her go, his breath coming ragged, fast.

"I guess I'd better not do that again . . . not now, anyway." He laughed.

"Hurry back," she whispered.

He nodded, gave her hand a quick squeeze, and was gone.

At first it was hard to concentrate, remembering the touch of Sable's soft body, but Lanse's pulse gradually slowed as he listened to the latest disturbing news about the community.

Shortly after eleven o'clock the previous evening, six to ten men (witnesses differed as to their number) had entered the Golden Horseshoe saloon. They had harassed the patrons for the better part of an hour, allowing no one to leave. Then they had stolen what money was in the cash drawer and as much whiskey as they could carry and had made their departure, leaving behind multiple bruises and one broken jaw.

Some time later, Jackson's Hardware store had been broken into, and though Nate Jackson had been smart enough to take the cash drawer home with him, the place had been turned upside down in a spree of wanton destruction.

Still later, in the small hours of the morning, a Mexican had been attacked and beaten, his house ransacked, his small hoard of gold taken. The man insisted he didn't recognize his assailants. His daughter, who was the only other person living at the house, was missing. It was believed that the marauders had kidnapped the girl, even though her father stubbornly insisted that she had gone to visit relatives. The girl had been seen on the previous evening still at home.

"I tell you, Lanse, the man is scared spitless," Tom Atkins exploded. "Chris and I talked with him not over two hours ago, and from the answers he gives, you'd think he was a blind man. He doesn't know what kind of horses they rode, doesn't know how many men there were or whether they were gringos or Mex. I'll leave it to Chris . . ." He appealed to the older man.

Chris Russell nodded his gray head in agreement. "The man knows more than he's telling. The story about the daughter going to visit relatives is balderdash, of course. They probably threatened him with Lord knows what if he talked."

"What about the witnesses at the saloon?" Lanse asked.

Chris shrugged. "They were all drinking pretty heavily. Each one tells a different story. You know how it is."

"But you think a gang from Sydney Town is responsible for all of it?"

"What do you think?" Tom Atkins asked angrily.

The talk grew even angrier when they arrived at Carter's place. "Sooner or later, we'll have to clean out Sydney Town. I say let's get it over with!" Tom drew himself as tall as his small stature would permit. He gave the oak table a resounding whack to emphasize his words to the dozen grave-faced men. The men had all held key positions in the citizens' group formed the previous year to resist when the Hounds had attempted to take over San Francisco in the absence of any effective, organized law enforcement. The citizens' group was known as the Vigilance Committee, its members, as the Vigilantes.

"Now, Tom," Jim Carter tried to calm the hotheaded young man again. "I didn't call this meeting to form the Vigilantes again. I don't think such drastic measures are warranted—but I do think we should keep a watchful eye on the situation."

"Gentlemen, you're making too much of this." The man who spoke was Luther Simms, a successful merchant. An old accident had left one side of his mouth scarred into a perpetual smile, which lent an incongruous note among the grim visages of his companions.

"Any community has to expect some violence," he said. "This isn't Boston; it's a rough, brawling boomtown. Just because we have a few robberies doesn't mean there's some sinister organization of criminals. A bunch of liquored-up bums hurrahs a saloon—so what? The greaser lost his poke of gold, but he'll get over the bumps and bruises. As for the girl, she may have gone along willingly, and if she didn't"—he shrugged his shoulders—"from what I hear it wouldn't be the first time a man has had her."

There were several nods of agreement, while Lanse eyed Simms coldly. There was something about the man's manner that always irritated him, and this day was no exception.

"What do you think, Lanse?" asked Jim Carter.

Lanse turned to his host and shook his head. "I don't know," he said. "Sydney Town is the root of it all—or at least a big part of it. There's no civil authority capable of handling it. The *alcalde* is all but helpless, and why wouldn't he be? It's like asking the mayor of New York to enforce the laws all by himself—it's impossible. Meanwhile, the Sydney Ducks eventually will force us to take some kind of action."

Lanse's statement was digested in thoughtful silence. "What about you, Chris?" he asked. "What do you think?" Chris Russell was the eldest member of the group, and his words always carried a certain weight. He had proved himself time and again an aware, astute man.

He was silent for a moment, as if conscious of this influence, then spoke: "I feel much as Lanse does. The time may come when we'll have no choice but to take action, but not yet, gentlemen, not yet. With all due respect to you, Tom, I think it would be foolhardy to go storming into Sydney Town. No one can accuse me of being a coward; but on the other hand, I'm not ready to hurry my departure from this world." There was a ripple of laugher through the room.

"Time, gentlemen . . . time is what we need," Chris continued. "The federal government might take steps soon to assist us, as it should. And besides, in the matter of the Regulators last year, the *alcalde* called for help. No one has made that request now."

There was a flurry at the door and Sam Brannan strode briskly into the room, his black eyes flashing with their customary vigor, printer's ink staining his hands.

"Sorry to be late." He threw his hat onto the table. "Heard what you said, Chris. I agree, of course. Meanwhile things go from bad to worse. How much worse? That's the real question." He sank into a chair. "My God, somebody pour me a drink of whiskey. A man needs his whiskey to keep his brains sorted out nowadays . . ."

After Lanse left for the meeting, Sable tried to occupy herself by working on the embroidered pillow cover she was making; the pattern was a large rose worked in satin stitch, in multiple shades of pink and red. But after repeated, unsuccessful efforts to concentrate on the small stitches, she laid it aside and went up to her room.

She leaned back against the closed door. Was it really only last night that she had leaned against this same door and shed such bitter tears?

Her happiness bubbled up and overflowed like a dancing fountain. She whirled around the room, skirts and petticoats flying; kicked first one foot and then the other, sending the small slippers sailing across the room. Breathlessly laughing at her own foolishness, she flung herself onto the wide softness of the bed.

In her mind she heard again and again Lanse's words to her, and she lay with her eyes closed, savoring them, holding them to her.

She didn't hear the horse coming up the drive at first; it was only after the rider was almost to the house that the sound penetrated her consciousness. She sat bolt upright, hoping that it was Lanse, but after listening for a moment, she made a wry face and sank back to the bolster, disappointed. She had come to know, oh so well, the way Lanse gave Satan his head when they reached the drive. They'd thunder up to the house, horse and rider perfectly attuned in a magnificent display.

A few moments later, Melissa's soft knock sounded at the door. "Miz Sable, there's a gentleman waiting downstairs to see you."

"Who is it, Melissa?" Sable asked, sure that Melissa was mistaken and that the gentleman was there to see Lanse.

"I don't know, ma'am. He didn't give me no name."

"All right, Melissa, ask him to wait. I'll be right down." Sable quickly made herself presentable again, running a comb through the mussed hair, retying the ribbon that had loosened, retrieving her slippers, and then, satisfied that her appearance met the requirements of the mistress of Wakefield Manor, she proceeded downstairs.

She felt pleased with herself, relishing the role of mistress of the house, sure that Lanse would approve her receiving the guest in his absence. She paused outside the double doors of the parlor long enough to assume a hospitable smile, then swept into the room.

Her smile became rigid, slowly faded. Her trembling knees refused to hold her erect and she sat down abruptly in the chair nearest to the door.

"You!" She mouthed silently.

Across the room from her, leaning casually against the mantel, Charles Gregg surveyed her with coldly insolent eyes; his mouth was curved into a smile of terrifying assurance.

Chapter 15

"Come now, my dear Sable," Charles Gregg said mockingly, "don't act so surprised to see me. After all, we did have an appointment, didn't we? Though I will admit to being a trifle late." He made a bow of feigned apology. "Forgive me, my dear, I should have addressed you as Mrs. Wakefield, shouldn't I?"

It was her old nightmare all over again, only this time she wouldn't wake from it. The tall, thin figure before her was only too real, and in the instant that she saw him, the happiness and security that she had found seemed to scatter like a handful of sand thrown into the wind.

"How did you find me?" she asked, the thought whirling repeatedly through her numbed mind.

"It wasn't hard . . . in fact rather easy." His manner grew boastful. "Oh, don't worry—it wasn't your precious Dora who gave you away, or that other dolt . . . let's see now, what was his name?"

"Wilfred," Sable supplied dully.

"Oh, yes, that's it. No," he went on, "they could have been blind, dumb, and deaf for all they admitted knowing." He crossed casually to the liquor cabinet and, scanning the supply, selected a bottle of fine old brandy, one of Lanse's favorites. He poured a generous dollop into a glass.

"Yes, it was rather easy," he repeated smugly. "You see, it was largely a process of elimination. I simply ascertained what you couldn't have or hadn't done, and after that it was easy to figure out. I knew approximately when you ran away . . . checked on the ships that had sailed around then, asked a few questions around the docks . . ." He left the sentence in mid-air. "Tell me, Sable, did you really imagine that you could go unnoticed among that cargo of man-hungry, drab old maids?"

She made him no answer, since he didn't seem to expect one, but watched him as he swirled the amber liquid gently in the bottom of the glass, sniffing appreciatively, then sipped it, testing the smoothness on his tongue.

"Excellent brandy," he commented. "Your Mr. Wakefield has very good taste . . ." For a moment his eyes rested suggestively upon her. Then he finished the rest of the drink in one swallow and set the glass down hard on the table.

"Stand up," he ordered. "Let's see if you've changed any in eight months."

Her mind was forming a refusal when she found that she was already standing; the abruptness of his order had caused an unthinking, almost reflex obedience. She watched him warily. The thin nostrils of his high-bridged nose flared slightly, the way she had seen Satan's flare at the nearness of the sorrel mare.

"Yes, you have changed, haven't you?" His eyes continued their inspection. "You're more of a woman . . . less a child. I suppose I have Wakefield to thank for that."

Ever the elegant dresser, he thoughtfully flicked a bit of lint from the sleeve of his obviously expensive, black coat. "You know," he continued, "I underestimated you, Sable. I once said that you'd rather share my bed than put yourself up for sale—which is, of course, exactly what you did." His gesture took in the house and furnishings and waved away her shocked rejoinder.

"Oh, it's perfectly all right. I've never understood some of the foolish ideas men have about women. I'll get just as much pleasure from you as if he hadn't had you first."

Sable gasped in disbelief, and her flaring anger helped to control the unreasonable, almost paralyzing fear she felt. "This has gone far enough," she said. "I think you'd better leave before my husband returns!"

"I'll be happy to leave as soon as you get your things together," he said matter-of-factly. "You won't need to pack much; we'll buy whatever you need." He stopped, anger breaking through the thin veneer of courtesy. "Do take that stricken look from your face—it doesn't become you. You're surely not going to use this so-called 'marriage' as an excuse?" His voice rose slightly. "I doubt very much if it's valid—and even if it is, I can have it annulled easily enough when we get back to New York."

Sable backed toward the door. "Melissa!" she called. The sound echoed back to her, high-pitched, frightened.

The doors swung open almost instantly; Melissa stood glaring at Charles Gregg, her lower lip stuck out in disapproval. It was obvious that she had been standing just on the other side of the doors.

"Melissa." Sable drew herself up to her full height and tried to keep the tremor out of her voice. "Melissa, Mr. Gregg is leaving. Would you show him out, please?"

"Pack Mrs. Wakefield some things," he addressed the Negress curtly. "She's leaving with me at once!"

"No!" Sable was crying a little now. She turned to Melissa in frantic appeal.

"I'll get Jace!" Melissa said, and ran from sight.

"Now look here, Sable." Gregg's voice was harsh. "When I set my mind on something, I get it, one way or another. I've been out considerable money and traveled thousands of miles to find you and take you back with me . . ."

She dashed suddenly toward the door, but his deceptively slim fingers closed around her wrist.

"You're mad!" she cried. Panic rose thickly in her throat.

He stood quite still. His eyes burned suddenly, like a flame bursting in the darkness. She had never noticed the color of his eyes before, but for one brief instant they gleamed yellow-green, like a cat's in the moonlight.

"Perhaps," he said softly, and then his head jerked suddenly at the sound of pounding hoofbeats close to the house, followed by Melissa's alarmed voice. Quick, heavy footsteps sounded at the front door and across the hall.

Sable held her breath for one agonized moment and then Lanse's big frame filled the doorway; behind him stood a scowling, menacing Jace, and beside Jace, Melissa's ebony face glowered beneath the snowy white kerchief.

"I suppose it's safe to assume that you're Wakefield?" Charles Gregg quickly recovered the pose of cool courtesy that he had dropped only moments before.

Sable felt the hold on her wrist loosen and she promptly fled, sobbing openly now, to Lanse. He encircled her with his left arm and drew her protectively to him, while his right hand strayed toward the bulge beneath his coat.

"Sable, what is it? What did this man do?" His voice was gentle as he addressed her, but his granite hard eyes never left Charles Gregg's face.

"I assure you I haven't harmed the lady," Gregg said suavely.

"I asked my wife."

"He was trying to make me leave with him," wept Sable.

"You'd better explain this, sir, and be damned quick about it!" Lanse advanced into the room, Sable still clinging to him.

"I'll be glad to explain, but first, allow me to introduce myself. Charles Gregg, sir—attorney, from New York." He casually plucked a rose from the vase on the table and examined it minutely, twirling the short green stem between his fingers. "I was her father's friend and I've come to take her back home where she belongs."

"No!" Sable wailed.

"It's all right," Lanse assured her. "You're not going anywhere with him. Mr. Gregg"—Lanse's voice took on a fine, thin edge—"my wife belongs right here with me, and that's where she's going to stay. I think we can consider the matter closed."

Gregg crushed the delicate blossom savagely in his clenched palm. One fragile petal fell free and floated to the carpet. "I don't think you understand, Wakefield—Sable and I were to be married. It was her father's wish."

"That's not true! He's lying, Lanse!" Sable cried.

Gregg ignored her outburst. His voice took on a man-to-man tone. "You know how unpredictable a young girl can be. Probably the shock of her father's death was too much for her. I expect that's why she ran off and joined that ridiculous expedition of females. At any rate, no great harm has been done. As an attorney, I'm sure an annulment can be obtained and Keith Flanagan's wishes carried out—"

"Lanse, don't listen to him . . . I tell you he's lying!" For one panicky moment Sable was afraid Gregg would succeed. Then Lanse spoke.

"See here, Gregg!" he said harshly. "I don't know why Sable ran away—I don't have to know, but I do know that we are legally married and we will stay that way. There will be no annulment. And now, Mr. Gregg, I suggest you leave my house at once!"

Gregg shrugged his shoulders in what seemed to be a gesture of defeat. "Very well," he said, "if that's your final word on it . . ."

"It is." Lanse eyed him stonily, while a sudden, inexplicable fear clutched at Sable. She watched Gregg warily. It's too easy, she thought. He wouldn't give up like that . . .

He came across the room and stopped squarely in front of Lanse.

"I'll leave, Wakefield. But I must say I'm somewhat

surprised . . . You don't look like a man who would be content with my leavings." His mouth drew down sharply. He glanced at Sable with contemptuous scorn.

For one shocked moment, her mind refused to comprehend. She saw Lanse's face turn gray-white under the summer tan, then, seemingly without effort, his long arm shot out, his closed fist catching Gregg squarely in the mouth with a sickening thud of knuckles against flesh. The impact sent Gregg reeling against one of the big chairs, his arms outflung; the crushed rose he had held fell in a shower of bruised petals to the carpet.

Before Gregg could disentangle himself from the chair, Lanse heaved him up by the lapels of his coat and slammed him violently against the mantel; a small porcelain figurine tottered and crashed to the hearth.

Gregg stiffened as though to throw off Lanse's restraining hands, but then his eyes flickered warily toward Jace, who had advanced into the room and now stood crouched, leaning forward a little, his fists like two giant hammers.

Lanse, still holding Gregg pinned to the mantel, leaned closer and spoke, slowly, softly, but every word like a pistol shot in the room's dead silence. "If I ever catch you on my property again, I'll have you horsewhipped! If you ever so much as say my wife's name again . . ." His voice dropped even lower. "I'll kill you!"

He shoved Gregg away. "Get out!"

Blood trickled from the corner of Charles Gregg's swollen mouth. His thinning hair, always meticulously combed, hung limp, but his eyes were slits of burning fury in a colorless face. He settled his coat across the shoulders, brushed his shirtfront, and walked from the house without a word.

Sable, cold, shaken, felt a sudden intense need for Lanse's strength. She leaned against him weakly, resting her head against the broad expanse of his chest, speaking his name in a hoarse whisper. Something . . . some almost imperceptible stiffening, made her look wonderingly into his face. Then she saw his eyes.

She drew back from him. Oh, no . . . no! she thought

wildly. He couldn't believe Gregg's lie! From somewhere she heard the sound of a woman's laughter, high-pitched, hysterical.

Lanse grabbed her by the shoulders and shook her, hard. "Stop it!" he said sternly.

"Melissa," he commanded, "take your mistress upstairs and put her to bed." He handed her over to the comforting arms of the old Negress. "I have to go out for a while," he said, his eyes avoiding Sable's.

Lanse studied the glass of whiskey intently, as though in it lay the truth he was both anxious and reluctant to find. It wasn't very good whiskey. It was the best served at the Eureka, but still, not very good whiskey. He drained it at a gulp, choking a little at the raw, harsh taste.

He tipped the bottle and filled the glass to the brim once more. He looked at his hands curiously. Not a tremor. Steady as rocks they were. Not a man in the room could have guessed how drunk he was, except maybe Mac.

The stocky barkeep wiped the top of the bar, worn smooth by countless bottles and glasses, polished by endless elbows. Every now and again he peered over at Lanse with a puzzled look on his beefy face. Mac knew he never drank this much—couldn't fool old Mac.

It was quiet in the Eureka—only a half dozen men were scattered through the room, plus two in the corner who stacked their poker chips neatly and then carefully rearranged them again, all the while peering at the cards in their hands; and one pimply-faced youth who stood at the bar, one heel hooked over the tarnished brass footrest, nursing his drink sullenly.

Outside, the wind blew in sudden gusts and thunder rumbled deeply. A thunderstorm was a most unusual event in San Francisco. There was a general rush for the front, where the men crowded to peer curiously through the small, streaked panes of the one window. Lanse strode as firmly, as steadily across the pitted, scratched wood floor as if he weren't already on his second bottle of whiskey. The two poker players, their cards forgotten for the moment, elbowed to get a better look.

"Nine years it's been," said the one. "Nine years . . . and if that ain't the truth, I'll buy you a bottle o' Red Eye. Had it straight from an old-timer. Why, he come here when this was nothing but a clump of adobe huts." His companion eyed him skeptically and there was a general shaking of heads.

Lanse gave one more restless glance out into the darkness. "To hell with it!" he said finally, and made his way back to his table.

He gulped the fiery liquid once more, gazing at the painting over the bar in its ornately carved, gold-painted frame. Funny, he thought, how much better she looks now than when I first came in. May as well take a good look, by God; it was my money that paid for it. Only way I could get old Mac to part with that mirror.

The nude woman in the painting stretched sensuously on a red velvet couch, her short, plump body arched enticingly, her full, almost pendulous breasts thrust out sharply. There was something vaguely familiar about her.

Lanse studied the dark eyes, the jet black hair, parted in the middle and pulled back tightly over the ears, the nose a little too big but nicely balanced by the wide mouth . . . Damned if it didn't look like Lita, that Mexican whore he'd had once at Lil Carstairs's place. Wonder if Porter got her to pose for it?

He had been playing a game with himself ever since he left the house to ride wildly through the night, finally pulling up, Satan's sides pumping painfully, in front of the Eureka. The trick of the game was to think of anything but what was really on his mind.

The painting blurred a little. His eyes began to play tricks on him; the plump body grew slimmer, the legs longer, the heavy breasts became high and firm. The straight, black hair changed to flaming curls, and where the face of Lita had been, Sable now looked at him with taunting blue eyes, her mouth curved into a provocative smile. He looked quickly away and emptied the glass in front of him in one fast swallow, not even aware of the taste of the liquor anymore.

He swore softly under his breath. What kind of man would say a thing like that about a woman if it weren't true?

Sable stood at her bedroom window and watched the forbidding clouds scudding rapidly across the face of the moon and then piling into one dark thunderhead. The wind had grown stronger now, setting the iridescent chiffon peignoir billowing out behind her. The deep bass of the thunder spoke again, louder, more insistently.

She welcomed the violence of the approaching storm; it matched the violence of her own feelings.

Downstairs, the big clock struck. She counted the chimes . . . ten, eleven . . . twelve. Midnight, and still Lanse hadn't come home. She bit her lip . . . no more tears, she told herself sternly. There had been enough tears earlier.

If only she'd told Lanse about Charles Gregg that first night! Her every instinct had told her to, but she had kept silent. If she had told him everything at first, he would have taken Gregg's vile suggestion for what it was—a last desperate attempt to accomplish his purpose.

Strangely enough, she could think of Gregg now almost dispassionately. She would never be afraid of him again. He had done his worst; now, no matter what happened, he couldn't hurt her more than he had already.

Lightning zigzagged across the sky, for one brief instant etching the clouds in silver. The low, beginning rumble increased in volume, building to a high, discordant crash.

On a sudden impulse she walked silently, her feet bare, across the room to her door. Opening it, she peered cautiously up and down the empty hall, conscious of the near-transparency of the chiffon peignoir and gown. Satisfied that Melissa and Jace were safely asleep in their rooms back of the kitchen downstairs, she ran down the hall and into Lanse's room, leaving the door slightly ajar, fearful that in closing it she might make a noise and wake them.

She looked about her, and realized why she had come. She wanted to feel Lanse's closeness, as she had always felt it in this room. She wanted to feel again that odd force and vitality that seemed to emanate from his belongings.

She reached for his brush, ran her finger over the raised silver "W" on the back, held it the way he must have held it that morning.

She put it back as she spied something on the carpet behind the chair. Melissa must have missed it, she thought, as she picked up the wrinkled shirt. Lanse probably threw it across the back of the chair and then it slipped and fell to the floor. The smells she associated with Lanse still clung to the shirt—a mixture of tobacco and brandy and saddle leather and . . . maleness.

She hugged the crumpled cloth to her, buried her face in it, shocked at the hot, surging tingle that coursed through her body at the touch and smell of his shirt.

Oh, God, she wailed silently, do *decent* women really feel this way? She remembered his kisses and his chest pressing against her while she lay on the grass and then . . . his hand on her breast . . . She gasped at the memory.

His bed loomed large before her and she turned quickly away, ashamed and painfully aware of her body; her breasts thrusting against the thin chiffon, the nipples erect and hot . . .

With a low moan she buried her face in the shirt once more, then suddenly stiffened. She had not been conscious of any sound except the wailing of the wind, the occasional boom of thunder, but somehow she knew . . . she felt his presence. She saw the heavy oak door swing slowly, silently, back on oiled hinges and there in the doorway, as she had known he would be, was Lanse.

She wondered, without really caring, how she had failed to hear him. Perhaps the noise of the storm. But, it didn't matter . . . All that mattered was that he had come home and now she could tell him everything, could make him understand . . .

"Lanse . . ." Her voice broke. "Lanse . . ."

He shut the door behind him and walked to her, his gray eyes smoldering, fastening her to the spot. With a wrenching effort she turned away.

"Lanse," she said. With her back to him, she could speak. "Lanse, you have to believe me . . . Everything that Charles Gregg said was a lie. I swear to you . . . if you'll just listen to me, I'll tell you what really happened." The words tumbled out. "I . . . I should have told you before, I know that now . . ."

He turned her slowly to face him, and she suddenly realized that words were not what he wanted from her. She felt her body tremble and go weak in a strange, female mixture of anticipation and fear. As their eyes met and held, the promise of the storm was fulfilled; the first dashing raindrops pelted, unheeded, through the open window.

Lanse stood back, grasped the filmy top of her nightgown. With one motion, he ripped it from her.

She didn't flinch. In fact, with a gesture to match his own, she let the chiffon peignoir slide off her arms and fall to the floor.

Unhurriedly, his eyes made their inspection. Her hair hung unbound, falling over her shoulders like tongues of flame. His gaze, tangible as hands, moved slowly, hotly down to the two perfect, white mounds of her breasts, the coral-colored, virginal nipples standing out taut and hard; then down to the slim, sweeping line of waist and hip and thigh, unbroken save for the flame-red triangle.

Sable bowed her head, unable to hold the proud pose any longer, fearful that his silence meant displeasure. He cupped his hand beneath her chin and made her face him, his touch setting her to trembling violently.

"Sable," he murmured, his voice filled with incredible longing and need. Her trembling legs refused to hold her any longer and she would have fallen, but now she was in his arms. He lifted her easily and carried her to the bed, where he laid her gently down.

She watched him as he undressed, every gesture, every move. She knew a *decent* woman would have looked away, but she didn't care.

He stood naked now at the bedside, looking down at her, and she returned that look, glorying in the hard leanness of him, the tall, muscular stretch of his body. She looked shamelessly on that man part of him. She had known that a man was different . . . those times when Lanse had held her, pressed close against her, she had felt, through the layers of clothing . . . but she had never known—never really *known* . . .

She shivered, her heart beating as if she'd been running. She held up her arms to him and, with a hoarse cry, he was beside her, his big hands pulling her to him.

"Sable . . . Oh God, Sable . . . I want you . . . I've wanted you for so long . . ."

"Dearest . . . my dearest," she was saying, but it was muffled by his kiss, his mouth so gentle, so tender that she wasn't frightened when his tongue came between her lips, pressed at hers . . . sucked at it. She gave herself over to the urgent need that was coursing through her flesh, a need she did not fully understand yet.

He touched her breasts, caressed them, ran his hands over every part of her. He covered her with the full length of his body, that beautiful man's body, the weight of him exciting in a way she had never dreamed possible. She moaned, wondered why she had ever been afraid.

Even when he moved her legs apart, she didn't resist, caught up in the wonder of his touch. But then, there was a sharp, painful pushing, and she cried out, pulled back.

"No, please . . . it hurts," she said. "Please . . . no . . ."

"I'm sorry . . . sorry," Lanse said, his voice at once tender and harsh with the enormity of his passion.

Instead of drawing back as she had thought he would, he grasped her hips firmly with both hands, and thrust again and again, the pain stabbing deeper and deeper within her . . . stinging, scalding.

"Lanse . . . no . . . please!" She was crying now, crying aloud, but he covered her mouth with his to muffle the sound . . . and no matter how she squirmed, she couldn't get away from him.

But suddenly, surprisingly, even with the hurt, there began a slow, diffused throbbing that grew within her, focused into an astonishing, sweet-hot need. She stopped resisting, started to move against him . . .

And at last when her mouth was free, she said the same word again, "Please . . ." But this time it was a welcome . . . a cry for that hard, thrusting length of him to push deeper . . . deeper . . .

Torrents of rain lashed at the house unnoticed. All she could see or hear or feel was Lanse . . . his face above her in the half-light, intense, almost fierce, his breath exploding with each long, slow movement . . . and through it all, her own whimpering cries of ecstasy.

Chapter 16

Sable awoke without the usual gradual transition from deep slumber to complete wakefulness . . . awoke to absolute contentment, to warm, vibrant happiness, almost unbearable in its intensity.

Her mouth curved softly at the sound of Lanse's deep, rhythmical breathing close to her ear. His arm lay possessively across her, his hand covering one of her breasts.

The air smelled as clean as a freshly sliced lemon after the violent rainfall of the night, and the sunlight spilling through the open window promised another beautiful day.

She knew she should feel strange, or at least shy, at waking to find herself naked, curved comfortably against Lanse's warm contours, but somehow she didn't. She raised her head, looked into his face, and immediately felt a rushing flood of tenderness. His tousled, dark head, the lines of strength and pride now softened by sleep, looked defenseless, somehow.

"Husband . . . my own dearest husband." She formed the words soundlessly. Very carefully, she smoothed the black hair back from his forehead and then traced lightly over his dark brows with the tip of her finger.

Now she knew what it really meant to be wedded—to be husband and wife. A man in a black coat saying words over you was only the first step. Last night was the true union—a woman giving herself to a man completely, holding back nothing, feeling no shame or fear once his hands were on her, welcoming even the first sharp pain and then the urgent, frenzied wanting, building and building to that exquisite final fulfillment.

She pressed her lips ever so lightly against his and then held her breath as he stirred, but the deep, regular breathing reassured her. She wanted his waking to be perfect. She'd go back to her own room and put on her prettiest gown and wrapper . . . and she'd fix her hair. She ran her fingers through the snarled curls. Then she'd go down to the kitchen and get a breakfast tray and a pot of coffee for the two of them. And when she came back, she'd wake him with a kiss—not a whisper of a kiss as she had given him just now, but a real one.

She slid easily out from under his arm, pulled the light blanket carefully back over him. Her nightgown was a complete loss, ripped from neck to hemline, and she knew that the transparent peignoir would do nothing to hide her nakedness. It took her only a moment to decide what to do. She tiptoed across the room and silently eased the washstand drawer open, smiling as she remembered another day when one of these towels had stood her in good stead. Wrapping it around her and securing the ends, she took one last look at Lanse and then quietly left the room.

The soft click of the closing door penetrated Lanse's slumber. Startled, he sat bolt upright, then, seeing the empty room, sank back to the pillow. He, too, for a moment had a feeling of mental well-being, despite the throbbing pain in his head and the soft, furry taste of his mouth —but only for a moment. Then the stunning, painful memory of Charles Gregg's visit came back to him.

He lay staring at the ceiling above him, reliving the whole thing clearly. He remembered leaving the house and riding like a madman until arriving at the Eureka. After that, things began to get hazy.

He narrowed his eyes in concentration . . . remembered beginning his second bottle of whiskey. "Goddamn!" he swore, "now didn't that solve a hell of a lot!" From the feel of his head, he knew he must have put away a good bit of it.

But what then? What happened after that? A fuzzy black curtain hung between him and the events of the night, and he couldn't see past it. He stopped trying. What difference did it make? Nothing mattered except what Gregg had said.

He consciously avoided thinking of the words, but all the time they were there, biting, corrosive. He could demand the truth from her . . . but what if she admitted Gregg wasn't lying?

He tossed the blanket off and swung out of bed, pausing halfway with a groan, then easing the rest of the way in deference to the hot little hammers beating behind his eyes.

He crossed to the curtained closet, took out a pair of trousers and pulled them on. Then, squinting at the bright sunlight, he noticed for the first time the dark half-circle of moisture on the maroon carpet beneath the open window.

The storm— His eyes opened wide. He remembered the storm, remembered the zigzag streaks of lightning, the crash of thunder and then the rain. And through it all ran the memory of a woman's body, soft and warm and tantalizing.

Beads of perspiration formed on his upper lip despite the cool air coming in the open window. Yes, by God! After he left the Eureka, he must have gone to Lil Carstairs's place.

He sank down on the side of the bed. The business with Gregg wasn't bad enough, he had to get himself crazy, blind drunk and then go off whoring last night.

He started at the sound from the next room . . . Sable's

room. He couldn't face her—not now. Not until he found answers for himself.

He finished dressing, hurriedly, carelessly, feeling only the urgent need to get out of the house. He tucked his gun into the snug shoulder holster, buttoned his coat, and strode out the door, passing without a glance the soft heap of iridescent chiffon, lying in mute testimony on the rug.

He paused briefly in front of Sable's closed door, feeling a surge of conflicting emotions. He could hear her humming softly inside. He wavered—but Gregg's words came rushing back to him. No, he swung off down the stairs. Best for both of them if he got away for a while. Think things over without her nearness to cloud his thinking.

"Morning, Mist' Lanse," Melissa called from the bottom of the stairs.

"Good morning, Melissa," he said shortly. "Where's Jace?"

"Still in the kitchen. He ain't finished his breakfast yet. We didn't expect you'd be up this early . . ." she said, puzzled.

"I'm in a hurry," Lanse said, as he hurried toward the back of the house and into the kitchen. He brushed away Jace's greeting with a gesture.

"Saddle up for me, Jace, and step lively. I want to get into town in time to take the ferry for Sacramento."

"For Sacramento, sir?" Jace's fork hung motionless midway between his plate and his mouth.

"Yes . . . business." Lanse was conscious of Melissa's sharp black eyes. "It's been much too long since I visited the mining camps," he continued briskly. "Well, don't just sit there . . . hurry up!"

"Yes, sir. I'll get Satan ready."

"No, not Satan; saddle the bay gelding," Lanse called after Jace's retreating figure. Satan was too flashy—open invitation for a horsethief.

"I'll fix you something to eat, Mist' Lanse." Melissa reached for the big iron skillet.

"No, no, there won't be time for that." Lanse stole a

200

quick look at the door leading to the front of the house. "I want you to give your mistress a message for me—"

"I thought I heard Miz Sable up and stirring . . . I'll go get her."

"No!" Lanse said firmly. "We won't disturb her. You just tell her where I've gone and that I'll be back in about a month . . ." He hesitated. "Tell her she's not to worry—and, Melissa, look after her."

"Of course I will, but Mist' Lanse, don't you want me to pack you some clothes?"

"I'll buy whatever I need in Sacramento."

Down at the stable, Lanse found Jace pulling the cinch tight on the bay gelding. The horse stood placidly, displaying none of Satan's impatient spirit, but Lanse knew that he would be strong and dependable on the rough, rocky trails of the Sierra foothills.

In a nearby stall, the big black stallion whinnied plaintively, as if aware that he was being left behind. Lanse took a piece of sugar from the bag that was always on the shelf and held it out for Satan, then gently scratched the huge black head, murmuring words of comfort.

"He's all ready, Mist' Lanse," Jace called.

"Good." Lanse gave Satan one last pat. "Mr. Rob will be over sometime today. I should have written him a note, but there wasn't time. You explain things. Tell him to take care of business and tell him to see that Mrs. Wakefield has whatever she needs."

Jace nodded his understanding.

"And, Jace, I'm trusting you to protect the mistress while I'm away. I know I can depend on you."

The man's already huge chest swelled out a little more.

"That means no more sneaking off at night until I get back . . . understand?"

Jace's big dark eyes widened. "Do you mean . . . ?"

"You know very well what I mean," said Lanse. "I've known all along about the woman."

Jace hung his head sheepishly, then looked at Lanse and grinned.

Lanse grinned back. He clapped Jace fondly on the

shoulder. "I couldn't leave if I thought that your mistress would ever be left alone without a man to protect her. I don't have to tell you what's going on in this town; you know as well as I do."

Jace lifted his head proudly. "You don't need to worry none, Mist' Lanse. I'll take care of things till you get back."

Lanse tightened his grip on Jace's shoulder, then swung up into the saddle.

The big Negro watched his master ride away. A month was a mighty long time . . . His belly quivered as he thought of the last time he'd gone to his woman, then he turned resolutely toward the house, his shoulders squared with responsibility.

The kitchen door burst open abruptly and Sable ran out, clutching the edges of the blue wrapper close around her.

She stopped as she saw Jace. "Lanse . . . ?"

Jace looked from Sable to Melissa standing in the doorway and then back to Sable again. "Mist' Lanse done gone . . ."

The hope in Sable's eyes faded, and was replaced by a look of hurt disbelief. She turned and walked slowly back to the kitchen door.

"He just didn't want to disturb you, Miz Sable, honey." Melissa patted her arm.

"Yes . . . that's it, of course," she said bleakly. "He didn't want to disturb me."

Chapter 17

The bay gelding picked his way steadily, surefootedly along the rough trail, occasionally sending a small shower of pebbles down the slope, now and again startling a rabbit or ground squirrel into the dense thickets of manzanita.

Though it was early September, the deciduous trees along the riverbottoms looked like giant puffs of colored smoke, red, yellow, bronze, purple . . .

In the two days since Lanse had left Sacramento, he hadn't seen a living soul, and that was the way he wanted it—gave him time to think. Not that he had yet brought himself to face the doubts that created a dull pain somewhere within him, but he was getting closer all the time . . .

He shifted in the saddle, conscious of a stiff soreness in his legs and back. From force of habit he reached for his watch, only to find the pocket empty. Of course, he'd left home in such a hurry he'd forgotten it. But the sun far down in the west told him that he had at best another hour before darkness.

He'd been so certain that he'd reach Red Rock Camp by now. Maybe he'd taken a wrong turn. He would have to

camp out again tonight and then start fresh in the morning.
His mouth pulled down at the corners in a distorted grin.
He didn't particularly relish the idea of another night in
the open, rolled up in the rough woolen blankets that he
had purchased in Sacramento along with the other supplies.

But, Lanse consoled himself, even if he'd made Red
Rock, his lot would have been little better—a hard cot in
some miner's rough shack.

The mining camps weren't designed for comfort or
even permanence. Shelter was thrown together out of
whatever was at hand—usually one-room rough lumber
shacks, the doors and windows covered with canvas. The
men who inhabited them were interested in only one thing
—the gleaming yellow metal. If the diggings started to
peter out, they moved on in search of better pickings.

Oh, what the hell, thought Lanse. It did a man good to
get out and rough it, away from soft beds, soft carpets. His
eyes narrowed . . . and the soft, rounded form of a girl
. . . a girl with blue eyes that crinkled at the corners when
she laughed . . . a girl with hair that turned to fiery copper
when the sunlight was on it.

He groaned inwardly. Why don't you face it, Lanse
Wakefield? You love her, you want her . . . want her more
than you've wanted anything before in your life. You can't
stand to think that that bastard might have been telling
the truth. That's why you ran away like a scared rabbit—
afraid to talk to her, afraid you'd find out it was true.

The dull pain stirred, grew sharper until his eyelids
closed and the muscles along his jawline twitched.

The gelding stumbled and Lanse snapped to full attention once more. "Easy," he soothed, rubbing the warm
neck as the big horse returned to its steady gait.

The air was growing chilly now. The sun had dipped
behind the pine-covered ridge to the west. He knew he
was near Red Rock, for a moment was tempted to go on,
then thought better of it. It was too easy to get lost in the
darkness.

Lanse made camp, and later, sitting on a folded blanket,

the warmth of the fire and the steaming hot coffee stealing through him, he was glad that he hadn't reached the mining camp. If he'd made Red Rock, he'd be circled right now by a ring of bearded, tobacco-chewing men, pathetically eager in their rough way to hear all the news from San Francisco, asking endless questions until far into the night.

There was a contentment here—the campfire throwing a circle of light, and beyond that the darkness of the night full of small scurrying animal noises. Tethered to a nearby tree, the bay gelding whinnied his contentment at finding food and rest after a long, hard day.

But Lanse knew that his own contentment was an illusion. Lansing Wakefield had never run away from anything before, and it rankled to do so now. Besides, with things the way they were in San Francisco, it wasn't exactly the best time to be away. Anything might happen.

The criminal element of the town was growing steadily. Every ship that sailed through the Golden Gate swelled their number. The scum of the earth they were, flocking to the easy money of a town gone crazy with gold fever.

But he could depend on Jace. He knew that. He laughed softly to himself, remembering Jace's look of consternation when he mentioned the woman.

He'd known about it for months. From the very first, when Jace had been missing at night with increasing regularity, Lanse had suspected a woman. After all, Jace was a young and virile man.

Lil Carstairs had confirmed his suspicions—Lil in her white tucked shirtwaist and prim black skirt, looking, except for the slight touch of lip rouge, for all the world like a schoolmarm instead of madam of the fanciest bawdy-house in San Francisco.

"Rose Hampton's having trouble with her main girl, and she's blaming you for it."

"Me?" Lanse had said.

Lil had thrown her dark blond head back and laughed. "You know Rose's place, over on Kearny Street—all high yellows."

Lanse had nodded.

"Well, her main girl—I've seen her. Pretty little thing. Skin like café au lait. She was pulling in men like a honeypot draws ants, so Rose said. Then all of a sudden, she was 'sick' three nights a week. Rose found out that big black rascal from your place was coming through the window those nights—for free, mind you.

"Well, she was gonna let the girl go at first, then when she simmered down she thought better of it. She just looks the other way. The girl keeps happy with that big buck, and Rose's customers are happy the other nights. Must be a lotta man there!" Lil had fingered the prim black velvet bow at her throat and one eyelid had dropped in a naughty wink.

Now, Lanse poked the fire with a slim branch, shook his head, grinned. Who'd ever have thought Jace would be such a hit with the ladies? Of course, it was going to be interesting to see what happened when Tish came.

Jace didn't know about that yet. Lanse had written his family months before, asking that she be sent out if she was willing to come. The answering letter had said that she would arrive around Christmas time, depending on the time it took the ship to make the voyage.

Even before they left Virginia, Jace was beginning to eye the young Negro house girl, who gave every promise of developing into a buxom beauty. The two years they'd been away should have taken care of that nicely.

If Lanse had not been so engrossed in his own musings, he would have noticed the shadowy figure that crept through the brush behind him. In fact, he might have seen Gregg at least a dozen times in the past two days—waiting in the bushes across from the Wakefield Manor drive, later on the ferry to Sacramento, when Gregg had turned a corner and almost walked into Lanse, only to turn away and pretend to talk to a man leaning against the rail while Lanse passed him by without a glance. Charles Gregg was not very adept at following without being seen, but Lanse's perception had been dulled by the warring elements within him.

Gregg had left Wakefield Manor that day hating Wakefield. Lanse stood between him and the woman who had become an obsession with him. Lanse had laid violent hands upon him, and no man had ever done that before. And the one dominant urge running through his twisted thoughts was to destroy Lanse Wakefield.

Only a man's length away now, the red glow of the fire flashed dully along the blade that jutted from his right hand, and all the while Lanse sat motionless, gazing into the dancing flame.

It was not until Gregg's last, exultant lunge that the crackle of dry grass warned Lanse. He threw himself instinctively to the left.

With a searing, white-hot agony, the blade plunged into his right shoulder. Lanse's breath hissed through clenched teeth with a harsh, inhuman sound. He wrenched away and turned to face his assailant. The knife jerked free and a surge of pain nearly caused his legs to buckle.

The two men faced each other for a brief moment. Lanse felt something very close to relief. For the first time in days, his mind was swept clean of shadowy doubts and he realized, with a growing elation, that Gregg was capable of doing or saying anything to get what he wanted—even maligning an innocent girl.

In spite of the pain Lanse laughed, low and deliberate and contemptuous. Then the bloodstained knife slashed toward him again. Too late he remembered the gun in the snug holster beneath his arm, but he caught Gregg's wrist with both his hands. The force of Gregg's attack carried them both to the ground, where they rolled with a wild threshing of arms and legs. The coffee pot was kicked violently into the fire with a hiss of steam. The bay gelding pawed the ground nervously, rolling his eyes in fear, pulling at the rope.

Taller, more muscular of build, Lanse could have easily subdued Charles Gregg under ordinary circumstances. But now, every movement sent a shock of pain through his shoulder, and the fingers of his right hand, grasping Gregg's knife-hand so desperately, grew numb.

Back and forth they rolled, both pairs of eyes fastened to the blade held stalemated between them. Their hands shook with the intensity of effort.

Lanse grew weaker with every passing moment; the bright blood spread across his shirt and dripped down his arm. Now, the knife and death were only a half inch away from his chest and he saw Gregg's thin lips draw back from his teeth in a icy smile of victory. But with a strength born of despair, Lanse gave a sudden heave and Gregg was caught off balance and toppled to his side. Then Lanse saw the sharp rock on the ground beside them and shoved Gregg's hand hard against it.

Gregg cried out with pain, and the knife flew across the clearing, out of reach of both men.

A burning fury filled Lanse, and he struck out at Gregg savagely, again and again, oblivious to the scalding pain that surged through him.

And Gregg with an equal ferocity rained blows upon his injured opponent. They didn't speak a word, but grunted like two hotblooded animals—like two stallions who fought to the death for a mate and for life. And the bay gelding frothed at the mouth and screamed his terror.

The strong, sweet smell of blood was heavy in Lanse's nostrils and, maddened, he brought his knee up hard into his assailant's groin. Despite his weakness, Gregg rolled away, clutching at himself, moaning and cursing in pain.

Lanse knew Gregg would soon finish him unless—the gun, his senses screamed it at him . . . the gun . . . He could feel it, hard beneath his armpit. If only he could get it before . . .

He forced his unwilling fingers to do his bidding. They probed beneath his coat with maddening clumsiness and at last grasped the gun butt only to slide off, slippery with his own blood.

He could hear Gregg stumbling to his feet and even greater frenzy seized him.

"Damn—goddamn!" Lanse croaked, as his fingers slipped again.

Gregg started to laugh and Lanse could hear him scratching through the grass. Then Gregg stood over him, still laughing from deep within his throat, and his eyes were gleaming their odd, yellow-green color.

Gregg dropped to his knees and raised the knife high. It was only then that he saw the gun pointed at him. Lanse discharged it full into his chest. Gregg's eyes opened wide, blinked rapidly while his free hand groped helplessly at the wound. He swayed, righted himself, then pitched forward across Lanse.

The gun slipped slowly from Lanse's bloody fingers, and for a few merciful moments darkness slipped over him, shutting out the sharp smell of gunpowder and the sick-sweet smell of blood. But then the heavy, limp weight pressing across his chest nagged at him, and he fought his way back to consciousness.

He struggled, pushing at the body that had become incredibly heavy, gritting his teeth and straining. At last, the thing that had been Charles Gregg toppled off him.

He lay there for a moment, resting, panting from his efforts. Then slowly, painfully, he dragged himself to his knees. It was then that he heard the horses, nearby and coming closer, crashing through the dry underbrush, pulling up just beyond his camp.

"Hello," a rough male voice called. "What's a going on here?"

Lanse wanted to answer, but it seemed to take all his strength just to stay on his knees.

"Wait a minute," came a second voice. "Wait till I get this here lantern lit." Saddle leather creaked; a moment later a match flared and then sputtered out. "Dammit," the second voice muttered. Again the flame flickered; this time it caught and held.

Three men, one of them holding the lantern up in front, stepped cautiously into the clearing. They wore the rough, sturdy clothing of miners. The one in front was tall and spare, his streaked beard more gray than black. The middle one, who held the lantern, was shorter and heavy-set with a jet-black beard. The third couldn't have been more than sixteen, with only a fine yellow fuzz on his chin.

"God almighty!" the older one breathed as he took in the scene before him.

The bay gelding still trembled, and there was a trace of foam at its mouth. A thin spiral of steam rose slowly from the coffee-stained ashes, and Charles Gregg lay sprawled face down, his arms outstretched. Beside him, Lanse, his clothes bloodstained and torn, his thick shock of dark hair obscuring part of his battered face, swayed weakly on his knees.

"What in tarnation's happened here, mister?" Without waiting for an answer, the older man turned to his companions. "You, boy, fetch me that canteen." He turned to the other. "Best take a look at him, Adam." He jerked his head at the body.

The old man set the lantern on the ground and turned back to Lanse. "Appears like you're in bad shape. Let's take a look." He took out a pocket knife and competently cut the sodden cloth away from the wound in Lanse's shoulder.

"What happened?" he asked again.

"He"— Lanse winced with pain—"he knifed me."

The old man smiled. "Yes, I can see that."

"He jumped me from behind," Lanse gasped. "Would've killed me if I . . . hadn't . . . shot him."

"Likely after gold . . . or your horse and gear. Must have been new out here though, or he'd have thought twice before trying it." The old miner removed Lanse's shirt, draping the coat back around him to keep him warm, and tore what was left of the shirt into strips.

"Time was when a man didn't dare lay down and go to sleep," he went on, "but that's changed some now. Sometimes when there ain't no law, a man's got to make his own. And that's just what we did." He shoved a wad of cloth against the wound, ignoring Lanse's jerk of agony, and bound it with the remaining strips of cloth.

"Nowadays when a man commits a crime, he's tried fair and square by the other men in the camp. And if they find him guilty he's sentenced just like in a legal courtroom . . ."

The one called Adam had rolled Charles Gregg over on his back and now stood looking down at him. "This one's done for," he said.

"Just as well," the old man retorted dryly. "Save us the trouble of hanging him."

The boy came back holding the canteen by the strap. His steps slowed as he passed Gregg and his face blanched at the wide, staring eyes, the bloodstained chest. He held out the canteen with a trembling hand.

The old man pretended not to notice. "Best get one of them blankets, too." The youth fled gratefully.

The old man held the canteen for Lanse, who rinsed his mouth of grit and then drank deeply.

A light of recognition flickered in the old man's eyes as he slowly recapped the canteen. "Wait a minute." He peered closer. "Ain't your name Wakefield?"

Lanse nodded weakly.

"Why sure, I remember you. You stayed two, three days at the camp one time when I was panning up around Dead Dog. Last year it was. Best strike I ever had, too, till she petered out."

The black-bearded man squatted on his heels beside them. "Guess I'd better bury him." He jerked his thumb at the body.

The old man chewed at his tobacco-stained underlip and nodded his agreement. "Yeah, I expect even a thief deserves burying." And then to Lanse, "You know, son, it's a lucky thing we happened along and heard that shot. We was on our way to Red Rock. Ain't more'n three mile from here."

Lanse heard the voice of the garrulous old man but he was watching the lantern, watching the light, first red and then yellow. Then the blackness started at the top and poured down like water until the vivid hues were obliterated and only darkness remained.

Chapter 18

The mournful tolling of a bell shattered the stillness of the night, while Sable raised herself to one elbow and stared, puzzled, at the odd yellow light that filtered through the lace curtains at her window.

Lanse had been gone for two full weeks; that was the way she reckoned time now, counting the days until his return. It was September 17, or at least it would be when morning came. She passed her hand over her eyes, trying to wipe the sleep from her mind.

She and Amanda had spent that day at Willa's house. Bitsy's puppies had arrived two days before; three of them there were, two white ones like Bitsy and the other peppered with black spots. Must be like its father, they all said.

Sable had been fascinated by the mewling, blind little creatures, never having seen anything that young before. And at first, she had been alarmed at their helpless state until Willa assured her that it was quite normal and that in a couple of weeks they'd have their eyes open and be trying their first shaky steps.

Rob had come by for them late in the afternoon, and Willa had insisted that they all stay for supper. Jed, her husband, had to get right back to the hotel afterwards, so they kept Willa company for a while, then Rob and Amanda had driven Sable home.

At Wakefield Manor, the Coopers had made their goodbyes and she had gone to bed almost immediately, feeling an unaccustomed weariness. Melissa had brought her a glass of warm milk which she drank sitting up in bed. Then she must have fallen asleep almost instantly, because that was the last thing she could remember until the steady ringing of the bell roused her.

She was wide awake now, though still puzzled. The peculiar light wasn't the sun, of that much she was sure; no sunrise had ever looked quite like that. There was an eerie, unreal quality about it.

Thoroughly alarmed by now, Sable caught up her robe, ran to the window, and drew the curtains aside. There to the north, toward town, the sky glowed as though from a thousand lanterns.

She couldn't see the front drive from her room, but she heard horses' hooves pounding furiously toward the house. Somewhere below her on the lower floor, Jace's deep voice boomed.

Hastily thrusting her feet into a pair of soft leather slippers, she hurried from the room and started down the stairs. The big front door stood open; outside she could see Jace gesturing toward the light in the sky and still shouting. Melissa came into the main hall from the rear of the house, still tying the ends of her white head kerchief.

"What is it?" Sable almost screamed.

Melissa looked up, startled. "Fire!" she said. "The whole town's burning."

"Oh, no! Willa!" Sable ran down the remaining stairs and out the front door with Melissa right behind her, just in time to see the Coopers' buckboard come to a clattering stop before the house, with a white-faced Amanda clutching the seat.

214

The horses reared; Jace jumped lightly forward, caught the nearest bridle, and quieted them.

"Rob," Sable shouted, with a trace of hysteria, "is the whole town really burning?"

Rob leaped from the buckboard and swung Amanda down to the ground. "No, no, it's not anywhere near that bad," his words were calculatedly calm but his eyes betrayed his anxiety. "Don't worry," he said, "we'll put it out."

Amanda clung to his arm. "What about Willa?"

"I'll try to find out," he said, with a certain male impatience to be gone. He leaned down and kissed her and then gently disengaged her clinging hands. "You'll be all right here. It's far enough away to be safe." He vaulted back to the wooden seat but Jace still blocked his way.

"Should I come to help you, Mist' Rob?" Jace's conflict was written on his face.

"No! I'll feel better if you're here to look after the women."

"Rob!" Amanda's voice was strained, unnaturally high. "Rob—be careful!"

He nodded, grabbed the reins. The buckboard lurched forward, showering gravel to the rear.

Amanda looked scared, Sable thought, for the first time since she had known her. She put her arm around her. "Let's go in," Sable said gently.

"No . . . wait."

So they stood there together and watched until the buckboard turned onto the road that led to town—toward the light, glowing yellow in the sky, that held terror and destruction and death. And for the first time, Sable was glad that Lanse had gone, because she knew nothing she could say would have stopped him from going to the fire, too.

The buckboard disappeared behind the dark line of trees that edged the road. Sable shivered, drew her robe closer at the throat; the air held a chill in it.

"Now," she coaxed Amanda, "let's go in." They turned toward the house. From the corner of her eye, Sable saw

Jace, still looking toward town, and she sensed the strong man's reluctance to be left behind with the women in this time of danger, but then the big man's shoulders squared, and he followed them into the house.

Sable led the way into the sitting room. "We can see toward town from the french doors," she said.

Amanda turned her head to one side, listened. "The bell . . . it's stopped ringing."

"So it has. But where was it coming from?" Sable asked. "We're too far from town to hear the bell from the firehouse."

"Tom Atkins's place," Amanda explained. "It's almost halfway to town and he can hear the firebell from there, then he rings his bell to warn us."

Sable motioned to the tufted velvet couch beside her and Amanda sat down. She was clad only in night clothes, as Sable was.

"Are you cold?" Sable asked her. "I'll have Jace light a fire. It'll take the chill off the room."

"No, I'm all right . . . whatever you want . . ." Amanda's voice was vague, her eyes still fixed on the french doors.

Melissa appeared in the doorway carrying a tray. "You got to keep up your strength," she admonished. She placed the tray on one of the carved mahogany end tables, pulled it closer to the couch. There were thin slices of buttered bread and a small dish of grape jam, and she poured steaming coffee into the two cups.

Amanda shook her head. "I don't want anything."

"Of course you do." Sable took the cup from the Negress's hand. "Melissa's right. It may be a long time. You drink this," she said firmly. Amanda meekly obeyed and Melissa nodded her satisfaction and left the room.

Sable drank her coffee too, grateful for its warmth, but neither of them touched the bread. The china clock on the mantel, its delicate numerals outlined in gold, read four-thirty. The pendulum swung back and forth with maddening regularity, but the slender hands seemed to stand still. And they waited.

The light in the sky grew brighter, more intense, until it glowed saffron like a huge blacksmith's forge. And still they waited . . . waited as women have always waited and will always wait. And the waiting was worse than the going.

Swaying precariously atop the Volunteers' fire wagon, Rob shouted encouragement at the galloping horses and hoped that the frantic, clanging bell would clear the street in time to prevent him running anyone down. People turned to watch as the engine passed, their faces slack and frightened.

Nothing, Rob thought, nothing could rip this town to pieces like the word "fire." Maybe because the towns-people had faced it three times before, and each time they'd known the whole town could go.

Looks to be north of the Plaza, he thought. By now, he could see the yellow flames reaching into the dark, rolling masses of smoke.

The shouts and screams along the milling streets melted together until meaning and words were lost in the cacophony of sound. A wagon, loaded down with furniture, careened crazily toward the fire engine, the driver's mouth working frantically. Rob jerked the reins, narrowly avoided hitting it.

"Look!" Jim Carter pulled his arm as they turned onto Montgomery Street. A line of men passing buckets waved their arms and shouted as Rob pulled up the horses.

The heat seared his face, even though the nearest burning structure was four buildings away, but from there the fire looked solid for at least three blocks north.

The men piled down from the fire wagon. Rob's feet had hardly touched ground when he heard a loud report, then the unmistakable whine of a bullet as it scorched the air past his ear.

The horses reared and Rob dove for the lead mare's head, Jim Carter and Tom Atkins close on his heels as the sound of rapid gunfire burst upon them.

"Must have got to an ammunition box," someone shouted hoarsely.

"Jesus Christ!" another screamed. And the men in the line scattered, ran. Some threw themselves flat down in the dusty street, folded their arms over their heads.

Rob held the horses with his entire weight. He heard a dull whump among the sharp, staccato bursts and the mare moaned softly, shuddered and then went slowly down.

There were a few more scattered shots and it was over. Rob straightened up, looked around him.

"Anybody hurt?" Tom Atkins shouted out. For a moment no one answered.

"Got me in the leg," someone said.

Several of the men went to help. Rob turned to Jim Carter. "Loan me your gun, Jim," he said. And he leaned over the gasping mare and ran his hand gently along the sweat-soaked neck.

"It's all right, girl . . . all right . . ." He held the gun close and fired into her head. She jerked, lay still. He looked down at her, patted the neck once more. "Cut her loose, boys," he said. "Let's get started."

It was well into the morning when Rob turned into the drive at Wakefield Manor and started for the house, astride one of his horses and leading the other. He'd left the buckboard at the edge of town and it had disappeared.

Amanda saw him first and ran outside, followed by the others. Rob pulled the horse to a stop and slid to the ground, swaying a little from weariness. His shirt was gone and his right trouser leg was ripped from knee to ankle. His close-cropped blond hair was scorched and dirty and he was covered with soot from head to toe, his face and chest and back streaked with sweat.

Amanda took it all in at a glance. Laughing and sobbing her relief, she threw herself into his arms.

"Nothin' to cry about, Mandy, honey." He grinned, his

teeth showing white through the grime. "Everything's all right." He patted her shoulder.

"The fire . . . it's out?" Sable asked.

"Yes." He nodded, his voice tired and flat. "It's out."

"What about Willa and Jed?" asked Amanda, brushing the tears from her cheeks.

"They're all right. I went by before I left town. The fire didn't get as far as the house. The hotel was damaged some, but not too bad, from what Jed said. He'd just gotten home when I was there."

"It must have been awful." Sable looked toward the north, where the dark gray haze still hung stubbornly.

"Like the day o' judgment," Melissa chimed in.

Rob drew a deep breath, wiped his mouth. "It was bad . . . though not as bad as some we've had. Hard to reckon the damage yet. I heard some say maybe three million dollars' worth."

They were silent for a moment.

"What about the office?" Amanda asked.

"It's still there. Papers and everything safe. Got one of our warehouses, though, and some of our investment property, but we were lucky at that. The warehouse wasn't more than a quarter filled, and we've still got the land—that's the main thing. We were lucky," he repeated. "Some lost everything they had . . . wiped out . . ."

As he talked, Sable saw the deep lines of exhaustion that etched his face, saw the barely perceptible swaying.

"Goodness," she said. "Here we stand asking you silly questions when what you need is food and rest. Melissa, will you prepare some food, please? Something hot."

"Yes, ma'm." Melissa hurried toward the kitchen.

"You'd better help Mr. Rob upstairs, Jace," Sable directed. "We'll put him in Mr. Lanse's room." Jace gazed at her in sober surprise. It was the first direct order she had ever given him but he hesitated only a moment and then ran to obey.

"I can make it," Rob protested. But as Jace's strong arm slipped around him he accepted the support gratefully. They went up the wide staircase with Jace on one side of Rob and Amanda on the other and Sable following behind.

Upstairs, Sable went ahead of them to open the door of Lanse's room. She crossed to the bed and pulled back the quilted coverlet. Even now, she couldn't enter this room without feeling a momentary surge of bewilderment, a quick, stinging hurt, but she shook it off at once.

"Bring him in," she directed as they reached the doorway.

Rob brushed away the helping hands. "I tell you I don't need any help. Nothing wrong with me that eight hours' sleep won't cure . . ." He saw the snowy linen. "I'll get it all dirty," he mumbled.

"It doesn't matter," Sable said, motioning him on. He lay back, drawing a long sigh as he sank into the deep, soft goose-feather mattress. Amanda started to tug at his boots and Jace dropped to one knee to assist her.

"I'll just close these drapes," Sable said, "then I'll see if I can hurry Melissa along with the food." She swept the heavy maroon velvet across the front window, then did the same at the side. She walked back to the bed, watched them remove the other boot, then glanced at Rob.

"Tell Melissa, never mind," she told Jace, her voice low. "He's asleep already."

Late that evening, the newspaper came out with a full account of the fire, predicting that the property losses might go even higher than three million dollars. It also contained a partial list of the unfortunate victims, and an editorial which praised the valiant bravery of the firefighters.

Rumors flew thick and fast as to the fire's origin. There were those who said it had been set deliberately by the hoodlums of Sydney Town to afford them the opportunity to loot. Preachers walked through the seared streets, preaching as they went, saying the fires were the punishment of a wrathful God on this city of wickedness, this Sodom, and urging repentance before it was too late.

And already the people were cleaning away the debris and starting to rebuild.

Chapter 19

In the noisy interior of the Golden Nugget saloon, a swaggering young man propped his booted feet atop the table, brought the cocked pistol close to his face, squinted along the blue-black length, then slowly squeezed the trigger.

The fly-specked lamp globe shattered, showering glass over the floor, while the fancy girls ran, yelling shrilly, and startled patrons jumped to their feet, chairs overturning. The barkeep advanced upon the young rascal, a threatening look in his eye.

But the center of attention just gave a slow grin and flung a handful of gold on the table before him. "That oughta take care of it . . . and all the rest of 'em, too." He waved a hand toward the remaining lamps cradled in their brass holders around the paneled wall. "This is one day I aim to celebrate!"

"You and me both, friend!" a voice piped from the back of the room. "Shoot the other ones, too," another man joined in. And the barkeep, his eye quickly calculating the worth of the coins on the table, clapped the young man on the shoulder, threw back his head and roared with laughter.

In the assay office, a bearded miner ran one finger, crusty with dirt and tobacco stains, over the black letters of the calendar and read aloud, "October eighteenth, eighteen fifty . . . I ain't never going to forget that date."

"You'll forget it, and quick," the clerk shot back sourly, "if the news ain't true. Rumors trickling overland have been false before."

"Ain't true? Sure it's going to be true," the miner retorted with supreme confidence.

Along the streets, banners and streamers hung from second-story windows, and crudely lettered signs hung across storefronts. The red-and-white barber pole in front of Jansen's gleamed with fresh paint, and the small glass panes of the Eureka window had been washed sparkling clean, the first time in anyone's memory.

The city pulsed with excitement, for after endless months of delay and tempestuous debates in Congress between abolitionist and proslavery factions, each wanting to add California to its own ranks, the vote had finally been cast. The steamer *Oregon* was on its way to San Francisco now, carrying official notification of the result of that vote —California's exclusion from or admission to the union.

The tension built as the hours of waiting continued, and the people of San Francisco kept an eye on Signal Hill, watching for the sign that would mean the *Oregon* had been sighted. Faster ships had brought the news that the *Oregon* would reach the city that day. The city found it galling to realize that they, who were so personally concerned, would be the last to know. Of course, the eastern states had gotten the news almost immediately.

Shopkeepers left their stores, businessmen locked their offices and joined the waiting throng, but the saloons had stayed open and were doing a lively business.

The sun was warm, almost hot, glorious as only an Indian summer day can be, but Sable was beginning to grow a little weary amid the noise and confusion, and suddenly she longed for the quiet, cool garden at Wakefield Manor.

Rob and Amanda had insisted that she come along.

224

"We'll make a day of it," Amanda had said, displaying the wicker basket piled high with food. "You can't miss the biggest news that California ever got," Rob had added.

And so she had come with them, though she was beginning to feel a bit guilty. They spent so much time with her, took her so many places. It was because Lanse was away, she knew, and they hated to leave her alone so much.

Now, they sat waiting in the carriage, the big open one with black leather seats and shining brass-rimmed wheels. The sleek dapple grays wore their best harness, the fine silver trim polished to a deep luster.

The three occupants themselves were dressed as for a most special occasion—Rob in gray linen with gleaming black boots and a black brocaded vest, Amanda's frock in her favorite color of yellow silk, and Sable in green taffeta with a bonnet to match that set her red hair off to perfection.

"There it is!" Rob shouted excitedly, his eyes turned toward the hill where the wooden slats of the signal mill at last proclaimed the approach of the *Oregon*.

A low murmur of sound washed through the crowd as they saw the signal and then the sound subsided and they waited, all eyes turned expectantly toward the sun-drenched stretch of water.

Sable's weariness fell from her and she felt a queer tightening in her throat. For the first time, she realized that this was as vital to her as it was to the rest of the people gathered here. No longer was she just a spectator; this was her home, too.

And then the *Oregon* rounded Clark's Point and came into full view, with flags flying in the wind. There was complete silence for a moment, as all strained to see. Then a deafening cheer arose, for there, at the very top of the mast, a banner streamed out with the wind, and on it were the words, CALIFORNIA ADMITTED, in great, black letters.

Rob whooped, pulled Amanda from the carriage seat, and danced madly around on the grass. All around them people were dancing, singing, shouting, beating each other on the back, shaking hands, and some just jumping up and down.

The two cannon in Portsmouth Square boomed, and then all the ships in the harbor followed with their guns until the echoes filled the air.

Forgotten for the moment, Sable sat quietly in the carriage, smiling a little at the jubilation, but at the same time feeling a sudden hollow regret that Lanse wasn't with her to share this moment. She knew this was what he had waited and longed for, what he had wanted most for this California that he loved so much.

He'd been gone for six weeks. He should have been home by now . . . surely tomorrow . . .

She jumped as a string of firecrackers went off nearby, then felt a tug at her skirt.

"Don't tell me I'll have to set off firecrackers to get your attention," Amanda said, laughing. "I spoke to you twice and you didn't hear me."

"I'm sorry . . . I was thinking of something else."

"We're going to have a party," Amanda went on, her face glowing pink. "Everybody is invited to our house. We'll ask Willa and Jed, Tom Atkins and Chris Russell." She counted them off on lace-gloved fingers. "And you'll stay the night with us," she added, settling it with a nod of her head.

All through the town, similar plans were being made. Impromptu parties and dances were held, groups formed in the streets and marched up and down, singing at the top of their lungs and banging cymbals together, fireworks sounded again and again, and rockets splashed against the night sky, spilling out their brilliant splendor. In the saloons, liquor poured freely and glasses clinked. The celebration continued until dawn.

And, as if this weren't enough to mark the occasion, eleven days later, on October 29, an official Admission Day was held. This time the events were better planned, more organized, but the people entered in with the same high enthusiasm, the same jubilation.

Cannon were fired at dawn to proclaim the start of the celebration. Later in the morning a parade was held, starting with the officials of the city, following them a brass band, and then the fire companies, the engines polished until they appeared to be fashioned of huge red mirrors, each one drawn by four prancing white horses, red plumes bobbing atop their heads.

Rob Cooper, riding in the Montgomery Street engine, leaned far out and waved to Amanda and Sable as they watched from the sidelines.

A company of soldiers, their backs ramrod straight, marched along. And then came the sailors; they were from the *Presidia*, which was anchored in the bay.

A goodly segment of the Chinese population marched in their brocaded silk trousers and high-necked jackets, throwing strings of exploding firecrackers. The proud Spanish *caballeros*, splendid in velvet suits, rode easily by on their beautiful horses.

A group of miners marched also, dressed in sturdy trousers tucked into the tops of rawhide boots, red or blue flannel shirts, and slouch hats that shaded bearded faces. The miners came with no rhythm or order but rather seemed to sprawl along, their high good humor evidenced from time to time by rousing cheers.

Finally, the flag of the Union was carried by, and the crowds reacted wildly, many of them weeping openly.

That afternoon there was speechmaking in the Plaza, and the crowds gathered to listen. Afterward the men collected in the bars and saloons and drank toasts to the new state. "To California! To President Fillmore! To the thirty-first state in the Union!" The streets echoed their cheers.

Several large balls were planned for that night, the most notable one to be given by Chris Russell, but Sable returned home after the parade. She remained adamant in her refusal to attend even though the gallant old gentleman himself called on her that afternoon and asked her to come.

Two weeks later, Sable sat on the silk cushioned stool in front of the dressing table and brushed her red hair. The face that looked back at her from the oval mirror was pale, the eyes touched with faint circles.

If only Lanse would come home. Tears stung her eyelids. Two whole months now. She knew something had happened to him, else he wouldn't stay away this long, no matter how he left.

Even Rob had to admit that it was unusual. Yesterday, he had promised that if Lanse wasn't back within the week he'd go after him, himself.

Her brush stopped in mid-stroke as her stomach sickened. She swallowed hard, twice, before she mastered the hot warning in her throat, then leaned forward against the table, resting her head against her folded arms.

She straightened up quickly and resumed the steady, even brushing as she heard light steps outside the door. The door opened just enough to admit Melissa's white-turbaned head. Her black eyes swept the room; as they came to rest on Sable, a wide grin broke across her face.

"I thought you was still asleep," Melissa said, chuckling.

"No, I've been up for a while."

"I was fixing to sneak in real quiet and gather up your things. Jace is heating the wash water, but I'll go down and get you some breakfast, before I start."

"No, wait." Sable stood up and placed the ivory-handled brush back on the dressing table. "Don't fix anything yet. I think I'll go back to bed for a while." She slipped out of the flowing pink wrapper and climbed into bed, propping the ruffled pillows behind her back, pulling the intricately embroidered top sheet up to her waist.

Melissa watched her, a frown wrinkling her brow. "You ain't sick, is you, honey?" she asked.

"No," Sable lied. "I just didn't sleep very well last night, and I'm still tired."

"Oh." Melissa's forehead smoothed. "Well, I'll just git these clothes and then get out so you can rest."

Sable watched her as she gathered the clothing strewn

around the room and then checked the drawers and the closets to make sure she hadn't missed anything. She was almost to the door when Sable called to her.

"Melissa . . ." The voice held a plaintive note. "Stay and talk to me a little while. Do you have time?"

Melissa put the bundle of clothes down on a chair and came back, smiling, to the bedside. "Of course I do, honey."

Sable patted the sheet beside her and Melissa sat down.

"That Mist' Lanse, he better get himself home, because I thinks Miz Sable's getting mighty lonesome for him." Her deep, throaty laughter filled the room and Sable smiled in spite of herself. "Now," the Negress said, "what do you want to talk about?"

"I don't know . . . anything." Sable shrugged. ". . . I do know, too." It had been in the back of her mind since that last day she and Lanse had spent together, and she had meant to ask Melissa before. "Tell me about Jace's real mother."

Melissa's face sobered suddenly. "How'd you know about that, Miz Sable?"

"Lanse told me."

Melissa shook her head and looked away. "That's a long time ago . . . You don't want to hear about that, honey."

"Yes, I do," Sable insisted stubbornly, but Melissa kept silent, reluctance written across her dark features. "Was she pretty?" Sable prodded.

"Yes, ma'am . . . She was pretty, all right . . . I never will forget the first day I saw her." She spoke slowly at first, spacing her words. "Lena was her name. Mist' Clay, that's Mist' Lanse's papa, had bought a new bunch of field hands. There they was outside of the house, just shuffling their feet and her standing right in the middle of them, tall and quiet-like."

"What are field hands?" Sable interrupted.

"They work in the tobacco fields and such-like. Just the smartest ones get to be house servants," she said with pride.

"Oh . . . all right, go on."

"Well, Miz Susan—that's the mistress—she saw Lena and she knew right off that she wasn't no field hand. 'What's your name, girl?' she asked her. 'Lena, ma'am,' she says. Then Miz Susan ask her some more questions, and sure 'nough she been trained as a house servant. Her old mistress sold her wid dis bunch o' hands 'cause the master been lookin' at her wid hot eyes." The words came faster now as Melissa warmed to the telling.

"Miz Susan, she brought her in the house and put her to work. Mist' Lanse was about two months old and I'd been spending most of my time taking care of him," Melissa explained.

"Everything worked out just fine for a while. Lena, she was a good girl, hard-working. I guess she'd been there about five or six weeks when the trouble first started." Melissa's eyes narrowed, and she seemed almost to forget that Sable was listening.

"He was good at making trouble, that Rath. Mean one. Hot-blooded, too. I guess he'd had most of the girls on the place, because they all afraid of him and scared to say no. Then he saw Lena and he sure took a shine to her, but she wouldn't have nothing to do with him. When he kept on a-pestering her, she come and told Miz Susan and asked her to make him stop. Miz Susan told Mist' Clay and he warned Rath to stop bothering Lena, but I saw Rath's eyes and I knew he just bide his time."

Sable lay quite still, fascinated by the story.

"It was right after that," the Negress went on, "when Mist' Clay's cousin came from Atlanta for a visit. Back home, any kind of visit at all lasts for three or four months," she laughed. "He brought his man along with him, of course. Biggest buck I ever saw. Caesar was his name . . ." She fell silent for a moment.

"Yes, ma'am." She nodded her head. "From the first time they saw each other, everybody knew how it was between Lena and Caesar. They sneaked off every chance they got, so they could be together. And Rath, he just watched them and burned, but he didn't dare do nothing because he was scared of Caesar. He knew Caesar could squash him like a bug if he wanted to.

"Then, after they been there about three months, Mist' Clay's cousin, he took Caesar and left, and that night I heard Lena cry and cry. But the next morning she acted like she forgot all about it.

"We all thought that was the end of it. Then about a month later I saw Lena's belly was starting to swell out, and Miz Susan, she saw it, too, but she didn't say nothing. She just shake her head. Miz Susan always said, 'Melissa, when the milk is spilt there ain't no use a crying over it.'

"That was the winter it was so cold . . . Don't usually get so cold back home. But then, the spring came early, and first thing we knew it was hot summertime again . . . and the tobacco green and growing in the fields and the bees buzzing around the honeysuckle in the garden . . ." She inhaled deeply through her nose as if she could still catch of whiff of its fragrance.

"Over at the Miller plantation, their daughter was getting married, and they gave a big party. All day long it lasted, with cooking outside and dancing that night. Everybody was invited. Even the house Negroes had their place to celebrate.

"Everybody went except Lena. She was big as the side of the house, and that morning she said she didn't feel so good. Miz Susan was going to let me stay with her, but Lena said no, her time wasn't for a couple more weeks yet, and she'd be all right by herself."

Melissa chuckled. "That party sure was something. Everybody laughing and singing and eating fit to bust. And Mist' Lanse, he was just walking and almost ran my legs off getting into everything. He was so excited with the goings on that I couldn't get him to take no nap, and it was plumb dark that evening before I could get him to sleep."

Melissa's face was soft with the memory, but then the smile left her lips, and the lines from nose to mouth deepened. "I just couldn't get Lena out of my mind. I had seen lots of birthings—didn't I help my own Miz Susan with her four? I knew Lena a big, strong girl and I wasn't worried about her having no trouble, but . . . I found Miz Susan with the other ladies and she said I could go along home and see about Lena if I wanted to.

"The moon was big that night, lit up everything like bright daylight. I took a shortcut through the woods and came out at the field back of the house and then past the stone wall by the garden. That's where I first heard her. I hadn't ever heard nothing like it before . . ."

Melissa stared unseeing, her eyes narrowed to glittering slits, and Sable wished fervently that she hadn't insisted upon hearing this story out of the past . . . a story that Lanse had refused to tell her. But it was too late to stop it now. Melissa seemed almost in a trance.

"I ran. Fast as I could go . . . and every step, I could hear her screaming. I had to go through the kitchen to get to her room at the side.

"I pushed open the door and there she was, laying on the bed, her face all twisted and gray, far gone in the birthing. And standing over the bed looking down at her was Rath, his face like the devil's, if the devil got a black face. He'd tied a rope tight around her legs, way up high," she ran her hands along her thighs, "so she couldn't get the baby birthed. And he just laughed while she twisted and screamed something terrible.

"I guess when he saw me he thought everybody'd come back, because he ran right past me and I could hear him going out the back. I tried to get the rope undone but the knot was too tight so I got a knife from the kitchen quick as I could and cut it.

"Pretty soon, that baby was born and I said to myself, ain't no use—that child's dead. So I didn't even fool with it, because Lena was bleeding so bad and I was doing what I could to stop it. Then I saw nothing would stop it. She started to scream at me. 'Take care of my baby . . . See to my baby.' I started working with it just to please her, because I didn't think there was no use at all, but I was wrong. Pretty soon that child started to suck in air like he never going to get enough, and he let out a good yell. Lena, she started smiling and she said, 'Everything be all right now . . .'

"I asked her to tell me what happened. Her voice was getting weaker, almost whispering, so I leaned down real close. She said we wasn't hardly gone that morning before the pains started. But it was going easy with her and she wasn't even scared. Then that devil came . . . that Rath. He told her he was going to make her sorry she thought she too good for him and he said go ahead and scream, because there wasn't nobody to hear her . . .

"She was quiet for a while after that. Then she said, 'Don't you cry, Melissa, because it don't hurt so much no more,' and she put her hand out to the baby and closed her eyes. She never opened them again."

There was a long silence. Sable pressed her trembling palms, clammy and cold, against her face.

"You'd . . . you'd better get to the washing now, Melissa," she choked, but Melissa, still staring at the wall, didn't seem to hear her. She shook her head slowly.

"That Rath, he ran clean off, and nobody ever heard from him again . . ."

Sable knew she'd scream in a minute. "Melissa!" then more softly, "Melissa, you'd better get to your work."

"Oh . . . yes, ma'am . . ." The Negress blinked her eyes, picked up the bundle of clothes, stopping to get a stocking that had fallen to the floor, and left the room, her face thoughtful.

Sable clapped her hand to her mouth. Then, gagging, she frantically pulled the chamber pot from beneath the bed and retched into it miserably. She lay back on the pillow, white-faced and trembling, tears squeezing from beneath her tightly closed lids.

It's not true, she thought, forming the words carefully in her mind. It's not true. I'm not going to have a baby. I'm not. But the picture Melissa had painted so vividly rose before her . . . a picture of a woman crying and twisting in pain.

She sat up and fought down her panic. All I need is a little air, she told herself, then I'll be all right.

She swung her legs over the side of the bed and stood up, weak-kneed and shaking.

"Just a little fresh air," she said aloud. It would be cool outside. There had been a nip of autumn in the air the last few days—not too cold, just right.

She'd ride. Why, it must be over a week since she'd had Princess out. No wonder she hadn't felt well, cooped up in the house and moping.

Sable dressed herself quickly in the beige riding habit, then stood in front of the full-length mirror and set the matching hat jauntily to one side of her head, ignoring the pallor of the face that looked back at her, the lips drained of color.

Halfway down the wide, curving staircase, dizziness overcame her for one awful moment. She clung to the railing, closing her eyes as the steps and hall and ceiling seemed to tilt crazily. Then the vertigo passed and she made her way down the remaining stairs.

Outside, she gulped the cool air hungrily, and walked toward the stable. She could hear Jace calling to Melissa around in back of the house, but she didn't stop. She could saddle Princess herself. She knew she could. She'd seen Jace do it lots of times.

She went straight to Princess's stall, and the little sorrel mare whinnied. "Glad to see me, aren't you, girl?" she said, and Princess agreed by nuzzling her arm playfully.

"All right now, let's get ready." Sable opened the stall door and led the mare out.

The well-trained animal stood patiently as Sable reached for one of the bridles hanging high on the wall. Suddenly her nausea rose sharply once more. She stumbled against one of the smooth, round pillars and clung to it, grateful for anything that felt solid. There was a roaring in her ears, but through the roaring there was a voice speaking to her, and as if in a nightmare she saw a black face above her, all wavy and distorted. Suddenly the dark face that swam above her was Rath and she screamed sharply in terror . . .

Then the voice became words, deep and crooning and gentle. "Now, now, little Missus, everything's going to be all right now . . . I'll get you to the house. It be all right now."

She was lifted and carried, the voice still murmuring words of encouragement, and in that last instant before she lost consciousness, she knew it was Jace. She felt an overwhelming rush of relief, a feeling of complete safety. And she wondered why she had ever been afraid of this huge man with the gentle voice.

Sable pushed the bottle of smelling salts away blindly, choked and coughed. She opened her eyes to find Amanda and Melissa bending over her anxiously.

"What are you doing here?" she asked Amanda, half sitting up. She was back in her own bed, still fully clothed in the beige riding habit.

Amanda pressed her back to the pillow. "You lie back there and rest until we're sure you're all right. Rob and I drove up just in time to see Jace carrying you to the house. My soul, it almost scared me to death!"

Melissa poured water into the white china bowl and wet a washcloth, wringing it almost dry between her strong, dark fingers. "This'll make you feel better, honey," she said, folding the cool cloth across her forehead. A knowing look in her dark eyes left Sable vaguely uncomfortable.

"Rob's gone to town for the doctor," Amanda said.

"I don't need a doctor . . . I'm perfectly all right now." Sable pushed the cloth away. "I just got a little bit dizzy, and then Jace came . . . Where is Jace? I want to see him."

Jace must have been waiting outside in the hall, for Melissa had scarcely spoken his name before he was there, bending his head slightly to walk through the doorway.

"Come closer," Sable commanded, and almost reluctantly, he came and stood at the side of the bed, his huge hands moving restlessly at his sides.

She wanted to explain why she had screamed. "I was awfully sick . . ." she started. "Everything seemed all . . . funny and . . . and twisted . . ."

"Yes ma'm," he said simply, but the brown eyes were filled with such warmth, that more explanation seemed unnecessary. Sable expelled a small breath of relief.

She smiled up at him. "Thank you, Jace," she said. He ducked his head, but couldn't stop the grin that spread across his face.

None of this exchange had been lost upon Melissa, and she, too, was smiling broadly. "You ain't had no breakfast, Miz Sable," she said. "I'm going downstairs and fix you some hot, strong tea. That's what you need right now. Come along, Jace." She gestured with her turbaned head toward the door, and he followed her obediently out.

"Which drawer do you keep your nightgowns in?" Amanda asked. "We'd better get you out of those clothes."

It was almost an hour later when they heard horses out in front. "That'll be Rob with the doctor," said Amanda.

And for the fifth time Sable protested irritably, "I don't need a doctor! I tell you I'm perfectly all right now!"

"Well," soothed Amanda, "now that he's come all the way out here, there's no harm in seeing him."

Downstairs, the big front door opened and closed again; voices sounded in the hall, and a moment later, footsteps on the stairs.

Amanda stepped outside the door to meet the doctor and a short consultation was carried on in hushed tones. Then a man carrying a scuffed black leather bag stepped surely into the room.

"Mrs. Wakefield?"

"Yes."

"I'm Dr. Bush," he stated.

He reminded Sable of Dr. Blair, the *Betty Kay*'s doctor. He had that same air of self-assurance.

"Mrs. Cooper," he called over his shoulder, "I'd like you to be present please. Would you come in? And close the door after you."

He took the chair by the bedside, setting his bag on the floor nearby, while Amanda did as he had asked her and stood unobtrusively near the closed door.

"Now then," he said, placing his fingers on Sable's wrist, his eyes fastened attentively to the face of his pocket watch, "let's just see what the trouble is."

The next few moments seemed like hours to Sable. Dr. Bush continued the somewhat superficial examination, and plied her with questions, delicately worded but pertinent, the answers to which pointed out all the things she had refused to ackowledge. A dull flush crept hotly to her cheeks and she stole a glance at Amanda, whose eyes were wide with delight.

The doctor leaned back in his chair. "I understand Mr. Wakefield is out of town at the present time on business."

"Yes."

"When do you expect him back?"

"I . . . I'm not sure," Sable stammered. "Soon, I hope."

"Hmmm . . ." Dr. Bush's eyes narrowed in thought, his thumbnail tapping absently against his front teeth. "I see no cause, madam, to subject you to . . . a more thorough examination. No reason to suspect complications . . . and with Wakefield away . . . could be deucedly awkward . . ." He seemed almost to be talking to himself for a moment, then: "Mrs. Wakefield, all the indications seem to point to one very simple fact. As you no doubt are already aware, you're going to have a baby."

At the matter-of-fact, dispassionate words, Sable turned her face away, hiding her eyes, not knowing herself what emotions they might betray. Mistaking her reaction completely, the doctor hastened to reassure her.

"There is no real need for alarm about what happened today. These little discomforts you're suffering now are perfectly normal for the first few months, and I'm sure you'll have no trouble carrying the child. However," he said, as he rose from the chair and picked up his bag, "to be sure, I'd suggest you stay in bed for the next few days—possibly a week."

"We'll see that she does, Doctor," Amanda said. Then they were at the door and the doctor said something about leaving powders in case she had trouble sleeping, and Amanda thanked him for making the trip out . . .

Sable was suddenly conscious of the warm, comforting pressure of Amanda's hand on hers. "Amanda," she wailed. "What shall I do?"

"You'll have a beautiful, healthy baby—that's what you'll do," Amanda said calmly.

"But it doesn't seem fair . . . I never thought about having one," she said with painful honesty. "While you . . . you want one so terribly and you've waited so long . . ."

For a moment Amanda's mouth compressed into a hard, straight line, then the pain in her eyes was replaced by reproach. "But you surely didn't think that I'd begrudge you . . . that I'd be jealous of you."

Sable drew a long breath, put her hand across her eyes. "I don't know what I thought . . . I don't even know how I feel about anything . . ."

"What is it? What's the matter?"

"I don't know," Sable said. She was quiet for a moment, then: "My mother died when I was born." She suddenly realized how much those words had been in her mind, pushed far back in the darkness, yet there all the time.

"And . . ." Amanda prompted her.

". . . and I'm afraid," she said defiantly.

To her surprise Amanda just nodded her head and said, "Of course you are. It's a big undertaking to have a baby."

"You mean you would be, too?"

Amanda's brown eyes were very serious. "I'm sure I would . . . a little. Maybe there's always a risk attached to the things that are worth having, I don't know . . ." They were silent for a moment and then Amanda's laugh broke the mood.

"You just haven't had time to get used to the idea yet," she said. "You're a fine, healthy young woman, and you'll probably have a dozen before you're through. Anyway you'll feel better once Lanse gets back home. Wait and see."

"Lanse," Sable said softly. "Do you think he'll be glad?"

"Glad?" Amanda's dark eyes sparkled, "He'll be the proudest man in San Francisco."

Chapter 20

"Lanse!" Rob's elation sounded in his voice as he saw a tall, dark-haired, familiar figure. He ran across the muddy street, deftly side-stepping a team of mules pulling a wagonload of new lumber.

Lanse turned, an answering grin on his face, his hand outstretched.

"Lanse! You old son of a gun!" Rob grabbed the extended hand and wrung it heartily. "You were beginning to worry us there, boy! What in hell took you so long?"

"Missed me, eh?" Lanse laughed and then continued more soberly, "I'll tell you about it later. Right now, I'm anxious to get on home. Everything's all right, isn't it?"

"Everything's fine." Rob was aware that his grin was betraying more than he intended when Lanse peered at him, suddenly suspicious.

"Sable is all right, isn't she? You're positive?"

"I'm positive," Rob assured him, sternly controlling the grin.

"And how's Amanda?" Lanse asked, relaxing.

"Oh, Mandy's fine. She's down at Dartman's right now

buying some new dress goods and things she's been wanting for the house . . . seems like that woman never gets through fixing the house. Say"—Rob put his hands on Lanse's shoulders and took a good look at him—"you look like you've lost some weight. You've been away from home too long."

"Yes—much too long."

In his enthusiasm, Rob missed Lanse's earnestness. "Come on," he urged. "Let's go down here to the Eureka and have a drink to celebrate your homecoming."

"Well," Lanse hesitated, then gave in. "All right, but just one, mind you. Then I'm heading home. I only stopped in town to buy Sable a present—you know how women like things like that." They swung into step beside one another on the rough plank sidewalk.

Rob poked him boyishly with his elbow. "Something tells me that if you just bring yourself home that'll be present enough." He laughed heartily at Lanse's pleasure and embarrassment.

They pushed through the double doors of the Eureka, stepped up to the bar and ordered whiskey.

"You know, of course, about our admission to the union," Rob said.

Lanse nodded. "Man almost rode his horse to death bringing the good news to Red Rock. Damn!" he exploded, "I wish I'd been here."

"Sure was something," Rob agreed. "Whole town turned out, and when the *Oregon* steamed around the bend with that big pennant flying from the mainmast, people went wild, dancing and singing and hollering."

"I can imagine," Lanse said, laughing. "They did some pretty fancy celebrating at the camp, too. Broke out a keg of whiskey they'd been saving for a special occasion. One of the old boys had made it himself." He shuddered, grinning. "Damn stuff so strong it almost ate the enamel right off my teeth. After they all got good and drunk, the miners decided to have a dance. Not a woman within a hundred miles, but some just pinned flour sacks around their middles and took the ladies' parts. You never saw such high stepping in your life."

Rob was convulsed. "And what about you? Did you win yourself a dance with one of the 'pretty ladies'?"

Lanse snorted. "I wasn't away that long." He tossed off the drink.

The tall, lean man standing at the end of the bar finished his beer, pushed the glass away and walked over to them.

"Good day to you, Mr. Cooper . . . and Mr. Wakefield, isn't it? We met once before, sir . . . at a dinner party, I believe. I'm Randolph Bush—Dr. Randolph Bush," he prompted.

"Yes, of course," Lanse said vaguely.

The doctor shifted his scuffed leather bag to his left hand and held out his right. "I'm delighted to see that you're home from your business trip. Women feel more secure at a time like this, when their husbands are with them . . . if I may run the risk of sounding professional." He chuckled, and as Lanse accepted his handshake, said, "Allow me to congratulate you, sir."

Lanse frowned, gave the man a wondering look.

"I think we'd better be going," Rob put in quickly, "Mrs. Cooper is waiting for me."

"Certainly," the doctor said gracefully. "I'm off on a call myself." He turned back to Lanse. "As I told your wife a few days ago, I foresee no complications. Feel free to call on me any time, of course. Good day, gentlemen." He touched the brim of his beaver hat and hurried on his way.

The two men looked at each other, Rob grinning awkwardly, Lanse's dark brows drawn into a straight line.

"What did he mean?" Lanse asked dully.

Rob jerked his head toward the door. "Come on . . . let's get out of here." He stood aside for an incoming patron, then went through the swinging doors. Outside, Lanse took his arm, swung him around.

"Rob . . . what did he mean?"

Rob nervously shoved his hat to the back of his head.

"That jackass would have to let the cat out of the bag. Course," he went on, "he didn't have any idea that you hadn't been home yet. But just the same, Mandy will think I told you. She'll kill me for sure."

"Rob . . ." Lanse's fingers tightened convulsively on his arm. "Rob . . . ?"

"Sure, you lucky rascal!" Rob pounded him jubilantly on the shoulder. "You're going to be a father! But, damn it all, you weren't supposed to find out this way. Now, Lanse," he counseled, "you've got to pretend you don't know anything about it. You know how women are. They like to pick their own time and place to tell a man these things."

His face immobile, Lanse turned without a word and ran almost awkwardly down the street toward his waiting horse.

"Well, I'll be damned!" Rob said, then shrugged his shoulders and chuckled softly to himself.

Lanse threw himself into the saddle and tore off without even an upraised hand, the big bay's hooves throwing mud wildly.

Lanse pulled the sweating animal to a stop, kicked his feet free of the stirrups, and slid to the ground. Forcing himself not to run, he crossed the verandah and entered the house.

As the big door slammed shut behind him he heard a joyful shriek from the stairs. "Praise the good Lord! Mist' Lanse done come home!" Melissa descended the few remaining steps with skirts flying.

"Where's your mistress?" he asked brusquely.

Melissa gestured toward the staircase, too excited to notice his tone. "Miz Sable's in her room. And it's about time you got yourself home here," she scolded, "because that little missus about to worry herself to death. Afraid something had happened to you . . ."

Lanse was already climbing the stairs, the sickness churning inside him as it had on the street with Rob. He had wanted to run then . . . run like a wounded animal to a quiet, dark place. But there could be no running for him now—not now.

How often he had imagined coming home . . . and home had meant Sable. It had kept him alive. During those long, pain-racked days, his body on fire with fever, he had called her name. And when finally he had started to mend, he had counted the minutes, the hours, the days, until he would be strong enough to come back to her. Never in his wildest, most feverish dreams could he have imagined it would be like this . . . his love, his pride, his manhood, bleeding, broken things.

He thrust the door open without knocking, kicked it roughly closed behind him. She was sitting propped up in bed, the plump, beribboned pillows at her back. Her blue eyes opened wide with surprise and for an instant she sat motionless, unable to believe that he really stood before her.

As if to mock him, she had never looked more chaste, more virginal. She was clad in a nightgown of pure white, a gown that covered her modestly to her throat. Her hair was tied demurely back with a white ribbon. And in that instant, as they stared at each other, he felt raw anguish surge within him. Then his pain turned to outraged fury. Somehow anger, no matter how terrible, was easier to bear than the hurt.

Then Sable gave a glad, little cry and was out of the bed and clinging to him, her arms around his neck, her face buried in his shoulder. "Oh, Lanse! My darling! Lanse!" She murmured his name, half laughing, half crying.

Despite everything, desire scorched through him at her touch. He reacted violently, flinging her arms from around his neck.

"You bitch!" he choked. "You filthy little bitch!" And he struck her full across the face with the back of his hand.

The blow slammed her back into the bed, and she crouched there, looking up at him, a remnant of her welcoming smile still on her lips for an instant. Then her face registered horror, and she folded her arms around her middle, by some age-old instinct seeking to protect the child she carried within her slender body.

He snorted. "Don't worry, my dear, they say it's hard to unseat a bastard!"

She stared at him, uncomprehending. "You know about the baby . . . but who . . . ?"

"Yes, I know," he cut her off sharply. "And what does it matter who told me?"

"Lanse . . ." she said, trembling, "I don't understand." Two great tears welled up in her enormous, bewildered eyes.

"God, what an actress you are!" He laughed bitterly. "But then, I've been exposed to that talent before. 'Please, give me a little time,'" he mocked. "You played the innocent-virgin act to the hilt. And all the time you must have been sneaking off to the woods and laying with Gregg."

Lanse's hands clenched and unclenched at his sides. "What happened with him, anyway? Did you decide that you'd made a better deal with me? Did you like the clothes and the big house? Did you like being Mrs. Lansing Wakefield?"

She sat watching him, listening, chalk-white except for the scarlet mark of his hand on her face.

"And then that last day," he sneered, "you said you were ready to be my wife. Were you already pregnant? Did you figure to palm the brat off as mine?"

He stood over her. "It doesn't matter now what your scheme was. I know I can't be the father. I've been taken for the worst kind of fool a man can be. Me! Lanse Wakefield!" He drove his fist violently into his open palm. "You pinned the horns on me, all right. But nobody's going to know it except you and me. You're not going to make me a laughingstock. As far as anybody knows, you're still the respectable Mrs. Wakefield, and you'll go right on playing the part whether you like it or not. And the first time you step out of line, the first time you do

anything that would bring scandal to the Wakefield name
. . . I'll break your goddamned neck.

"And just in case you're worried that your lover will
let the cat out of the bag, don't be. He's dead. I killed
him."

Sable's eyes flashed with new shock.

"Yes," he said, mistaking her reaction. "I killed the
son-of-a-bitch! But maybe it'll be some comfort to you to
know that he did this to me first."

He tore off his coat and shirt, turned his back to her to
show the ridged, angry-looking scar on his right shoulder.
Sable covered her eyes.

He drew his shirt back on and buttoned it slowly, replaced the coat.

The hot violence suddenly drained from him. "There
was a time," he said, his voice tired and flat, "when I
loved you as I never thought it possible to love a woman
. . . but now . . . now I feel nothing but contempt for
you."

He turned away and walked from the room, the taste
in his mouth as bitter as ash. Sable just sat, staring at the
closed door, white-faced, shattered.

The big clock in the hall struck nine before Sable left
the sanctuary of her room the next morning. She had
barred the door last night, and only after Melissa had
knocked repeatedly did she call out that she was tired
and wanted to be left alone.

Now she descended the stairs, head held high, only her
reddened eyes hinting at the long hours of heartbroken
weeping that had finally ended in exhausted slumber.

Lanse stood up from the table, napkin in hand, as she
entered the dining room. "Good morning, my dear."

At his pleasant greeting, her hard-won composure almost slipped. Then she saw Melissa standing nearby and
realized that it was all for her benefit. She got a good grip
on her emotions. "Good morning, Lanse," she said, her
voice firm and level.

"Miz Sable," Melissa said, outraged, "you know you

ain't supposed to be out of that bed yet! That doctor said you ought to stay in bed for a week—and the week ain't up until tomorrow."

"I feel fine, Melissa, really I do," Sable said patiently.

"Of course she's fine," Lanse said. "Come have some breakfast. The sausages are delicious." His face was carefully bland, expressionless, though a very close scrutiny would have revealed a tiny muscle in his jaw that pulsed intermittently.

Sable saw Melissa's eye rest uneasily for a moment on Lanse and then flicker back to her. "About time you ate something. You ain't had a bite since yesterday noon. First thing you knows, you going to be sick," she scolded.

"I am hungry," Sable lied. Lanse pulled out the chair to his right, where Melissa had set a place for her, and stood waiting, a mocking smile on his lips. Sable wanted to scream at him, but she calmly seated herself, shook out the fine white linen napkin and placed it across her lap.

"I'll get the biscuits," Melissa said. And with her exit, Lanse applied himself with vigor to the remaining food on his plate and not by word or gesture or look did he acknowledge Sable's presence in the room.

Melissa came back with the tray of biscuits and then Lanse said, "Thank you, Melissa, that will be all for now." They were alone again . . . alone with that terrible wall of silence that Lanse had put between them.

Sable reached nervously for the platter of eggs and sausages, saw the grease half congealed around the edge, and looked quickly away, feeling the familiar tightening in her stomach, the hot waves pressing upward toward her throat. For a moment she thought she'd have to leave the room, but then the nausea subsided, and she nibbled slowly at a dry biscuit and drank from the glass of milk before her.

Lanse finished his meal without once looking at her, then rose from the table and started for the door. She watched him walk away, and almost before she realized it she was on her feet and running after him.

"Lanse! Please wait . . . I must tell you . . ." At the sound of her voice he turned, but the icy coldness in his eyes froze her to the spot.

"There is nothing you can tell me that I want to hear," he said, and then he was gone.

That was the beginning, then, of their strange relationship. That first breakfast together set the pattern for things to come, except that Sable never repeated her pleading outburst.

In the days after Lanse's return they were flooded with invitations, and Lanse accepted them all, as if to make sure that no one should guess there was anything amiss between them. As long as they were in the presence of others, they were to all outward appearances the devoted young married couple. This was especially true of Lanse. He was thoroughly courteous, even gallant, but with an underlying mockery that only Sable could detect. She could hardly force herself to go along with the deceit, did it only to keep the remnants of her own shattered pride.

Other than these scenes enacted for the benefit of others, Lanse ignored her completely and went out of his way to avoid her. He left for work early and stayed late. And on the evenings when they weren't entertaining or being entertained, he excused himself from the dinner table and went immediately to the study, where he worked on endless stacks of business papers until well after Sable was asleep.

On one of these nights, some weeks after Lance's homecoming, Sable sat alone in front of the big stone fireplace. It had turned colder, and the wind gusted past the windows. Sable stretched her feet out closer to the flames, feeling the warmth penetrate slowly to her toes. A delightful woody smell permeated the room, bringing back memories of cold winter nights spent before the fire with Papa, roasting chestnuts, peeling back the brown, crisp shells while juggling them from one hand to the other because they were still scorching hot, then dipping the meaty kernels into bowls of melted butter, savoring the taste of them in your mouth . . .

She sighed, a quivering, deep-drawn breath, and ran a hand speculatively over her abdomen. Still flat. But of course it would be. Not quite three months yet. When does it first start to show? Maybe she'd ask Amanda.

She jerked her hand almost guiltily away and hurriedly straightened her skirt as she heard Melissa's footsteps behind her.

"Now then," Melissa said, in the hearty tone she always used when she wanted Sable to do something that she suspected Sable would resist. "I thought you'd be getting hungry just about now." And she set the copper tray with its brown earthenware mug and pot filled with warm chocolate on the table by the sofa.

Every night Melissa brought the chocolate and every night she spoke to her as one would address a child, Sable thought. But it was easier to drink it than to argue.

"Thank you, Melissa."

The Negress's face assumed a satisfied expression as Sable raised the mug of chocolate, rich with cream, to her lips. It was another victory in Melissa's battle to keep her mistress "eating for two," as she put it.

She lingered by the table to rearrange a bowl of late-blooming chrysanthemums, and Sable suppressed a smile. She recognized Melissa's action for the ruse it was, an excuse to stay and see that the chocolate was finished. The flowers had been perfect. She herself had taken them from Manuel and arranged them only that afternoon.

The log in the fireplace burned through and shifted, spurting a parade of sparks up the soot-blackened chimney.

"It's getting colder," Sable said, shivering a little at the moaning wind outside.

"Yes, ma'am." Melissa eyed the empty log basket. "I expect I best get some more wood from the pile."

"Let Jace get it."

"Jace ain't here."

"Where is he?" Sable finished her chocolate and replaced the mug on the tray. "Did . . . did Lanse send him out?"

"No, ma'am. He's just out gallivanting about somewhere like he used to before Mist' Lanse went away. Mist' Lanse hadn't been home two days before he was at it again." Melissa's mouth drew down disapprovingly. "I'll get the wood."

"No, don't bother, Melissa. May as well let it die down. I'm going up to bed soon anyway."

"Can I get you anything else, Miz Sable?"

"No, thank you."

The flames grew lower and Sable leaned her head back against the soft tufted velvet of the sofa back, watching the dying firelight flicker against the high ceiling.

"Miz Sable, honey." Melissa's voice was low and rich. "Don't you think you'd best tell him the truth before it's too late?"

Sable started violently, looked into the piercing black eyes. Then she sank back against the cushions of the couch and sighed wearily. "Do you know everything that happens in this house, Melissa?"

"No, ma'am," Melissa answered. "But it ain't very hard to figure out what's going on now. Remember, I heard what that Mist' Gregg said to Mist' Lanse that day. Course I knew right off wasn't a word of truth in that. But there ain't nothing sets a man off like another man hinting he's laid with his woman."

Sable sat silently, biting her under lip, while Melissa spoke out of the shadows.

"Late that night I heard Mist' Lanse come in and go up to his room. It was storming . . ." She waited for a long, slow moment and still Sable sat mute.

"You know," Melissa went on conversationally, "I remember well the first time Mist' Lanse ever got drunk. Fifteen he was. His Pa like to had a fit. Drank a whole bottle of whiskey because one of the Bailer boys dared him to, then him and the boy got into a fight. It took half the hands on the place to separate them. Funny thing was, next day Mist' Lanse couldn't remember a thing about it . . ."

"Stop it, Melissa!" Sable cried. She pressed her finger-tips to throbbing temples. "I don't want to hear it! I don't want to talk about it!"

"Don't be a fool!" Melissa snapped, in a tone Sable was sure she had never dared use before with a white woman. But for that one moment they were no longer servant to mistress, black to white, they were just woman to woman.

Melissa pressed her advantage. "Don't expect him to give in and come to you first. I've been with the Wake-field family most of my life. I helped Mist' Lanse into this world. I love him much as I love Jace, but Mist' Lanse is just like all the other Wakefield men—proud—too proud. Go tell him the truth . . . right now."

"No," Sable said, low but firm. "I . . . I tried to talk to him, but . . . he wouldn't listen."

"Why don't you show him this?" Melissa reached deep into the wide pocket of her apron and drew forth a wisp of gossamer thin material.

Sable's face flamed as she recognized the nightgown, ripped from neckline to hem. Until this moment she had forgotten it completely.

"I found it that morning in Mist' Lanse's room . . ."

"It doesn't make any difference . . . I can't go to him again."

Melissa turned resolutely away. "Then I will. Some-body's got to get things straightened out."

"Melissa!" Sable jumped to her feet, snatched the ma-terial away. "Give that to me! Don't you dare tell Lanse any of this. If you do I'll . . . I'll . . ." Her voice was high-pitched and taut. She saw Melissa's mouth stiffen and then tremble slightly.

Instantly contrite, Sable took the two dark hands be-tween her own. "Forgive me, Melissa," she said, quick tears springing to her eyes, "I didn't mean to speak so harshly—truly I didn't. But I want you to give me your word you won't say anything to Lanse . . . promise me?"

Melissa was quiet for a moment, pity in her eyes, and

then she nodded reluctantly. "All right, Miz Sable, I promise, if you're sure that's what you want."

The two women stood for a moment regarding each other solemnly, then Melissa turned and went from the room, making a soft, clucking noise with her tongue and shaking her head slowly from side to side.

Sable picked up the chiffon nightgown from the arm of the couch where it had fallen, rubbed its softness against her cheek. The tears flowed unheeded down her cheeks as the memories came rushing back . . . memories of Lanse's arms around her and murmured words of love on his lips . . . when she had thought her heart would burst with loving him.

Their union of body and spirit had been fierce and primitive, older than time, yet it had also been hallowed . . . sacred.

But only to me, she thought bitterly, only to me. To him it was just a vague, alcoholic dream.

Lanse had rejected her, shamed her. It was almost unbearable to her. And now, Sable wanted to strike back and hurt him as much as he had hurt her.

If he had ever really loved her, she told herself, he would never have forgotten their night of love, never believed Gregg's awful lie. And as for the Wakefield pride —she was tired of hearing about it. After all, she had pride, too. Never, never, would she go to Lanse and humiliate herself further by begging him to remember that he was the father of her child . . .

The fire was now merely a glowing bed of coals. Sable held the gown above them and let it fall. For a second, the thin chiffon writhed and twisted as if alive, then a flame flashed and it was gone, leaving only a few dark, charred remains to show where it had been.

Chapter 21

"Gentlemen, consider that just a few years ago this was nothing but a sleepy Mexican village—a handful of adobe huts ringed by hills of chaparral and scrub trees and, on the other side, the Bay."

Sam Brannan removed the stub of cigar from his mouth and ground it out in the ashtray before him while the other men around the table looked toward him expectantly.

"Yerba Buena," he said, "the place of the good herb. Rechristened San Francisco on January 23, 1847. But mark you"—he wagged a forefinger—"this is the most important part. In '48, when gold was discovered in California, San Francisco still had no more than eight hundred inhabitants . . . eight hundred," he repeated.

"So what do you have? Magnificent harbor. Key position to act as a gateway to the mines and—boom!" He made a sudden, explosive gesture. "Less than three years later we're trying to deal with a population of at least forty thousand, probably more."

There was a general shaking of heads, a murmur of

conversation around the table. Tom Atkins, impatient as always, jumped to his feet.

"Damn it, Sam," he said, his face gone a dull red, "the reasons don't matter . . . it's the fix we're in, that's what matters." He waved a copy of the *Herald* before them. "It's all right down here in black and white. Ain't a one of us that hasn't fought fire in this town. We've seen what it can do. Yet those Ducks was able to sneak right into the office of the Pacific Mail Steamship Company and set the damned place on fire so they could steal what they wanted. And is anybody arrested, anybody jailed? Hell no! Because there ain't no jails, ain't no government, ain't no damn nothing, if you ask me."

Lanse suppressed a grin as he winked at Rob. Tom reminded Lanse of nothing so much as a Bantam rooster, cocky as all hell and itching for a fight.

"Now, Tom." Chris Russell attempted to smooth the ruffled feathers. "We know how serious this is—that's why we're here. Luckily, no harm was done yesterday. Though the criminals got away, the fire was put out before it could spread."

"Might not be so lucky next time." Tom's tone was still peppery, though he did resume his chair.

Sam Brannan reached over and took the paper from Tom's hand. "The *Herald*," he said. "Damned fine newspaper—even if they are competitors of mine. Guess you've all read this." He ran the tip of his finger down the column, while there was a universal nodding of heads.

"I was particularly interested in this last paragraph." His black eyes snapped from one face to another and then he held the paper closer and read aloud: "We do not advocate the rash and vengeful infliction of summary punishment on any person against whom the proof is not positive . . . but we nevertheless believe that some startling and extraordinary correction is necessary in San Francisco to arrest the alarming increase of crimes against property and life, and to save the remainder of the city from destruction."

"That says it right out plain," Tom said, thumping the table.

Jim Carter, the banker, pulled his spare frame erect. "God almighty, man, be reasonable. How many men do we have here? Fourteen. Fourteen men to clean up San Francisco!" He snorted his derision. "The only thing to do is keep on petitioning the government for help. They can't ignore us now that we're a full-fledged state."

"Like hell, they can't," said Rob Cooper. "They're doin' a pretty good job of it right now. Trouble is, we're so far away."

Lanse nodded his agreement. "Besides," he said, "we're not the only ones in this town that want something done. I know others myself. Maybe fourteen men can't fix things, but two hundred men would be a different story . . ."

It would go on that way far into the night, for the meeting was typical of many Lanse attended in the weeks following his return to San Francisco. The lawlessness seemed, if anything, to have increased. To find a body floating face down in San Francisco Bay was an almost common occurrence, and the numbers of robberies and feared cases of arson were on the rise.

Lanse would have taken an active part in the affairs of the community in any case, but, though he didn't actually admit it to himself, he welcomed the conflict now, welcomed the challenge. Civic affairs took up where his work left off . . . together they allowed him to fall into bed at night so tired that his mind could escape the torment of his thoughts.

As Christmas week approached, the town, like a willful child, changed its violent mood abruptly, relaxed and took on a holiday air.

There were dances and dinner parties, and the Wakefields and the Coopers attended many of them; Lanse and Sable were together much more than they had been at any time since Lanse's homecoming in October. Sable found herself wishing the holidays were over, for the discomforts of early pregnancy were still very much with her. But no matter how ill she felt, she didn't beg to be excused. In her own mind that would have been a defeat.

She dressed in her prettiest and held her head high. She could match Lanse Wakefield party for party—could even match him in the hated playacting he had insisted upon, though God alone knew the effort it required. She much preferred his long hours away from home, his studied indifference. She hated putting on an act of affection for him, because of course, she told herself firmly, any feeling she had ever had for Lanse Wakefield was completely dead. She soon found how wrong she was.

One night, with Christmas less than a week away, she was preparing for bed when a firm knock sounded at the door and she opened it to find Lanse standing there.

Her heart throbbed suddenly, uncontrollably. Deep down inside her, a small, cold deadness stirred, warmed . . . became a singing that filled her. And she stood trembling, waiting for him to hold out his arms. She'd rush into them and all the hurt would be gone and she'd tell him, My darling, I've missed you so . . . I love you so . . .

But he didn't hold out his arms. He just stood there awkwardly. His eyes dropped briefly to her waist and then quickly away.

"I . . . I wonder if I might come in?" he asked, and then with more assurance, "I want to talk to you about something."

The singing died within her, turned to bitterness. She felt her cheeks burn. Had her face given her away? Had he known that she was ready to throw herself into his arms?

She nodded assent, then turned quickly and walked across the room to the washstand, pressed her hands against the cool, pink-veined marble, her back to him, hot waves of humiliation beating against her.

She heard the soft click of the door closing and then the sound of his footsteps as he crossed the room and stopped a few feet away from her. She broke the awkward silence.

"Won't you sit down?" Her voice sounded brittle.

"No. No, I'll just stand . . . I know it's late, so I won't take up much of your time . . ." He waited, as if expecting her to turn around and face him, but she didn't. He cleared his throat nervously. "Had you given any thought to Christmas?"

"Christmas?" she echoed numbly.

"It's only a few days away now. We . . . we'll be expected to have gifts for each other. It wouldn't look right if we didn't."

She was silent.

"I've made arrangements with the merchants. You can go into any of the leading shops. Select whatever you want, and it will be taken care of . . . What I mean to say is, whenever you want anything . . . anything within reason, you're free to do that. That's certainly one of the privileges you're entitled to as my wife."

"I understand," she said stiffly.

"As for the gift, a watch would do fine . . . this one doesn't keep good time anymore. Sheffields's is the best place to go. They have some excellent things . . . In fact, I'll probably select something there for you. Jewelry's always a good choice."

"I'll take care of it tomorrow," she said, her voice carefully level.

There were a few moments of strained, shrieking silence and then: "Sable . . ."

She whirled to face him, her mouth stiff with pain. She could stand no more. "I said I'd take care of it. Now just get out! Get out!"

For a moment Lanse's eyes were unguarded and there was a look in them that she didn't understand, then they veiled over, became deep and opaque. He turned without a word and left the room.

Later that night, Lanse moved restlessly on the rumpled bed. The longed-for sleep had been slow in coming and now it was filled with fitful dreaming.

She stood once more with her back to him, and he was drawn to her, robbed of his will to resist. His fingers groped and found the shimmering mass of hair and underneath her neck shone with a dazzling whiteness. He bent his head and kissed the warm, soft skin, felt his own flesh leap, go hot as his mouth moved down her throat and across her bare shoulders . . .

He jerked awake, groaning, sick with desire. A sharp disgust filled him that he could still want her so terribly —even now, knowing that she carried another man's child.

He sat up, rested his elbows against his knees, his head bent, his fingers thrusting through his hair. He could, he told himself savagely, go in there right now and take her, by force if necessary. But he wouldn't go. There was too much pride in him and too much bitterness.

That pride, that bitterness had come perilously close to melting when he had been in her room earlier. She had looked so defenseless standing there with her back to him. And before she turned away, he had been almost certain that there was hurt in her eyes . . .

Maybe . . . maybe Gregg had forced her . . .

Damn you to hell, Lanse Wakefield, he thought. Now you're snatching at straws. You got just what you deserve. Who in his right mind would marry a woman he didn't even know just because she looked young and helpless and frightened?—and so goddamned beautiful . . .

He stiffened. There had been a sound from her room . . . a sound like muffled sobbing. He strained to hear. But no . . . there was nothing now but silence.

He stood up, pulled one of the pipes from the rack on the table and carefully filled it with tobacco. He lit it, drew the rich smoke deep into his lungs, then settled himself comfortably in the big chair by the bed.

The room was dark but for the periodic glow of his pipe. And then it came again . . . the sound. And this time he was sure of it. She was crying . . . crying for Gregg . . . The bitterness of it slashed him.

It was some moments before he realized that his teeth were clamped so hard around the pipestem it was ready to snap. He took it from his mouth with a muttered oath, then climbed back into bed and lay staring at the ceiling until dawn.

Somehow they both got through the strain of Christmas day. Lanse sported his new watch and Sable dutifully wore the exquisite diamond brooch for the benefit of the inevitable callers.

Melissa scurried back and forth the entire afternoon and evening carrying trays of dark, sliced fruitcake and cups of creamy eggnog, heavily laced with whiskey and dusted lightly with nutmeg.

Amanda Cooper and Willa Mason were the only women guests, but there was a continuous stream of assorted males, many of whom Sable had never seen before. The house resounded with the deep bass of their voices and sudden bursts of laughter.

Sable did her best to play the role of gracious hostess, but by the middle of the evening her head began to ache with the din of voices.

"Are you all right?" Amanda asked anxiously.

"Yes, I'm fine."

"You're white as a sheet. Why don't you lie down and rest for awhile?"

"No, I can't!" Sable answered vehemently, determined not to give in. And then she saw Amanda's questioning eyes and hastily amended her words. "What I mean is . . . it wouldn't look right for the hostess to leave her guests."

"Nonsense," Amanda said firmly. With a wave of her hand she caught Lanse's attention.

"No, please, Amanda," Sable protested, but it was too late.

Lanse excused himself from the group and walked over to them, his dark brows raised.

"Just look at this girl!" Amanda said to him, "she's worn completely out . . . and in her condition, too. I can't do a thing with her. She has some foolish idea that a good hostess doesn't leave her guests even if she faints dead away right in the middle of them." She added scoldingly, "Talk to her!"

Instantly Lanse was all solicitude. "Why, of course it's all right, my dear. You go along and rest and I'll make your excuses for you."

Sable couldn't bring herself to look at him. How could he sound so sincere, so concerned—when she knew that if she looked deep into his eyes she'd find nothing there but icy contempt. Her head throbbed dully, and when she felt Amanda's gentle tug at her arm, she went along without protest.

On New Year's Eve they attended a party at Chris Russell's; on the following day, at Lanse's insistence, they themselves gave an oyster supper. The guest list numbered twenty-four and included, of course, the Coopers, the Masons, Tom Atkins, and Chris Russell. One of the town's leading bankers, Jim Carter, was there, and Sam Brannan, focal point as always with his bombastic speech, and young Will Coleman, who owned the Coleman Building and Contracting Company. Even a visiting senator attended; all in all it was an illustrious gathering.

The evening went smoothly except for one bad moment at the end of the meal, when Chris Russell got to his feet and raised the thin-stemmed crystal glass, glittering with reflected lights.

"Ladies and gentlemen . . ." He paused until all eyes turned his way. "I think a toast is in order. While there has been no official announcement from the parties concerned—" He looked first at Lanse then at Sable, his eyes twinkling mischievously. "—I'm going to take advantage of an old man's privilege and be the first to toast our host, our most charming hostess, and the young heir —or heiress—that's on the way." He raised his full glass higher.

All the guests jumped to their feet, their glasses raised,

calling out their congratulations. Sable's face grew hot with embarrassment. She glanced at Lanse and saw the red creeping slowly up from his collar.

Later that evening, as they were bidding their guests goodnight, Chris patted Lanse fondly on the back. "You're a lucky man, Wakefield!" he said, giving Sable a wink.

"Yes, I am that . . . a lucky man." Only Sable caught the dry irony in Lanse's tone.

The big-boned Negro girl shifted her weight uncomfortably from one foot to the other, as she stood just inside the big front door. She would have felt more comfortable if she'd gone around to the kitchen, but Lanse had told her to come in this way while he went to fetch Jace.

"Tish!" Melissa's glad cry rang out and the girl's lips curved in a wide grin.

"Glory Hallelujah! Tish is done come!" Melissa laughed and gave the girl a hug of welcome. "We've been expecting you for three or four weeks now."

"Lord," Tish said, "I didn't think we'd ever get here. Never seen so much water in my life! If I'd known how long it was going to take and how that old ship would go up and down and up and down, I don't think I'd ever have come."

Their shrill laughter rang out in unison. Then they turned as the double doors opened and Sable came into the hall.

"Miz Sable, this girl, Tish, finally done come—all the way from Virginia." Melissa gave the girl a little push forward. "Tish, this here is the mistress."

The infectious grin split Tish's face, and she bent her long legs in an awkward curtsy. "How'd do, ma'am."

Sable smiled back at her. "We're so glad to have you, Tish," she said. "I hope you'll be happy here with us."

Heavy footsteps sounded outside of the door and Melissa opened it to admit Jace, a scuffed and battered suitcase hoisted to one shoulder.

"Mist' Lanse say he got to get on back to town," he

said, bobbing his head to Sable, then grinning delightedly at Tish.

"Thank you, Jace. I'll leave you and Melissa to get Tish settled."

Several hours later, Sable called, "Come in," in response to the light tap on her door, fully expecting it to be Melissa with the inevitable hot chocolate. But the door opened to reveal Tish looking rested and crisp with a snowy apron tied around her waist and a starched white cap perched atop her head.

"Miz Sable, ma'am, I hope I ain't disturbing you, but this letter's for you." She reached into the apron pocket and pulled out an envelope. "Miz Susan, she says to me, 'Tish, you take good care of this letter, and when you get there you give it to my new daughter-in-law.'"

Sable reached out and took the unexpected communication from Lanse's mother. The outside was somewhat the worse for wear after the months of travel, but the name written across the front in pale violet ink was still quite legible: Mrs. Lansing Wakefield.

"And she said to give you this, too." Once more Tish's hand went into the apron pocket and this time emerged holding a small packet tied securely with blue ribbon.

"Thank you, Tish."

Tish shifted her weight uncomfortably from one foot to the other. "Anything you want me to do before I go, ma'am?"

"Not just now, Tish, thank you."

The young girl left and Sable broke the seal of the letter, then removed the single sheet covered closely with the delicate, slanting script.

My Dear Sable,

It is difficult to know how to begin this letter, since we have never met one another, and yet I feel very close to you somehow. When Lansing wrote to tell us of the marriage, he described you glowingly, and his words added up to a very lovely, well-bred young lady. He is obviously very much in love with you.

Sable stopped for a moment and looked away until the hot swelling in her throat was mastered. Lanse must have written the letter months ago.

They always accused me of being partial to Lansing—and perhaps it's true. He's my youngest, you know, and so like his father. Even as a child he was the image of Clay, not only in looks but in actions. They have the same fierce pride, the same hot temper, but underneath they're really quite vulnerable. But do forgive me for running on so. Suffice to say, since Lansing loves you, that in itself makes you very precious to me, my dear, and I feel that at last I have a daughter. And oh, how I long for a grandchild . . . But perhaps it is tactless of me to speak of that with you and Lansing married less than a year.

I'm sure that Tish has given you the ring already. It is my wedding gift to you. It belonged to my mother and her mother before her, and though I am not a superstitious person, an old slave woman used to say that the ring had magical powers and that the woman who wore it would have a long and happy marriage. It's nonsense, of course, though our marriages have been very happy. But the marriages involved had a far more potent magic to see them through—the magic of deep and abiding love. And that is what I would wish for Lansing and you.

I must face the fact that I am getting older now, and a long and difficult trip to California would be impossible for me. But I cherish the hope that you and Lansing will come home soon for a visit and I will meet you at last. I know he has made a great success there in California, as I knew he would, but don't let him work too hard. Try to persuade him to take some time off and we can have a nice, long visit.

The whole family—George, his wife Anna, and the other boys, Edward and William—send their congratulations. And of course, Clay and I send our very best wishes and our deepest love. I will be looking forward to hearing from you.

Susan Wakefield

At the bottom there was a postscript:

Tish is a good girl. She was born and grew up right here on the place. I'm sure you will be pleased with her.

For a moment Sable just sat with the letter in her hand, then she placed it on the table and opened the ribbon-tied packet. She held the ring before her and involuntarily exclaimed at its beauty.

The stone was a sapphire, brilliantly blue and clear, with great depths of cool, blue flame. The gold setting was severely simple. She slipped it onto her finger, pleased to find it almost a perfect fit.

I must write and thank her at once, she thought, and she pulled the pink satin bell cord. A moment later Tish stood at the door.

"Tish, bring me pen and ink and paper, please. I know we have some downstairs. Ask Melissa."

"Yes, ma'am." Tish sped away as if anxious to prove herself to her new mistress.

Sable paced back and forth impatiently.

What could she write? What could she possibly say to Susan Wakefield besides thank her for this beautiful and unexpected gift? Wouldn't Susan be able to read between her words and guess the truth—that her marriage to Lanse was a mockery?

She stopped abruptly and stood quite still. There had been something—a faint movement deep within her. She waited, close to panic. There! There it was again! Only this time stronger, a firm, definite stirring that sent a shiver of excitement through her. She laughed at her own surprise. Naturally the child would move. It was a living creature . . . though she had never thought of it that way before.

Until now it had been a vague, formless thing that frightened her, that had made her ill in the mornings at first, that would swell her slim body to shapelessness, that one day would be expelled from her body with terrible agony, that would perhaps bring death to her . . . as death had come to her mother. But now these small movements brought it home with awesome force. She was going to have a baby . . . a baby.

She closed her eyes, happiness within her for the first time in months. A baby . . . a part of Lanse and a part of her, growing inside her . . . sheltered, protected inside her . . . tiny hands and feet that could already move. It was a glory and a wonder in her.

Now she knew what to write to Susan Wakefield. She'd tell her of her grandchild. The grandchild she'd prayed for. For it was Susan's grandchild . . . even if Lanse wouldn't acknowledge it.

That evening Lanse came home unexpectedly early and made a smiling, hearty entry into the dining room. They always used the formal dining room now, never the small intimate sitting room.

He was acting for Tish's benefit, Sable thought grimly. By now she was almost inured to it. And sure enough, as soon as they were alone the expected stony silence began.

But suddenly, Lanse's fork dropped with a clatter to the table and Sable looked up in astonishment to find him staring at the ring on her right hand.

"Where did you get that ring?" he demanded.

His vehemence frightened her a little but she forced herself to sip a few drops of wine before she answered him.

"It's a present from your mother. A wedding present," she retorted calmly.

"But how . . . when . . . ?"

"Tish brought it." Sable laughed shortly, bitterly. "She wanted me to have it because there's some kind of legend about it. It's supposed to have magical powers. Brings undying love to a marriage." She gulped more wine to keep her mouth from trembling.

"I know all about that ring," he snapped. "I've seen it on my mother's finger since I was a child." He toyed a moment with the food on his plate.

"She wrote to you?" he asked suspiciously.

"Yes."

The tall white candles between them flickered, and the sapphire caught their dancing light, transformed it into tongues of ice-blue flame.

"I suppose you'll write to thank her," he said, trying to sound casual.

"I already have."

The pulse at his temple throbbed. "What did you say to her? If you—"

"I told her the truth," she interrupted.

"Damn you to hell!" His hand shot out and closed over her wrist in a grip that made her wince. "You won't tell my mother anything that will hurt her, do you understand? Besides, I told you before if you ever let anybody know the truth, I'll break your goddamned neck . . . Understand?"

Despite the pain of his bruising fingers, Sable looked straight into his eyes and faced his rage calmly. "I don't want to hurt your mother any more than you do. She'll never find out from me what our marriage has become. I give you my word that the truth I told her will only bring her happiness."

He looked at her a long, slow moment as though trying to fathom the puzzle of her words. Then he dropped her wrist, as if it had burned him. He shoved his chair violently back, stood up, and strode from the room.

Chapter 22

Sable and Amanda stopped short just inside the door of Willa and Jed's neat white-washed cottage, blocking the door completely for Rob and Lanse, who stood on the porch behind them.

"Carrie!" Amanda cried.

"Carrie Thorne!" Sable echoed, and held out her hands to the smiling girl. "It's so good to see . . ." Her voice faltered as she saw the ugly purple bruise on Carrie's freckled cheek. ". . . so good to see you," she finished, after exchanging a quick glance with Amanda.

"When did you get here? We heard you were living in Sacramento. Willa told us," Amanda said.

"Yesterday," said Carrie, flushing a little and gripping Sable's two hands tightly. "On the afternoon ferry."

"So that's what Willa meant when she said she had a surprise for us and we were all to come here for dinner tonight." Sable looked around the room. "Where is Willa?"

"Oh, she'll be right in." Carrie let go of Sable's hands, looked awkwardly from one to the other of them and sighed . . . a long, defeated sound.

"Ain't no use pretending you don't see it."

"Your husband?" Amanda asked hesitantly.

"Yes." The answer was low but Carrie held herself with quiet dignity. "There's more where they don't show."

The two men had stood, forgotten, at the open doorway until Rob's voice crackled across the room.

"Dirty bastard!" he said, very distinctly. And then as the women turned toward him, he gave Amanda a quick look of apology. "Sorry, hon," he muttered.

"Rob Cooper," Amanda said primly, "this is one time I agree with you." Rob stared at her for a moment in utter amazement then burst out laughing.

They all turned as Willa, her face flushed becomingly, entered the room, the irrepressible Bitsy at her heels, short tail wagging a delighted greeting.

"Mercy me!" Willa said, brushing a wisp of dark hair back from her face, "what must you think of me. I don't know how I come to be so late." She shivered as a gust of wind blew in the open doorway. "You menfolk, come along in here and close that door. We'll all catch our deaths."

Willa gathered their wraps and took them into the bedroom, for the modest cottage had only one closet. Carrie still had her things packed in the cardboard suitcase.

As soon as Lanse was seated, Bitsy bounded into his lap and would have licked his face if he hadn't held up a restraining hand.

"Bitsy!" Willa scolded as she came back into the parlor. "Stop that!"

"She's all right," Lanse said. The small creature settled down beside him in the chair and promptly went to sleep.

"Where are the pups?" Amanda asked.

"Jed built them a pen out back. They're all three bigger than Bitsy now, and Jed says one dog in the house is enough. He thinks I'm crazy anyway because I was set on keeping all of 'em, but"—her big, brown eyes went liquid soft—"how could I give Bitsy's puppies away?"

"Jed workin' at the hotel tonight?" Rob asked.

"No. He ought to be here right now," Willa replied. "He's getting some fellow to take over for him. I told him tonight was real special, with Carrie here and all . . . Supper's all ready, soon's he comes."

And so it was. Jed barely had time to wash up before Willa had the food dished up and on the table. Then after they had eaten, the men went back to the parlor to enjoy their smokes and talk over the latest shocking crime that had been committed but two days before.

"Talk around town is Jansen may not live." Jed Mason coughed explosively on his cigar; he had just recently taken up smoking. To appear older, Lanse thought.

"Small wonder, with that clout on his head," Rob said. "They're getting bolder and bolder. Nobody would have been surprised if they'd busted into the store after it was closed—but to go in there, big as life, with every store on the street open for business, hit Jansen over the head, and walk out calm as you please with two thousand dollars . . ."

"You two there last night when the crowd gathered outside the city office and raised all the ruckus?" Jed asked.

"That wasn't a crowd, Jed; that was a mob," said Lanse. "Came damned near to tearing that place apart, taking those two out and lynching them."

"We were still over at the office," Rob explained. "When we heard what was going on, we hightailed it over there. All hell was about to break loose! And it would have, too, if Will Coleman hadn't started talking when he did."

"What did Will say?" asked Jed.

"He said plenty. Funny thing, too. Will's always seemed so quiet. He sure surprised me. Anyway, when he'd finished talking, he'd persuaded the mob to set up their own judge and jury and hold their own trial. Well, they went through all this rigmarole, but then the jury couldn't agree on the thing."

"Nine said they were guilty," said Lanse, "and three held out they were innocent. But by that time they'd all lost some of their steam, and everybody went on home."

"So now," Jed said, "it's all up to the town officials."

Lanse snorted. "Good God, Jed! You ought to know what a joke *that* is. How many killings have you heard about since you came to this town? How many robberies, how many beatings? And now think hard. How many criminals have been tried in the courts and lawfully punished for their crimes? Not a single goddamned one!"

"But, sir," Jed stammered, "you sure don't think a lynch mob is the answer?"

Lanse noted the "sir" immediately, for he and Jed had been on a first-name basis for some time. He softened, leaned over, and clasped Jed briefly on the shoulder. "No . . . no, of course not. Mob law would be worse than no law at all," Lanse went on. "But the fact remains that the city officials are either corrupt or just downright ineffectual."

They were silent for a moment, listening to the clatter of dishes from the kitchen.

Rob shook the ashes from his pipe. "There's only one answer to the situation—an organized committee to keep law and order, even if it takes a few hangings to show them we mean business."

"Exactly," Lanse said.

"But isn't that pretty close to what happened last night?" Jed argued.

"Not at all," Lanse shot back. "We're not talking about a bunch of whiskey-soaked miners that decide to string somebody up. We mean the leading citizens of San Francisco. Men like Sam Brannan and Will Coleman . . . men like you, Jed, and Rob here and, yes, like me. Men who live here and work here. Men who care about this town and are willing to take full responsibility for their actions."

"None of us like the idea of taking the law into our own hands, Jed. But when there is no law enforcement by proper authority . . ." Rob shrugged.

"Have any definite plans been made?" Jed asked, half-convinced.

"No . . . nothing but talk so far," said Lanse.

"I don't see how we can wait too long," said Rob. "Things are changing fast around here. Why, just take us three—all of us married and Lanse here starting a family. A year ago the sight of a respectable woman was enough to gather a crowd in San Francisco. Not that they're real plentiful now, but still, there are a few of them. Chris Russell's wife is coming out to join him this spring, and there'll be more—if we can assure them they'll have a safe, decent place to live."

Lanse stood up, shoved his hands deep into his pockets, and went to the window to stare at the bleak, muddy street. No matter what the subject, he thought, sooner or later there was something to remind him of Sable and the child she carried. Always something to lay bare the wound inside him. And it could only get worse; he knew that. After the child was born there would be a living, breathing reminder before his eyes constantly . . .

Behind him in the room Rob said, "Jed . . . talking about the womenfolk, I been meaning to mention something to you. Now, don't take offense! I know you're man enough to take care of your own affairs, but . . ." Rob finally came right out with it. "With things the way they are, do you think it's safe for Willa to be alone until all hours of the night?"

Lanse turned back. "Rob's right," he said. "It isn't safe for her. We're not trying to run your life for you, but . . ."

"I know," Jed interrupted with a wave of his hand. "I worried about it myself, until I bought a pistol and showed her how to shoot it. Made her promise not to open the door to anybody she don't know, when I'm away."

"That's good," said Rob.

"I've even thought of taking her over to the hotel with me," Jed went on, "but you know how it is. There's always some drunk spouting nasty talk or a fella bringing some tramp in to spend the night with him. And right now I can't afford to turn any paying customers away.

"Just six months. That's all I need. Six months more and I'll be in the clear. Then I can hire somebody to take care of things at night and be home where I belong."

"I guess . . . you wouldn't let us help—with money, I mean?" asked Lanse.

"No." Jed's face showed his gratitude for the offer, but his voice was firm. "I've got to make it on my own."

Lanse looked long and hard at the boy, then nodded his understanding.

In the kitchen Willa scoured the last dirty pan vigorously. Sable and Carrie dried while Amanda put things away.

Sable finished polishing the glass in her hand and set it on the spotlessly clean white tabletop. As she turned to reach for another one, her full skirts caught against the table leg and pulled back tightly to outline her figure.

"Sable . . ." Carrie said in a small voice. "You're . . . in a family way."

"Yes. Isn't it wonderful?" Sable said warmly.

She heard a muffled sob and turned to find Carrie sitting at the table, her face hidden against folded arms, shoulders shaking with grief.

Stricken, Sable made a move to comfort the crying girl, but Amanda wisely waved her back.

"Let her get it out of her system," she said softly, "she'll feel better for it."

And they waited in strained helplessness as the sound of Carrie's bitter sobbing echoed through the room. Finally it grew weaker, and the girl lifted her head, the tears still streaking down her freckled cheeks.

"Mrs. Wesley Thomas Spencer . . . Sure has a fine ring to it, don't it?" Her words were wedged between small, gasping sobs. "I tried so hard . . . so hard to make it work, but it just wasn't no use. He was so nice to me at first. Seemed like he needed somebody bad as I did . . ."

She hunched her shoulders a little and rocked back and forth in the straight-backed chair.

"Then he was late coming home one night. He'd been drinking. He came in, latched the door in back of him and then smiled at me—a real funny-looking smile. And then he just drew his hand back, slow and easy like, and hit me across the face hard as he could . . ." Behind the shiny brightness of her tears her eyes went dull. "He hit me again and kept on hittin' me, and all the time smilin' that awful smile like he got some unholy pleasure out of hearing me crying and begging him to stop . . ."

Her voice trailed off and she rocked back and forth in silence, her memories too ugly to be shaped into words. After a little while she picked up the wet cup and started once more to polish it.

"Next morning, when he seen what he'd done to me, he cried like a baby and promised he'd never touch another drop of liquor." Her voice was calmer now. "He kept his promise almost a month that first time . . . Second time, he held out for two weeks."

"Oh, Lord, Carrie, I'm so sorry!" Willa wrung the dishrag in her hands, her big, soft eyes ready to brim over with tears.

"Isn't there anything we can do?" Sable asked.

"Yes, let us help you." Amanda touched Carrie's shoulder, but the girl just lifted her chin proudly and shook her head.

"Ain't nothin' anybody can do. I made up my mind he won't ever get the chance to hit me again. I'm going back home, soon's I can get enough money. I stole enough out of his pocket for the ferry. He'd passed clean out. When he got like that, nothin' could wake him. Figured he owed me that much anyway. A . . . a harlot gets more than that . . ." She kept wiping the cup, long since dry. "I'm beholden to Willa for letting me stay here a few days till I can get myself a job, then I'll be moving out."

"Now, Carrie," Willa broke in, "you know I want you to stay here permanently."

"I won't stay here with you, Willa," Carrie said with finality. "You and your man need to be by yourselves. All married folks do. Besides, soon as I get enough money for my passage, I'll be going back to my folks." She laughed bitterly. "Pa always did say I'd wind up an old maid. Well, I guess I ain't quite that, but he's going to be stuck with me just the same."

Rob poked his head through the doorway and Carrie turned her face away. "Hey," he yelled, "aren't you ladies ever going to finish those dishes?"

"We'll be right there, dear," Amanda answered, "just as soon as we finish putting things away."

When Carrie had regained her composure and the last pot was tucked neatly into the cupboard, the women removed their aprons and joined the men in the parlor. Amanda with her usual forthrightness came directly to the point.

"Carrie wants to go back home to her folks," she said. "But she can't leave until she earns enough money to pay her passage. Couldn't you men help her to find work?"

Lanse and Rob exchanged surprised glances.

"Mrs. Spencer . . ." Rob began hesitantly.

"Oh, please, call me Carrie."

"All right, Carrie . . . Just what kind of work did you have in mind?"

"Well . . . I don't rightly know. I was raised on a farm. I can milk and feed livestock and churn butter . . . I'm good help around the house . . ." she finished lamely.

Lanse and Rob exchanged another look.

"Carrie," Lanse said, "why don't you let Rob and me take care of your passage for you?"

"Yes, I think that would be best," said Rob.

"Why, I can't let you do that!" Carrie said. "Please— don't think I don't appreciate it, but . . . I just can't do that."

"But you don't understand. A decent woman . . ." Rob gave up, threw a hopeful look at Lanse.

"Carrie," Lanse said patiently, "there just aren't any jobs for an unmarried . . . that is, an unattached woman out here. The kind of work you mentioned is done by Mexicans, or even cheaper, by Chinese laborors. You'd be an old lady before you could save passage money out of what they make, even if you put every bit of it away. If you weren't married, there'd be men lined up to court you, but as it is . . ." He spread his hands. "You're in a real predicament. It does you credit that you want to get out of it on your own, but in this case, believe me, we know what's best for you."

Sable watched him as he spoke, watched his concern

wipe away the taut, hard lines that were forever in his face now. She felt a sudden, bittersweet stab of longing as she contrasted this kindliness with the distant coldness in his eyes when he looked at her. Her interlocked fingers gripped tighter. That kind of thinking could only lead to more hurt, she thought. In a few months, she'd have her baby. That was what mattered now . . . what had to matter.

"Now you listen to Lanse," Rob was telling Carrie. "He's telling you right." And then to Lanse, "Why couldn't we fix it with Captain Harlow to take her on the *Seawind?*"

"My thought exactly."

Jed Mason looked questioningly at the two men. "You've decided definitely to buy her?"

"Yep," answered Rob jubilantly. "Within the week, Lanse and I will be the proud owners of our own merchant vessel."

Sable jumped with surprise, suddenly became aware that Amanda was watching her with the questioning concern that had often been in her eyes lately. Sable forced her features into studied, deliberate composure. She'd have to learn to be more careful.

"I must admit," Rob was saying, "when Lanse first mentioned the idea, I was a little leery of it, but now I'm convinced it's the best deal we ever made. With our own ship we can have our agent buy goods at rock-bottom prices back East and then turn a nifty profit when we sell them here."

Lanse smiled quietly at Rob's enthusiasm. "Listen to him," he said. "Before long he'll be insisting the whole thing was his idea." While Rob laughed, Lanse turned to Carrie. "She'll be provisioned and ready to sail within three weeks. Your quarters might not be too fancy, but I'm sure Captain Harlow will take good care of you."

"But . . . I don't know how I could ever pay you back . . . any of you," Carrie said, weakening.

"Then don't try," Lanse said firmly.

Eighteen days later, they waved goodbye to Carrie as she stood on the deck of the *Seawind,* the deep-pink traveling coat a delicate complement to her fair complexion. The dark bruise had faded, replaced by a faint rosiness; she looked almost pretty as she held her lacy handkerchief high to flutter in the breeze.

Amanda buttoned the collar of her high-necked, long-sleeved nightgown as she came into the room.

"Hadn't you best be getting ready for bed?" she asked Rob. "It's after eleven."

"In a minute." Rob patted the couch seat beside him, and as soon as she was seated, started pulling the carved bone hairpins from her chignon.

"Oh, you!" She chided him, but the soft curve of her lips belied the words and she made no move to stop him as he released the dark mass of her hair.

He put his arm about her and pulled her back against him. Her head rested comfortably against his shoulder. It had rained during the day, leaving the air damp and chilly, but inside, the fire crackled smartly and the room was warm and cozy.

"You have to meet Lanse early tomorrow morning at the office, don't you?"

"Yes. Something about buying another piece of land."

"Another deal?" she asked, surprised.

"I know what you mean," Rob said wearily. "I sometimes wonder myself if we don't have too many irons in the fire. We've sure been going off in all directions lately."

"Lanse's idea?"

"Mostly," he admitted. "Course I will say it's paying off so far, but . . . Seems like there's something driving him. He's just not the same man he used to be. Works night and day, and if there isn't anything to do he invents new work for himself. Oh, I don't know, there's nothin' that I can really put my finger on, but . . ."

Amanda shifted slightly in his arms and turned to face him, her brows twisted in concern. "I know," she said.

278

"I've been worried about Sable, too. What you've said just confirms my suspicions."

"You mean there's something wrong . . . that way?" He was incredulous.

"I'm afraid so."

"But what? Lanse has never even hinted that there was anything wrong between them. And with the baby on the way . . . you must be wrong, hon," he said.

But Amanda shook her head stubbornly. "I've noticed too many little things . . . woman things that you wouldn't understand. I know Sable too well to be fooled. I wonder . . ."

"What?" he prompted.

"I wonder if it could have anything to do with Charles Gregg?" she mused aloud. Then, conscious of the question in his eyes, she laughed softly. "All right," she said, "I'll tell you everything I know."

She slipped her hand into his and told him the whole story, beginning with her meeting of Sable that cold day in the park, Sable's subsequent plea for help, and her intense fear and loathing for Charles Gregg.

"I know her better than anyone else," she said. "Gregg was the only reason she decided to come out here."

Rob looked at Amanda a long time, for the hundredth time wanted to ask her her own reason for coming and for the hundredth time denied himself as he saw the vulnerability in her eyes.

At last he said quietly, "I still don't see why that would have anything to do with Lanse and Sable now."

"But you don't understand," she said. "Gregg followed her here."

Rob tightened his fingers around hers. "When was this?"

"I think it was just before Lanse left on that trip to the foothills. From what I could gather, she had never told Lanse about Gregg. When Gregg came to the house, Lanse ordered him out. I don't know exactly what was said, but it must have been very unpleasant for her. From all she told me, Charles Gregg can be a very unpleasant man. He must have left town after that; she's never mentioned his name again. And once, when I brought it up, she got a funny look on her face and made some excuse to avoid talking about him."

"She should have told Lanse whatever there was to tell, right from the first," Rob said deliberately. "There's no room for secrets between a man and his wife."

Her hand suddenly became icy in his. "Maybe she didn't think it was important," her voice sounded unnatural. She hurried on. "Besides, there was absolutely nothing between Sable and Charles Gregg."

Rob was silent for a moment, then: "I'm sure there wasn't. Anyway, it isn't any of our business."

"No," she agreed quickly. "Now, we really do have to get to bed." She slipped from the circle of his arm, walked over to the round table and picked up the lamp. "You hurry up, now," she said, avoiding his steady gaze.

She went as far as the door and stood for a moment, her back still to him. Her shoulders slumped a little and she turned back to face him, looked into his eyes. "There are things I should have told you, too, Rob . . . I lied to you . . ." Her words were a bare whisper.

His arms reached out to her and she put the lamp down and fled to them.

It was much later when she stopped talking; the fire had died to glowing embers and her face was marked with tears, but there was a new quietness about her, as if a terrible burden had been lifted from her. No matter what his reaction, she was glad that she had told him at last.

He had been silent, had made no move to interrupt or prompt her, even when her voice had broken into sobs he had waited quietly for her to go on, his arm a reassuring pressure about her waist.

She shivered with the growing chill of the room.

"You're cold," he said. He stirred the remaining coals with the iron poker and added a new log. Flames licked up around the dry bark. He brushed his hands, sat down beside Amanda again, and pulled her firmly back against him.

"Did you love him . . . your husband? No, don't answer that," he said quickly. "I shouldn't have asked it. It's not really important."

"I want to answer it," she said calmly. "I want no more shadows between us. Did I love him?" She searched for the answer.

"I thought I loved him, at first. But I didn't know what it was to really love a man. I do now." He started to speak but she rushed on.

"I was so young then. When he first came to court me he seemed so handsome, so dashing. Two of my best girl friends had gotten married that summer, and all of a sudden they were different in my eyes, not girls any longer but fashionable young matrons. So when he asked me I said yes. It was fine for a while . . . like two children playing house. We entertained our young friends and they entertained us.

"A year went by . . . two years, and all the couples we knew had a child. Some had a second on the way. His men friends began to make sly remarks, remarks that made him feel . . . less a man. I know, because I overheard some of it by accident. He blamed me for it—and rightly so." She broke off suddenly. "But, I've already told you all of that. What I'm trying to say is, any mature love between Jim and me was crushed by resentment and guilt before it had a chance to grow."

This night had answered so many of Rob's questions. Now he knew why Amanda had shown such agitation every time he mentioned children, why, in spite of her obvious desire, her body had gone stiff with tension every time he made love to her.

He ran his fingers along the back of her neck, entwined them in the thick, soft strands of her hair. "Mandy, Mandy honey," he said, "I want you to listen to me and listen good. I didn't want a wife to be a broodmare for me. There's lots more to being married than that. There's talking together and sharing together and waking up in the night and finding the other close beside you in the dark . . ."

"But I know you want a family," she said miserably, "just like Jim did . . . and one day you'll come to hate me the same as he did . . ."

He touched her mouth. "I don't ever want to hear you say that again," he said firmly. "We are a family—you and I. If the good Lord sees fit to send us children, of course I'll be happy about it. And so will you. But if He don't see fit, then who are we to argue with Him?"

"If only I could believe that," she said.

"You've got to believe it . . . because it's true." He saw the doubt fade slightly in her eyes, saw the first glimmering of hope. He kissed her, gently at first and then more urgently.

"Rob," she said softly, her face against his shirt. "Could I ask you a question?"

"What is it?"

"Did you know?" She hesitated. "On our wedding night . . . did you know?"

He smiled. "That I wasn't the first?"

She nodded.

"Well," he hedged, "I suspected it."

Her eyes grew big with wonder. "And you didn't say a word. Why, for all you knew I might have been one of those women that . . ."

"No," his voice was very sure. "You might give yourself to a man you loved, but you'd never sell yourself. I know that now and knew it then. As for the rest, it's all past. We're what matters now."

He buried his face in the soft, dark mass of her hair. She had washed it that morning in rainwater and sweet-smelling soap, and the fragrance clung to it. He pulled her closer and kissed her eyelids, her temples, her mouth, his lips opening a little on hers. His hands caressed her, lightly at first and then increasingly impatient at the nightgown in his way.

The fire was warm in front of them, the couch was wide, and she had never felt so soft and yielding in his arms before.

Chapter 23

Rob set his unfinished drink down and looked across at Lanse, noticing the new tightness about the mouth, the fine, new lines that fanned out from his eyes.

They sat in the lush new El Dorado, glittering chandeliers overhead. An hour from now, a band on the balcony would play the latest tunes, but right now a lone piano player methodically pushed the keys, the sound tinny and hollow in the big room.

Two men played poker quietly in the corner. Three more stood at the bar, tall glasses of beer in front of them. And nearly a dozen gathered around the leather-covered gaming tables, the croupier's toneless "Make your bets, gentlemen" sounding periodically.

They had put in a hectic day, and Rob wanted nothing more than to get home as quickly as possible, but Lanse had been so edgy all day that when he asked Rob to stop in and have a drink with him, Rob had agreed.

The weather had taken a sudden warm turn—freakish weather, everyone said. It couldn't last. It was too early. But it had set the trees to budding, and only that morning,

Amanda had pointed out a tiny clump of wildflowers near the porch.

"You do think it's a good idea, then, to make a few small loans provided the party has sufficient collateral?" Lanse was saying.

"I guess so," Rob said resignedly, "provided we don't drain our own funds to a point where we'd be in a pinch in an emergency."

"Naturally not. But the interest rates are too good to pass up. Why, I heard of one fellow collecting ten percent a month, compounded. I don't recommend we go quite that steep, but there's still a pretty penny to be made." Lanse swallowed the rest of his drink, made a wry face, then poured another from the bottle between them on the table.

"Besides," he said, "have I steered us wrong yet?"

Rob studied him a minute before he answered. "No, Lanse, you haven't," he admitted.

"Then what are you worried about?"

Rob toyed with his glass, rolling the liquor from side to side. "I know it's a good idea," he said at last. "There's no doubt but what we'll make money on it. It's just that . . . don't you think we might be going at things a little too hard?"

"I've taken on most of the extra work, haven't I?" Lanse's voice was sharp.

"That's just it, Lanse. You look tired. You drive yourself too hard. You know, it's no good winding up the richest man in the graveyard."

Lanse snorted. "I'm fine. Don't worry about me."

The man at the piano played on, the thumping sound of the brass pedal came to them with monotonous regularity. A disreputable-looking pair at the bar ordered another round of beer and continued their discussion of the merits of the various bawdyhouses they had visited, their words carrying clearly to Lanse and Rob.

"You oughta try that'un," one said enthusiastically. "She's got the purtiest little ass . . . all round like . . ."

"I wish they'd shut their goddamned mouths!" Lanse said savagely.

Rob watched him, puzzled, watched how his hand shook as he set the glass back on the table. "Just two drunks, Lanse," he said quietly, "two drunks spouting off a little. Don't pay any attention to them." He tried to shift the conversation to more familiar ground. "How's Sable feeling?"

"Oh, fine, fine."

"Let's see now," Rob said, leaning back in his chair, "it shouldn't be too much longer . . . about three months or so?"

"Yes." Lanse's voice had a dry edge.

Rob grinned hopefully at him. "You lucky son-of-a-gun. That's going to be great. Imagine you a father."

"Just imagine."

There was an awkward silence. Snatches of the lascivious conversation at the bar drifted to them. Lanse poured his third glass of liquor, and his scowl deepened.

"Lanse," Rob said. "Maybe I shouldn't say anything . . . and if you want to tell me to mind my own business, go right ahead. But we've been friends for a long time . . . I can't see you go on like this without trying to do something about it."

"What in hell are you talking about?" There was a forced smile on Lanse's lips, but Rob stood his ground, deadly serious.

"There's something wrong, something's eating the hell out of you, burning you up inside. For God's sake, Lanse, get it out in the open! Maybe it won't seem so bad."

"I declare," Lanse drawled, "you're getting worse than any woman I ever saw. Seeing all kinds of things where there's nothing to see."

In their enthusiasm the pair at the bar had raised their voices once again. "You mean to tell me you ain't seen that new gal at Big Bertie's place?"

"No," came the reply.

"All the way from Paris, France," the first one snickered. "Why, she's got a dress with two little holes in it here." He touched either side of his chest. "She takes that red stuff they use to paint their cheeks and puts some of it on the ends of her tits and lets them stick out at you." He made an obscene sound with his tongue. "Sure makes a man itch. Worse'n if she was stripped . . ."

Lanse jumped to his feet, perspiration beading his upper lip. "Let's get the hell out of here!" Then, more calmly, "It's too hot in here . . . and too noisy." He turned and made for the front, while Rob pulled two coins from his pocket, threw them on the table, and hurried after Lanse, overtaking him just the other side of the double doors.

It was dusk; a pale sliver of a moon lay just above the horizon. They walked together, their boots thumping hollowly on the wooden sidewalk. The street was relatively deserted, it being the dinner hour for most.

Rob grabbed Lanse's arm. "Lanse," he said, "I'm only trying to help—"

Lanse turned, his mouth a thin scar across his face. "I don't need any help."

"Oh, yes you do. I know you too well. This iron front you put on doesn't fool me a damned bit!" The two men stood glaring at each other, then Lanse's eyes wavered and fell.

Rob pressed his advantage. "Surely you don't think there was anything between Sable and that man Gregg before she came out here?" he blurted.

The result was the inevitable explosion. Lanse's face filled with blind fury. He grabbed Rob's coat and pulled him up sharply, his closed fist drawn back.

Rob made no move to defend himself, just looked steadily at Lanse with something close to pity in his eyes.

Lanse slowly dropped his fist, made a strangled sound, and turned away. Rob straightened his coat and watched with worried eyes as the tall figure disappeared into the twilight.

The angels must have watched over Lansing Wakefield as he walked the streets of San Francisco that night, for he gave no heed to where his feet took him. His feelings, suddenly unchained, filled him so completely that he was blind and deaf and dumb to anything else.

He walked along back streets, past gambling casinos, not hearing the clatter of the roulette wheels or the clinking of coins, past dancehalls and saloons, past dark houses with windows tightly closed and shuttered. Occasionally deep voices boomed out in a rollicking song or bellowed a curse. Once a woman's cry echoed, shrill and plaintive, but he passed on, unhearing.

His thoughts burned feverishly. He wanted his wife . . . wanted to hold her and let her bring comfort to him, wanted to pull her close and ease the hunger of his body for her. But Sable hated him. He had heard her crying in the night for her dead lover . . . crying for the father of the child she carried. Rob must have guessed . . . must know all about it. Maybe everyone did . . .

He thought deliberately of the drunken pair in the saloon and their lewd conversation. Remembered each phrase, each obscene uttering, and hated himself for the hot, animal feelings they roused in him. But, oh God, it had been so long . . . and they must all be laughing now, laughing and whispering about the high-and-mighty Lanse Wakefield. His wife had been another man's property . . . damaged goods.

Well, he would show them it didn't matter to him . . . didn't hurt him. One woman was as good as another . . . it didn't have to be Sable.

For the first time he stopped, became aware of his surroundings. He was somewhere on the docks. The stench of decaying fish mingled with the smell of salt in the night air. The water made a soft music as it lapped gently against wood pilings. He turned and walked away, and this time he knew where he was going.

There was a light knock at the door and then a blond woman with pale skin and light blue eyes poked her head inside.

"Guess who's downstairs?" she said in a whisper.

"Lanse Wakefield. Lil's sending him up to you." The face disappeared.

Lita got up quickly and straightened the bed. She walked to the mirror and smoothed the heavy black hair tightly back over her ears. She studied her reflection closely and smiled, satisfied that the faint light of the single flickering candle hid the telltale lines across her forehead, the shadowed circles under her eyes.

Lanse Wakefield downstairs. Imagine that. Maybe he'd asked for her. She smiled at her reflection again, turning first this way and that.

She'd heard that that pretty, red-headed wife of his was pregnant. Some women were so touchy at a time like that. Maybe . . . just maybe, if she played her cards right . . . It wouldn't be the first time a rich man set a bawd up in a plush apartment.

The heavy footsteps coming toward the door broke into her wild imaginings. She turned and struck a pose, a fixed smile on her lips.

Without a word, Lanse turned the knob and entered the room, shoving the door closed behind him. He walked directly to her. There was no word of greeting, no smile.

"Take it off," he said harshly, indicating the robe she had on.

She smiled pathetically, coquettishly, undid the sash, and slipped out of the garment. He pushed her roughly onto the bed.

There wasn't even a pretense of tenderness. He took her savagely, brutally. And even used as she was to all manner of men, she had to set her teeth to keep from crying out as he took out all his pent-up longings, his anger, his hurt pride, on her. But for all his burning, anguished violence, it was no good. She sensed that much, dimly. Even in the moment of jetting release he could not find ease for his torment.

Afterward he lay quietly on the bed beside her, not speaking, not touching her, then stood up and adjusted his clothing.

She looked up at him resentfully and then saw his face,

saw the terrible disgust, the utter loathing stamped on his features . . . and her resentment grew, turned bitter.

"You needn't look like that! You know it takes two!" Her voice was coarse and brassy to hide the sudden shame she felt inside . . . something she would have sworn was dead and buried long years ago.

Lanse turned slowly and looked at her with haunted eyes, as though he saw her for the first time. His face softened a little.

"If I feel contempt, madam," he said slowly, wearily, "I assure you it is for myself." And he turned and walked from the room.

It had turned cloudy and much cooler during the night. Rob put several sticks of wood into the kitchen cookstove, stretched tall to get the kinks out of his back and yawned broadly, at the same time scanning the gray sky through the side window. It was then that he saw Lanse ride up. He dismounted, tied Satan to the rail, and headed toward the front porch.

Rob flung open the front door before Lanse had a chance to knock. He didn't say anything, just clasped Lanse on the shoulder and motioned him into the house.

The big Virginian's face was haggard, his eyes puffy, his chin bristling with stubble.

"You're out mighty early this morning," Rob said. "Had your breakfast?"

Before Lanse could answer, Amanda, dressed in crisp green muslin, came down the stairs, pushing the last bone hairpin into the bun at the nape of her neck.

"Lanse," she called. "I thought I heard someone come in."

"Set another place for breakfast, hon," said Rob.

"No," Lanse protested, "I'm not hungry."

"Nonsense. Course you are." She exchanged a quick look with Rob. "I'll call you when it's ready."

"Well," Rob said heartily, once they were alone, "sit down."

But Lanse remained standing. "Rob," he said, holding

out his hand, his voice nearly breaking, "I don't know how to apologize . . ."

Rob wrung the outstretched hand warmly. "No need to," he said gruffly. "I had no right to pry into your affairs."

"And who'd have a better right?"

"Come on. Let's sit down," Rob said.

Lanse obeyed him wearily, leaning back against the bright yellow cushions, his shoulders slack, his hands lying limp and still in his lap.

"You were right about everything." There was pain in Lanse's voice. "These last months have been hell. I made a terrible mistake when I married Sable."

"Oh, now, it can't be that bad . . ." Rob was distressed to see the proud, arrogant man so humble.

"It is, and worse." Lanse lifted a hand to stop Rob's protest. "What could I have expected? After all, to marry a total stranger, someone you know nothing about . . ." Stricken, he grasped Rob's arm. "You know I don't mean anything against Amanda. She's a fine woman . . . anyone can see that. You were a lucky man to get her."

Rob nodded. "I think so. And now tell me, just what's so wrong with Sable?"

Lanse looked straight ahead, his voice flat and toneless. "She . . ." He swallowed hard. "She . . ." His face twisted. "Rob, I can't . . . If I could talk to anybody in the world it would be you, but I just . . ."

"All right, all right." Sometimes things went so deep in a man he couldn't put them into words—especially a man like Lanse. Rob didn't make the mistake of mentioning Gregg again. He simply said, "Now, Lanse, listen to me. The first thing you got to do is let the past be past. Start from right now."

"I wish it were that simple."

"Maybe you've been expecting too much. After all, you've been married less than a year, and with Sable in a family way . . . I always did hear that a woman could be a little hard to get along with at times like that. As for you, give yourself a little time. You know sometimes . . ."

sometimes loving doesn't come all at once, sometimes it comes along slow-like . . ."

"Love her?" Lanse groaned and buried his head in his hands. "Oh my God, if only I didn't love her! I've tried to put her out of my mind, tried to throw myself into the business, work so hard and so late I'd be too tired to think. But it didn't work. I tried liquor and that didn't work. And last night . . ." He paused, met Rob's eyes, "Last night, after I left you . . . I went to Lil's place. That didn't help either."

They were both silent for a moment. The pleasant aromas of frying bacon and strong black coffee wafted from the kitchen. They heard the clang of the oven door.

"Lanse," Rob said finally, "you admit to loving your wife . . . and anybody with half an eye can see how she feels about you. Why, when you were away in the camps, she couldn't wait for you to get back. Made me promise I'd go after you if you didn't come home the week you did. You'll soon have a family started. Things ought to be mighty sweet for you just about now . . .

"But," he drew a sigh, "every man knows his own troubles better than another. All I'm saying is this. Nobody can tell you how to get things straightened out. That'll have to come from you."

Lanse nodded and his shoulders squared just a little.

"Now come on." Rob made a fist and hit Lanse lightly on the arm. "If my nose is right, breakfast is almost ready. What you need is some good food in your belly, and after that we'll see what we can do to get that brush-pile off your face." Rob ran his hand over the light blond shadow on his own chin. "Fact is, I could use a shave myself."

Lanse hung back a moment before entering the kitchen. "Rob," he said, "does everybody know about Sable and me?"

A wide grin split Rob's face. There was that old devil pride, rearing its head again. That sounded more like Lanse. "No," he answered. "Nobody except Mandy and me."

Sable rubbed sweet-smelling white cream into her swollen abdomen, slowly, methodically. It felt cool to her fingertips, to her skin, and disappeared almost as soon as it was applied, leaving only a soft, satiny feeling.

Melissa had given it to her weeks ago, and cautioned her to use it daily if she wanted to escape ugly stretch marks: a usual result of pregnancy. Sable looked down at her white skin and envisioned the faintly purple streaks which Melissa had described marring the smooth surface. She frowned slightly and quickly rubbed in more of the cream. She touched a bit of it to her breasts, swollen, tender, the nipples aching.

There was so much more to having a baby than she had ever imagined. Six and a half months and already she felt enormous. Even her walk had changed. Now, she held her head and shoulders farther back to balance the extra weight in front and walked with a side-to-side swing . . . like a duck, she thought wryly and wrinkled her nose in distaste. She must look hideous.

The baby moved inside her, a long drawn-out stretching motion followed by a sharp kick that made her smile.

"You're getting impatient, too, aren't you, little one?" she said aloud. "Not much longer now . . . not much longer."

Despite the discomforts, as the baby grew stronger with each passing day, so did her love of it, her joy in it. The baby was her anchor and had made these last months bearable.

Sable capped the jar of cream and set it on the nighttable, then turned her face toward the door as voices sounded in the hall—Jace's, deep, muffled, then Tish's high-pitched, "Ain't I done told you, no!" punctuated by a small shriek that ended in a giggle and light, running footsteps followed by heavy, slower ones.

Sable tried to set her mouth in the stern lines that the situation demanded but the laughter in her bubbled out. Tish was having a hard time with Jace. Only yesterday when Sable had gone in search of Melissa to go over the dinner menu, she had been stopped short by a startled squeal, and Tish had come scooting out of the kitchen, her white starched hat askew atop the curly black hair. Jace had followed her, grinning broadly, wickedly.

At sight of Sable, Tish had hurriedly straightened the cap and bustled off upstairs, muttering something about the furniture needing to be dusted, while Jace tried to look innocently unaware. But there was still a certain gleam in the big, black eyes.

Properly, Sable supposed, as the mistress of the house she should speak to Jace . . . but that would be embarrassing. And, of course, it was impossible to go to Lanse . . .

She sobered, closed her eyes. In the last two weeks, he had somehow changed. It puzzled her, but it was there . . . something different in his eyes. Or maybe something was gone from them that had been there before.

Just this evening, at the dinner table, he had made a point of telling her that he stopped by to see Dr. Bush and asked him to be on call in case the baby should arrive early. It was true that he had said it in front of Melissa, and yet . . . Sable had had an unmistakable feeling that he was talking to her . . . really to her, not showing false concern for the benefit of the others.

Melissa had been highly insulted by the whole thing. "My Miz Susan never had no doctor when her time came. She always said to me, 'Melissa, you are the best hand to deliver a baby of anybody I ever did see,'" she had grumbled, her lower lip thrust forward.

Lanse had soothed her hurt feelings by telling her that they couldn't possibly get along without her, but had added firmly that the doctor would be called just in case.

Lanse's concern for her warmed Sable, but, unbidden, through the soft stirrings of something not quite hope, but almost, came the memory of Lanse's visit to her room that night just before Christmas . . . the memory of herself, humiliatingly eager.

Her mouth set in a tight, hard line. Nothing was changed . . . would ever change.

Manuel Garcia shaded his eyes with one dark-skinned, calloused hand and squinted into the late-afternoon sun, then hurried along the narrow dirt road. Days like these were truly a gift of the Virgin, he thought; the sun bright and life giving, the air sweet, the earth beneath him warm, stirring. It had felt good, as always, to work in the soil with his hands, to sift it through his fingers, making it ready to receive the young plants that *Señor* Lanse expected any day now. Plants that he had ordered from a far-off place called "Virginia."

Manuel had spent the entire afternoon with his employer, carefully planning where each plant would go, speculating whether they would live in this land so far from their home. "We will see. We will see," he had said.

His pace slackened as he heard the ring of ax against wood. "Ho, Pedro," he called and raised his hand as the tall young man turned and flashed a smile.

"Wait. I will walk with you," the young Mexican called, as he gathered the freshly split firewood into a burlap sack. He threw the bundle over his strong, young shoulder, picked up the ax, and Manuel and he fell into step, side by side, along the rutted road toward the rise, beyond which lay their homes.

Manuel had been the first to build a simple one-room cabin there well away from the city, for himself and his wife Rosita. He had been unhappy amid the squalor and noise of the Mexican quarter, where shacks were jammed so close there wasn't room for green, growing things between them.

His old friend Juan Ramirez soon built a second house near to Manuel's where he lived with his son and two daughters. Then less than six months ago, young Pedro Gonzales had brought his bride, Maria, and built the third house.

Manuel and Juan's son had helped the young bridegroom raise the roof over his new home, with much advice from old Juan. Manuel's wife, Rosita, and Juan's two young daughters had sewn curtains for the four windows and had scrubbed the place shining for the new bride. Was it any wonder then that their little community now felt such joy to learn that Maria was with child?

Pedro had called them all to his house only a week ago, and, his face flushed with pleasure, made the announcement. They were only just sure of it themselves, he had admitted, but the news was too wonderful to keep longer. Rosita and the Ramirez sisters had bundled the blushing mother-to-be off to their house, whereupon Pedro had brought out a jug of tequila and the men had celebrated until the wee hours of the morning.

Now Manuel threw an amused, sideways glance at Pedro, as that young man strode along beside him with just a hint of a swagger.

"Oh ho, my young rooster," Manuel teased, "now you strut along and say to yourself, 'What a man's man am I to accomplish so much in such a short time!' But just you wait"—he wagged a finger under the grinning young man's nose—"until next year and there is another one, and the next year another one, and the next year . . ." He raised his shoulders in an exaggerated shrug. "Who knows? Maybe twins. Then your Maria will be saying, 'Enough, enough!' and you'll find yourself on a pallet in front of the hearth."

Manuel roared with laughter in which the younger man joined good-naturedly. But suddenly Pedro's grin faded. "Look!"

Manuel's eyes followed Pedro's gesture and saw a woman running toward them, heavily, awkwardly. As they watched, the woman stumbled and fell, her shawl slipping from her shoulders, but she heaved her stout figure up and ran on without it.

"It's Rosita," Manuel said, astonished, and he set off to meet his wife, with Pedro right beside him.

"What is it? What is the matter?" Manuel cried.

Rosita was panting heavily. "There . . . are men there. I was frightened. I ran away."

"What men? Who frightened you?" Manuel prodded.

"Begin at the beginning, Rosita," said Pedro.

"I do not know them." She turned to Pedro. "I had

gone to the spring to get water. As I returned, I heard voices—loud voices. I crept up slowly and saw horses and men . . . many of them. I heard old Juan shouting angrily inside his house, and then two of the men went into your house, Pedro. I was afraid they would see me. I ran away."

The young man's face blanched. "Maria," he said hoarsely. He flung the sack of wood aside, gripped the ax tightly, and set off toward the top of the hill.

Manuel ran after him. "Pedro, wait!" He grabbed the young man's arm. "Not that way, they would see us clearly against the sky. We must cut away from the road and go through the trees and bushes as Rosita came to us."

Pedro nodded curtly and plunged into the brush.

"Slowly, slowly," Manuel cautioned. "We mustn't let them hear us coming." He gestured to Rosita to fall in behind him.

They crawled the last few yards through thick bushes, the briars scratching their hands and faces, until at last they had a clear view.

The houses had been built in a semicircle, with Manuel's to the left, Juan Ramirez's in the middle, and Pedro's on the right. Eight saddled horses were tied at the other side of the clearing, though only four men were now in sight, bunched in front of the Ramirez house. Old Juan and his son lay in the dirt of the clearing, bound securely hand and foot. Juan seemed dazed, but his son glared at the intruders sullenly, his eyes dark and burning; the bruises on his face, the bloody gash over his left eyebrow bore witness to the fight he had put up.

Pedro tightened his grip upon the ax, readying himself to spring out into the open.

Manuel gestured frantically. "No," he whispered, knowing that the slightest sound would betray their presence. "They are heavily armed. We must wait for our chance."

A shout came from Manuel's cabin and a fifth man appeared in the open doorway. "Look what I found me," he bellowed and ran to join his four friends.

Manuel recognized the small bag he was waving under the others' noses. In it there were five gold coins, his life savings.

"I bet this here'll bring a good price, too," the man said. The rosary swung back and forth from his hand, glittering brightly. It was Rosita's and had been given to her by her mother for her First Communion. The man shoved the silver beads into his pocket.

From the cabin nearest them, Pedro's cabin, came scuffling sounds and a loud crash. Pedro's eyes went frantic. "I must get to Maria!"

"But how?" said Manuel. "They will see you before you can get to the porch. You can't help Maria if you are caught."

Then Juan's two young daughters burst screaming through the door of the middle cabin. With loud guffaws the men caught the girls and held them squirming, while a sixth and seventh member of the group came out of the cabin, one nursing an injured hand.

"Blimey," he said, betraying an accent often heard in Sydney Town, ". . . blimey, if the little scut ain't bit me!"

Pedro nudged Manuel with his elbow. "Look," he whispered, "there are eight horses and seven men in the clearing. One man only must be in my house . . . with Maria. If you could draw their attention long enough, and I got to my house without being seen . . ."

Manuel would never know the rest of what Pedro had intended to say, for at that moment, from the cabin nearest to them, came a muffled gagging sound, followed by a long scream that ripped the air with its terror. A second later Maria, completely naked, ran from the house.

She was beautiful, full-bosomed and wide of hip, her pregnancy not yet in evidence, and the men out front stared at her as if mesmerized. Several of them moved toward her, one emitting a low, bestial sound from his throat.

She stopped still as she saw them, her face drained of color. The sun was still high enough to cast an unmerciful light upon her and her hands moved in a pathetic attempt to hide herself.

Suddenly a curt command crackled through the air, and in the cabin doorway a lone figure stood: a Negro, not overly tall but of powerful build, with muscles that bulged beneath his clothing.

"She's mine," he barked. And his men fell back a pace, sullen, but accepting his authority.

The Negro advanced upon Maria, his eyes glittering, cruel lips drawn away from his teeth in a sensual grimace. He grasped her by the wrist and Maria shrank back, wailing.

Pedro had lain like a man turned to granite, but his wife's cry freed him from the trance. He lunged from his hiding place in the dense thicket, swinging the ax in a high arc above his head, his roar of rage splitting the air. The attack was so unexpected that for a moment his was the only movement. Then, just as the ax rose to come crashing down, the still-grinning Negro whipped the pistol from his belt and fired.

The ax poised in mid-air, then fell to the ground with a thud as the young man clutched his chest, his eyes going helplessly to his wife, then pitched forward heavily, his face in the dust.

"Pedro!" Maria's scream was agony carved in sound. She lunged toward her fallen husband, but the Negro's arms had already closed about her.

Old Juan sat stunned, unseeing, but his son twisted and strained at his bonds as the men ripped his sisters' clothing from them, and fought among themselves for possession of their bodies. And in the bushes, Manuel could only clutch at Rosita, who had crawled up beside him, and force her face down so that she could not see the hell that was before them.

As for himself, he watched . . . almost welcoming the pain it caused him, as if to atone for his helplessness. And the worst pain of all, the sight that burned into his memory, came when he saw Pedro, not yet dead after all, lift his head, his face streaked with dirt, to stare with horror-crazed eyes at the man who grunted like an animal atop the writhing, screaming body of his wife. Then a thin trickle of blood ran from the corner of his mouth, and his head lolled sideways once more into the dust.

There comes a point at which a human being can feel no greater pain, when the brain can absorb no more, and Manuel had reached that point. Having had their fill of the women, the marauders finished ransacking the houses, then set them on fire, but Manuel could only watch with dulled eyes. Finally the Negro leader went to the women, lying on the ground in senseless stupor as the men had left them, and then to the uncomprehending Juan, and lastly to his shouting, struggling son, and very coldly shot each of them through the head with a rifle, but Manuel could only feel a growing numbness and clutch Rosita even tighter to him.

Shouting to one another, laughing coarsely, the eight men mounted their horses and rode away in the night, the flames from the cabins, like three giant torches, casting huge flickering shadows before their retreating figures.

Manuel lay still for a long time. The cabins were just smoking, charred rubble when he felt Rosita stir against him. He released her at last, crawled from the thick bushes and stumbled to his feet, his legs aching and stiff, barely able to support him at first.

He sat for awhile, while Rosita walked round and round, slowly, seeing, yet unable to accept what she saw.

He stood then and searched through the still-hot rubble of his cabin till he found the small tool case which he kept on the back stoop. Though it too had burned almost completely, the metal part of the shovel was still unhurt, and a charred stump of a handle remained.

It took Manuel a long time to dig three shallow graves, and when he had finished, his hands were raw and bleeding. Rosita sat and watched, dazed, whimpering a little.

It was hard work; the bodies were heavy, but he carried them tenderly . . . Old Juan and his son in the first grave, then his two daughters to share the second . . .

Last of all he untied the neckerchief from around his throat, wiped the dirt from Pedro's face, and smoothed back the black hair before he placed the young husband, with his wife beside him, into the dark damp earth.

Chapter 24

The sun was a huge orange fireball balancing on the rim of the horizon, when Lanse burst into the kitchen, his shirttail not yet tucked into his trousers, his hair all on end, in answer to Jace's urgent summons.

"Manuel! Good Lord, what's happened?" His gardener was streaked with dirt, clothes torn, his face crisscrossed with cuts and scratches; and beside him, Rosita was in almost as bad condition, her eyes vacant with fatigue and shock.

"*Señor* Lanse"—there was near-hysteria in Manuel's voice—"I have brought my Rosita here to be safe . . . I tell her, when we get there, *Señor* Lanse will help us."

"Yes, yes, of course." Lanse took a steadying hold on Manuel's arm. "Take it easy now."

He motioned to Melissa standing near the stove, and she poured two mugs of coffee and placed them on the table. When Lanse shook his head at her questioning look, she replaced the pot on the back of the stove and cast a practiced eye at the thick slices of bacon in the iron skillet and the bubbling pot of mush.

"This here food be ready in a jiffy," she said.

"Drink that. Settle down now," Lanse encouraged Manuel as he gulped the steaming coffee gratefully but Rosita sat bewildered, paying no attention to anything until Melissa took her hand and gently placed the warm mug within her fingers.

"Now," Lanse said, when Manuel's cup was empty and the tremors that shook his body were subsiding, "come with me to the study. We can talk better there. Melissa, take care of the woman." He turned to Jace, who had stood near the door all the while. "You come, too."

In his study, Lanse waved Manuel to one of the black-leather chairs, then turned to close the twin paneled doors, but saw Sable standing uncertainly at the foot of the stairs, one hand raised to her throat, her eyes wide with inquiry.

"There's nothing to be alarmed about," he said quietly. "There's been a little trouble, but everything is all right now." Their eyes held for one disturbing moment and then he swung the doors closed.

"Now," he said, seating himself in the swivel chair behind the desk and turning to face Manuel. "For God's sake, man, tell me what this is all about."

Only the day before, Manuel would have felt uncomfortable at being ushered into the study and offered a chair, but now it was of no consequence. Once started, his words were like floodwater pouring over a dam. Lanse listened to the terrible story, listened as horror mounted upon horror, the small muscles along his jaw twitching spasmodically.

"And so," Manuel finished, spreading his hands, dark with soot and crusted blood, "I did not know where else to turn. Everything is gone—everything." His voice trailed off and he sank deeper into the soft leather of the chair.

Jace clenched his big fists, jammed them into his pockets, and turned to stare out the window, while Lanse sat for a time unable to speak.

He was stunned, angered to the point of rage, ashamed
. . . yes, ashamed that such a thing had been allowed to
happen. The so-called leaders had allowed it to happen,
the men of substance such as himself who were supposed
to form the backbone of this new state. A backbone
with damned little grit in it, he thought caustically.

"*Señor* Lanse," Manuel broke into the painful thought.
"I was a coward," he said, his voice filled with ruthless
self-reproach. "I should have tried to help them . . . Instead, I lay hidden in the bushes like a woman . . ."

"But what could you have done against their guns?"

Manuel was silent for a moment, then his level gaze
met Lanse's with a quiet sureness. "I could have died . . .
with my people."

"My friend," Lanse said, deeply moved, "sometimes it
takes more courage to live . . . and fight. And we will
fight. You won't be left defenseless again. I promise you
that. From now on you will carry a gun. You, too, Jace."

"I want Manuel and Rosita to stay here. We'll build
you a new cabin—right in front of that clump of willows
west of the vegetable patch would be a good place—"

He broke off as he saw Manuel's face working convulsively. "I need you," he assured the gardener. "Not only
for the garden and the grounds, but more important, with
things as unsettled as they are, I need another man here
in case of trouble. Will you stay?"

Tired as he was, Manuel's body straightened at the
challenge in Lanse's voice. "I will stay," he said.

"Now tell me." Lanse leaned forward in his chair. "Do
you think you would know any of these men if you
saw them again?"

Manuel's brow knotted. "I do not know," he stammered, "I do not think so . . . except . . ."

"Except what?" Lanse prompted.

"Their leader. He was a man of his color." He pointed
to Jace.

"Manuel, are you positive?" Lanse was incredulous.

"I am sure, *señor*. I saw him clearly and I heard the
others call his name. I never heard this name before—

except once. It was after the big fire and a man in black was going through the streets with the Holy Book in his hands and he was saying, 'Repent, repent, or the fire of God's wrath will burn again.' "

Lanse and Jace exchanged puzzled glances.

"That was what they called this man," Manuel said. "Wrath."

Jace's head jerked up, the wide, dark nostrils flaring. Lanse held up a restraining hand, and said, "You heard them call the man . . . Rath?"

"Yes."

Jace and Lanse stared at one another, the air between them heavy with their shared knowledge.

"No, Jace," Lanse said, "it couldn't be the same one." He rushed on as if to convince himself. "It's impossible . . . after all these years . . ."

"Yes sir, Mist' Lanse." The words were docile enough but Jace's eyes flickered strangely. Buried deep in this big, good-natured man, Lanse knew, was a spark of hate that had stayed alive over the years. Now, at the mention of Rath's name, it flamed up, burned brightly within him.

Drawing a long breath, Lanse broke the silence. "You can go along to the kitchen, Manuel. Melissa will feed you."

The old Mexican stood up stiffly and went to the door. With his hand on the knob, he turned back for a moment, the pain leaping, alive, in his eyes once more.

"Not even a priest to give them the last comfort of the church," he said.

"You eat now and rest. Then I'll ride with you to the mission," Lanse said. "They'll have their priest . . . I promise you."

Lanse's fury deepened, if that was possible, when Rob brought news later that morning. The massacre in the clearing had been only one of many outrages that had happened through the night. Gangs of bullies had descended upon the Mexican and Chilean quarters to loot and ravage, murder and rape. Then they had roamed through the streets searching out more victims.

Planning to do some shopping, Rob and Amanda had driven into a town strangely quiet, where small knots of people gathered to speak hardly above whispers. While Rob was listening to an account of the night's terror, the first newspapers were rushed out onto the streets, the ink still wet upon them.

Now Rob handed one to Lanse and paced back and forth impatiently while he read. Lanse's scowl deepened, the muscles along his cheek knotted white.

"And where," he said bitterly, "where were the so-called decent people while all this was going on? Didn't anybody try to stop it?"

Rob stopped his pacing. "As far as I could find out, nobody raised a hand."

Lanse exploded with profanity.

"I know how you feel," Rob said, "but in a way, I can understand. It would take a hell of a lot of guts to go up against a bunch of armed rowdies, especially when you know there was no law to protect you and you didn't know if there was one other man in town that would back you up. They were too scared to think about right and wrong. Most of them were just thanking their lucky stars that their skin was nice and white."

"I know . . . I know." Lanse paced a step or two and then wheeled, his feet planted wide apart. "But there's got to be an end to it."

At nine-thirty that same evening, Lanse was standing in the middle of Tom Atkins's dining room, repeating the same words.

"Gentlemen, there's got to be an end to it!"

"Great God, Wakefield," sneered Luther Simms, "every time one of these greasers runs a splinter in his ass you get yourself all in an uproar."

Lanse controlled himself with difficulty.

"You know how these people are," Simms addressed the whole group, "always fighting among themselves. That probably accounts for at least half of what went on last night. As to the rest of it"—his voice hardened—"I'm not risking my life to save some dirty ignorant Chileno's neck—or his wife's virtue, either. Most of those sluts would lay down in the street for you if you gave them a copper penny."

Rob Cooper spoke up heatedly. "What happened last night puts a blot on the honor of every man who calls himself a citizen of San Francisco."

There were several vigorous nods of agreement, while Luther Simms snorted his contempt and turned away to light his cigar.

Jim Carter, the banker, perspiring profusely, said, "I'd planned to bring my family out here, but after what's happened"—he shrugged—"I don't know what to do."

"I'm expecting my wife any day now." Chris Russell rose from his chair by the hearth, his ruddy face unnaturally grave. "She may head right back to Philadelphia when she hears. Can't say as I could blame her."

"The question is, what do we do about it?" Jed Mason asked quietly.

"I'll tell you what we'll do about it," Tom Atkins bellowed. "We'll get together enough men, arm them to the teeth, and swoop down on Sydney Town and whip them Ducks within an inch of their lives. We'll teach 'em a lesson they'll never forget."

Lanse laid a restraining hand on his host's shoulder. "No, Tom, that's not the way. We'd be putting ourselves on a level with those hoodlums last night if we go tearing out there not knowing who's guilty and who's innocent."

"But how can we find out which ones were at the bottom of it?" Tom shot back.

"Chances are we never will," Rob interposed. "But maybe we could see that it never happens again."

"It's not the first time a Vigilance Committee has been proposed," said Lanse, "and now things have gotten to a point where it's the only answer. A handful of men is not enough, but the combined weight of the decent men of this town is.

"Let them know we mean business. Draw up an official constitution. Have an armed patrol on the streets at night. Send a committee aboard every ship that drops anchor and ban any more convicts from the British Penal Colony. What's more, all known criminals should be given a specified time to collect their belongings and leave the city. We must set up our own courts to try offenders and mete out justice according to the merits of the case."

"I'll say 'Amen' to that," Chris Russell joined in the chorus of assent.

Lanse reached home to find Jace and Melissa waiting, dressed all in black as for a funeral, silent and dark as the shadows in which they stood.

"What's the matter, Jace?" Lanse asked quietly as he relinquished the reins.

Jace countered with a question of his own. "You going to be home for the rest of the night?"

"Yes."

"I'm going out for a while. Melissa, too. We be back before morning."

Lanse, tall man though he was, had to look up to meet the eyes of this dark young giant. After a close scrutiny, Lanse finally nodded his head.

"I understand," he said. As Jace turned away, Lanse put a hand to his arm. "Jace," he said. "Jace . . . take care."

Only Jace's eyes acknowledged the words and then the two of them were gone, merged into the darkness. Lanse tried to quiet the apprehension that formed a cold knot in the pit of his stomach, while nearly twenty years rolled away and he had a vivid memory of two small boys, one black, one white, crouched hiding beneath the bed as Melissa told the awful story of Jace's birth.

And later when they had escaped, undetected by Melissa, the small dark hands had clutched his own, the dark face twisted with emotion, the child's black eyes glittered hate for the first time. And he had said, "Sometime I find him. I kill him!"

The clouds parted slightly and a pale moon gleamed. Lanse massaged the flesh along the back of his neck where the muscles ached most with weariness, then walked slowly toward the house.

The two figures crouched, motionless, behind the clump of bushes, heedless of their cramped, stiff muscles. Their black clothing and dark skin blended into the night until only the whites of their eyes gleamed dully in the shadows.

Raucous laughter echoed from the sprawling shack not more than fifteen yards from their hiding place, a shack their careful inquiries among fellow-servants and freed slaves had led them to. A coarse voice shouted, "I think you're bluffing, dammit; I'll raise you ten."

Then suddenly the door opened, throwing a shaft of light across the gravel path, and a man, far gone in drink, stumbled out, staggered along the path past Melissa and Jace and disappeared for a moment behind the far side of a rough shed, a good distance from the shack. He lurched once more into view and started back toward the open door only to stop, cursing volubly, just in front of the bushes that held the silent watchers.

For one terrible moment, Jace and Melissa didn't even breathe, for this was Sydney Town, and any intruders here would have their throats slit before any questions could be asked or answered. But luck was with them. The man's curses were directed at the trouser buttons that drink-befuddled fingers were having difficulty in closing . . . and after much fumbling, the man nodded his satisfaction and entered the house once more.

During the next hour the pair continued to crouch like two dark statues, watching the shack. Inside, the laughter and shouting rose to new heights, then one voice rang out unsteadily in song. Another joined in, and another, until the night air rang with it.

The door opened a second time and a man was silhouetted briefly against the light before the door closed behind him.

They could hear the crunch of his footsteps along the gravel and the lantern he carried illuminated the powerful shoulders, the thick-set neck, the narrow, glittering, black eyes.

Melissa stared for a second, her lips drew back from her teeth, her eyes rolled in her head and she raised her hands in front of her, rigid, fingers spread, like some ancient African high priestess. She turned to Jace and nodded her head slowly.

Jace's eyes burned into the darkness as he watched the powerful shadow in the pool of lantern light disappear into the shed. Like a giant black panther, Jace eased himself to his full height and walked soundlessly, on the balls of his feet, after the man who had killed his mother, the man he had sworn someday to kill.

The air inside the shed was dank, fetid, heavy with the smell of manure and horses. The lantern hung high on a nail near the ceiling, and Jace could make out the crude partitions that divided the stalls for the four horses stabled there. A movement in the shadows against the far wall betrayed Rath to him and he watched, the sour taste of hate in his mouth, while Rath scratched through his saddlebags, searching intently for something.

Jace pulled his knife from the sheath at his waist, clutched the carved bone handle in his big fist. Crouching, he felt his way silently, step by step across the refuse-strewn earth floor. He raised his big arm high above his enemy's broad back. The powerful muscles from wrist to shoulder corded, stood out. One stab, he told himself, one stab down . . .

Rath continued to search through the saddlebags, muttering curses under his breath, and still Jace did not strike. In the distance, dimly, he could hear the drunken shouting and singing from the shack. Seconds went by and the hand that held the knife began to tremble. Perspiration gathered along his brow, ran together, traced its way down his face and neck.

Jace thought of his mother and of Manuel and his people, of the hideous crimes the man before him had committed. And yet, something deep inside him revolted, sickened. He could not kill a man in cold blood—not any man.

He flung the knife from him and it clattered against the wall, then dropped with a dull thud to the dirt floor. Rath wheeled, visibly struggling to clear his head of liquor. His eyes focused on Jace's features, leaped wide with shock, in that one second he went cold sober.

"You . . . Caesar!"

Let him think that, Jace thought, his lips drawing back from his teeth in a distorted grin. What could be more fitting than for him to think that Caesar had come to take revenge after all these years . . . Caesar, his father, the giant buck who could split a rail with one blow of his powerful fist.

Jace had never known how much he resembled his father, but now it was evident in Rath's twitching upper lip, the sudden slackness along the jaw line, the eyes, red-veined, staring.

The first stunning moment gone, Rath sprang quickly to one side and snatched up a pitchfork. His legs set wide apart, he turned and thrust all in one motion. Jace weaved away, escaping by a hairsbreadth the glistening, sharp points.

The horses whinnied nervously as the two men crouched, regarding each other cautiously, Rath, despite his weapon, respectful of the great size and strength of his opponent.

Jace gave ground as Rath came toward him, his eyes never leaving the wickedly sharp steel of the hay fork, moving backward slowly, step by step. Then, unknowingly, Jace stepped back into a low feed box, and though he struggled wildly for balance, the soft grain shifted and he crashed backwards to the hard-packed dirt.

Rath growled hoarsely, triumphantly, and thrust again with all the strength of his massive chest. Jace jerked convulsively away, but grunted with pain as one steel prong stabbed through the flesh of his left arm, just below the elbow.

Rath heaved the fork up, ready to strike again, this time a mortal blow, but Jace was too quick for him. He grasped the wooden shaft of the fork and gave it a yank that all but sent Rath sprawling. He yanked again, tearing it away from the grasping hands, flung it away to bury its sharp points into the soft wood of the wall.

Rath fought wildly, but few men could have withstood Jace's great strength, even wounded in the arm as he was.

The horses reared and snorted. One broke through the flimsy partition that held it and lunged madly about the small confines of the shed.

But Jace, heedless of the flying hooves, heedless of the hard, wracking sobs that shook him, and of the tears that streamed down his cheeks, hammered his great fists again and again against the man who had killed the mother he never saw, the man who had raped and burned and tortured and stolen.

And Melissa, watching from just outside the open door, muttered curses on Rath's soul.

"And I know you want it so, don't you, my darling?
"Just like Kit did . . . wanted you to . . .
me the same as he did . . ."

He touched her mouth. "Don't you
say that again," he said firmly. "We are a couple—
you and I. If the good Lord sees fit to send us children,

Chapter 25

Lanse gathered the papers on his desk into the leather case, tucked it under one arm, and left his study.

"Tish," he called in the hallway. "Bring me my coat— I think I left it in the dining room."

Tish came in a moment with the tailored dove-gray coat and held it while Lanse thrust his long arms into the sleeves.

"Jace all right this morning?" he asked.

For no apparent reason, Tish looked at the floor and giggled foolishly. "Yes, sir, he's fine. That arm getting better every day."

"I suspect he's enjoying all the attention he's been getting," said Lanse, setting off another burst of giggling.

Though Lanse's words were light, he felt deeply relieved and thankful that the thing was finally ended. Unable to sleep, he had waited through the dark hours of that night, one week ago. Finally, just before dawn, Jace had staggered in, leaning heavily upon Melissa, his face the color of wet ashes with shock and loss of blood.

Lanse had asked no questions, but had helped Melissa

clean and bandage the wound, undress the big man, and put him into bed. He knew, by Jace's wound and by the veiled look in Melissa's eyes, that Rath was dead. And there was unspoken agreement between the three of them. It would never be mentioned again.

Later that morning, the rest of the household were simply told that Jace had had an accident down at the stables, and since that time the invalid had been pampered completely, with Tish, especially, anticipating his every wish—almost.

Shaking his head, grinning over the helplessly giggling girl, Lanse turned to pick up his case. It was then that he saw his wife coming down the stairs, and though the smile on his lips didn't fade, it lost a certain spontaneity.

Despite the heavy bulge of her figure, her carriage was erect and she held her head high as if she were immeasurably proud of the burden she carried. Lanse contrasted her bearing with the hangdog, almost apologetic look he had observed in some pregnant women, as if they would give anything to be able to hide their bulk. Sable had matured these last months, lost the childlike look that he had first found so appealing. Now when he looked at her he saw a woman, and that in a new way was even more appealing.

His thoughts were disturbing to him, and to hide that fact he made a great show of greeting her.

"You should have slept later," he chided, and took the stairs two at a time to slip his arm through hers and, with Tish looking on, assist her down the stairs. "It's still quite early, you know."

Sable flushed slightly. "I was restless," she said. "I've been awake for a long time."

"Maybe you can take a nap later in the day," he suggested. "You remind her, Tish."

Her arm was still locked in his and their eyes met and probed for a long, agonized moment, discounting the light words spoken between them, reflecting the disturbing nearness of each to the other.

And silently something deep inside Lanse was crying out, Is there no answer to this . . . Is there no way back to those first days . . . weeks? Now, finally, he admitted to himself that in spite of everything, without her to share his life there would be no happiness for him. He wanted her for his wife. Not the playacting marriage that had been of his own making, but fully and completely his wife. He wanted her body—and more . . . he wanted her love. Wanted to hear her say, "I love you, Lanse."

She had never said those words, but once she had offered herself to him . . . had returned his kisses with such fervor that he had been sure. But that was just before he found out about Gregg . . . For one brief instant, he wished desperately that he had never found out, had continued blissfully unaware, had bedded her that night. Then the whiplash of his pride stung once more and he released her arm abruptly.

Sable dropped her eyes, two bright spots of color touching her cheeks and Lanse turned awkwardly away and saw Tish, still nearby, regarding the two of them with a puzzled light in her eye. As if on a sudden afterthought he turned back to his wife.

"Better not wait dinner for me," he said. "We're having another meeting tonight. Civic affairs, you know. We're getting together at Chris Russell's."

"All right." Sable's voice sounded perfectly normal. "Give Chris my best regards. And his wife, too. I believe she just arrived?"

"I'll do that." Noticing Tish's still watchful eye, Lanse suddenly, impulsively, took Sable by the elbows and brushed his mouth lightly against hers, then, without looking at her, turned and went quickly through the door.

Once outside, his normally long stride quickened. It was necessary, he told himself. Purely for Tish's benefit. Nevertheless, the startled tremor that he had sensed in Sable now echoed through his own flesh, and though the kiss had been light as a drop of summer rain, his mouth burned as if his lips were still pressed against hers.

Lanse attended the meeting at Chris Russell's that evening, and on the following days another and still another, and all with the same result: talk.

The decent men of the town, the men of substance, were alarmed, uneasy, but they still discussed formation of the Vigilance Committee, endlessly, and could not agree quite how to do it.

Meanwhile, Rob and Lanse prudently hired four trustworthy men to guard their two houses, and Rob, despite Amanda's protests, found a Mexican couple who would act as gardener and housekeeper, and who also would be an added protection for her when he was in town.

One night, Lanse hunched himself deeper into his black-leather chair and tried to concentrate on the book he was reading. He was fully clothed, though it was nearing two in the morning, the rest of the household dark, its occupants fast asleep.

Unable to sleep himself, he had for the better part of an hour been scanning the well-worn pages of his volume of Shakespeare, when he started half out of his chair at the sudden loud banging on the front door.

"Good Lord!" He tossed the book onto the table and hurried toward the front entrance.

He could hear a muffled stirring from the servants' quarters and a door opening on the upper floor. He felt a rising irritation as the hammering continued.

"Wake everybody in the house . . ." he muttered. He drew his small pistol from the holster beneath his shoulder, then drew back the bolt and threw open the heavy, oak door.

The man, his fist still upraised, gaped at the pistol in Lanse's hand, his mouth dropping slackly away from toothless gums.

"Before God, Mister Wakefield, I ain't up to no mischief!"

"Then speak up," Lanse said crisply. "What's your business here at this time of night?" One of the men he had hired sprinted from the direction of the stable. "It's all right, Tompkins." Lanse waved him back. "I'll take care of this."

The oldster shuffled his feet and whined, "Young fella sent me, he did . . . Give me this here gold piece . . . Said he'd give me another'n if I took a message to you . . . asked me if I knowed who Lanse Wakefield is. Sure, I says. I seen him plenty of times . . . him and that pretty, red-headed woman of his." He pointed one grubby finger past Lanse. "That's her," he said, "that's her right there."

Lanse glanced over his shoulder and saw Sable, her eyes still heavy with sleep, standing near the stairs. He shifted his bulk, blocking the other's intent survey, and with difficulty held back his rising irritation.

"All right, you know who I am," he snapped. "Now just who sent you and what is the message?"

"Said to tell you Mason—"

"Jed Mason?"

The old man shoved the grease-stained hat to the back of his head and pondered with exasperating slowness. "I can't rightly remember what his first name is. He's the one runs that there hotel over on . . ."

"Yes, yes, I know all that. What did Jed want you to tell me?"

"He said to get Mr. Cooper and come soon as you can."

"To the hotel or the house?" Lanse prodded.

"To the house . . . yes, that's it—to his house."

"All right." Lanse dug into his trouser pocket and came up with another coin. "Here, head back to town and buy yourself some whiskey." And then: "Tompkins," he called to the shadowy figure that leaned against the hitchrail, while the old man shuffled down the steps, "see that he goes on his way."

Lanse turned back from the doorway with only a perfunctory glance at Sable. He jerked off the brocaded satin smoking jacket and stood in his shirtsleeves, the shoulder holster and gun chillingly apparent.

"Now where did I leave that damned coat?" he muttered.

"Here it is, Mist' Lanse." Melissa glided silently from

the shadows at the back of the hall and Lanse hurriedly put it on, then wheeled to the door.

"Wait!" Sable's voice stopped him. "I want to go, too."

"Nonsense. You go back to bed."

"No." She clasped at his arm. "I heard what that man said. Something must be very wrong for Jed to send for you in the middle of the night. Maybe Willa's sick or something. I want to go," she repeated stubbornly.

"Sable," he turned back to her and for the moment the conflict between them was almost forgotten, "I'm going to ride hard to get Rob and then on to town. Look at you"—he gestured toward her waist—"in . . . in your condition . . . you couldn't stand that kind of jolting." He tried to pull away, but Sable's eyes widened with new thought.

"What if it's a trick?—a trick to get you away from the house. What if Jed didn't send that message?" And then at his surprised stare, "You don't really think we women are so gullible we don't know the things that have been going on, do you?"

He looked at her for a long, drawn-out moment. "I'll be careful," he said, then turned and hastened on his way.

Thirty minutes later, Lanse dismounted and tied the hard-breathing black stallion to the gatepost in front of the Masons' cottage, eyeing the empty rig and patient horse waiting nearby.

"I'll knock," he threw over his shoulder to Rob Cooper, hard behind him.

"No, wait," Rob said. "I see a light in the kitchen. Let's go around back."

A cricket chirped noisily as the two men made their way around the house to the back door, while from the wire pen almost lost in the shadows at the far corner of the yard came a soft, low whining.

The door was already slightly ajar. Lanse looked questioningly at Rob and then nudged it open. Jed Mason sat hunched over in one of the cane-bottomed wooden chairs, motionless, his head buried in his hands.

"Jed."

He started up, his face drawn and set. "Thank God you've come!" he said and motioned them in.

Lanse and Rob exchanged looks as they saw the evidence of violence in the room; the overturned chairs, the broken flowerpot with dirt spilling onto the floor, bare roots starkly exposed; the cabinet drawer that looked as if it had been yanked part way out and then had fallen to stand crazily on one end—and in the corner, on the floor, the blanket-covered heap.

"What's happened here, boy?" Rob asked.

"He looks like he could use a drink," Lanse interposed as he saw the small twitching movement of Jed's mouth. "You have any whiskey in the house?"

"No." Jed made a visible effort to bring himself under control. "I don't want it, anyway."

"What happened? Where's Willa?" Rob pressed him.

"In there. The doc's with her." Jed jerked his thumb toward the bedroom, then started to pace back and forth, talking in harsh, jerky sentences.

"It was almost one o'clock before I could leave the hotel. When I got here, the door was unbolted. I thought that was mighty funny . . . and then . . . then I heard them—inside here. I ran in—there was four of them." He ran his fingers distractedly through his hair. "I shot . . . killed one of them. The others got out through the bedroom window."

The silence lay in the room like an ugly, vile thing.

"You don't mean . . ." Lanse hesitated.

Jed nodded bleakly and turned away.

"Oh, God, no!" Rob breathed. He and Lanse looked helplessly at one another.

"I don't know how they ever tricked her into letting them in," Jed went on after a moment, his back still to them. "I told her never to let anybody in the house less it was somebody she knew. There was a gun there in the cabinet . . . I think she tried to get it." He gestured to the upturned drawer. "But they must've taken it away from her . . . when I picked her up she was crying . . .

wouldn't say a word to me . . . just looked right through me like I wasn't even there . . . and kept on crying."

He turned back to face them, his voice carefully controlled now. "I had to shoot the dog. Found it laying in the corner over there." He motioned toward the stove. "Its back was broke. I guess it must have took in after them and they kicked it or something . . . I don't know. It's out in back. She sure set store by that dog."

He kept glancing at the closed door to the bedroom. "They threw some kind of meat to the pups, to keep them quiet."

Rob cleared his throat noisily. "Then that . . . ?" He nodded toward the covered heap on the floor.

"Yes."

Lanse drew back the blanket, and he and Rob stared for a moment at the crumpled man beneath it, then covered it over once more.

"We'll make arrangements to . . . have this taken care of," he said.

Jed nodded woodenly, then held out his hands in a helpless, pleading gesture. "Why?" he asked. "Why? . . . When there must've been a hundred bawds they could've . . ." He broke off and shook his head.

Lanse's answer was quick and firm. "Because that's the kind of scum they are. Because there's no law in San Francisco that isn't a mockery. No order. No protection for the people. And because nobody has raised a hand to stop them."

It made Lanse sick, deep down. Next it will be us, he had told them. If we close our eyes to this violence, if we look the other way, it will be our homes, our women, next. But the solid citizens still urged caution . . . caution while people were being terrorized. It was just the low classes, the foreigners, they argued, quarreling among themselves as they always would . . .

"I'm going in there." Jed's voice broke into Lanse's thoughts.

Rob stepped between Jed and the hallway. "I don't believe I would," he said gently.

But there was no need for further argument, for the door opened and the tall, lean form of Randolph Bush emerged, his face lined and tired-looking. He came into the kitchen, set the black bag on the table, and nodded curtly to Lanse and Rob.

"Is she all right?" Jed asked hoarsely.

The doctor rolled down his shirtsleeves and fastened the cuffs. "She will be," he said, the professional note of reassurance strong in his voice. "I've given her some powders. Should make her sleep until almost noon. I'll be back tomorrow to see her."

He snapped the open edges of the bag together and tiredly reached for his coat. He turned for a moment at the door.

"For her sake, this must be kept as quiet as possible," he addressed the three men. Then his next remark was for Jed alone. "Be very gentle with her," he said. "Don't force her to talk about it. Let her be the one to bring it up."

Jed nodded, his mouth compressed into a thin, straight line, then: "Did she say anything to you?"

"She didn't speak a word."

Lanse lifted Sable from the buggy in what he hoped was a completely impersonal manner and set her gently on the ground.

He tried to persuade himself that he didn't feel any concern over the tired little lines about her mouth or the faint purple smudges beneath her eyes, but his words betrayed him.

"Are you sure this isn't too much for you?" he asked. "After all, Melissa was here yesterday and saw to the washing and cleaning, and Amanda's here every day . . ."

"I feel fine," Sable insisted shortly.

"All right. I'm going to chop some wood for the Masons before I leave," said Lanse, and gave her his arm around to the back of the house.

It had been five days since that awful night, and Willa Mason was like a doll who waked and slept, eyes straight ahead, looking neither right nor left, to all appearances not hearing or seeing anything. When food was forced between her lips, she offered no resistance and swallowed by reflex action, but she never uttered a sound and didn't even seem to be aware of it when the women bathed her or tended to her other needs.

Dr. Bush visited twice daily, and each time emerged from the bedroom with the small lines of worry ridged deeper between his eyes.

"I can't find any physical reason for the state she's in. It's just as if she's shut everything and everybody out . . . put up a fence around herself. I don't know what to do to bring her out of it . . . I just don't know . . ." He patted Jed helplessly on the shoulder and left.

Never talkative, Jed had withdrawn even further into himself now. He sat by Willa's side almost constantly, watching her face anxiously for any sign of recognition, lifting his head only to give a grateful glance whenever Sable or Amanda came near.

"Is she any better?" Sable asked as she entered the Masons' kitchen.

Amanda shook her head. "Just the same," she said. She filled the pan with potatoes from the split basket in the bottom of the cupboard.

The two women seated themselves at the table and started to peel the potatoes.

They were silent for a moment and Sable fought back the exhaustion that threatened to overwhelm her by concentrating on the task before her. The knife in her hand was old, worn thin by use, its mid-section honed away until the blade curved inward to a bare half inch at its thinnest part.

"They're pithy," Amanda said, wrinkling her nose slightly. "What I wouldn't give for new potatoes—those little ones, boiled, with lots of butter on them, and a bit of parsley . . ." Her voice trailed off sadly.

Sable shook her head, suddenly moved almost to tears. "This place . . . ," she said. "Sometimes it's too much. The fires, the violence . . . what happened to Willa . . ."

"I know." Amanda looked at her, understanding in her eyes. "But one day it'll be better. Men like Rob and Lanse will make it better. Besides," she said simply, "it's home."

Sable regarded her soberly, drew a long breath. "It is, isn't it," she said. "Home for us . . . and for this one, too." She rested her hand lightly against her rounded belly, and Amanda smiled.

Lanse banged the back door open, entered with an armload of cut firewood.

"I'll be on my way," he said. "Work's piling up at the office. Besides, I'm going to stop by Mason's hotel and see that the man we got to take over is doing a good job." He hesitated, started to leave, then turned back. "Are you sure you feel like staying?" he asked.

"Very sure," Sable said, deliberately avoiding his eyes.

"All right. I'll be back later."

She steeled herself against the softening in him, the almost-but-not-quite tenderness in his voice, for too often it was followed by cold harshness that she failed to understand was his protection against himself. She only knew that love had brought her pain, and she numbed herself against loving him.

It was only occasionally, when she woke in the dark stillness of the night, that the hardness melted and the soft, inner heart of her cried out to make him listen . . . tell him the truth. But in the cold light of morning the weakness was gone. It was too late to tell him . . . too late.

Sable looked up at the small hand-painted china wall clock that was Willa's pride. Five o'clock. The feeling of exhaustion that had bothered her earlier in the day had deepened, and the very nerves of her body seemed stretched to the raw, aching limit. I can't give in to it, she thought grimly.

"I'll take the tray in and feed Willa," she told Amanda, forcing a smile to her lips.

"Good. Tell Jed I'll have his supper on the table in just a minute."

Sable heard the rasping scrape of the iron soup ladle against the side of the kettle as she walked into the narrow hall, balancing the tray carefully in front of her. The bedroom door was closed but the catch had not quite fastened, so after several loud footsteps to make sure that Jed had heard her approach, she turned sideways and nudged the door open with her elbow.

Jed sat, as usual, by the bedside, his head bowed, his hand clutching Willa's, while Willa just lay and stared at the ceiling, her only movement the light rise and fall of her breathing.

Sable made room for the tray on the night table. "I've brought some soup for Willa. Amanda has supper ready anytime you're—" She stopped as Jed raised his head despairingly.

"She hasn't moved . . . not the whole afternoon." He jumped to his feet and slammed his fist into the side of the tall mahogany wardrobe. "The doc's tried everything." He paced up and down, nursing his bruised knuckles absentmindedly, and then threw himself back down in the chair. "What now? What now?"

Sable stood quietly, knowing that he didn't want answers from her, that he just had to say the words out loud.

"The doc even . . . slapped her." He reached out gently and stroked Willa's pale cheek. "It made me mad at first, till he told me he'd hoped to shock her out of it . . .

"It was all my fault. I never should've left her alone. I thought I was doing right, trying to make the hotel pay . . . but I was wrong."

His lower lip trembled suddenly and he clamped his mouth tight, looking very young, and Sable, watching him, felt much older and wiser than her nineteen years. She saw Amanda standing in the doorway, her eyes questioning, but she held up a restraining hand.

"She's never going to be better," Jed said, and his mouth trembled again. "The doc says he doesn't know what else to do for her . . ."

He was silent for a moment, then: "I ain't never been much with words . . . I guess I get that from my pa. He didn't talk much, neither. I never told her how . . . how much nicer it was after she come. I wish I'd told her that . . ."

His voice broke with a harsh, cracking sound. Sobs tore him, and he buried his face in the blanket and covered his head with his thin arms, his shoulders heaving spasmodically.

Sable had never seen a man cry . . . and she had had no idea of how terrible it would be. She wanted to reach out, to comfort him . . . anything to stop the terrible sounds that wrenched from his throat, but she could only turn helplessly to find her own distress mirrored in Amanda's eyes.

It seemed to go on for an eternity—the hoarse gasping, the fingers clutching deeper into the blanket with each shuddering sob, while Sable and Amanda stood by feeling powerless to do anything.

But if their attention hadn't been so focused on Jed, they would have seen that a change was taking place in the still figure on the bed.

Willa's eyes began to flicker strangely, as her husband's weeping continued, her face lost its wax-doll look. Lines of pain etched themselves across her forehead, around her eyes, her mouth twisting suddenly with grief.

She turned slowly, looked at Jed's bowed head, his face still hidden in the covers, and the tears welled slowly in her eyes, trembled for an instant, spilled out.

"No, Jed . . . no," she pleaded. She reached out her hand to touch his shoulder, while Sable had to clap her hand over her own mouth to keep from crying out.

Jed raised his head, hesitantly, as if fearing to believe his senses, his shoulders still heaving. He saw Willa's hand reaching out to him, the recognition in her eyes, and he clutched her to him, pressing his face against hers. They both were crying, their tears mingling.

Sable felt a tug at her elbow. "It'll be all right now," Amanda whispered close to her ear. "They'll be all right."

And the two of them tiptoed from the room and closed the door gently behind them.

They looked at each other and then away, embarrassed, for they had witnessed something too personal to be seen by even the friendliest eyes. And Sable's feeling of maturity and wisdom suddenly deserted her and was replaced by a numbing sense of loneliness.

"I want to go home," she said, and she could feel her whole body droop.

Amanda quickly held out a hand to her. "Sable, are you all right? Have you had any pains?" Her voice was sharp with concern.

"No . . . no pain. I just want to go home."

Chapter 26

Slowly the routine of everyday living returned. The days were warm and glowing with sunshine, and Manuel could be seen daily working in the garden. Already he had brought early blooms into the house for Sable to enjoy. And she enjoyed them all the more because she was so closely confined now, with her pregnancy nearing its end.

Rob and Lanse, during the crisis at the Masons', had gotten a reliable man to take over at the hotel. Now Jed kept him on as night man so that he wouldn't have to leave Willa alone again, and time began to heal the young couple.

Plans for the Vigilance Committee were moving, and if all went well it would soon become a reality. And none too soon to suit Lanse, for scarcely a day went by that didn't bring some new incident. The Ducks grew more confident and at the same time more cunning. Even a traveling peddler was suspect and barred from the San Franciscans' homes, what with all the robberies and assaults. Men on the streets looked guardedly at one another when dusk drew near.

Forming the Vigilance Committee took time and

thought and careful planning, and Lanse, together with others who shared his views, had done more than his share. And now he sat at the big desk in his study, catching up with the long-neglected bookwork of his own business.

The deep creases across his forehead smoothed, disappeared, as he studied the sheet of figures before him. He calculated rapidly, sometimes in his head, sometimes scrawling the numbers around the margin. Finally, a pleased expression swept across his features. Quite a nice profit already this year—and if their venture with the *Seawind* did as well as he hoped it would . . .

The sun slanted in through the window behind him, and a low branch of the big sycamore rustled immature leaves gently against the pane. Lanse swiveled the black-leather chair around, relaxed, feeling the warmth of the sunlight right through his light wool trousers.

A sparrow perched for a moment on the branch outside the window, wisps of straw jutting from her beak, then she darted off to her nest. Lanse had a sudden feeling of loss that she was gone.

"Spring fever!" He snorted aloud, derisively. There was still work to be done, and here he sat like some calf-eyed schoolboy, staring out of the window and half-hoping that the sparrow would come back.

But he didn't turn back to the rows of numbers, the stacks of papers; instead, he sat quite still, closed his eyes, and let the sun sink into him. And he remembered a day in September when an equally brilliant sun had been in the sky, and underfoot the grass had been lush and thick and green. He had pointed out the chattering birds to Sable and they had laughed together . . . and he had helped her over the fallen log that blocked their path and . . . she had been in his arms.

He didn't hear the first knock at the door, but the second caused him to start with something close to embarrassment.

"Come in," he called. He heard the door open, at the

same time swung the chair around to see Jace standing tall and broad in the open doorway.

"Mist' Lanse, I got to talk to you about something."

Despite his great size, Jace reminded Lanse at that moment of a small schoolboy standing in front of the headmaster's desk.

"Well, shut the door and come on in," Lanse said warmly. He reached for his pipe, then lit it, while Jace shoved his big dark hands nervously into his pockets.

"Sit down." He gestured toward the other chair and Jace obeyed. "Well, let's have it. It's not your arm, is it? Last time I looked at that, it was almost healed."

"No, sir. That arm's done well." Jace rolled up the sleeve of his blue cotton shirt, displayed the small round scar, puckered and faintly pink.

"What is it, then?" Lanse prodded.

"It's Tish . . . me and Tish, we want to get married." He grinned broadly.

Lanse, surprised and pleased, removed the pipestem from between his teeth. "Jace! I couldn't be more pleased! But," he went on more cautiously, "are you sure?"

"I sure am . . . because Tish don't believe in no carrying on. She won't let me touch her unless I get the preacher to say the words over us."

At this frank admission, Lanse couldn't hold back his delighted laughter. "Jace," he said, getting up and clapping the big man on the back, "there's been many a man married for the same reason, but you're the first one I ever heard admit it." A new thought crossed his mind. "You won't be making any more trips to town . . . ?"

"No, sir, I won't," Jace emphasized. "Tish don't believe in that neither. She'd have my hide for sure . . ."

The wedding was held at the house the following weekend, with Tish in a new white dress looking shy and embarrassed, and Jace in his Sunday-best suit looking suitably nervous.

Manuel had filled the room with flowers, and in doing so had stripped practically every garden in the area, for it was still early in the season. The long table set up out on the side verandah groaned with Melissa's handiwork.

Tompkins and Bates, the hired hands, watched the ceremony from the open french doors; inside the room, Manuel stood arm-in-arm with his Rosita, who beamed unreservedly, even though she couldn't understand a word of what was being said. Melissa stood to one side, the black eyes beneath the spotless white kerchief suddenly suspiciously damp.

Several chairs had been arranged in the center of the room. Rob and Amanda, who had insisted that they wouldn't miss the wedding for anything, sat in two of them with Sable beside them in a third. Lanse stood just behind Sable, his hand resting lightly on the back of her chair.

The preacher ran one finger back and forth beneath the limp string tie at his throat, then took the book from the pocket of his black wool coat and began.

When the brief ceremony was over there was a moment of silence; Lanse was the first one to step forward to offer his congratulations, wringing Jace's hand warmly and thumping him soundly on the back. Then everyone was talking at once.

Sable stayed quietly seated until the commotion had died down a little and Lanse watched her rise and come forward. Heavy as she was, he thought, there was still something of grace about her . . . the way she held her head above the slim, white support of her neck.

"I do hope," she said, "that you'll be very happy." The quiet simplicity of her words affected Lanse more than he cared to admit to himself. She looked up at him briefly and he saw the sudden flare of something—loneliness, sadness—in her eyes.

From long habit, Tish bobbed her a curtsy, but Jace just nodded, a slow smile breaking across his face. "We thank you, missus," he said with equal simplicity. His dark eyes went from Sable's face to Lanse's and back again, and it was as if he were saying, "Happiness to you, too— in spite of the trouble between you . . ."

Lanse looked away to the sunny verandah, where Melissa was urging Tompkins and Bates to join the festivities, and the preacher, needing no urging, had already piled his plate high and was regarding it with relish.

A chord vibrated, hung sweet in the air, died, instantly to be replaced with another. Manuel, eyes half-closed in the marvelously seamed face, threw his head back and caressed the strings of his guitar with long, sensitive fingers, sun-darkened almost to mahogany. He sang in a rich, strong voice the songs traditional for a wedding among his people, and the music filled the house, vibrant, throbbing, joyous.

Later, when Lanse found the opportunity, he took a small, heavy, leather pouch from his pocket and pressed it into Jace's hand.

Jace eyed it for a moment, knew what it was. "You done too much already," he said, and for the first time in years left off the servile "Mist' Lanse."

For an instant, time turned back for Lanse, and he and Jace were boys again . . . ten years old?—yes, about ten. They had fished that morning, and the fish lay all in a row on the bank, the sun shining on them. His brother William was there, too, . . . fifteen he was, and tall—as broad through the shoulders as many a grown man. "Don't you let me catch you calling him Lanse again," his brother's voice had cracked through the air. "You call him, *Mister* Lanse, you hear me, boy?"

"No, no, he doesn't have to do that," his own boyish words sounded.

Then he heard the low "yes, sir" from Jace and the moment's pause, then the "Mist' Lanse," directed at him. Lanse had looked once into Jace's face, and then, turning blindly away, had run into the woods and thrown himself face down on the hard, scratchy ground. He had cried . . . the last time he remembered crying.

Jace was trying to give back the gold, but Lanse shook his head, pushed the hand away. "Save it for your firstborn," he said, and then, a little embarrassed, laughed shortly. "Anyway, I'm damned glad you decided to stay on here. Who else could bring me cold shaving water in the morning?"

On May 4, 1850, San Francisco had suffered its second serious fire. Now, by some odd chance, flames seared the city for the fifth time almost exactly one year later. It was said that this fire started in an upholstery shop on Clay Street, but that was of little importance. For, ten minutes after it started, it spread in a wild holocaust. The weather of the past month had been sunny, beautiful and very dry. The wooden shops and houses were like tinderboxes. They didn't just burn, they exploded into flame.

This time when Sable heard the frantically tolling bell echoing from Tom Atkins's place, she knew immediately what it was. There was no dreamlike quality this time, but a harsh reality about the sound that grated along her backbone, set cold perspiration dripping from her armpits.

She struggled into her wrapper, pulling it tightly across her swollen abdomen. She could hear Lanse stirring in the next room and then shouting, his voice hoarse with urgency, to Jace downstairs to get horses ready.

Sable started toward the window, stumbled, almost fell, then caught the bedpost awkwardly. She reached the window, swung back the heavy overdrapes and the thin curtain. She gasped at the yellow glow that in spots deepened to bright orange, like a false sun filling the horizon. It would have been beautiful had the source not been so deadly.

She remembered that sight, the fear, the waiting . . . the thankful relief that Lanse was gone and away from the danger. But Lanse wasn't gone now. She felt suddenly chilled.

She was almost to her door when she heard Lanse leave his room, heard the heavy sound of his boots along the hallway to her door and then . . . silence.

He was there . . . on the other side . . . only a few inches of wood separated them. And her whole body cried out to him. She wanted to open that door . . . wanted it more than she'd ever wanted anything in her life, but she stood as if paralyzed, her eyes fastened pleadingly on the knob, waiting for what seemed an eternity for it to turn, waiting for a word from him ... anything ...

The sound of his footsteps echoed again, faded, as he went away and down the steps. And she walked slowly back to the bed and sat down, dry-eyed, a raw, burning ache in her throat.

The lower floor of the house was utter confusion. Tish's voice rose in a frightened, discordant wailing, and she clung helplessly to Melissa, while Manuel dragged Rosita into the house through the back door. That good woman remembered only that she had lost one home in a night of terror and fire, and now she was determined to stay in their new cabin. Every few steps she let loose a torrent of Spanish ... At the front door there was a hearty thumping.

Into this confusion Lanse brought a quiet authority that was a calming force.

"Tish! Stop that caterwauling at once," he said firmly. "Melissa, see who's at the door."

Bates, the hired man, stepped into the front hall and planted his feet. "By God, Mr. Wakefield," he said, gesturing with one muscular arm in the general direction of town. "By God it looks like a bad one."

Lanse nodded grimly. "Rob Cooper should be here any minute," he said. "We'll take Jace with us. You and Tompkins and Manuel will stay here. Better put Tompkins in the stable and see that he has enough ammunition—there's plenty in the bottom of the gun cabinet. You and Manuel take care of the house. Close all the shutters and bolt them. Be prepared for anything ..."

There weren't so many people to be seen now. At first they had been like ants in a flattened hill, confused, frightened, but trying to salvage what they could. Shopkeepers, some cursing, some weeping, beat the encroaching flames with rugs and blankets; men threw sand and carried dripping buckets of water; some fought to save their papers, others staggered under the weight of trunks or bedding, still others were content with the clothes on their backs. But now, most had given up and gone to safer parts of the city.

Lanse's eyes stung and his chest ached dully as he drew smoke-laden air into his lungs and put his weight into the rhythmic swing of the pump handle. Across from him, Jace grinned, his naked torso gleaming with perspiration in the dancing light of the flames—and Lanse grinned back from a face which he was sure by now was black as Jace's own.

The big man's endurance surprised even Lanse. It took four men to work the pump, two on each side, and Jace had outlasted two groups of men and now worked one side alone while Lanse and Rob took their turn opposite him.

But even Jace's great strength wouldn't be enough to stop this, Lanse thought as he watched the flames spurt even higher, showering burning material and red-hot sparks onto the dry, wood-shingled roofs nearby. The puny stream of water which their backbreaking effort flung at the fire did little good.

A horse, terrified to madness by the roaring, the heat, the sun-bright glare, his mouth dripping foam, reins flapping about his legs, bolted down the street toward them. He reared, screamed shrilly as hands reached out toward him, then veered away toward the next intersection and into the chaos that the town had become.

"My God!" Rob's voice cracked with the effort of working the pump handle, "I've never seen anything like this before. We don't have a chance against that damned wind."

The men handling the hose turned and waved at them, presenting an almost nightmarish picture, their faces covered to the eyes with wet handkerchiefs against the smoke, the searing heat. Tom Atkins ripped the cloth away.

"Back up . . . back up," he yelled, his voice barely carrying above the noise. "It's gaining on us!"

And so they retreated, foot by foot, down the gentle slope.

A man, tall, loose-jointed, ran awkwardly up the street toward them. "They sent me to tell you . . ." he panted, brushing the lank strands of hair away from his eyes, ". . . to tell you if you can't hold her back, best get the hell out of here." He jerked his thumb in the direction from which he had come. "Warehouse about midway in the next block. Got a big store of gunpowder . . ."

"Gunpowder . . ." The word was repeated through the small cluster of dirty, exhausted men. "Gunpowder!" one said, his voice rising with fear. "It'll blow this place right clean to hell . . ."

"Wait!" Lanse held up his hand. "Let's don't waste time talking about it. Get this pump going again." And as Rob and Jace joined him on the pump handle, the other men grimly pulled the handkerchief over their noses and took up the hose.

But it was no use. Inch by inch they lost ground, and when they were a quarter of the way into the next block, they had to acknowledge their defeat. They pushed and pulled the engine to a place of safety and waited for the powder to blow.

Rob broke the exhausted silence. "Great God Almighty," he said. "We should've had six engines to make any headway against that."

"The others have their hands full, too." Lanse swept his arm in a wide arc. "Look at that sky."

A rider came by at a fast trot . . . drew his horse up sharply as they waved to him.

"How bad is it over that way?" Rob shouted.

The man shoved the wide-brimmed hat to the back of his head. "Must be ten, twelve blocks a-burning like Hades itself. Can't do nothing with it long as that wind's a-fanning along like it is. Them corrugated metal buildings over on Sansome Street was glowing like cookstoves when I got out of there . . ."

There was a series of small explosions then one mighty boom as the flame reached the stored gunpowder in the warehouse. Wood and debris shot upward, reaching into the night sky along with the new burst of flame and swirling, black smoke. The horse arched his back, tried to buck his rider off, but the man just yanked his hat down tight, dug his heels in, and sent the animal sprinting along the street.

"That's it," Lanse said. "Let's get back to work . . . Somebody see if you can find a well. Have to get the water going again."

They took up their new position, but within twenty minutes were driven from it . . . then another, and another, until the night seemed to be an endless series of defeats as the fire reached out to fasten destructively on structure after structure.

"Son-of-a-bitching fire!" one of the men cried. "Ain't enough water in the whole goddamn ocean to put it out."

"We'll get it out," Lanse spat. "Put your backs into that pump."

He turned impatiently at the tugging on his sleeve, drew back as the whiskey-fouled breath hit him full in the face.

"Oh, sweet Jesus! You got to get him out of there," the man sobbed. "My brother's in there . . . you got to get him out . . ."

"Where? Tell us where!" Lanse shook him. The man's head rolled limply upon his shoulders while he pointed an unsteady finger at a two-story house already in flames.

"I left him in there," he said. "We was just drinking a little . . . only we run out of the stuff, and I said, 'I'll go get us a bottle.' That's what I said . . . and I left him upstairs there. . . See, here's the bottle . . . just like I said . . ." He fumbled, pulled the full bottle of whiskey from his coat pocket.

"Which room did you leave him in? Can you remember?" Rob Cooper pressed him.

The man squinted. "That one—that one right there on the end."

"What do you think, Rob?" Lanse said.

"It's going fast. Never get in through the house. Besides, he might have gotten out by himself." They looked at each other and then back to the burning building. "If we could get a ladder up to that window . . ."

Lanse nodded. "Get that hose over here," he yelled. "Put it right up there."

The men maneuvered the engine into the right position and started the stream of water against that side of the burning house, while Jace brought the big ladder.

The three of them, Jace, Lanse, and Rob, edged up closer, trying to get the ladder against the house just under the windowsill, the heat scorching right through the wet cloths over their faces. But the fire had eaten through the supports. The tortured frame shuddered . . . cried out with a weird, nearly human sound . . .

"Lanse, look out!" He heard Rob's voice. Then a bright flash of pain exploded in his head.

It was quiet in the house now . . . quiet with a stillness that hung heavy and thick about them. Sable deliberately tapped the silver spoon against the delicate rim of the china teacup and listened while the pleasantly ringing sound melted away the sticky silence.

"Do you think they'll come back?" she asked.

Amanda turned from the window. "Those riders?"

There had been eight, maybe ten of them, not two hours past, riding boldly up the carriage drive then dissolving into the bushes and trees as the first warning shots were fired from the house and stable. They had held back for a few minutes, letting the night shadows shield them, then one had edged away from the thick row of hawthorn and bolted for the house. But the quick flurry of gunfire drove him back. There was a hoarse, guttural shouting and the riders regrouped, rode quickly away.

"They won't be back." Amanda let the thin lace curtain fall back across the window. "It'd take them half the night to get into this house, and they know it. Plenty of other places where they won't have anyone to stop them."

"What about your place? Will it be all right?"

Amanda nodded. "The Mexican couple is there—and Rob hired that new man last week. I'm glad he did, now."

Sable pushed the tea tray to the far side of her night table. "I should have Melissa come for this . . . have her bring some hot tea, if you'd like."

"No, thanks." Amanda sat down on the side of the bed and gestured toward the pillow. "Why don't you stretch out for a while?"

Sable rested her hand lightly on her abdomen, felt the dragging weight that had become a part of her now, pressing downward. "I think I will," she said, and felt the relief as soon as she was off her feet.

The two lamps with their frosted-white round globes and painted pink rosebuds were unlit. Bates had sent word upstairs by Melissa to keep the lights out as long as they had the window shutters open. But they weren't really necessary. In the past two hours, the glow at the window had brightened until now the spidery lace pattern of the curtain was etched softly in light and shadow against the opposite wall.

"Any pains?" Amanda said.

Sable smiled and shook her head. "Just uncomfortable. I still have almost a month to go."

"Babies have been known to come early, you know."

"I wish it would be a little early . . . it'll be good to have it over." Sable looked away. In these last weeks, even her love for the child she carried couldn't soften her fear. Always, woven into the fabric of that fear, like a dark thread coming back again and again, the thought . . . *my mother died when I was born*.

She looked back at Amanda, saw the strange half-smile playing about her lips, the soft pink color in her cheeks.

"I've been wanting to tell you . . ." Amanda traced the patterned stitching of the quilt beneath them with one restless finger. "I missed . . . and now it's time again . . . past time, and there's no sign. I think I'm that way."

"Amanda!" Her own fears forgotten, Sable covered the moving hand with her own. "I'm so glad for you—so glad!"

"At first, I was afraid to believe it . . . But now . . . I think maybe it's true . . . after all this time."

"What about morning sickness?"

Amanda nodded her head eagerly. "Yesterday and this morning, too." The color in her cheeks deepened. "Besides that, my breasts are sore . . . and they seem heavier. I guess part of it could be my imagination . . ."

"Nonsense! You have all the signs." Sable's voice held a positive note. "Just listen to me," she said. "I sound like an expert."

"And who'd be a better one?" Amanda retorted gravely. They both looked solemnly at Sable's swollen abdomen and then shook with muffled laughter.

"Does Rob know?" Sable asked.

Amanda nodded. "And he's about to burst with it. Can't wait to tell Lanse . . . but I made him promise me he'd wait a little longer until we're sure."

At the mention of the men, Amanda frowned and looked toward the window. "I wonder how it's going?" she said. She got up from the bed and went back once more to the window, pulling the curtain aside . . . stood for a moment, looking.

"Sable . . ." she said quietly—too quietly, "come here."

In a moment Sable was standing beside her. The bright orange halo that seemed to hover in the night sky had changed. No longer was it the motionless glowing it had been . . . now there was a definite movement, slender fingers that pulsed, reached upward, then fell back to be lost in the mass of color.

They watched for a moment in silence.

"It wasn't like this the other time. You couldn't see the flames." Sable's voice sounded thin and too high-pitched. "That must mean it's a lot worse."

"Maybe not . . . Maybe it's just because the sky's so clear . . ." Amanda's words were reassuring, but somehow the sound of her voice made them a lie.

Then suddenly there was the steady pounding of hooves toward the house and Sable instinctively felt for Amanda's hand.

"They've come back—those men have come back!"

Amanda's grip was tight on hers for a moment. "We'd

341

better get these shutters closed and fastened," she said, her voice carefully calm.

Sable nodded, and they peered, cautiously at first, at the garden below them . . . carefully scanning the shadowy rows of hibiscus toward the far wall, the orderly plantings of rose bushes and chrysanthemums, the dark patches of prepared beds where the tender plantings would soon go . . . dahlias, four o'clocks, zinnias.

The thudding of hooves seemed to be right in front of the house now. A horse whinnied . . . and another answered.

"I don't hear any shooting. Why doesn't Bates do something?" Sable said, her voice a hoarse whisper.

Amanda put a finger to her lips, her head turned to one side. "Listen!"

The front door slammed shut and there were male voices in the downstairs hall.

"It's all right," Amanda said. "It's Rob . . . that's Rob I hear." She started toward the door, but Sable just stood for a moment, an uneasiness creeping upward to her throat. Then she followed Amanda into the hall.

Amanda had stopped, turned to look at her . . . stepped aside. Then Sable saw Jace at the top of the stairs carrying Lanse hanging limply across one of his big shoulders, and for one awful instant she couldn't move. She screamed, clapped her open hand across her mouth to smother it.

"He's going to be all right," Rob assured her, patting her hand in that awkward way a man comforts a woman not his own. "It takes more than a good whack on the head to hurt Lanse Wakefield . . . you'll see . . ."

They stood by the big mahogany bed, and though Sable nodded, she never took her eyes from Lanse's still face, watching intently as Melissa gently wiped away the partially dried blood, the streaked dirt. She saw the scratches, the small burn on his cheek . . . another at his throat, his forehead.

"Jace and I . . . we'd better get back, hon. You sure you can handle things here?" Rob's words, Amanda's answers were blurred sound to Sable. She could only hear the crying inside her . . . please, please don't let him die . . . I love him so . . . don't let him die.

There was a gentle tug at her sleeve and Jace blocked her view of Lanse.

A slow smile warmed the brown eyes. "Missus," Jace said, "if I didn't think Mist' Lanse was going to be all right . . . I wouldn't be going back to town and leaving him."

"I know, Jace . . . I know." Her mouth felt stiff. Then the big man was gone and Melissa's dark fingers probed quickly, competently, through the thick strands of Lanse's hair, gently separating the sticky mass to expose the bruised swelling, the cut scalp, edges faintly blue and oozing slightly. She reached for the wet cloth.

"Let me," Sable said, and Melissa turned to look at her, startled for a moment. Then the smallest smile tugged at the corners of her mouth and she pressed the washcloth into Sable's outstretched hand.

"I'll take this water, Tish," Melissa said, taking the basin from the young woman's hands. "You run down to the kitchen and look in the bottom drawer of the cupboard. Fetch me my doctoring basket up here. Hurry up, now."

Melissa put the basin of warm water on the night table and drew the lamp closer. "Seems like I been patching this boy up half of my life," Melissa rambled on, seemingly to herself. "Many's the time they come carrying him in, and him nothing but a youngster . . . looking worse'n this. And I say, 'What's this child been up to now?' and they say, 'Another fight with the Bailer boy,' or some such."

She turned knowing black eyes on Sable. "You all right, honey?"

Almost immediately, Amanda's voice sounded from behind them. "Why don't you let us do this, Sable? We can take care of Lanse."

"No," Sable said firmly. "I want to myself."

Tish returned with the wicker basket, and Melissa

quickly went through the neat contents, then held out the small pair of scissors.

Slowly, carefully, Sable trimmed the thick, dark hair away from the wound, then, following Melissa's instructions, swabbed it thoroughly with pungent liquid from a dark brown bottle. She relinquished the sewing to Melissa, acknowledging the old Negress's great experience, but insisted on watching, even though the first thrust of the needle, the first pull of the strong white linen thread made her so ill she thought she would faint.

When it was all through, she was ready with the soft strips of cloth which she had found tucked away in one corner of the basket.

"Ain't nothing makes such good bandages as old sheets what ain't good for bed linens no more," Melissa said as she tied the last two ends securely, and Sable gently lowered the bandaged head back to the pillow.

Amanda took Sable's arm. "Won't you please come with me now and lie down? You can see he's going to be all right. One of us will sit with him, if it will make you feel better."

"No." Sable shook her head. "I think I'll stay here for a while."

It was much later. Lanse had lain so still for such a long time. Sable pulled the blanket closer about him, wishing she had had them put him in another room—but how could she have explained that? How could she have said, "I can't bear the pain of being in this room with him; there are too many memories . . ."

Don't think about the room. Don't think about this bed. Don't remember.

He stirred . . . moaned slightly, fell quiet again. The small burn was a livid patch against his pale face.

We should have put something on that, she thought, and went through the contents of the basket, removing the tops from the various jars of creams and ointments until she found the one she thought was right.

She sat on the side of the bed and with a gentle forefinger applied the soothing ointment to the burns, first the one on his cheek then the smaller ones on his forehead, at his throat. Her face was very close to his. She could feel his breath, warm on her skin.

"Lanse." She said his name softly, and somehow she was kissing him, her lips pressing hungrily against his.

"Oh, Lanse . . ." She pulled away, her head bowed, tears washing her face. "Why didn't I tell you the truth while there was still time . . . when you might have believed me?"

She searched her pocket and found the wisp of handkerchief. Amanda might come in . . . or Melissa or Tish . . . She couldn't let them find her this way.

She heard the stirring, drew in her breath sharply and turned to him. Lanse was staring at her, his eyes sleepy, confused . . . the lids lowered slightly as if he were trying very hard to concentrate.

He raised his hand to her face, but the effort seemed too much and he let it fall back to the bed; his eyes closed again and soon his breathing came in the deep, normal rhythm of restful sleep.

Chapter 27

Lanse opened his eyes, raised his hand to his head and felt the edges of the bandage. He cautiously moved his legs and then his other arm. Must not be too bad, he thought. Everything seemed to be working properly.

He lifted himself to his elbows, winced at the sudden throb of pain the movement produced, eased back to the pillow.

He recalled clearly Rob's shouted warning, the cross-beam crashing downward . . . and after that, only vague shadowy forms and movement. There had been the pain in his head, and once he had heard Jace's voice . . . but later . . . *had she really been here?* She had touched his face and kissed him . . . she was crying.

No. That couldn't be. It was a dream. It had to be a dream. She had said something . . . what was it? His head ached dully now, and trying to remember made it worse. What was it she had said? Something about telling him the truth before it was too late. But what did that mean?

"So!" Melissa's voice startled him. "You finally decided to wake up. Right around the clock you been laying there." She bustled into the room, pulled back an edge of the bandage and peered beneath it.

"Poor little Miz Sable, she been trotting back and forth to see how you doing. And I been telling her all along, 'Miz Sable honey, that sleep the best thing for him . . .' How's your head feel?"

"It's all right."

"Aches, don't it?" she said dryly.

Lanse grunted, watched her straighten the bedcovers. "Sable . . . your mistress was here?"

Melissa turned her head, birdlike, to one side and looked at him for a long uncomfortable moment. "Yes, sir . . . course she was. Why, she tended to that cut herself. I had the hardest time persuading her to let me do the stitching. I declare, that poor little thing almost fainted dead away while she was watching me."

Lanse saw a gleam of amusement dance wickedly in Melissa's black eyes. He looked away. "The fire is out?"

"Yes, sir. It was mighty bad, though."

"Rob and Jace all right?"

"Yes, sir, but Miz Willa and Mist' Jed burned plumb out. The house and hotel both gone."

"Damn!" Lanse swore softly. "You'd think those two had had enough trouble for awhile. Where are they? Here at the house?"

"No, sir. Mist' Russell come for them. Took them home with him."

There was a sound at the door, and Sable's anxious face appeared. The throbbing in Lanse's head became a pounding as he saw the blue eyes widen, the sudden color in her cheeks.

"You . . . you're awake?" she said, making no move to enter the room.

"Yes . . . finally."

She twisted her hands. "Are you all right?"

"Oh . . . I'm fine . . . fine," he repeated and felt like a fool.

"I'm very glad." The words were so low he almost

348

didn't hear them. Then she was gone and he wanted to call after her, but Melissa was watching him with that same devilish amusement.

"Damn it, Melissa, get out of here," he sputtered. "Get out of here so I can put my pants on."

Melissa planted her hands firmly on her hips. "You ain't getting out of that bed today."

"You see if I don't," he said. "Get me some breakfast. I'm hungry."

Rob Cooper walked into the study and grinned at Lanse, who, in spite of Melissa's firm pronouncement of the morning, was indeed up, dressed, and downstairs.

"Well, sir," Lanse drawled, taking in the fine gray suit, the pale green silk vest, "you surely look different than the last time I saw you."

"You look a mite different yourself," Rob said. "How do you feel?"

"Fine"—Lanse ran his fingers lightly along the bandage—"considering. Sit down." He gestured toward the chair, then reached for the tray with its decanter of brandy ringed by small glasses. When two of the glasses were filled, he handed one across the polished top of the desk to Rob, cradled the other in his own big hand, and settled back in his chair.

"Well, let's have it," he said.

Rob sobered. "It's not so good, Lanse. The office is gone . . . all the papers with it . . . four warehouses."

"Goddamn! They were nearly full!"

Rob nodded, swallowed part of his drink. "I know."

Lanse forced himself to speak more calmly. "What else?"

"All that property on Clay Street's leveled . . . Course we can build on it again, when we get outselves out of the woods. Some of the loans we made'll just have to be written off—like Jackson. His saloon's nothing but a pile of ashes. He didn't have a penny's worth of insurance."

Lanse swiveled his chair back and forth. "That's something we'd better get right onto—filing our insurance

349

claims. Probably take some time to collect, *if* we can collect. You know what happened last time. Some of the companies just folded, couldn't make good. But . . . we can still count on the *Seawind* and her cargo . . ."

"Yes, and don't forget," Rob said, "we've got some money tucked away in that bank back East. We can draw on that."

Lanse raised the glass of brandy, inhaled the fumes, tasted it. "If I recall, that was your idea . . . and a damned good one, too."

Rob ignored him. "We'll be all right . . . just take a while."

Lanse nodded. "I heard about Willa and Jed. They're going to stay with the Russells?"

"Yes. Vinnie, Chris' wife, wouldn't have it any other way. She's a good woman. Sent Chris after them just as soon as she found out. I talked to Jed for a few minutes. He's counting on the insurance. Wants to rebuild right away."

They were quiet for a moment. Lanse finished his drink, put the glass down on the desk. "Have you been back into town?"

Rob nodded. "It's worse even than I thought it would be. Whole business district's practically gone. I heard a rider had come in from Monterey, said they could see the glow from there."

"Why, that must be ninety . . . a hundred miles away!"

Rob stood, walked to the window to look out at the rapidly fading light. "The looters have been at work," he said. "While the town was burning, lots of the outlying houses were broken into . . . robbed. They came here—to our place, too, but a few shots sent them on. In town, everything that wasn't burned or nailed down's been carried off."

"The Ducks?"

"Sure. And that's not all. Yesterday morning, bands of them rode through the streets yelling and shooting it up. They nailed a couple of dozen of these up."

Rob reached into his inside coat pocket, unfolded the crumpled, dirty bit of paper, and tossed it on the desk.

The crudely lettered words stared up at Lanse: *Sydney Town—the new ruler of this city.* Anger smoldered, became a white-hot thing in him. "But God, we'll see about that!"

Rob grinned suddenly. "That's exactly what Sam Brannan said when he first saw one." He sobered again. "Sam's called a public meeting at the Plaza tonight. That's where I'm headed when I leave here."

Lanse got to his feet. "Just wait until I get my coat. I'm going with you."

"Do you think you should?" Rob caught at his arm. "That was a pretty good crack you took."

Lanse shook away the restraining hand. "I'm going," he said.

The dry dust of the street stirred under the hooves of the horses, and Lanse could feel it in his nostrils along with the ashes and smell of the hundreds of burned substances—wood, cotton, liquor, gunpowder, flesh . . . yes, that, too . . . flesh, bone. For a moment he could feel again the persistent tugging at his sleeve, the whiskey-fouled breath hot against his face. Had the poor wretch's brother been in that upstairs room, or had he been lucky enough to get out in time?

"See?" Rob's voice broke into his thoughts. "That whole section of wharf's burned right through."

Lanse's eyes followed Rob's outstretched hand along the charred, irregular remains of the wharf out to the cut-off ends of the piers, the water black and quiet around them.

They passed what had been one of their warehouses— Full two days ago, Lanse thought disgustedly.

But a few blocks farther and Lanse's spirits lifted as he saw two men working, an upright pole shoved into the ground to hold the lantern. They patiently shoveled the debris into a wheelbarrow and emptied it into the waiting wagon. It was the corner lot and Lanse thought back to the small shop that had been there—dry goods, that was it, dry goods. The two men straightened, one threw up his hand at them, the other smiled, his teeth looking too big, too white, in the soot-blackened face.

There were others like them, still working despite the fact that daylight was several hours gone. On some lots there were already stacks of new wood, its pungent smell strangely identifiable among the hundreds of others.

Rob grinned at him. "She's quite a town, isn't she?"

"Damned right, she is!"

There was a large tent where the Eureka had been; painted on the canvas were big, black letters: OPEN FOR BUSINESS. Raucous laughter echoed from the lighted interior while several male voices, one of them slightly flat, rang out with "Oh, Susanna," accompanied by the familiar-sounding piano.

Lanse pulled Satan to a standstill. "Can you tell me how in hell Mac managed to save that piano?"

Rob laughed. "Story is he ran out on the street and talked three men into helping him carry it out. Said he'd had it brought overland all the way from St. Louis and he'd be double damned if he'd let it burn. Saved that, and a wagonload of whiskey, and that big picture he kept up over the bar—you know, the one you had painted for him when you traded him out of that mirror."

Lanse nodded. "I know the one you mean."

They were a few minutes late getting to the Plaza, and the meeting was already under way. There was a good crowd, solid businessmen rubbing shoulders with bearded miners. There were sailors in port for a week or two and curious to see what was going on, a young dandy—gambling man by the look of him, Lanse thought—and farther back in the crowd, two dancehall girls, long capes covering their short skirts.

Lanse and Rob circled the crowd until they finally found a spot where they could tie up the horses to a nearby hitchrail, keep an eye on them, and still have a good view of the proceedings.

Sam Brannan spoke, his feet planted firmly apart atop

the empty packing crate, his chest thrust out in a fighting posture.

"Some of you were here yesterday," he was saying. "Some of you saw the Ducks ride through the streets of this town. You heard what they said. You saw these." He held up a piece of paper that matched the one in Lanse's pocket.

"You there, Tom Atkins!" Sam's arm flashed out; Lanse's eyes followed the pointing finger to see the slight figure edge forward in the crowd. "I hear your place was one of those robbed."

Tom's face reddened; he raised his fist. "By God, that's right, Sam! And what they didn't steal, they just plain broke up! Looks like they took an axe to it!"

Sam nodded shortly. His black eyes swept on. "And you, Harley Baker . . . your store burn, Harley?"

"No, sir." The big man who answered stood quietly, but there was a sullen, hard anger in his voice. "But when I come back after the fire was out, all my goods was gone."

Sam went on calling on one here, one there, while Lanse and Rob turned their attention momentarily to Chris Russell and Jed Mason, who had elbowed their way over to them. They shook hands around.

"Glad to see you're up and around, Lanse," the older man said.

"Thanks, Chris." Lanse turned to Jed. "Sorry about the house and hotel, Jed. We'd be glad to have you at Wakefield Manor. Stay as long as you'd want."

"Oh, here now!" Chris Russell raised a protesting hand. "We've only just gotten them settled with us. Why, I haven't seen Vinnie so happy since the children were still at home. She and Willa were clucking over a piece of needlepoint when we left . . ."

Sam's voice rose sharply and they turned back to listen as he snatched the tall black hat from his head and threw it violently to the ground.

"I'm very much surprised"—his voice was pure sarcasm—"to hear people talk of grand juries, or recorders, or mayors. I'm tired of such talk. Fires, murders, beatings . . . these are the realities.

"Sydney Town is a growing hellhole . . . spreading . . . being fed by the constant stream of Australian convicts . . ."

Lanse heard the whispering rustle of silk, and turned to look down into the very green, very feminine eyes of Flossie Tucker.

"Lanse Wakefield, ain't it?" She touched his arm lightly with one gloved hand. "I bet you don't remember me?"

Lanse covered his surprise, inclining his head slightly. "On the contrary, Miss Tucker. I remember you very well." How could he help it? he thought wryly—though at least Winston seemed to have taught her better taste in clothes. His eyes moved over the pale ivory silk of her dress, from the soft folds over the generous hips to the nipped-in waist, coming at last to rest in near fascination on her half-exposed bosom, the tops pushed high and round above the lace-edged neckline.

He heard her laugh, soft and faintly mocking, and looked quickly up to find the green eyes regarding him with amusement.

"I been wanting to talk to you," she said, still smiling. "I saw you here in the crowd and thought this would be a good chance."

"Well—" He cleared his throat, aware of the sidelong glances of his male companions. "Well, perhaps, we'd better move right over here." He steered her firmly out of the crowd, back to a clear spot in the dusty Plaza, then waited for her to speak.

"Hurt yourself?" She tilted her head to one side, eyed his bandaged head.

"No, no, it's nothing," he said quickly. "Just got in the way of something I shouldn't have."

She nodded. "I'm leaving San Francisco tomorrow," she said. "We're sailing for New York."

"Oh . . . I hadn't heard that Winston—"

"I ain't with Winston no more," Flossie cut him off.

"He's bringing his wife and son out. They'll be here next month. I'm going back with Luther Simms."

Simms. Lanse could see the scarred mouth, the eyes with their bright, hard cynicism, the hint of sadistic cruelty. "Oh," he said, embarrassed, hoping that his voice didn't betray the pity he suddenly felt for her.

"Anyway," she went on, "with me leaving and all, I wanted to ask about Sable. I ain't seen her since that day on the street. I ain't tried to. I could tell you didn't like me speaking to her . . ." She waved away any protest he might have made. "It's all right . . . I understand how you feel. I hear she's . . . in a family way. That right?"

Lanse nodded.

"Will it be soon now?"

"Yes . . . less than a month."

"Well," she said, "you tell her goodbye for me. And tell her I hope . . . no, I *know* things are going to be just fine."

"I'll do that," Lanse said.

Flossie suddenly smiled forlornly. "I can't remember how long it's been since I . . . liked another woman, but I liked her. Right from the first time I seen her, I says to myself, Flossie, that's a good kid. She took care of me when I was sick . . . those others, the bitches, would've let me die before they'd lifted a finger to help me. Did she tell you that?"

Lanse shook his head.

"Well, it's true. Stood right up to them, she did . . . and her better'n any of them," Flossie said proudly.

She twisted her silk-gloved fingers in the gold chain around her neck. "God, I was scared . . . so scared I swore if I got well I'd change . . . find myself some man out here and be a real wife to him. She told me I could do it, too. Ain't that a laugh . . ." The gold chain snapped, swung free in Flossie's fingers. She looked down at it for a moment.

"The first week I was up and around, I was right back in Judd's bunk where I wanted to be . . . Judd Grayson, he was the captain of the *Betty Kay*," she explained. "I guess she was disappointed in me, but she never said nothing . . . not a word."

She slipped the gold chain into the small reticule that matched her dress, then tilted her head to one side and her green eyes were laughing at him once more. "Goodbye, Lanse Wakefield," she said softly. "You take care of her now . . . you hear?"

Lanse watched her walk away, then turned and pushed his way back through the crowd.

"These men are murderers, I say, as well as thieves." Sam Brannan's fist raised high in the air. "I know it, and I will die or see them hung by the neck. The laws and courts never yet hung a man in California, and every morning we read fresh accounts of murder and robbery. I want no technicalities. Such things are devised to shield the guilty . . ."

Despite the distance between them, Lanse could see the black eyes flash, but even Sam Brannan's eloquence could not hold his attention now.

Lanse swept back the velvet drape and let the moonlight into the room, stood for a moment looking up at the source of that light . . . not its usual pale yellow, but a fat, ripe peach against the night sky.

His head ached with an annoying persistence and he turned away from the window, stripped off his trousers, and climbed into bed. He pulled the top sheet over his nude body and shifted the pillow to a more comfortable position.

It was here . . . right here beside him that she had sat. And her face was soft against his and she had kissed him . . . His big fingers moved across his mouth . . . Or had he dreamed that part?

He had almost gone to her when he had come in, but stopped when he saw there was no light showing under her door. Besides, what would he have said? Did you really kiss me?

He punched the pillow. He'd almost made a goddamned ass of himself. And yet, the memory was so real.

Far off in the night, a hound caught the scent of his quarry and sent up a frantic baying. Lanse's laugh was short, dry. He had heard that dog on other nights. How many nights had he lain here awake, wanting her until it was an ache in him? And every time it was as though he knew every rise and hollow, every sweet, tormenting line of her white body—yet he had never possessed her. But Gregg had . . . Goddamn him to hell. He'd touched her, held her, sated himself upon her . . . She carried the proof of that right now.

Always before when he reached this point, he had retreated from the agony of it, forced his mind to a safe, dark numbness. But not this time.

With a conscious effort of will he remembered that day when he had returned home from the meeting at Tom Atkins's to find Gregg. It surprised him that after all this time he could remember so explicitly every word they had exchanged . . . the way Gregg's thin lips had twisted downward. *You don't look like a man who would be content with my leavings* . . . His knuckles tingled with the memory of smashed flesh beneath them . . . Sable's face, white, her eyes wild, disbelieving . . .

Later, at the saloon, the whiskey had been raw. It had scorched his tongue, the back of his throat, but it had done what he wanted it to . . . dulled his mind until he could almost forget what Gregg had said. And the woman in that damned painting had seemed to mock him and invite him at the same time, her breasts and belly, the curve of her hip and thighs thrusting out to him . . . only somehow it wasn't Lita anymore, but Sable.

He guessed that was what had made him go to Lil's place . . . It all blurred, ran together after he left Mac's. He remembered holding his face up to the cooling air, jolting as Satan stumbled over a dry, sun-baked rut in the road. And lightning had ripped the sky apart and lit up that big cliff, the one that was all jagged with rocks. In the light, the rocks were a bright, clear pink that muted, dulled with the returning darkness. After that, his only memory was the soft woman-flesh beneath his hands and his urgent need for her and the rain starting slowly, hesitantly, then pouring in a complete release.

Lanse's eyes suddenly narrowed. There was something wrong with that. That cliff . . . with the outcropping of pink rock . . . He knew it so well, for he had never seen rock back in Virginia of such a brilliant hue. That cliff was near the creek crossing, and that nearly home. He must have been at Lil's first . . . but no, the road that wound around the foot of the cliff had been dry. Satan had stumbled and he remembered the deep, dry ruts. Then how could he have been in town at Lil's place when the rain started? How could he have held a woman in his arms? Unless . . .

The sudden pounding in his temples was like a series of small explosions.

Chapter 28

Sable propped her feet atop the low footstool, leaned her head against the tall cushioned back of the wicker chair and looked up through the green vines to the delicate blue sky. It was pleasant here under the arbor, the breeze softly stirring the leaves, scarcely changing their pattern against the white wooden lattice. A bee buzzed noisily among the lacy clusters of pale yellow flowers . . . What was it Manuel had called them? She'd have to ask him again.

Her eyelids felt heavy. She hadn't slept much through the night. She'd been too uncomfortable . . . no position eased the pressure of her swollen body now.

She had heard Lanse come in—it must have been two or after, and yet he was already gone to meet with the insurance adjustor when she had come down to breakfast. She was worried . . . not about his head injury, that seemed to be all right. At least, he told her it was.

No. It was the constant comings and goings, the meetings, the undercurrent of something happening.

Small groups of men, men she'd never seen before, came to the house to talk with Lanse. Even worse, their own friends, Rob, Jed, Chris, Tom Atkins, came often, but there was something different about them . . . Their pleasant courtesies were somehow superficial, and underneath was a brittle intensity that frightened her. Sam Brannan came, too, and while she had always liked Sam, she knew that he was the leader, the driving force in their meetings, and his visits to the house unsettled her.

She had read the newspapers the men carelessly left in the study—the inflaming editorials that cited the shocking statistics on crime in San Francisco, that bitterly accused the Federal Congress of failing to pass legislation to aid the situation, and that openly urged the decent men of San Francisco to band together to enforce their own laws until such time as the government would accept its responsibility.

Each day the Ducks found new ways to taunt the helpless citizens, and the front pages were filled with stories of their violence.

Sable wanted so much to talk to Lanse, to find out what the men were planning to do. But there was a new unease between them . . . had been since the fire two weeks past. There were times when she was sure he remembered her kissing him, times when he looked at her with the strangest expression in his eyes . . . when he seemed on the verge of saying something. But he never did. Was he angry with her? Was he pleased? Oh, God, if only she could know!

The sound of a carriage brought her abruptly back to her surroundings. Wheels crunching on the fine white gravel, it came along the drive and swung round in front of the house. But she couldn't see for the dense growth of privet that sheltered the garden on that side.

It couldn't be Amanda. She had told Sable yesterday that she was going to make soap today, and there was no task about which Amanda was quite so particular as soap-making.

Melissa came out of the twin doors onto the side verandah and along the flagstone path to the arbor.

"Miz Sable, honey, there's a gentleman here to see

you. I done told him and told him that you ain't receiving no callers right now, but he says he ain't leaving until I tell you he's here." Melissa's lower lip thrust out in its most disapproving manner.

"But who is it, Melissa?" Sable was completely puzzled.

Melissa's hand measured about four and a half feet above the ground. "About this tall, with great long arms and ugly as sin. Says his name's Nimrod, or some such."

"Nimrod! Oh, it couldn't be!" Sable started to rise, then remembered how uncomfortable walking was now. "Bring him here, Melissa," she said eagerly.

"Miz Sable," said Melissa, shaking her head, "I ain't never heard of no lady receiving gentlemen callers when she was almost ready for her confinement."

"Oh, Melissa, do hurry." Sable waved her away impatiently. "And, Melissa, could you fix some of the orange and lemon juice with water and sweetening the way you did the other day? And bring some of those little iced cakes, too, please."

Moments later, the slight figure with its well-remembered rolling gait came along the path toward her. One of the abnormally long arms shot upward to snatch off the faded seaman's cap, and the wizened face suddenly broke into a grin.

There was a quick stinging beneath Sable's eyelids, a hot constriction of her throat. She had only known this little man for the few months spent aboard the *Betty Kay*, but now as he came up and made that funny, rapid bob of his head, it was like seeing someone from home. She wanted to throw her arms around his neck and hug him soundly, but instead, she smoothed her skirts and smiled up at him.

"Nimrod," she said, "I'm so gald to see you."

"And I'm sure enough glad to see you, too, ma'am," he said, still grinning. She saw him glance at her middle and then look quickly back to her face.

"Sit down." She waved him into the matching wicker

chair across from her own. He sat down, placing an oilcloth-wrapped bundle on the footstool between them.

"When did you arrive in San Francisco? Are you still with Captain Grayson?"

"Oh, yes, ma'am, I'm still first mate on the *Betty Kay*." He turned the faded blue cap in his hands. "We dropped anchor the day before yesterday. First thing we heard about was the fire. It sure enough must've been a bad one . . ." He gestured toward the house. "Guess you wasn't hurt none."

"No . . . We're far enough away to be safe from the fires, but my husband lost some of his business holdings, and some of our friends . . ." She stopped suddenly and smiled at him. "No matter about that—tell me where you've been since I saw you last."

He opened his arms wide. "We been everywhere! First we went to them Sandwich Islands . . . you'd sure enough like them, Miss Sable . . . big, tall, brown-skinned people, always smiling. They meet every ship, bring food and put flowers around your neck and—" His voice trailed off and the smallest gleam appeared for an instant in the black eyes. "They're just right friendly. Course," he laughed dryly, "them missionaries don't give you much of a welcome . . . they ain't got no use for us seafaring men."

Sable shifted in her chair, trying to get more comfortable, saw Melissa walking toward them with a tray in her hands.

"Here's Melissa," she said, "with something cool for us to drink."

Nimrod snatched the bundle off the footstool to make room for the tray and carefully put it into the seat beside him, while Melissa favored him with a disapproving look and left.

"Please do try some," Sable urged him, "it's really very good." Then, with sudden misgivings, "Perhaps I should have had her bring something stronger . . ."

"Oh, no, ma'am, this here'll do just fine." He raised the tall glass to his mouth and drank. "Just fine."

"And have some cake, too."

He fumbled for a moment with the white linen napkin, finally put it awkwardly across his lap, took one of the small iced cakes gingerly. But once he had bitten into it, he relaxed and munched happily. "Good," he said.

She leaned back against the cushion and sipped her own drink. "Not as good as turtle steaks and fruit grunt," she teased. Then, suddenly serious: "I think that was the best meal I ever had. Do you remember?"

"Yes'm. It sure enough tasted good. That must've been nearly a year ago . . . don't seem like that long." He put the unfinished piece of cake down on the napkin. "Though you've changed some, Miss Sable." He suddenly looked stricken, his eyes leaping briefly to her swollen abdomen, his face turning a violent, deep red. "I . . . I didn't mean . . ."

She laughed at him, felt the slight heat in her own cheeks. "I know you didn't," she said.

"I just meant you . . . you look even prettier now—like you'd all growed up."

"Thank you, Nimrod, that was a very nice thing to say." Her voice sounded a little husky in her own ears, and she quickly sipped a bit more of her drink. "Now," she said, "you were telling me about the places you've been."

"Oh . . . yes, ma'am." He settled back in his chair and, between bites of cake, resumed his story. "After them Sandwich Islands, we dropped anchor at Shanghai and Hong Kong, then we went all the way down to Fiji before we come back to Frisco. Them Fiji islanders are sure enough something—got the kinkiest hair, sticks way out to here." He held his hands bowllike around his head. "And they wear necklaces made out of teeth . . .

"Now, Hong Kong," he said, "I didn't like so well. Ain't nothing much there." He finished his second cake and wiped his hand across the napkin in his lap.

"I like Shanghai better. Course, it's crowded and smelly close around the harbor, but farther into the town it's nice. I bought some stuff off a merchant there . . .

went right to his house, I did. He was wearing red satin pants and a jacket that had this big dragon stitched right on the back. A little house girl brought us tea in porcelain cups without no handles. Anyway, like I said"—he put the napkin aside and fumbled for the bundle beside him—"I bought some stuff off him and . . . and I brung this to you . . ."

"To me . . ? Why, Nimrod, you didn't have to do that."

"No, ma'am, I wanted to. Soon's I saw it, I knew you ought to have it."

He pulled back the edge of the oilcloth and Sable made a small sound of admiration at the vivid, clear blue color revealed. Then Nimrod pulled the bolt of material free, turned it around several times, and a length of the fine, silk fabric hung free, shimmering, the light bringing out the barest hint of green.

"Oh, Nimrod, it's so lovely . . ." Sable ran her hands along the soft, rippling cloth. "I don't know how to thank you. It'll make the most beautiful dress for after . . . I mean in a few weeks from now. See"—she held the cloth up near to her face—"this color will go well with my hair."

"It sure enough will, ma'am," he said softly. "It just sure enough will."

Sable put the cloth down. It had been a silly, vain thing for her to say—but it seemed an eternity since she had been slim, since she had cared about having a pretty new dress.

She looked hesitantly up at Nimrod. "I can't remember when I've been so pleased with anything," she said. And Nimrod's face paled, then reddened and the faded cap between his hands was twisted almost into a figure eight.

"How are things here for you, Miss Sable? I mean, are you glad you come out here? Are you happy here?"

"Of course I am . . . I'm very happy," she answered quickly.

"I'm sure enough glad to hear it, ma'am. I did a lot

of thinking after we left Frisco last year—about you and them other ladies we brought. This here town maybe ain't the best place for ladies . . ."

"Well, we've managed. Only one that I know about went back home. That was Carrie Thorne . . . you remember Carrie?"

"Yes'm, I do. I'm sure enough sorry."

"We were, too, but it was for the best that she go back."

They were quiet for a moment.

"And what about Miss Amanda?" Nimrod broke the silence. "Do you ever see her?"

"Oh, all the time. Her husband and mine are business partners. Amanda's fine. I've never seen her happier."

"That's right good news to hear. You give her my best next time you see her."

Sable nodded. "Why don't you have some more cake, Nimrod?"

"No, ma'am, I had plenty . . . besides, I'd best be getting along back to town. Cap'n be needing me."

"So soon . . . How long will you be in San Francisco? Will you come see me again?"

Nimrod stood up. "Doubt if there'll be time, ma'am. We'll be here a few more days, but there'll be lots for me to see to . . . then it's back home to New York. Course, we'll make port here once in a while, and when we do I'll hire me a rig and come out again . . ."

"I'm going to take that for a promise." Sable stood, felt the downward pull, the aching strain against muscle and tissue. "I'll see you to the door," she said.

"No . . . no, ma'am." Nimrod was firm. "You stay right here."

"All right . . . Thank you again for the material. I love it. When you come again, I'll show you the dress."

"I'll sure enough ask to see it," he said. "Well, goodbye, Miss Sable." He made the quick, small gesture with his head.

"Goodbye, Nimrod," she said. And she watched him go along the path, pause at the door to clap the battered cap upon his head and give her a jaunty salute before he disappeared.

She sat down, pulled the free end of the silk across her lap and touched it to her cheek.

Lanse felt his shoulder and arm muscles move, release their power into the wood and metal of the axe, heard the clear, good sound as the blade bit into the felled tree. And as his arms swung up, Jace's swung down, the two men working in a perfectly attuned rhythm.

Lanse had wanted this field cleared for planting since before the house was built. He could have sent Bates and Tompkins to do it, but the truth was he wanted to get away from the pressures of trying to rebuild a damaged business, from insurance claims and plans for the Vigilance Committee—and most of all from the doubt that had been with him since that night . . . the sleepless night spent pacing the floor of his room, when he had tried to remember what exactly had happened on that night after Gregg had left Wakefield Manor. It was impossible . . . it was fantastic. And yet, she had sat on the side of his bed when she thought he was unconscious and said, *I wish I'd told him the truth before it was too late.*

The wood cracked, made a hollow sound. Lanse brought the blunt side of his axe down viciously and the trunk parted.

They rested, drawing the air deep into their lungs, grinning at one another. Lanse wiped his arm across his forehead, then stripped off his shirt and threw it to one side, while Jace, who had shed his shirt more than an hour before, drank from the canteen, held his head back and let water run over his face and dribble down his chest.

"Let's eat," Lanse said. "I'm hungry."

"Me, too," Jace agreed. And they walked side by side to the thick clump of trees at the field's edge where the horses grazed.

While Lanse retrieved the jar of fresh buttermilk from

the cool creek, Jace took down the basket from a wide fork in one of the trees.

Tish had packed thick slices of beef and wedge-shaped chunks of cornbread, a jar of beans, and fried apple pies. They disdained the white napkins and tablecloth, filled their plates, and stretched themselves out on the grass to eat.

"You know," Lanse said, gesturing toward the field, "now that we have the trees all down, we'll just strip off the limbs this afternoon. Tomorrow or next day I'll send Tompkins and Bates up here with a crosscut saw to cut up the trunks."

"Some of them biggest pieces going to have to be split."

Lanse bit into the thick, brown undercrust of the bread, chewed, and swallowed before he answered. "I'll tell them to bring a wedge and sledge hammer along."

Jace grunted, refilled his tin cup with buttermilk.

The sky, so bright and sunny when they left the house that morning, had gone a dull gray. The air felt heavy, close.

They ate the rest of the meal in silence. Jace washed the last bite of fried pie down with buttermilk, wiped the back of his hand across his mouth, and rolled over on his back with a contented sigh.

It had always been that way with them, Lanse thought. They could talk or not talk, as they pleased. There was an easiness between them that banished the need for conversation. That was why he had asked Jace to come with him today.

The horses had come closer, nibbling at the sweet, tender grass, and now Satan ventured even nearer, nuzzling at Lanse's pocket where he had so often found a bit of sugar.

"Sorry, boy," Lanse said, laughing. "Nothing in there today." He shooed him gently away.

It had grown darker in the past few minutes and Lanse stood up, walked to the edge of the clearing and looked up at a sky that was a rolling, troubled mass of dark gray clouds, shaded almost black to the horizon.

"Looks like we might get wet," he said.

Jace came to stand beside him. "There's that old hay barn back of that rise. We could ride over there until it passes."

"Good idea," Lanse said. "You go get the axes and our shirts. I'll put this stuff back in the basket, get the horses and come out to meet you."

But Lanse was scarcely into the saddle before the first rain fell, scattered drops almost as big as his thumb that hit the ground with dull, flat thuds. Then closer and harder they fell until he could hardly see ahead of him.

The big, bay gelding he led whistled through his nostrils and jerked his head continuously, but Satan, though nervous, soon quieted under his master's familiar touch.

Lanse heard Jace call, then saw him holding the sodden shirts high and waving them like a flag.

"Come on," Lanse yelled above the sound of the rain, and handed the bay's reins to Jace.

It wasn't very far to the hay barn, but they had to go slowly, letting the horses pick their way carefully over the slippery ground, lest one fall and break a leg. Then suddenly, through the downpour, it was there before them, rickety, one side of the roof sagging badly where a support had given way and been propped up, gaping holes here and there in the weather-grayed walls.

They rode through the wide opening, doors long since gone, and swung down.

"Whoooee . . ." Jace threw his head back and laughed, slapping the water from trousers plastered to his skin, his muscular torso, in the half-light of the barn, looking like carved black marble. Lanse shook the water from his hair and eyes, stamped his feet upon the hard-packed earth floor.

"Just like upending the spring and dumping it on you," Jace said.

Lanse looked out at the downpour. "Looks like it might last awhile, too." He was aware of a steady drop of water on his bare shoulder, shifted to avoid one of the many leaks, then took a good look around their shelter.

"That corner looks drier than the rest of it," he said. "Probably gets some protection from the loft."

There was even a bit of old hay, musty smelling and faintly green with mold, but they heaped it up and sat down to wait out the rain.

"Just don't seem right," Jace shook his head, "that there ain't no thunder, ain't no lightning with a summer rain here. Remember when we was younguns and Melissa'd look up at the sky and say, 'The old lady's beating on her frying pan again'?"

Lanse nodded, laughed.

"And you know, I really did used to wonder if there was some old woman up there making all that racket."

They were quiet for a moment. Jace said, "Ain't heard thunder nor seen lightning but one time since we come out here . . . that was last fall. Don't seem natural . . . why you suppose that is?"

Lanse's stomach suddenly seemed to shrivel, but he kept his voice carefully level. "I don't know. Maybe the mountains have to do with it . . . something like that . . ."

"I got caught in that storm, too." Jace chuckled, while Lanse felt his heart pound in a slow, forced way.

"What do you mean?" he said carefully.

"I heard you come in that night and I went out front to see if you wanted me to put up Satan. And I found him standing out there loose. I never knowed you to do that before. I meant to say something about that, but you left sudden-like next morning, and I guess I clean forgot about it until right now.

"Anyway," he went on, "I took him on down to the stable . . . going to rub him down. And I was hardly in the door when that big storm started. I stayed down there until it was over."

For a moment Lanse felt numb, and then his body went hot all over, in spite of the rain-cooled air.

It was true, then. He had come home before the rain started . . . and the woman he had held . . . the woman had been Sable.

Lanse was vaguely aware of Jace saying something,

rising and going to stand before the door, but he sat quite still, his mind seething with questions. Why . . . why hadn't she told him? Why had she let him believe the worst for all these months?

There was a flash of anger so intense that it left him breathless, replaced instantly by a guilt of equal force as he thought what he had said to her. He had called her a bitch. He had hit her . . .

Oh God . . . could there be anything left for them after that? What could he say to her?

Chapter 29

Amanda took off her pert green bonnet, patted her hair and turned to her husband and Lanse with a smile.

"Is it all right if I go ahead upstairs?" she asked.

"By all means," Lanse answered. "Willa is already up there with Sable."

"Oh, good . . . I'll see you before you leave," she said to Rob.

"All right, hon." They watched her go up the gracefully curving staircase and then went into the study.

"How is Sable?" Rob asked as Lanse waved him into a chair.

"She's doing well, thank you . . . anyway, as well as we could expect." He sank into the chair behind his desk, tilted it back.

And what did he really know about how she was doing? he asked himself bitterly—he'd scarcely laid eyes on her in the last two days. Of course, their relationship had hardly been close these last months. And this damned Vigilante thing would have to boil over right now.

You could make the opportunity, he jeered at himself,

even if you had to walk right into her bedroom in the middle of the night. You're afraid of what she might say.

"She's going past time, isn't she?" Rob's voice jarred him back.

"Yes . . . a little. Melissa says it isn't anything to worry about. I thought I might stop by Bush's office and ask him to come out and see about her. She can't manage the stairs anymore. She's taking all her meals in her room."

"So that's what I have to look forward to."

Lanse was in the process of filling his pipe, and for a minute Rob's words didn't register, then he looked quickly up, saw Rob's big grin.

"Do you mean . . . Amanda . . . ?"

Rob nodded and Lanse came around the desk, wrung Rob's hand. "Well, congratulations! This calls for a drink!" He glanced at the decanter on the desktop. "Not this—I have something really special in the liquor cabinet. I've been saving it for an occasion, and I can't think of a better time."

He led the way across the hall through the double oak doors.

"I bought three bottles of this from a ship captain's private stock—about four or five months ago. He needed some gambling money in a hurry." Lanse reached into the deepest recesses of the cabinet.

"Apricot brandy," he said, "distilled so smooth it rolls right off your tongue—but it'll kick like a mule. Hand me two of those glasses."

Lanse poured, passed the drink to Rob, took his own, and raised it high. "To your son," he said.

"And to yours," Rob echoed him, and his words caused the strangest feeling in Lanse. He hadn't really thought about that part . . . that Sable's child would be his own.

They drained the glasses. Rob caught his breath, blew it out. "Did you say 'kick'?" He laughed.

Lanse held out the bottle. "Have another?"

"No thanks, I want to be able to walk when we get there."

The big clock in the hall struck seven, the sound echoing through the house.

"Does Amanda know what we plan to do tonight?" Lanse said.

"Yes . . . I didn't want her to know especially in her condition. But Mandy has a way of getting things out of me." He grinned. "Did you tell Sable?"

"No." Lanse's answer was short. He replaced the cork in the apricot brandy and put it back in the cabinet. "Chris and Jed were here earlier . . . said they'd meet us there."

Two hours later, Lanse stood in the California Engine House, crowded shoulder to shoulder, listening to Sam Brannan clear his throat solemnly, his black eyes sober and quiet.

Sam held up the paper and read: "Whereas it has become apparent to the citizens of San Francisco that there is no security for life and property either under the regulations of Society as it at present exists or under the laws as now administered, . . . therefore, the Citizens whose names are hereto attached do unite themselves into an association for the maintenance of the peace and good order of Society and the preservation of the lives and property of the Citizens of San Francisco and do bind themselves unto each other to do and perform every lawful act for the maintenance of law and order and to sustain the laws when faithfully and properly administered . . . but we are determined that no thief, burglar, incendiary or assassin shall escape punishment, either by the quibbles of the law, the insecurity of prisons, the carelessness or corruption of the Police or a laxity of those who pretend to administer justice."

And minutes later, Lanse's hand was firm and steady as he scrawled his name boldly beneath the growing list.

Sable held up the pair of knitted blue wool soakers that Willa had made for the baby. "Oh, Willa," she said, "you've gone to so much trouble . . . thank you. Did you see the little outfit Amanda made?" Sable tried to get up but Amanda waved her back.

"I'll get it for you," she said.

"Would you? It's in that top drawer."

Amanda came back and showed Willa the exquisite dress and bonnet set, made of the sheerest batiste and embroidered in blue around the tiny collar and brim of the bonnet.

After it had been duly admired, Amanda put it back in the drawer along with the new soakers and came back to join them.

They had arranged chairs in one corner of Sable's bedroom. Amanda and Willa both worked on needlepoint. Sable earlier had made an attempt at her embroidery, but had long since put it aside.

"I'm so uncomfortable," she said, shifting the small throw pillow behind her back. "I don't think I can stand it much longer."

"Why don't you lie down? We can pull the chairs up closer to the bed," Amanda suggested.

Sable laughed. "I guess it's not quite that bad," she said, "though sometimes I feel like it is. I thought for sure it would happen last week . . . but here I am." She looked down at her huge abdomen with disgust.

"I heard if you take a big dose of castor oil . . ." Willa offered.

"Don't you dare!" Amanda countered. "A neighbor did that with one of hers and came near to dying from it." She waved her needle at Sable. "That baby'll come when it's ready to."

"I guess so," Sable agreed halfheartedly. "But I wish I'd start in labor right now." Even as she said the words, she knew it wasn't true . . . she feared it, with a cold, hard chill inside her. And in spite of her good friends, in spite of Melissa and Tish and all the others, she had never felt quite so alone.

Her guests worked on in silence until Amanda gave a small exclamation of pain and quickly put her thumb to her mouth. "Stuck myself!" she managed to say in spite of the mouthful.

"Is it deep?" Willa asked.

Amanda took out the injured thumb and looked at it . . . shook her head. "No . . . I just wasn't watching what I was doing."

And suddenly, Sable was aware that Amanda had been nervous all evening. She remembered the slim fingers picking at the lace across her pocket, pulling at a loose tendril of hair. Willa had been fidgeting, too.

"Amanda," she said, "are you all right?"

The answer was quick and almost too cheerful. "Of course I am . . . why wouldn't I be?"

"Willa?" Sable turned to the young girl and saw her hesitate, saw the withdrawal that happened sometimes now, as if one touched some raw, hidden place in her. And they were never quite sure what they said to cause it.

At last she answered. "I know what they're doing tonight. Jed says . . . he says it's something he has to do."

The room seemed suddenly very quiet, and Sable looked from one to the other of them. "Then that just leaves me . . . doesn't it?"

The insurance agent, Homer Claypool, peered nearsightedly across the desk at Lanse and wiped the lenses of his gold-rimmed spectacles with his handkerchief. He'd covered every inch of ground, sifted through rubble, gone over every estimate of loss, and managed somehow to pare every one of them at least a third less than Lanse's original claim. Sometimes he wouldn't even allow half.

It had been a bad day right from the beginning. Lanse had had every intention of talking to Sable that morning, but Melissa had soon ended that.

"Don't take that tray up to Miz Sable," she had called to Tish. "I just peeped in the door and she was sleeping like a baby. Poor little missus . . . don't think she closed her eyes last night."

Lanse had swallowed the last drop of his coffee, telling

himself stiffly that if he wanted to wake his own wife in his own house, he'd do just that, when Rob arrived and insisted they were going to be late for their meeting with Claypool.

They had ridden into a town where the uneasiness was a smell in the air, a taste in the mouth. Small knots of men gathered here and there, talked, moved on. There was a quietness, a waiting that was unlike the sprawling, lusty town they knew.

As they tied their horses to the hitchrail outside Claypool's office, a tall, lank man sidled over to them, a gold toothpick sticking out of one corner of his mouth.

"Say," he said in a conspiratorial voice, "did you hear about the Vigilantes signing a constitution last night?"

"We heard," Rob said.

The man pulled the toothpick from his mouth. "What do you suppose the Ducks are gonna do about it?"

It had been the same all day, with every man in town looking as if he were sitting on eggs. That is, Lanse thought, every man except this fat, little bastard across from him who had gone about his business sublimely unaware of it all—too goddamn busy trying to cheat them out of the money his company owed them.

The spectacles at last polished to his liking, Claypool hooked the thin gold sidepieces over his ears, ran his handkerchief over a head nearly bald, then deposited the wrinkled square of linen in his coat pocket.

"Now then." He quickly looked down the row of figures. "I think when we come to terms on these last items, we can make a complete estimate of your claim against my company and conclude this part of our business, gentlemen."

One pink, well-kept nail slid across the page. "Now really, Mr. Wakefield, Mr. Copper, this one is completely out of the question."

"For God's sake!" Lanse leaned forward aggressively, but Rob's hand was at once on his arm.

"Wait a minute, Lanse," he said. "It's almost ten o'clock . . . we've been here all day. Let's get this thing over with and go home."

Lanse hesitated. "All right, what are your figures on it?"

Claypool went rapidly down the page, scratched out some entries, wrote over others, then handed the paper to Lanse, who looked it over, handed it to Rob. In a moment Rob nodded his head.

"We'll settle for it," Lanse said. "Where do we sign?"

"Mr. Claypool," he said when their business was done, "if you ever decide to change your line of business, we'd sure like to have you working for us."

The insurance adjustor pursed his mouth, but there was the barest hint of amusement in his eyes.

It was an unusually fine night, the sky clear and luminous, with a pleasant, summery breeze. Lanse and Rob had barely closed the door to the insurance office behind them, barely stepped out onto the rough plank sidewalk, when they heard the measured, somber tolling from the fire house. It was not the frantic ringing that signaled another fire, but a deliberately spaced sound that caused the two men to stare at one another, their eyes filled with knowledge.

The challenge had been given. For twenty-four hours San Francisco had been a powder keg, its fuse carefully prepared . . . and now the spark was struck.

Sam Brannan had been made president of the newly formed Vigilance Committee and had offered the use of his offices, near the corner of Sansome and Bush streets. This was where they headed.

A crowd had already gathered, standing along the sidewalks beneath the Committee room windows, spilling out into the dusty streets and around the nearby corners, and Lanse and Rob had to push and elbow their way through to the doors.

Inside the narrow hallway, Tom Atkins was just coming down the stairs.

"Tom!" Lanse hailed him. "What's happened?"

The slight, sandy-haired figure took the last two steps in a single stride. "We got a man named Jenkins upstairs,"

Tom jerked his thumb over his shoulder. "Caught him red-handed stealing the safe out of one of the shipping offices down on Long Wharf . . . must be ten or twelve witnesses saw it. When they caught up with him, he threw the safe in the Bay. Some of our boys came along, took him into custody, and brought him here."

"How long ago did this happen?" Rob asked.

"This evening before dark. Some way the word spread . . . That crowd outside started gathering even before the bell rang. There's a few upstairs wanting to sign up with us. Lafe Walker's talking to them."

"Well, let's get up there," Lanse said.

When they came into the outer room they saw fifteen, maybe twenty men waiting in front of the table where Lafe Walker sat. There was some pushing and loud guffawing.

"You tell them, Bertie," one man called out, his beefy face red with laughter. The cause of the merriment planted her beringed fingers flat on the table and leaned so far over that it looked as if her enormous bosom might pop right out of the faded pink satin dress.

"You ain't go no right to turn me down, Lafe Walker," she said. "A bunch of them Ducks come in my place, took their pleasure with my girls, and then roughed them up so much they wasn't fit to take care of customers fer a week. Didn't pay me a cent. Sign me up. I'm here to sign up!"

"Now, Bertie," Lafe pleaded, "I told you we ain't signing up no women . . ."

Lanse and Rob exchanged quick grins and went into the big meeting room. There were a good number of men already present. The prisoner sat apart from the rest, his big frame looking as if it might shatter the plain wooden chair.

He coolly stared at them, his small, deep-set eyes insolent in a face dominated by a protruding lower jaw.

President Sam Brannan hurried over to them.

"We met Tom downstairs," Lanse said. "He told us what happened."

Sam removed the ever-present black cigar from his mouth. "We'll start hearing testimony as soon as they've all had a chance to get here."

"Seems to me I've heard about this man Jenkins before," Rob said.

Sam nodded his head shortly. "One of their main bully boys. You name it, I suspect he's done it. Ducks way of calling our hand."

It was nearly half an hour later when the shipping agent, having been duly sworn, shifted uneasily in the witness chair and pointed a finger at John Jenkins.

"Yes, sir, that's the man . . . there's no doubt about it."

The prisoner laughed—a cold, brittle sound. "You better be thinking on what you say, little man," he said derisively. "You don't expect they're going to keep me here?"

There was a stirring in the room. Sam Brannan's voice cracked. "The prisoner will keep silent until he's called upon to testify in his own behalf!"

The shipping agent's face had paled noticeably beneath the green eyeshade he still wore pushed back slightly on the light-brown hair. His long, thin fingers nervously buttoned and unbuttoned the gray silk vest.

"Please go on," Sam addressed the witness. "Tell us what happened."

"Well," the agent began, "it was sailing time and I left the office and stepped out to the pier head to tend to some last-minute things. I turned around and saw this man," again he pointed to Jenkins, "with the safe hoisted up on his shoulder, coming out of the office door.

"There were lots of men there on the wharf. I yelled, 'Stop that man . . . he's a thief!' Some of them did try, but he just knocked into them and got by.

"He went down underneath the wharf—had a boat there waiting . . . shoved off and started rowing. Some of the men ran along the pier, and kept him in sight, while about a dozen more of us put out in rowboats and took after him.

"Guess we must've chased him for fifteen minutes or more before we caught up to him. Anyway, we was coming at him from all sides, and when he seen he couldn't get away, he stood up and laughed at us, heaved the safe overboard, so we couldn't get to it . . ."

Sam flicked the white ash from the tip of his cigar. "And do you, sir, personally know what the safe contained?" he asked.

"Yes, sir. Close to two thousand dollars."

Jenkins's eyes narrowed and glittered, his heavy jaw thrust sharply forward as he pointed a finger at the witness. "And that's just where you going to wind up, little man, right down there at the bottom of the Bay. Listen . . . listen to that crowd down there." He jerked his head toward the windows. "My friends'll come in here and bust this place wide open!"

Sam Brannan pounded on the desk with the flat of his hand, shouting for order, while Lanse saw the shipping agent's face go even paler, saw the beads of perspiration glisten along his upper lip.

With quiet at last restored, the witness nervously answered a few questions from the floor and then gratefully slipped from the chair and disappeared.

Twelve witnesses in all were heard, each one corroborating the shipping agent's story. When the last man stepped down, Sam rapped his hand smartly against the desk.

"We'll have a short recess now," he said, "so that you gentlemen can attend to whatever you need to"—there were grins throughout the room—"then we'll hear what the prisoner has to say."

Lanse and Rob went into the outer room and stood alongside Chris Russell and young Jed Mason, looking out of the second-story window at the crowd that filled the street and the opposite sidewalk. People hung out of the windows across the way. Torches blazed here and there.

"Must be more than a thousand men out there waiting," Chris Russell said.

Rob's face was sober. "What we do here tonight concerns them just as much as it does us. I just talked with Tom Atkins. He says the talk through the crowd is that the Ducks are gathering. But a lot of them down there are saying they'll back us, whatever we decide on."

"Look how many are here waiting to sign up!"

Lanse looked along the lengthening line of men, stopped suddenly, caught by a familiar figure, rotund, balding, owl-eyes behind gold-rimmed glasses . . .

Homer Claypool saw him, inclined his head slightly, and Lanse nodded in return. "Mr. Claypool," he said under his breath, "I believe I owe you an apology."

"Safe? What safe? I ain't stole nothing. They're all a bunch of goddamned liars." Jenkins's voice dropped. "They'll be dead liars come sundown tomorrow . . ."

There was a buzz of conversation through the room.

"Cool enough bastard, isn't he?" Lanse said to Rob, who grunted.

Sam's voice brought quiet again. "Do you, sir, have anything at all to say in your own defense?"

The broad, flat lips drew back from tobacco-stained teeth. "This whole thing makes me laugh," the witness said. "You ain't never going to get me out of this building. When the Ducks get through with you, them of you as can still walk will be dragtailing it home to hide under the featherbeds. You gonna find out who's boss in this here town!"

"Will you gentlemen escort the prisoner into the back room and keep him there while we deliberate?" Sam said calmly. Four men in the front row rose and took Jenkins out.

Sam took one of the big black cigars from his pocket, carefully bit off the end, and lit it, puffing out small clouds of white smoke. He sat down.

"Well, gentlemen," he said, "we'd better talk about the verdict."

"No use to talk—he's guilty." Lanse recognized Tom Atkins's voice. And the chorus of "guilty" rang out as if from one throat.

"Anyone who votes not guilty?" Sam waited for a long moment. "I guess then the penalty is the question."

"Can't be no question—it's got to be hanging." The voice came from somewhere in the back of the room. "There ain't no jails . . ."

"We could run him out of town," another called.

"And if we did," Chris Russell countered, "he'd come right back before our backs were turned!" There was general agreement at that.

Jim Carter, the banker, stood up. "I hear in the mining camps they hang a man for stealing so much as a copper penny."

It was true; Lanse had seen it himself, and harsh though it was, he thought, it was the only way they had been able to maintain even the semblance of civilization.

Rob stood up, too, spoke quietly. "I think maybe that first man back there said it right . . . there can't be much question. We've challenged them. We've got to follow through, let them know we mean business. Because if we don't, we're gonna be worse off than we were before."

It went on like that for a good half-hour: each man had his say and then the vote was taken. Hanging was the verdict.

"We'll take him right now—to the Plaza," Sam said.

"No!" Will Coleman jumped to his feet. "They'll call us cowards, taking him out in the dead of night. We should wait until sunrise; that's always the time for any official hanging."

"I don't believe we can afford that luxury," Sam protested. "We may have trouble enough as it is. Let the Ducks think on this until dawn and Jenkins'll be right—we'll never get him out of this building." There was a chorus of agreement and Coleman was overruled.

Several men were sent ahead to prepare a place, and a preacher was brought in and closeted with the prisoner. Sam Brannan walked to one of the open windows and spoke to the crowd below, which had waited in awesome quiet all this time. With a few sentences, he explained what had taken place, and there was a sudden wash of sound.

"Do you approve of what we're doing?" Sam's voice boomed out. And if there were any dissenting voices, they were drowned out by the rousing cheer that went up.

There was quiet, if tense, activity in the Committee rooms. Most of the men carried pistols of their own, and now the Committee passed out rifles.

Lanse took the rifle that Tom Atkins handed him. The wooden stock felt cold in his hands. "Lafe Walker has all the ammunition you'll need," Tom said.

A bare ten minutes later, Lanse found himself marching cautiously along the dusty street, his shoulder almost touching Rob's, his thumb on the hammer of the rifle, his finger resting lightly on the trigger. The crowd fell back before them, casting long shadows in the flickering light of the torches. The prisoner, surrounded on all sides by armed Vigilantes, shouted an obscenity at someone and then laughed defiantly.

"He still thinks the Ducks are going to take us," Rob said under his breath.

"We'll see . . . we'll see." Lanse's eyes swept the street, probed along the shadowy sidewalks, the darkened doorways and windows. The throng that had waited so long outside the Committee-room windows marched along the sides of the column, followed in great numbers behind. Now and then a voice could be heard above the shuffle of feet through the dust, but for the most part, they were soberly quiet.

Through Sansome, California, Montgomery streets, they marched in eerie silence. Lanse felt some of the tightness in his chest ease and then he heard Rob's sudden, ragged intake of breath.

The column was almost into the intersection when suddenly they were faced by a large group of ruffians, some on horseback and some afoot. Lanse heard Jenkins laugh again, but he didn't look around. He just drew the hammer slowly back beneath his thumb and kept it there as the Vigilantes walked determinedly on.

"Now, you bastards," Jenkins shrieked, "now we're gonna whip you down to size. Then we'll tear up that paper you wrote last night and shove it down your puking throats!"

To Lanse's surprise, the crowd that had marched along with them didn't break and run. Instead, they moved in even closer, and some of them pulled out pistols and quietly pointed them at the Ducks, making an overwhelming show of force.

The rock-solid front of the Ducks shifted. For a moment Lanse thought they would charge, then felt the wavering, the indecision. The torchlight caught, snaked along the blue length of a rifle barrel.

The front cracked. Their moment gone, the Ducks fell back, the column marched on. Lanse realized that for the last few moments he hadn't been breathing and he sucked the cool night air into his straining lungs.

"All right, boys, you can pick them off in the Plaza . . ." he heard the condemned man call to his friends.

Light blazed from the windows of all the big gambling houses and saloons that flanked Portsmouth Square: the Bella Union, Empire, Parker House, the El Dorado. Tucked among the elegant brick structures, almost unnoticed, was a small adobe building, the last remnant of the village *Yerba Buena*. They gathered beneath a chipped and fading sign that read "City Hotel" above its door.

The bells started again, a death dirge in the clear night air. Someone brought a bottle of brandy and a glass, poured out a good dollop, and handed it to the prisoner along with a big black cigar that Lanse suspected was one of Sam's.

Jenkins raised the glass high and grinned at them, the torchlight playing across his face. "I ain't one to waste good liquor," he said, and downed the amber liquid with one swallow. He tossed the glass away and fingered the cigar. "Think I'll just save this for tomorrow," he said.

"I'll smoke it whilst some of you are nursing busted heads —them of you as are still living . . ."

The words were defiant as ever, but Lanse heard the slight cracking of his voice.

The rope was brought forward, the noose passed over Jenkins's head. His eyes went frantically over the crowd, searching from face to face. Dark stains of perspiration spread beneath his armpits, across the chest of his blue cotton shirt. A muscle in his cheek twitched violently.

The long free end of the rope was thrown over a wooden beam that jutted out from the tiled roof of the old adobe building.

Sam Brannan's voice rang out, "Every lover of liberty and good order lay hold of this rope!" Lanse grasped the rough hemp between suddenly damp palms, and he and the others put their strength into it, hoisted Jenkins's big body into the air. An awful, inhuman sound was cut off sharply as the rope tightened about the prisoner's throat.

There was complete silence, every eye on the struggling figure, the contorted, slowly purpling face. Lanse felt the hot, churning sickness inside him burn thick and foul-tasting into his throat. He turned his face away.

The torch flames rippled, undulated atop their long poles. The odor of pitch was heavy in his nostrils. Finally, he felt the rope pulled from his hands. Someone tied the end to a nearby post and Lanse looked up, saw Jenkins dangling quietly, turning very slowly, starkly outlined against the weathered adobe.

Across the Plaza in the gambling halls, he heard the renewed whir of the roulette wheels, the clink of gold coins, the rattle of the dice. A woman laughed, shrill and piercing.

Somehow, Lanse had gotten separated from Rob in the crowd. He pushed his way through.

Then a big hand closed upon his shoulder and he swung round to a sober-eyed Jace.

"Mist' Lanse. I been trying to find you for the longest time. If I hadn't had this, I don't think I'd ever got through that crowd." He pointed to the butt of the pistol that jutted from his belt, and stole a quick look at the slowly turning figure.

"What is it, Jace?" Lanse said.

"It's Miz Sable—her time. I come to fetch the doctor, like you said we should, but I ain't been able to find him, neither. Melissa said to stay until I found you. Miz Sable's calling for you."

Chapter 30

Sable clung to the towels Melissa had knotted to the bedposts, braced herself. Her body arced upward, higher, higher. She set her teeth against the pain, felt her lips draw back sharply, heard the awful sound that wrenched its way through the still-closed teeth. At last, the blessed lessening . . . she sank back exhausted, limp, her eyes closed. Melissa dabbed her face with the cool, wet cloth, murmuring encouragement.

It had been so slight at first, the small hot aching that spread across her back from time to time early in the afternoon . . . she hadn't even realized what it was. Then there had been a peculiar giving way, and water had run down her legs, drenching her petticoats. Her voice had been so shaky she was afraid they wouldn't hear her calling, but Melissa and Tish both came running, took one look, and half carried her to the bed.

Melissa had wanted to send for Amanda, but Sable had refused to let her. She knew Amanda would insist on coming and staying with her until it was over. And Sable couldn't let her run even the slightest risk of a miscarriage . . .

The pains had really started then, coming faster and harder. Time had somehow run together, blurred. Sable didn't remember just when she had started calling for Lanse. She just knew it must have been a long while ago.

It had grown dark in the room, and she had watched Tish carefully remove the frosted white globes from the lamps, light each one, and then just as carefully replace the glass tops so that their painted pink rosebuds glowed softly.

"What time is it, Tish?" she said.

"Never you mind, honey . . . it's still early," Melissa answered.

Sable wanted to press her, but another contraction seized her; the agony of it filled her, snapped her legs up beneath the thin sheet that covered her. Her head thrashed back and forth.

She hadn't been surprised at the pain of labor—Amanda had prepared her for that. But she hadn't been prepared for the awful violence of it, the terrible heaving and straining of the womb trying to expel the burden it had carried for so many months. This was the way her mother had died. And she was so tired . . . so tired. Maybe she would die, too . . . only she had to see Lanse first. Had to tell him . . .

"It won't be much longer now, honey," Melissa's comforting face was above her. Sable grabbed one of the dark hands between both her own.

"Melissa," she cried, "where's Lanse? Why hasn't he come? I have to see him!"

"He'll be here soon, Miz Sable . . . him and the doctor. I sent Jace to fetch them both. I'm doing just like Mist' Lanse told me, but there ain't nothing that doctor can do for you that I can't. If it's one thing I knows about, it's birthings."

Tish's voice came from across the room. "Jace should have been back long before now. Maybe . . ."

"Be quiet, Tish," Melissa snapped.

Sable tried to ask, Maybe what, Tish? But another pain claimed her, and her body twisted frantically, her hoarse crying almost drowning out Melissa's "Push, honey, push . . . try hard!"

Sable was barely able to get her breath when another pain was upon her. She wanted to shriek, *no more . . . no more . . . please,* but her throat was too dry. She could feel Melissa's hands on her, one on her heaving abdomen, the other between her thighs. She felt like she was being torn in two.

"Almost, honey, almost . . . it won't be long . . ." Melissa's voice came to her.

You said that before, she wanted to scream. But when she could speak again she said: "Please, Melissa, I'm so thirsty . . ."

Almost instantly Melissa's gentle hands were lifting her head, holding the cup to her lips. "Not too much, now," she said. "You can have some more later."

"They here!" Tish said.

Sable tried to lift herself up on one elbow, but Melissa pushed her gently back. "Lie easy, honey," she said.

In an instant the grinding agony was upon Sable again, and she was trying so hard to do what Melissa told her to, but her tortured mind cried out, I can't, I can't, while Melissa's dark hands probed and pulled beneath the sheet.

The room blurred around her. The anguished sound tore from her throat as if from someone else. Maybe this was dying, she thought . . . Only Lanse was coming . . . and she had to see him first . . .

When at last the pain eased, Sable could hear heavy footsteps in the hall. Tish hurried to the door and then Lanse was there in the doorway, looking over Tish's head, his face strained, his eyes uncertain. Suddenly Sable started to cry, something she hadn't done through all the pain.

"Lanse . . ." she said and held out her hand.

With one arm Lanse swept Tish aside and was into the room and to the bed. His hand grasped Sable's.

"Mist' Lanse," Tish's voice rang shrilly. "You can't be in here now . . . that baby's coming . . ."

"Hush up, Tish," Melissa said sharply. "You go along to the kitchen and get me them linens I left on the table. Hurry up, now." She shooed the girl out of the room.

But Sable had pulled Lanse down closer to her, her voice coming raggedly, her words almost incoherent. "Lanse . . . Lanse, I have to tell you about that night. Melissa knows . . . she can tell you it's true."

"No . . . no, sweetheart," he stopped her. "Don't try to talk now. It's all right . . . I know . . . I know."

Sable felt the pain start to swell in her. "Lanse," she cried frantically. "Help me . . . I can't do it!"

"Yes . . . yes, you can. Take my hands, feel my strength!"

And she hung on to those big hands as if they were her only link with life, trying so hard not to scream because Lanse was there, her tortured body almost lifting off the bed. She saw his face, her pain mirrored in his eyes, seamed into his mouth . . . and she did feel his strength as by force of will he gave it to her.

For the briefest moment she felt as if the pain was starting to recede, then it was worse than before. Her head jerked back, twisted from side to side, her body heaved convulsively, once, twice, and woven into her own screaming was Melissa's shriek of joy.

For a minute Sable lay perfectly still, reveling in the sudden freedom from pain. She heard the funny, mewling sound, a sharp crack, and then the lusty crying of her child.

"It's a fine boy, Miz Sable . . . a mite puny looking . . ." Melissa said. "Ain't half as big as his papa was when he was birthed, but he's going to be just fine . . ." Lanse laughed, a happy, relieved sound, and smoothed back her hair, touched his hand gently to her face.

"Did you hear that?" he said. "We have a son!"

She smiled up at him, her eyes overflowing with sudden tears, struggled to lift her head, but her exhaustion was too complete.

Lanse slipped his arm beneath her shoulders, lifted her, and she saw the tiny, blanket-swathed creature who had caused her so much pain and now was making so much noise.

Tish tiptoed in and looked from one to the other of them with awed wonder, her big, square teeth gleaming brightly out of her dusky face.

"Here." Melissa handed the baby to Tish. "Take this child over there and let his mama get a good look at him before you clean him up."

Sable looked at her howling son, saw the tiny, waving arms, the faintly blue skin streaked here and there with blood, the black hair wet and plastered to the small skull. She felt such a surge of pride, of love so complete that for a moment she could scarcely get her breath.

Lanse's hand tightened for a moment on her shoulder, then the baby was gone and he gently put her head back on the pillow.

She heard the murmur of their voices after that, was vaguely aware of Melissa's hands, and once she thought she felt Lanse touch his cheek to hers. She tried to open her eyes, but she had slipped too far into blissful sleep.

Lanse finished the last of the strong black coffee and looked at the newspapers spread out on the table before him. The *Alta* uppermost. With unusual and stark brevity it read:

> The Vigilance Committee is at last formed and in good working order. They hanged at two o'clock this morning, upon the Plaza, one Jenkins, for stealing a safe.

To say so little—and so much, Lanse thought.

Rob had brought the papers and then had hurried home to tell Amanda about Sable and the baby. It was long past breakfast now . . . past lunch even. After Lanse had finally left Sable, he had gone down to the study and sat there alone for hours before his exhaustion drove him to the sleep he so badly needed. There had been so much he had to think about.

Melissa came into the room, a laundry basket tucked under one arm. Her black eyes swept across the table with its lone coffee cup and papers. "Mist' Lanse, ain't Tish brought your breakfast yet?"

"No, I told her not to . . . I didn't want anything but coffee. Is Sable awake?" he asked anxiously.

Melissa grinned at him, nodded her head.

"Is she all right? How does she feel?"

Melissa's grin broadened. "I expect you better go right up there and see for yourself."

He started for the door, turned back. "Melissa," he said quietly, "I've been a damned fool."

The old Negress turned her head to one side, her eyes softened. "You ain't the first man to say that . . . now you get on up there!"

A minute later he walked as softly as he could along the hallway, fearful that she might have gone back to sleep. The door was slightly ajar. He pushed it open, stepped into the room.

Sable's face was turned away from him; her red hair, brushed shining and tied back with a pale blue ribbon, spilled out over the white pillow cover.

"Melissa," she said, all her attention focused on the baby in her arms, "do you really think he's taken enough?" And now Lanse saw that one side of her blue nightgown was pulled down and she was trying to coax the sleeping infant to wake up and accept the full, pink-nippled breast.

"It's me," he said. She turned, startled for an instant, then her mouth curved into a smile and her blue eyes crinkled at the corners . . . just the way they used to, he thought.

Suddenly she remembered the exposed breast and hurriedly adjusted the lace nightgown, her cheeks growing quite pink for a moment.

He came closer. "How do you feel?"

"Pretty well . . . rested," she said.

There was so much he wanted to say, but he didn't know how to start. He leaned over the baby, sat down on the bedside to get a better look.

Sable smiled proudly and pulled the blanket back to show the tiny face, skin a healthy pink color, hair a soft, black fuzz.

He nudged one of the tightly closed fists with his thumb, and the tiny fingers with their incredibly small, translucent nails uncurled slowly and then curled up again.

"Isn't he beautiful?" Sable said. Her face was radiant as she looked down at the baby. "Melissa says . . . she says he looks like you."

Lanse peered closely at the little face. In truth, he couldn't see a resemblance to anyone, but he felt foolishly proud that the baby might look like himself. He grinned sheepishly.

"I want to name him after you—if that's all right," she said.

"No, it isn't all right." He saw the quick dismay in her face. "I've already chosen a name for my son. He's going to be Keith Flanagan Wakefield."

She caught her breath. "Oh, Lanse . . . are you sure?"

"Positive." He nodded. "Then our next boy will be Clay . . . for my father. And the next one, that one we'll name after me."

Her blue eyes looked enormous in the delicate oval of her face, her lips trembled slightly. "Would you put him back in his cradle, please?" Her voice was very low.

He lifted his small son carefully, saw the tiny rosebud mouth purse and then relax, carried him to the hand-carved rosewood cradle, and placed him on the satin-covered pillow.

He stood with his back to her. "Can you . . . forgive a fool?" he said hoarsely.

"Lanse . . . don't say that . . . don't ever say that! I've been the fool! I knew the truth and was too proud to tell you . . . I'm the one who's done this to us!"

He turned back, saw that in her distress she was trying to get up. He hurried to her. "Don't, Sable . . . you'll hurt yourself . . ." And then his arms were around her slim body, holding her to him. His mouth found hers, and he could feel the tears on her face, taste them in his mouth. He felt an amazing tenderness . . . passion would come later . . . and he could wait.

The words came—all the secret, unsaid things between them, until later, much later he kissed her again. "Rest now," he said, and touched her cheek lightly. "I'll be back . . ."

He looked once more at his sleeping son. The window was open, the sunlight slanting in. And somewhere downstairs, he heard Jace's deep voice calling to Melissa.

He had made his peace with himself . . . found his answers. Last night in the Plaza had been wrong—completely wrong. And yet, it was the best they had for right now.

History would judge them. Let it.